BONDS

OF

LUST

AND

LOATHING

For the babes ready to reclaim their power …
Go on …
Take it.

PREFACE

Trigger warnings:

This novel contains scenes depicting or discussing abuse of all kinds, violence, torture, explicit content and BDSM kinks, including brat play, discipline, and restraint. In the primary relationships, consent is always present.

ONE

Getting kidnapped by a psychotic shifter wasn't Sylvie Hart's idea of a good time, but it wasn't the worst thing to happen in the last few months, either.

Her forehead warmed the glass of the black truck's back window as the driver sped along winding roads. The bear of a man, Ace, hadn't spoken a word since they left the parking garage, but his onyx gaze flicked to the rearview every few minutes. Bound uselessly in her lap, her hands trembled. She was spent. The adrenaline-fuelled rage from her initial capture, the fighting and cursing and screaming, had taken most of her energy until all she could do was slump and stare into the open sky and rolling hillocks. Had Kian and Elias noticed she was missing yet? It had been at least an hour. *Surely.* But the mark on her chest—Kian's mark—was dormant. Not a twinge of heat or emotion. She thumbed the gold and wooden band on her right ring finger. Her fae husband and vampire lover. *They* were her fated—her *mates*. Not the shifter responsible for her predicament in the vehicle ahead. *No.* Rowan Hex was deluded, and the mate bond he said he felt meant nothing. All he deserved was an unfathomable hate that burned to the deepest pits of her soul.

"Pull over," she croaked, nudging the driver's seat with her bare foot. "I need to pee." She wasn't lying, but the spattering of trees along the roadside was the true reason for her request. If she could get close enough, she could merge inside one, calling on her dryad nature, and wait for salvation. *Or be lost forever.*

A juice bottle with a few dregs at the bottom landed on the seat beside her with a wet thunk. Bastard.

"I'm not using that. My fucking hands are bound." With a silken necktie. She hadn't tried to free herself, but she could have. They clearly weren't planning a kidnapping when they first arrived for a meeting, but Rowan Hex was resourceful.

When Ace said nothing, she dug her foot into the seat where his back pressed. "Please—" Her words cut off as the truck lurched to a sudden stop and her face slammed into the back of his chair. She swore something cracked, and sure enough, as she pushed herself into her seat, her nose gushed blood.

Ace's drawn inhale and bass growl had her swallowing dread. *Fuck.* He would scent her, just like the other bear shifter by Elias's cabin had. What would Hex do with the information? That she wasn't just *his* mate? But when her eyes met Ace's in the reflection, confusion swam there. Suspicion.

"I need to pee," she said again.

His blink pulled him from whatever thoughts he was having and his attention returned to the road, the subtle shake of his head not missing her notice.

"Fine, I'll just piss all over your back seat then."

He braked again, but this time she wedged her feet between the door and his seat. She barely shifted. That fact seemed to irk him more.

"Do that," he said, voice grittier than shale, "and I'll use your head as a fucking mop."

Her resolve flickered, and she hid her face behind her hands, using the tie to wipe the smeared blood from her chin. He would not see her fear. She sniffed. At least the bleeding had stopped. Silence accompanied her as the midday sun blared through the tinted windows, and she squinted against it until the sparse trees blocked the sun. So many opportunities to escape thwarted by a locked door and monstrous male.

A buzzing from the centre console stole her attention before Ace picked up the object and put it to his ear.

"Alpha?"

The voice on the other end mumbled a string of instructions, but Sylvie couldn't distinguish one word.

"Yes. I'll head straight there. How long will it take? No. It's no issue. Thank you, Alpha."

More mumbles. Why did it seem like she wouldn't be seeing Hex again soon? She didn't like her chances with Ace. Especially with the hints of glee in his last few statements.

"Hey!" Her voice was thick with the state of her bloodied nose. "He said he'd meet us there." Ace ended the call and dropped the phone in the cup holders.

"Keep your mouth shut, *bloodwhore*." He pawed at her legs without looking, as if to hit her. She curled as small as she could in the cramped space. If he braked then, she'd probably fly through the windscreen.

But the phone buzzed again, and Ace let it ring four times before answering.

"Yes, Alpha?"

His body tensed as a barrage of words spewed out. This time, she could make out some.

Harm.

Kill.

Talk.

Understand?

Her heart thudded harder with each spat syllable.

"Can you hear me now?" Hex's voice echoed over the speaker, and she paused. Was he talking to her?

"Woman!"

He still didn't know her name. Kian would be proud.

"I hear you," she said.

There was a pause. A long one, and Sylvie straightened in her seat, peering over to the device in Ace's hand.

"Good."

She jumped. "Where are we going?"

"Ace will escort you to our holding cells while I handle pack business."

Pack business? Holding cells?

"They won't be as luxurious as the lodgings you're used to, I'm sure …"

He hadn't seen her apartment then, or the one before that. *Or the one before that.*

"But it is the safest place for you for now."

She swallowed, trying not to gag on the coagulated blood sliding down her throat. "But you said—"

"I know what I said. Ace will take care of it."

"By *it*, you mean me."

The call ended with a harsh click and Sylvie groaned, slamming her clenched fist on her knee. *Stupid cunting dog!*

"We're almost there," Ace said, growling the words like he was barely human. Were they human? Either way, she didn't want to see him in animal form. This was bad enough.

By the time the truck pulled to a crunching stop, Sylvie's bladder was almost bursting, and crusted blood flaked across the back seat. *Come on, come on, come on.* Ace took his time sliding from the driver's seat, the entire vehicle jolting when his feet hit the ground. He blotted out the sun as he passed her window and rounded to the trunk. Gods help her.

The sounds of clinking metal, crumpling paper, and crinkling plastic had her gulping as Ace pawed through the trunk, and when he returned with a roll of thick tape, the last of her adrenaline stores surged. She jerked away, kicking her feet in his direction as he opened her door. He caught her ankle with a bone-aching grip that drew a groan of pain, then pinned her against the truck with a forearm and tore a strip of tape off with his teeth.

"You already tied my hands," she gritted out. "What are you—"

He slapped the strip over her mouth and palmed it, cutting her words short and most of her breathing. Her eyes bugged as air squealed through her semi-blocked nostrils.

"Walk. Cause trouble and I'll tape your legs and drag you. Understand?"

She nodded and stepped forward, nudging his chest with her shoulder by mistake when he didn't retreat. His face contorted, and he pinched her nostrils shut with a forefinger and thumb. Hard. She jerked as the lack of oxygen and flaring pain sent off screeching alarm bells.

"Never touch me, *bloodwhore*." She nodded frantically, her vision spotting and body tilting sideways before he finally let go. Tears filled her eyes as she hit the ground, but she kept her gaze down, bringing her legs under her and standing, drawing slow, shaking inhales.

Don't show weakness.

She walked ahead of Ace towards the structure peeking from behind a bend in the narrowing gravel path. The single level building was imposing in the landscape. Maybe Hex was right. There was something awful about this place. Thick wooden beams formed an H shape, and each window was adorned with wrist-thick iron bars. Beyond the crunching of their steps, the only other sound was the soft chirrups of birds. They were alone.

Ace shoved her towards a rusted door with inch-deep slashes and dried blood dribbling from the cuts. It opened inward, and she tripped headlong onto frigid concrete floors.

It was clean enough; the disinfectant smell was not what she had expected. Where was the shit, piss, and mildew?

She turned, fingers brushing the tape on her mouth, but Ace nudged her with a steel-capped boot. "Leave it. I don't want to hear your voice."

She stood again, muscles creaking, and ogled the place. Six barred cells, conjoined by a solitary hallway and two iron doors at the farthest end of the building inside the last cells. Maybe that's where they kept the torture devices.

To her horror, Ace kept corralling her in that direction, tearing open the last cell and gesturing to the closed door within it.

"In there," he said.

She shuffled over and palmed the icy handle, dragging it down along with the fear. When it opened, she blinked. A washroom? A drain centred the space while three showerheads gleamed from the back wall, with fresh soaps hanging from wire shelves. She turned to Ace, questioning, but his expression turned her hope to unease.

"Stand against the wall."

He shoved her deeper inside until a thick hose came into view, suspended by giant hooks and controlled by a big red nozzle.

She just stared.

"I won't ask again."

Her eyes burned as she dragged herself to the brick wall, stopping next to a tray of bar soap.

"Take off your clothes."

She disappeared inside herself as she lifted her gaze to Ace. His tilting head and bored look was almost a comfort until he said, "Alpha's orders."

Alpha's orders.

The world slipped away. The room, the cold—it all disappeared until Sylvie was a silent observer, watching herself unbuckle her trousers, undo the buttons of her blouse, and stare defiant at the monster before her. Her blouse snagged around her elbows, but Ace didn't bother unbinding her hands as he lifted the hose and turned the nozzle, his glare stalling on the small indigo mark over her heart for a moment before his eyes glazed.

Kian's mark flared with a soothing wave that rippled down the bond. She hid her relief. Even with the distance between them, he would protect her. The glamour he'd woven over their marks worked like a charm. She thanked him for the mercy of anonymity even as ice water pelted her bare legs, then her stomach, throwing her body into the wall with blinding force, the bruising lashes tenderising her skin. The only respite from the cold was the urine that streamed down her legs.

Her muffled screams sprang free as the stream hit her lower jaw, ripping the tape off and throwing her skull into wire and stone. Oblivion followed.

TWO

Needles and ice. *Drip.* Teeth cracking. Cold and wet. *Drip.* Agony flooding through skin and bones. *Drip.* Screaming. *Who is that?*

"Stop." All Sylvie could manage was a mumble. The water pelted bare flesh, flooding her lungs until it erupted from her mouth and nose. Drowning. She was drowning. "Stop!"

This time, the water listened. The roar of its stream quietened to a trickling hiss, and she blinked the stars from her vision before smoothing back the matted hair in her eyes.

She was too cold to shiver. Too numb. The concrete walls of the space shrank inward, constricting the wheezing breath from her lungs as she lay in a curled position. *Is this Hel?* But when a striking force cracked her ribs and a presence hovered overhead, she finally returned to sense. Ace. Contempt sank into his features as he ducked and undid her wrist bindings. The blouse came away next in a sopping heap. *Alpha's orders.*

She coughed and spat as the last remnants of Ace's treatment stirred in her lungs. A fleck hit his cheek, and he recoiled, swiping it away as if it were acid.

"You will learn your place, bitch."

The venom in his words glanced off her.

"Why do you hate me so much?" Her sentence made her break into a fit of coughing, but he didn't answer.

He returned to his full height and turned away, disappearing behind the echo of a slammed door. A crack in the dam holding her emotions widened, and the tears she'd held back drizzled down her aching cheeks. It hurt to cry, the uncontrollable shuddering of her body jostling every bruise peppering her legs and torso, so she stopped.

Hours passed that way, then a night. The chill of the dark had her dragging herself to the shower nozzle and trying her luck. She had an hour of hot water warming her until the heat ran out.

She rubbed the scar down her cheek, a gift from her aunt, and let memories of Elias and Kian stave off the darkness.

When they found her, nothing would stop them from destroying every person who caused her harm. She warmed at the thought of tearing Ace apart, bathing in his blood and grinding his skull to dust. The violence spurred the flames at first, but eventually a sliver of ice wended down her spine. She couldn't lose herself here. Elias might relish the darkness within her, but Kian deserved better. He deserved someone who didn't get off on the suffering of others. Not after all the suffering he had endured himself at the hands of her fucking aunt. Her scar was nothing compared to the marks Lazuli had inflicted on him. He deserved peace.

She reached a shaking hand to her blouse and pants, wringing the water before hanging them to dry through the slats of the barred window. It would take hours, but she had nowhere to be, apparently. Then she tried the door. It opened to sheets and thin blankets dressing a cot, but the external barred cell door, as expected, didn't budge. She peered at her goose-pricked flesh. The thin sheets would do.

She tugged the mattress and bedding onto the floor, sliding it under the metal of the cot, and dragged herself atop it. The tight squeeze sent a wave of comfort through her, just as it did in her childhood when she'd hid from scathing words, beatings, and unwanted touches in the foster homes. It reminded her of the nestled warmth of the trees she had merged with, without the risk of getting lost for eternity, wrapped in their sapping embrace. She'd realised it soon after Kian pulled her free from her grandmother's bound tree in the Stone Court. The cost of her half dryad heritage without a bound tree was to be lost inside another. It was only luck and perhaps love that drew her back. But even that might eventually fail.

Pulling the blankets around herself, she pressed her spine into the wall, tucking her fingers under her armpits, and stared towards the door of the building as the sky burned away the darkness with honeyed light. The smaller she could make herself, the better.

She hadn't realised sleep had claimed her until a fracturing cold engulfed her face. Her horrified inhale drew water into her lungs and she coughed and retched, rolling to her side before another hard slam shoved her back into the concrete wall behind her. Something cracked and she screamed, her throat tearing through the water filling her lungs.

Nothing made sense. Unable to see, she flailed and kicked when something gripped her hair and pulled, lifting her to her feet even as they slid on the slick floor.

She coughed and wheezed and pried her eyes open, only wishing to close them again at the sight of hatred in the creature's face that held her, an empty bucket in his free hand.

"Hello, Ace." She attempted a wry smile, but the tightening of his fist in her snarled hair forced it into a wince.

The bucket dropped with a clatter and he jammed his fist into her side, right on her fractured rib. Her scream rattled the walls, the ground shifting subtly, as if groaning with her. But the cost of *that* sucked the energy from her bones until even her legs couldn't hold her. The only thing keeping her upright was Ace's grip on her hair. Hair that was surely about to tear clean from her scalp.

"What do you think you're doing, *bloodwhore?*"

"Fuck you."

His grip in her hair jerked as his fist slammed into her stomach, turning her yelp into a broken wheeze.

Her eyes dragged shut like her body wished to save her from suffering, but she held on. Just a bit longer. Gods knew what he might do to her body if she wasn't conscious.

"What do you want?" she wheezed, pushing through the rattling in her chest.

But Ace had gone still, his gaze tracking down her torso and legs. The ones that were almost black from bruises hours ago were now healed. *Fuck* . She'd always been a fast healer, but since marking Kian it had gotten ridiculous. Her nose, too, was absent of swelling or darkness around her nasal bridge. There was no claiming she was human.

"The bruising," he said, letting the rest of his sentence hang between them.

With rising unease, she noted the twitch of his lips as they curled up in the corners. She clawed at the hands embedded in her hair and squirmed, pushing down the lancing pain in her ribs. She healed fast, but not that fast.

"Get away." Her hiss did nothing but draw Ace's smile out, the feral gleam forcing her heart to thud through the last of her adrenaline stores.

"You're no shifter, but you heal like one." He tilted her head back until her neck lay exposed for him. She growled and clawed at his face. She wouldn't bare herself to him. No, only Kian and Elias had that pleasure. But Ace showed no desire as he dragged his nose up the column of her throat, stopping at the divot under her earlobe. "Vampire." *He knew.*

Maybe he noticed the thought flashing in her fearful glare, as the clutch she thought was impossible to tighten, did. This time her hair ripped, strand by strand. The pull on her neck strained every muscle and her eyes squeezed shut as she fought his grip, her feet skittering across the floor for purchase.

"Put me down," she gritted between clenched teeth.

And finally, a second away from breaking, he dropped her. The sharp, shooting pain up her knees as she landed almost stole the little consciousness she had left, and she blinked back a burning sensation. He would never fucking see her break. Never.

His head tilted as he crouched before her, his thumb pressing into his canine. "Perhaps I should just bite you and let my venom do the work for me."

Venom?

The question must have crossed her features, because Ace's smile darkened. "Don't you know, bloodwhore? Shifter venom kills vampires."

She settled for silence. Her head hung back onto the cot as she drew her battered knees to her chest. She would relish in Ace's death. Even as he stared down at her, plotting his next move, she imagined all the ways she could make him hurt, each one more grotesque than the last. Only the sound of a distant ringtone drew her from the images of eating Ace's heart, and she tucked her chin down, watching the exchange. Ace's skin shifted in pallor, going a fraction paler than before, as Hex's voice prattled down the line.

"Yes, Alpha. She's ready to see you now." A cruel smirk twisted Ace's lips, but Sylvie noted the twitch beneath his right eye. The subtle tell. Of what, she didn't know.

He hung up and stood, grabbing her under her legs and upper back before carrying her to the cell nearest the front door and setting her on the bed with a restraint she hadn't thought him capable of. As he disappeared into the other locked door opposite the showers, she lay on her back, not caring about her state of dress, or lack thereof. Ace had seen more of her than her supposed mate, and she couldn't help wonder if that fact would affect the shifter. The "alpha," no less. She'd read enough books to know what that meant. Did the bond feel the same for him as it did for Kian or Elias? Because all she felt for the shifter was loathing.

"Change into this." Ace's growl had her stomach stiffening, anticipating another kick that never came. Instead, a lump of clothes covered her face, and she grunted, pushing them off while glaring at him.

"Why?"

"Because if you don't, I'll rip all your teeth out, one by one."

She ran her tongue across them as she sat, noting how her ribs had already stopped screaming at each movement. Instead, her muscles hummed with a dull ache.

She pulled the long-sleeved shirt over her head, followed by a thick knitted jumper as she said, "Shall we make friendship bracelets out of them?"

Ace's expression darkened as she tugged on a pair of too-big sweats and tightened the drawstring.

When it was done, Ace gripped her chin, jutting her head back until he exposed her throat. "You will tell my alpha what he wants to know, or I'll make your stay here as uncomfortable as possible."

Too fucking late.

"Sure thing, shitstain."

The screech of brakes and tires skidding in loose gravel cut his growl short. "Tie it up." He threw a hair tie at her and gestured to the mess of hair around her head before leaving the cell, shutting the barred door and leaning his back against it with crossed arms.

She'd managed a messy pony at her nape with a few strands around her face hiding her scar and loose enough to stop the flaring pain in her scalp when the holding cells' front door swung open with a slam and the male of the hour filled it, hate in his eyes.

THREE

If intimidation was Rowan Hex's strategy, he'd already lost. Ace's glare held a poison that the alpha of the shifters couldn't quite match. Not when his burning golden eyes dragged a leisurely path down Sylvie's body, stopping at her bare feet. She leaned her elbows onto her aching knees, resting her chin atop her fists as he crossed to her cell, his boots cutting through the silence with each slam of his steps on the concrete.

Every thunderous crack had her mind flashing to Ace's torture and the sound of her anguished flesh battering against stone.

She placed a well-carved mask over her expression as he reached the cell door and swung it open, a brown paper bag dangling in his free hand.

"Unlocked?"

Ace dropped his gaze. "Yes, Alpha. I unlocked it when I heard you arrive."

They both went silent, eyes glazing, before Hex's attention returned to her and Ace scurried away, leaving the building completely. Sylvie stared after him, blinking.

"See something you like?"

Her attention turned back to the shifter before her, a look of malice shifting in his stare as he pulled a stool from the corner of the cell and sat atop it, the brown bag at his feet.

"Not at all," she rasped, her lashes flickering as she eyed the black whorls of the tattoos peeking from his unforgivingly tight tank top.

He stared at her in silence, too hard for her liking, but she had long learned the art of nonchalance. Nonchalance bolstered by disgust.

"Hungry?" he asked, nudging the bag at his feet.

She stared back, not even glancing at the bag. It was a game she would not play.

"What do you want?"

He exhaled through his nose, his mouth pinching into a straight line.

"What do you know about the fae artefact Animae Dimidium Meae?"

Mirroring her pose, he waited, jaw clenching every few seconds.

It took a moment for her brain to come online, the duress of the last twenty-four hours interrupting her long-term memory.

She lifted a shoulder to shrug but stopped herself. "Besides your email to Elias, nothing."

He tensed at Elias's name in her mouth, but she just shook her head, unfurling from her position to lay flat on her back. A faint sigh escaped from her parted lips while Hex's gaze drilled into the side of her face.

"Ace says your scent is unusual. What are you?"

She slowly turned onto her side. "A woman."

His brow quirked even as he kept his lips in a frown.

"Tell me," he said, stool screeching as he edged closer. "Are you his—" He paused, as if the words were too sick for him to even think. "Are you a pet? Does he feed from you? I hear they have powerful compulsion, so if you could not resist, perhaps it is forgivable—"

A huffed laugh escaped her mouth before she could stifle it, and when his expression thundered, she laughed harder, palming her ribs to steady them.

"What is so funny, woman?"

"Do you think I care if I'm palatable to you? Do you think your opinion really fucking matters? You are *nothing* to me, dog."

His hazel-green eyes flashed such a brilliant gold that she winced at the intensity of his gaze before settling her expression once more. She expected a kick, perhaps a slap across the face, but Hex didn't move an inch.

Disdain settled in her chest as she sighed. "Why am I even here?"

The quiet between them stretched for a few uneven breaths before he spoke again. "I told you."

Mates.

Insanity. Two was more than enough.

"You don't even know my name."

"Then tell me," he said, the vibration from his low, throaty voice waking something within her. Something ugly, prowling around the dimming fire. She smothered it as she pulled herself back into a sitting position, her back against the wall this time. How she was still functioning was beyond her.

"Names hold power, you know," she said. Kian's approving face flashed in her mind. She reached out to touch him across the void, her hand lifting before her awareness returned and she dropped it with a thud at her side.

He followed the motions, his throat bobbing a fraction.

"Not here," he said.

"How sad."

His lip curled. "Tell me."

"Get me out of here first. Away from him." She jutted her chin to the door, where she assumed Ace was waiting.

Hex's gaze narrowed, never leaving her face. "Ace is my beta and does as he's told."

Her skin prickled under the scratchy clothes. "And what is that?"

Tension rose in the space between them like a heatwave, the pressure suffocating.

"Your name, my mate."

She found the floor with her feet and stood, a scowl painting her face. "Don't call me that."

He didn't rise. "It's what you are."

"Not for fucking long."

His face pinched, the muscle in his temple jumping as he ground his teeth. She pressed closer, standing above him until he was almost close enough to touch. To strangle.

"Don't make me ask again," he said.

She took another stubborn step, the fire within her licking up her limbs and curling around her heart. "Don't tell me what to do."

She was above him then, his irises flickering between green and gold like they were malfunctioning. His throat lengthened as he tipped his head back, eyes aligning with her mouth. Too bad she didn't have a weapon.

"Sylvie," she said, before he could say another word. "Sylvie Hart."

Then she moved, aiming her fist at his throat with the last pool of energy she had, but before it could land, he snatched her wrist from the air faster than she could track.

"Careful, woman. I might like that."

She sneered, snatching her hand back from his, stumbling to the cot and planting on her ass. A flurry of micro expressions crossed his face as she slumped into the wall and curled her legs up. She was fucked. If her eyes closed, she'd be lost to the world.

"Natalie said you were human."

A sickening viper of unfamiliar emotion slithered up her throat from her stomach at his casual mention of her colleague. The woman who let her get kidnapped by a monster. She'd be dead by now if Elias had anything to do with it. Sylvie's only regret was that she hadn't been there.

Traitor.

What else could Natalie have shared?

"But your scent," he said.

"What about it?"

"It's strange."

Her pulse jumped. In the darkness of her fraying mind, thoughts slugged past until her brain hurt. What knowledge would hold the highest value? Information was currency, and she was fairly wealthy in that.

Her lids drooped. "That's because I'm mixed." She slid sideways, her head crashing on the solid metal bedframe. "Half none of your business, half fuck you."

Hex's dark chuckle barely breached the fog swarming her head.

"Rest up. We'll try this again soon. Maybe after another few nights, you'll be ready to cooperate."

She mumbled one last curse as he prowled from the cell, leaving the holding cell building without looking back. "I'll kill you."

Ace filled the space Hex left, his lecherous gaze dousing her in thick dread.

"What?" she groaned, even as exhaustion dragged her deeper into the abyss.

"Time to see how fast you heal."

* * *

"So disappointing. I thought you'd be more of a challenge to break."

Sylvie gulped lungfuls of air inside the washroom after Ace had pushed her to the brink of drowning by throwing a cloth over her face and holding her under scalding liquid for the tenth time. Maybe it was the eleventh. She'd lost count after blacking out and waking with foam bubbling in the corners of her mouth.

She rolled away onto her belly, dragging her limbs under her to crawl. Anywhere. Away from him. Away from the steady drip of the water from the tap. *He's my beta. He does as he's told.* Ace snatched her back, ripping her shirt to check her ribs. He'd smashed them twice with a well-placed punch and timed their healing. *Drip.* Four hours from bruising to unblemished skin. The deeper muscles still ached, but there was no proof. *Drip.* No evidence.

When he dropped her, she slid on her belly across the wet floor, tensing along her sides as she waited for the impact. Before every strike, he would inhale through his teeth as if tasting her fear in the air, and she wouldn't sit and wait for the soft cue. Slick with sweat and water, she crawled. Breathing shallow, skin raw from the scalding water. He would kill her. When she made it to the door and the hit never came, she peered over her shoulder at him. He was fidgeting with his phone, and Sylvie resumed her slow drag to the cot, sliding under and digging her fingers into the metal slats.

Ace's boots slapped the floor as he walked to her and knelt, peering under the bed with black irises. "We're not done."

She bit the inside of her cheek until blood pooled in her mouth.

"Why is he doing this?"

She'd asked it before, but Ace never replied. He just found new ways to hurt her, to test the limits of her healing. Pulled fingernails had taken the longest to return, her nail beds only just covered after what had to be a day, maybe two. She had no measure of time, not since he'd covered the small windows to the outside world with blackout fabric. Food was scarce. After Hex's bribery of takeout that he'd left on the floor, Ace had offered one meal since of stew with stale bread. He'd spat on it, but she was starving.

His gaze hollowed as he snatched her leg from under the bed.

"It's what all of your kind deserve after what you've done."

My kind?

Her fingers lost their grip as he wrenched her across the floor, his hands finding purchase in her matted locks. He growled, lifting the thick knotted snarls and pulled a blade from his pocket.

"No!"

It was over. He'd finally had enough of her. She was dead.

But it wasn't her throat he sliced, it was her hair. He sawed through it, cutting away the length until it pooled on the floor, knotted and lifeless. The fervid burn behind her eyes had her blinking. It was just hair. She wasn't going to cry. *She wasn't.* But her face had other ideas. It twisted and crumpled as her trembling fingers tugged at the mess he left behind. The longest strands scratched the base of her throat and the shortest curled up and frizzed around her head. Even Ace stilled, perhaps realising this was too far. Or perhaps it was because it wouldn't heal the same. He couldn't hide this.

Ace is my beta. He does as he's told.

She swallowed against a lump that threatened to choke her.

"I've done nothing to you!" Her shout startled them both, and he let her go—let her shove herself into a corner and swipe away her tears. "You fucking monster. I've done nothing!"

He snarled, striking her leg with his boot. "You're a filthy bloodsucker. I knew it the moment your blood spilt across my back seat."

"You're wrong."

"I'm not. I've smelled it before. Tasted it. Yours might be sweeter, but there is no mistaking the death in your blood."

She wiped away another tear trail with the heel of her hand. "It doesn't matter what I am. I don't deserve this."

"Yes, you do!" Ace was inches from her, his voice so thick and animal she shook. He would shift right there and tear the head off her shoulders. She'd seen the bear shifter at Elias's cabin. He was nothing compared to Ace. Ace would swallow her whole.

"You all do! You killed my sister, you stole our people, and now you mean to take our mates from us?"

Her lip quivered as fury mixed with terror. "I didn't do any of those things, you psycho. I'm innocent!"

Ace's laugh chilled her. "You're a killer."

"No."

"Can you say you haven't murdered someone in cold blood?"

Her skin prickled. "I—they—"

"Don't lie to me, bitch. And don't make excuses." The black of his iris bled into the whites of his eyes until nothing human remained. Ace was her reaper.

Her reckoning.

"Have. You. Killed?"

"Yes." She'd killed a man as a child. A monster who deserved worse for what he'd done. But it didn't matter to Ace. He had already made his mind up about her, and nothing would change it.

"Then you are no different from the beasts that killed my family. They took something from me, so now I'll take something from them."

FOUR

Filtered light trickled through a hole in the blackout curtains of the cell window as Ace clicked his stopwatch. "Still four hours." Sylvie had lost so much time. Nothing but the starvation in her belly and the dryness of her tongue signalled it had passed at all. Maybe it hadn't. Maybe she was in Hel or limbo or purgatory. Whatever. The punches hardly hurt anymore. She was just numb. Hollow.

Drip.

Her fire had turned to a wisp.

Drip.

Hex never came back.

Drip.

"What?" she croaked. But Ace slammed a hand over her mouth, the other holding a device to his ear.

"Yes, Alpha. Yes, fine. No. Didn't touch it. Alright." He hung up and gripped her biceps, dragging her to her feet, holding her up as her ankles buckled.

"Stand."

"I can't."

She hadn't slept beyond the brief moments of bliss when oblivion took her and her body wouldn't cooperate.

"If you don't stand, I will make you wish you were never born."

"I already do."

But she tried anyway, tensing her shaking colt legs and clasping the bars of her cell as he gestured to the main hall.

"Where are we going?" She tripped over her frozen toes, barely catching herself with the bars, wincing at the jagged scars along her palm she'd made a lifetime ago, now stained with rust.

Ace gave her a withering glare before grabbing her upper arm to walk her the rest of the way. "Outside. Alpha's orders."

As the main door clanged open, Sylvie shielded her eyes against the blinding light, blinking and squinting until her bloodshot stare adjusted. Beneath the sparse tree canopy, away from the cells, little sunshine caressed the moist soil underfoot. It crumbled between her bare toes as she moved, sticking to the flaking polish on her nails.

Ace shoved her towards the thicker forested area ahead, away from the gravel path they had first walked, and she couldn't stop the flicker of hope igniting in her heart. Like a single cinder coaxed with shuddering breath, a vision of her sprinting towards safety and throwing herself inside one of the larger orewoods flitted across her mind. With each trembling step though, it dimmed until only a pinprick of heat remained.

Soon, even that would extinguish and icy dejection would replace the fire and fury. Ace gripped her roughly, pulling her to an unceremonious stop as a lilting song speared through the trees. She followed it, almost losing herself in the memories of Evergreen and the night songs she'd grown to love.

The willowy female that split the tree line, with barely a hair out of place, looked like spring personified. Flowing red locks woven in an intricate braid framed her freckled cheeks.

"Rosalia!"

Sylvie scoffed. An apt name.

"Does Alpha know you're here?" Ace's coarse question only succeeded in drawing the female's brows together, lightly creasing her forehead.

"Rowan doesn't control where I run."

She padded closer, homing in on Ace's grip around Sylvie's arm before flashing a dimpled smile. "I'm Rose. And you are?"

Ace released her and she swayed, not having realised how much she was relying on his touch for support.

"Sylvie," she said.

"That's lovely." Rose's smile stretched, though the muscles around her mouth flickered. "And what are you, Sylvie?"

Ace growled, stomping between them, his hands curling into fists. They were the size of fucking dinner plates. No wonder her entire rib cage still ached with every breath.

"She's a fucking bloodsucker, Lia. Go run back to the pack house."

That time, Rose's gaze lifted, meeting Ace's lumbering frame with a raised brow. Then her head tilted. If Sylvie weren't almost comatose on her feet, she would've applauded the female.

"Hmm. That's not what Rowan said."

Sylvie raised her lashes, noting the way Ace had paled a few shades. But it went nowhere, and Rose's attention returned to her. "When's the last time you ate?"

It took a moment for her brain and mouth to communicate before she said, "I don't remember."

"You eat normal food?"

Sylvie nodded.

"Good. Well, wait here. I've got something for you."

Ace growled as Rose twirled on her toes, heading back the way she came. "I thought you were on a run."

She disappeared without a word and Sylvie sagged, dropping to her knees and sitting hard on her right hip, hands in her lap as her energy failed her.

"What are you doing? Get up."

She didn't respond until he dug his toe into her thigh. "I can't."

"I'm back!" Rose returned with a grin and a swollen tote bag, her cheeks dusted with a pink tinge. Sylvie had the impression the holding cells weren't close to the rest of Hex's pack, so either Rose was the fastest runner on Erus or she had planned this all along. The only question was, why? Rose tugged a blanket free from the top of the cotton tote and laid it on the dirt.

"Here. Come sit. Move your ass, Ace."

Ace growled but side-stepped as Rose sat cross-legged on the blanket. It took more than one readying breath for Sylvie to move, and if Rose noted the shaking of her limbs, she made no comment.

Instead, she pulled a thermos, two bowls, forks, and four mini bread loaves out of the tote and set the space. The fresh scent of baked bread had Sylvie's dry mouth filling with saliva, as did the sight of the stew Rose poured from the thermos. Dark rich stew with chunks of potato, greens, and some unidentifiable protein.

She didn't move to eat though, not until Rose took a bite out of a potato and didn't die. With a slowness she loathed, Sylvie slowly copied her movements, foregoing the cutlery and instead drinking from the bowl. She relished the burn against her palms, the heat reminding her she was alive as she swallowed the last broth dregs.

Rose poured her another serving. "It must have been a while since you've eaten if you like Rowan's cooking this much."

Sylvie almost choked, sloshing scalding liquid across her lap as she placed the bowl back down.

"Woah. It's alright. He's not gonna jump out of the soup and bite you."

Sylvie flushed from the admonishment but didn't move to reclaim the meal despite how desperately she wanted to.

"Please." Rose slid the bowl until it brushed Sylvie's legs. "Have some more. It's safe." As if to prove her point, she tore off a section of bread and dipped it before downing it in one bite.

Despite her inner protests, Sylvie resumed her eating, albeit even slower than before, with smaller bites and sips.

Ace growled, the sound making her flinch. She'd almost forgotten he was there, hovering over her shoulder with Rose's kind energy blasting her in the face.

Rose snarled back, her teeth temporarily morphing into needle points. "I won't remind you whose family I belong to. Back up. Now."

Even Sylvie leaned back against the power in the command. Whoever Rose was, she wasn't one to trifle with. Ace did as he was told, storming away until his footsteps faded. *Was he gone?* She didn't dare look, her dread building. No matter how ballsy this female was, Ace was still twice her size, and if Sylvie said or did the wrong thing, she'd pay for it later.

For all she knew, they were working together. Buttering her up to lower her guard.

"Don't be too hard on them. They're just stressed."

It took a few bites for Sylvie to realise Rose wasn't just talking about Ace.

"Why?"

Rose's lashes fluttered, then her lips quirked upward. "We're getting help to find an artefact we've been searching for since before I was born. It's a lot of pressure."

The Animae Dimidium Meae.

Sylvie swallowed past the lump in her throat. "What is it?"

Rose ripped more bread. "It's supposed to form mate bonds, or at least the illusion of them. It's the best idea we've got for our endangered species problem."

Yeah, because "turning" kills more people than it changes.

She left the thought unsaid.

"We haven't had a born shifter birth since me, so we're all on edge. Mate bonds are the life and death of a pack, you know."

Yet the alpha let his beta torture her for days. Perhaps he just missed the memo. Or perhaps she should just go easy on him, because he was *stressed.*

Fucking—

"No," she whispered, faint as a wraith. When Rose raised a brow, she clenched her jaw. "I didn't know that."

With a soft smile, Rose poured the last of the stew in Sylvie's bowl and deposited her half eaten loaf atop it before standing and swiping the crumbs on the ground.

"I better go, but you eat every bite, alright? You're wilting." Sylvie had no response. She just stared as Rose darted off, light on her toes, the bushes seeming to part as she leapt through them with the grace of a hare.

"Thanks."

Ace's heavy footfalls, a little faster than a brisk walk, jolted the soil under her.

"You're still here," he said.

She didn't bother answering, or finishing the food Rose left. Instead, using the little strength the meal gave her, she stood and stretched, each movement aggravating her deepest muscles.

"Why didn't you say anything?"

She glared, dragging her feet towards the cells again.

"Where are you going?"

"Sleep."

The trees were so close, she could almost sense their roots beneath her bare feet, but even her dryad sight flickered. A dying ember. Maybe it was over. Her body was shutting down anyway. She considered giving in, if only to stop the searing pain anytime Ace battered her flesh, but the image of her males finding her dead had her resolve to give in weakening. She was so, so tired.

Seconds away from dropping to the ground and begging for mercy, she froze at the sound of tires tearing through gravel and the roar of a revving engine before it cut off.

Hex appeared along the dirt-worn path, stone flecks flying from his boots as he stormed their way until he saw her and stilled. His expression, previously thunderous, fell, his lips parting. It wasn't until she tracked his line of sight did she realise. Her mask of composure slipped, and she bit her wobbling lip as her fingers darted to the sawn ends of her hair. She hadn't even seen it, but it felt ugly.

It shouldn't have hurt her the way it did, or mattered so much. It was only hair—it would grow back. Eventually. But Ace had taken away a piece of her identity. Her shield. Hex reminded her that the scar Lazuli gave her was now on full display as his dripping gold stare dotted along it to where it disappeared under the scratchy neckline of her jumper. He lifted his hand, something silver flashing in it.

His throat bobbed. "It's for you."

FIVE

Sylvie scrutinised the space between her and Hex's outstretched arm, the phone waiting in his idle palm. It was a test. Another game. If fatigue didn't tug at the fringes of her consciousness, she would have stormed to the cells, but she didn't trust her feet. She couldn't take another beating or disdainful kick if she fell.

Hex said nothing as he closed the gap between them and deposited the device in her hand. The screen flashed as an unknown number rang and rang. She scanned the display warily, glancing between it and the males scrutinising her before pressing answer and lifting it to her ear.

Her fingers shook, her tongue darting out to wet her dry lips, the swallow doing nothing to soothe the lump rising in her throat.

The voice that passed her lips was not one she recognised. Hollow.

"Hello?"

"Princess?"

A whimper slipped free before she could catch it, her free hand clapping over her upper face as it crumpled, the tears she thought long dried up searing down her cheeks.

"Kian?"

Banging clattered down the call while Kian's energy flowed between them, their voices enough to strengthen the stretched tether. Some of her pain eased, along with her fear, as he asked, "Are you safe?"

Relief saturated her when he didn't mention the sensations he was likely feeling through the bond, but the question still lingered in the airwaves. She wanted to ease his fears too, but the words wouldn't come.

"How did you find me?"

"Elias compelled Natalie."

Her heart squeezed the ember in her mind, which flared at the reminder of her betrayal.

"Dead?"

"No," Kian said softly. "Fired."

"I'm still thinking about it." Elias's irate tone sung to the vicious part of her that wanted nothing more than Natalie's death.

"What happens now?" she asked, sniffing and reining her emotions back in. She'd already shown too much to the shifter males.

A violent bang followed by Kian's firm, but smothered, "You're not helping," had love rushing through her chest. Something rustled, then a throat cleared. "We're looking for the artefact. The sprite that carries it has a portal key and uses it to enable her gambling habits in Sterling and the western continent. I've warded every casino in southern Erus, and when she appears, we'll have it."

She eased the pounding of her heart with a few shaky breaths. "And after that?"

"A trade." Hex's voice had her jolting. She dropped the hand covering her face and backed up half a step. His gold eyes followed each movement even as his expression twisted into contempt.

"Your *bosses* know we'll tear them apart if they set foot on shifter land. But I hear your new house will be the perfect neutral ground."

Her new house. A home bordered by an ancient forest. The orewood trees around her shimmied. *This ancient forest.*

She slumped as the past excitement tainted with disappointment. If Hex and Ace knew where she lived, she'd never feel safe again. She couldn't wait for them to find the artefact. Even four hours alone with the shifter was enough. So many things could be done and undone in four hours.

With a blank expression, she rocked on her feet, using the momentum to stagger back a few steps away from Hex. A few steps closer to a juvenile orewood.

She turned, gasping as if searching for what tripped her, and took three more ungraceful steps forward.

"When you find me," she started muttering as the tree expanded in her vision, thinner than she was used to, almost close enough to graze with the tips of her fingers, "make them pay." She turned, dropping the phone at her feet. Hex's head tilted the slightest degree, his brows furrowed while Ace looked on with unveiled contempt as she threw herself against the soft bark, her palms latching on and melding. It wasn't the same as in Evergreen. The trees on Erus were reluctant hosts, but it let her in eventually, moments before Ace's demonic huffs reached her skin—her bark.

She'd done it. She was safe and her males would find her. The orewood sap dragged her lids down and lulled her into a state of bliss. Energy wended through her fingertips, filling her with power—relief—as a shadow loomed and the ground shuddered.

Paws slammed against her hard flesh. The roots tethering her to the ground, connecting her to all other life, moaned and tore from the soil. A monstrous bear, fur as dark as the moments between night and dawn, huffed and growled, throwing its weight against her again and again. Then, screaming from pain and grief, the tree cast her out, dropping her at the feet of the creature, only to be dragged by a tattooed hand.

The touch of Hex's skin on hers had a current zipping up her thighs, and she squirmed, clawing her nails into the ground until they bent and bled.

Her blurred gaze captured the brutalised tree where Ace still prowled. "I'm sorry," she whispered to it before flipping onto her back to kick at the vice grip around her ankle. "Stop! I'm not going back in there. Let me go, you fucking bastard!"

Cracking and pained vocalisations sounded behind her, and when she twisted to stare, Ace in human form, naked, shoved the tree until its last tethered roots ripped free and it fell with a sickening thud, tearing limbs from neighbouring orewoods on the way down.

"Stop!" she howled, straining with everything she had. Maybe the last of what she had.

And he did stop. They both did. Ace sneered as Hex dropped her foot and knelt over her, clasping her hands together before she could swipe at his face.

"Tell me the truth." Hex bared his teeth as a stray knee hit him between the legs and he shifted until his inner thighs caged her legs together. "You're fae, aren't you?"

She turned her face away, cheeks burning.

"Not possible …" Ace's voice wavered. 'She's a vampire, Alpha. I scented her blood."

Hex's eyes shifted to gold. "Leave us!" He didn't look where Ace stood, and neither did she. She just bucked her hips and struggled until the grip around her wrists had bones grinding.

"Is it true?" he asked.

"Get off me! I hate you!"

The boost the tree gave her before Ace murdered it had already faded, and she squeezed her eyes shut, avoiding Hex's searching stare.

She'd lost her fucking chance.

The weight around her eased, and the pressure on her wrists shifted, her arms pulling upward. Her eyes snapped open as Hex brought her to her feet and let her go. She widened her base and curled her hands into fists as he observed her.

"Why?" he said.

She just shook her head. *Why what?* The surrounding forest was empty of any other shifters, and birdsong filled the air for the first time since she arrived.

"Why are you so desperate to get back to them?" Uncertainty and annoyance played across his face as she scowled, releasing an aggravated breath.

"None of your business."

He reached for her then, but she would not be handled by those males again. Hex or Ace. With the last of her power, she swung, wincing as her knuckles cracked against his bearded jaw. Time slowed as he blinked at the ground. Once. Twice.

She didn't dare move; her body wouldn't allow it. One wrong step and she'd collapse. The impulsivity controlling her in Hex's presence had her buzzing, and she watched in morbid interest as he spat a glob of blood, his red-stained teeth visible as his split lip pulled into a smile.

When he licked across his canines, she swallowed, wishing to stab her guts for the way they flipped.

"Your vampire nature wants to destroy me, but your fae side feels the bond, doesn't it?"

She sneered, her bleeding knuckles twitching as the skin wove back together. "All I feel for you is hate."

He darted forward this time, snatching her hands and spinning her. The length of his front pressed into her spine, and he squeezed her arms along her side, holding her still.

"Let go."

He ignored her, inhaling against her neck, his nose brushing her skin where her hair stopped.

"Why did you cut your hair?"

She shivered, wanting to scream at him, at herself as she tilted her chin down, baring more of her nape to the bastard. His breath fanned across her collar and she threw her head back until it hit something with a sharp crack. Her vision speckled as she threw herself from his loosened grip and faced what she'd done. Blood dotted down her back from Hex's crooked nose.

This time, he laughed darkly, pinching his bridge with a forefinger and thumb before snapping the cartilage back into place.

I've done it now.

Visions of Elias's punishments crossed her mind, ones she'd certainly deserve and enjoy if she had done the same to him. But Hex wasn't Elias. There was no safety to be a brat here. No trust stretched between them. With a gulp, she darted for the nearest tree, but the weight of a truck slammed into her back, knocking the wind from her lungs and pinning her face down in the dirt. Her muscles screamed at the foreign weight, the violence inflicted on her from Ace still roiling just beneath the skin.

"If you touch me, I'll kill you," she spat, barely disguising the wheeze of agony as her ribs creaked.

He curled his warm hand around her throat, arching her neck slightly and tilting her face towards him. "I'm already touching you. Anything else to say?"

"I'm not fucking begging!" But she was close to it. So close, with the way her bones themselves wailed like they were preparing to splinter. "You'll be begging, though," she rasped, using her toes to shift her weight. It didn't work. "If you don't get off me."

If you don't get off me, I'll fucking die.

The pressure on her spine lessened as Hex slid a hand into her hair, cupping her skull in his palm as he lowered his face to hers. Nose to nose. Sinful thoughts bubbled and burst as she thrashed. "Get off."

He tilted his head. Animal. Predator. "Do you *want* me to beg, my mate?"

If he so much as tipped his chin towards her, their lips would meet. Something new within her coiled, wrapping its lusting teeth around her throat. *No.* After what he'd done? She couldn't ever go there.

Time stood still as she sucked air between her teeth, trying to lessen the compression of her other organs as Hex leaned closer, tempting that unknown part of her.

"If you don't move, my fated will skin you alive before I set you on fire. Get the fuck off me, you animal."

And then he was off her, and a full breath swelled her lungs, her violet mate mark itching, as if acknowledging her *real* mate had dissolved the magic he'd placed there. When heavy breathing filled her ears and it didn't belong to her, she got the distinct impression she'd made a terrible mistake.

"What did you just say?"

Sylvie took her time getting off the ground, wiping the dirt from her clothes and the jagged ends of her hair. She sucked in a few full breaths, palming each spot that still ached. Her ribs, her abdomen, her scalp.

All she could do was delay the inevitable. The truth she should never have shared hung between her and Hex like a sick joke.

"Say it again."

She shook her head. It was a mistake. She was weak.

When she finally peered at him, his entire form trembled, his nails lengthening, skin sprouting dark fur. She didn't even know what kind of shifter he was. And they were supposed to be mates.

His words were soft, as if not speaking to her at all. "Why would they do this? It's impossible. Impossible."

She craned her neck, tilting her ear toward him to catch the last muttered statement.

"You can't be real."

When he faced her head-on, body slightly morphed, she stumbled back a step. His jaw sported a row of sharp teeth, the hair on his face growing coarser—darker. Not a hint of white framed his golden iris.

"Ambrose?" he asked, the bass of his dual-toned voice forcing chills to arc down her spine.

The birdsong fled, but she didn't retreat. Hex was an animal. One that could pounce and tear the flesh off her bones or poison her with his bite.

Sylvie held his stare.

Maybe she could be a predator, too.

"And Prince Kian of Evergreen." She lifted her right hand, adorned with his wedding band. "My husband." It was a marriage of necessity, but she wanted it. Wanted him. Her mark warmed.

Hex shuddered, his shoulders rolling like he was loading the added information on his back and preparing to carry the baggage.

"Do you have proof?"

She worked her jaw, the nerves easing as Hex reverted his shift, the whites of his eyes returning. He didn't give the impression he would strike her. No, Ace performed his dirty work with gusto.

With a sigh, she nodded once, fingering the collar of her top and tugging it downward. The neckline snagged long before revealing Kian's mark, but Hex closed the gap between them, peering down her shirt, their foreheads almost touching.

They shared breath as he regarded the indigo brand.

"Only one?"

She stepped back. "For now." She vowed the second she was back in Elias's arms, she would claim his mark. Hex would never want her then, never be allowed to have her. She'd kill him before that happened.

He worked his jaw, rubbing a calloused tattooed hand down his chin, the whorls and patterns on his skin flexing.

"Head back inside." His gesture to the holding cells had her fear flaring.

"No."

A frown pulled at his lips. "The second they find the artefact, I'll take you to them." But before that, he'd trap her at the mercy of a psychopath.

Ace does as he's told.

She crossed her arms as rage burned. The longer she was forced to be in Hex's presence, the faster she forgot the torture he'd put her through. A wild cat playing with its prey, making it feel like maybe it was safe, maybe it didn't need to fear the predator before it sank its teeth into their spinal cord and snapped it with one bite.

"Walk, woman."

"I can't go back in there."

But Hex didn't care. He stormed forward, dropping his shoulder and thrusting it into her abdomen, forcing her to fold over his back as she gasped and punched and shouted.

"No! You can't do this to me again!"

She cursed and spat and kicked until he threw her atop the cot nearest the door and locked the cell. He glanced over her once as she sprawled to the ground, the memories of the last few days bombarding her over and over until her skin grew slick with sweat. "Please," she gasped for air that wouldn't come as she looked at the showers, the cloth that Ace had used to suffocate her still dangling from a showerhead. Mocking.

"Please, don't send him back here." Her voice grew shrill. "Please!"

But Hex was already gone, and she was alone.

SIX

Sylvie was underwater. Ace plugged her nose, pinching until it broke, blood pouring down the back of her throat as he held her under. She choked and inhaled, her lungs burning and fighting as he plunged her deeper and deeper. Only one thing shone in the inky pitch of his demonic iris: a purple string of light that hummed, faded and thin, one end embedded in her flesh, the other far beyond the darkness. It flared and twined as she fought. Her mouth opened in a silent scream.

"Wake up."

"No! Stop! Please!"

Heat encased her as she woke, a grip around her body blocking every buck and thrown elbow until the buzzing lights of the cells and the scent of wood smoke enveloped her senses.

"No more! No—"

"Sylvie."

Her heart lurched. *Elias? Kian?*

But when her nightmare faded, it wasn't a crimson gaze that stared back, or dark umber with indigo flecks. It was gold. Hex.

His jaw set as he carried her from the building, down the gravelled path, and placed her in the back seat of his truck, behind the object of her nightmares. Ace said nothing. He didn't even look her way as Hex buckled her seat belt and left her staring in the rearview mirror at the soulless eyes in the passenger seat.

She set her features in stone. Disinterest. Disgust. Hate.

Ace would not see how much he had hurt her or bent her to the point of breaking. *Because of Hex.*

Pure exhaustion tugged at her as they pulled away from the gravel path and onto the asphalt. While Hex said nothing as he drove, she recognised the winding roads he followed. Kian must have found the sprite, and that meant she was going home. *Home.* Her first time seeing the house in person would be a fucking hostage exchange. It broke her heart, but she probably wouldn't live there long with psycho shifters knocking at their back door. She let her lids drift shut as the purr of the engine lulled her like a white noise machine.

Elias and Kian would be there, ready to hold her and make the pain go away. They'd destroy for her too, but with the threat of Ace using his bite against Elias, she wouldn't tell him the full extent of her treatment. She couldn't lose him. When they attacked, they would be ready. Ace wouldn't see them coming. Neither would Hex.

She floated in and out of sleep, voices penetrating the fog in her mind even if she couldn't make sense of the words.

"—should have told you sooner … my mate—"

"Impossible. Why would the Fates—"

Guttural growls vibrated beneath her as she adjusted, tucking her feet against the heated seats, and slipped back into oblivion.

"Who knows?"

"Only Rose."

The rest of their conversation garbled and mixed with the noise of her nightmares. She gasped awake as a pressure on her fingernails returned, the pliers in her dreams handled by Hex instead of Ace, his golden gaze drilling her spirit until it crumpled. Her fingers curled, tucking into her body. *Just a dream.*

They pulled up a winding path, the forest arching in a crescent around a farmhouse elevated on a slight slope. Gardens trickled alongside a paved path and at the base of it stood Elias and Kian.

With a sharp inhale, she fumbled for her seat belt, not waiting for the truck to stop before snatching at the handle. She whimpered at the child lock and slammed her fist into the glass. Kian stepped closer, his throat bobbing, but Elias held him back with a hand to the elbow, his own eyes so dark red they almost looked black.

"Let me out!"

The engine cut off and Hex was there, pulling the door open and stepping back as she slipped out the door, skidding across the dusty driveway to get to Elias and Kian. Her legs gave out moments before she slammed into Kian, his arms looping around her back and squeezing, the draining of her darkness so stark her head spun.

"Wait." The breathless demand stilled his siphoning, and she buried her forehead into his chest. If he took too much, she might lose her rage, and she needed it if she was going to get revenge eventually. And she would.

Elias gripped her chin and tilted her head up from Kian's arms.

"Are you hurt?" His low tone held a warning.

Don't lie to me.

He toyed with the remnants of her hair as if it were the only thing stopping him from using his hands to rip the throats out of their silent observers.

Her breathing hitched, and anger flared down Kian's mark.

"Tell him, Princess."

She swallowed, shaking her head and facing the two monsters she was lying for.

Hex studied them, his gaze not holding malice, but something else, something that stirred the writhing *thing* lingering around Sylvie's guttering fire.

Ace, though, Ace didn't spare any of them from the dripping scorn.

"What did you do to her?" Elias said, voice low.

Sylvie cut her attention to him, not missing Hex's head turning to his beta as she fingered Elias's collar.

"Please, don't, Elias." With her weakened, she would only slow her males down, and if it came to a fight, they'd risk themselves to keep her safe. Only one bite would hurt Elias. Kill him. Unthinkable.

"I'm fine. My hair got matted. *Look at me.* I just need rest. Give them the stupid thing and take me home."

Elias dragged his gaze back to her, running his thumb down her scar, a haunted look entering his expression. She stepped out of Kian's hold and stood at Elias's side as her husband lifted a box from behind him. Iron spirals carved through the dark wood, and a silver latch flicked up from Kian's light pressure. Inside sat a chalice the colour of strawberry wine with tiny gems flickering along the stem and a twisted band of gold sunken into the base.

Kian lifted the artefact and raised it between them. "Mixing the blood of two shifters inside and drinking it will form a bond between the couple. Not a true mate bond, but enough for reproduction."

Ace grunted low, surveying it warily.

Kian continued unperturbed, "I'd be wary of born shifters using it if they haven't found their mates yet. If it happened—"

"There hasn't been a mate bond formed in over two decades," Hex interjected, pointedly ignoring the one that was supposedly between him and Sylvie.

"Still," Kian said. "I wouldn't tempt the Fates."

Hex nodded once, reaching for it when his pocket buzzed. Ace's phone followed immediately after and only he answered, the echoes of distress peeling through the air.

Sylvie couldn't make out the words, but her stiffening kindred apparently could.

"What's happening?"

Hex's bass growl sent a shock wave through her, and she leaned into Elias's cool frame as the alpha hissed, "This is why you monsters deserve nothing but death. Every fucking one of you." Hex shook his head, taking the phone from Ace, and stormed a few steps away.

She swallowed. "What happened?" she whispered.

Ace's hate-filled glower saturated her. "Yet another vampire attack on our people."

"It's daylight," Kian stated with a furrowed brow.

What does that have to do with anything? Elias could be in the sun with no effect. The present moment being a prime example.

"Not turned vampires," Ace spat.

Elias spoke then, menace dripping from every syllable. "Born vampires haven't set foot on Erus since the Division. How do we know this isn't another infighting clan war incited by the droves of humans *you* turned?"

Sylvie barely followed along. There was so much she didn't know.

"Our species is dwindling, you vampire scum. All the humans we turn know the truth and the risks. They choose our life. But you and your brother can't stand it, can you?

Sending your thieves month after month," Ace said, "stealing our elders and women."

Sylvie suppressed the surprise that must have darted across her face. Her horror.

"Not possible," Elias said, cutting off her thoughts. "They'd need a powerful realm crosser to achieve what you're claiming, and they're all dead."

Except for Kian and Kerensa. But neither of them would do what Ace claimed.

Hex returned, handing off Ace's phone, his expression hard. "Don't preach our history to me, bloodsucker prince."

Sylvie stomached another gut punch as Elias said, "Why? You weren't there, pup. I was."

The stare down between Elias and Hex had her fated bond humming in warning. She let Kian's emotions wash over her, each one unravelling as she let them settle—disappointment, anxiety, relief, and acceptance.

"We should just kill them," Ace growled, his face morphing as he cut his black gaze to Sylvie.

Don't do it. Don't you fucking dare.

His teeth elongated, words garbled, "Finish what I started with that mutt."

The second the sentence left Ace's shifting maw, Sylvie closed her eyes with a sigh, defeated. *Now why the fuck did you say that?*

A cacophony of sudden violence tore apart the serenity of the space while a tug pulled her in the opposite direction.

"We have to move, Princess." Kian drew her up the path, but she dug her heels in and shrugged off his touch.

"Help him, Kian!" She turned towards the chaos, heart racing as Elias prowled around the ten-foot bear, who was already littered with deep wounds, while Hex seemed to be halfway through a shift. Ace's huge, glistening mouth dived towards Elias, and Sylvie found herself running, terror filling her with adrenaline.

"Stop!" Kian's following words were lost in the sound of the rapid thud of her heart against her ribs and the gasping of her breath as she barrelled into the bear's chest, knocking it back before its teeth collided with Elias.

"Get back!" It all happened so fast; she didn't see the three-inch claws until they dug into the soft skin across her chest.

"No!"

Blood drenched her as a burning pain lit her torso on fire, the force of Ace's hit sending her flying across the grass. The angle gave her the perfect view of Hex's completed shift. His wolf dwarfed Ace, with his colour and sleekness matching a raven.

He leapt with animalistic grace, digging his gleaming canines into the bear's throat, tearing and growling as Ace's claws raked his sides.

Kian knelt beside her, dragging his hands over her body, searching for wounds while she looked on in horror at Elias wrenching Ace's head back—so close to his fucking teeth—giving Hex better access.

"Wait," Sylvie called weakly, dragging herself to her feet and leaning against Kian for support. She curled her bloodied fingers around the chalice he still held and lifted it. "Don't kill him." Not yet.

Ace deserved death, but not like this. No, Sylvie wanted the honours when the time was right and she wasn't a shell of her former self.

She braced her core as she slid through the bloodied grass and shook her head at Elias. The noises coming from Ace weren't good, the rattle in his lungs suggesting he might not make it anyway, but she persisted.

Hex let go first, growling over the sounds of Ace's bellows, and once Elias released him he fell to the ground, whining. Ace seemed to realise how near to death he was and limped off into the forest, not daring to look back.

Sylvie swallowed. Letting him go could cost her, but for now, she didn't care. Kian had lived through enough violence for a thousand lifetimes. He deserved to witness mercy. Even if it was short-lived. Even if he already knew her intentions.

Hex edged nearer, focus locked on the chalice in her hands.

"Sylvie," Elias warned, but a soft, "Wait," from Kian had him silenced as she approached the solitary wolf.

Gore dripped from his muzzle and sides. Perhaps the wounds would kill him, but by the look of it, some of the deepest gouges were already healing.

A girl could dream.

He shook his body like a wet hound and the red droplets spread across the lawn and her skin, coating her in the flecks until she was certain it looked like she had the pox. Her shoulder wound hissed with the movement, but she lifted it anyway. "Here." She raised the chalice towards his snout, fighting the tremble from blood loss. He could kill her at this distance, or bite her hand off, but he carefully clasped his teeth around the cup instead. His warm, wet breath fanned across her front, his tongue lolling once and brushing the back of her blood-soaked fingers as he adjusted his grip on the chalice.

A faceless creature inside her purred, but before she could focus on it, Hex spun and sprinted towards the woods, leaving his truck behind. She held her stance for as long as she could, until the swaying of her body turned to complete collapse. Elias caught her and pressed his lips to her forehead as the world turned white.

SEVEN

"You should feed."

"I'm not letting her out of my sight."

Sylvie's hearing returned before her ability to move did, the strained voices of her males penetrating her mind. She could almost see their tense frames hovering about her.

"She's asleep, Elias."

Not anymore.

"It's my fault we're in this mess. It's my fault they hurt her."

"She's healed now—"

"I'm not talking about her shoulder. They did something to her."

Kian didn't respond, and the flurry of emotion down their bond told her to stay quiet. She schooled her features.

"Don't bother hiding it. I know what it looks like when a person is tortured, Kian."

Her heart hammered in her chest. What would he do if he knew the true extent of her treatment? She already had a fair idea. But there was something else in the statement. Another hidden accusation. A hint of fear down Kian's bond had the violet swirl on her chest itching, confirming what she felt.

"What's that supposed to mean?" he said. Even with closed eyes, she imagined a look spearing between them. One that referenced more than what had happened to her. She never shared Kian's history with Elias, and it looked like he hadn't either.

"I know you," Elias said, "I won't pry, and I don't expect an explanation, but I know the face of a survivor."

Tears prickled Sylvie's eyes and ran down her cheeks, past the lids that seemed glued together. Someone cleared their throat as Sylvie's body finally caught up with her consciousness.

"Princess?"

She reached blindly for the voice and had both hands grasped. One cold set of hands, the other warm.

"Sorry," she whispered, sniffling the emotion down.

"You did nothing wrong." Kian's breathy voice tickled her cheek as he pressed his lips to hers. Her lids fluttered open, and she smiled as Elias took Kian's place, kissing her lightly, as if he might break her.

She lay atop a soft surface, and as her mind grew clearer, she took in the surrounding room. Silvery drop lights shone from the high ceilings gleaming above. Beneath her were towels to catch the blood from her shoulder, now completely healed and cleaned.

"Did you heal me?" she asked Elias, sitting up, using Kian as support.

He shook his head, his skin a little paler than she remembered. A jolt of fear sank into her stomach. "Did you get bit? Are you okay?"

"I'm fine—"

"I healed you. He just needs to feed," Kian interrupted, glancing at him sidelong. Reprimanding.

She blinked. "Go feed."

He grunted, standing up to pace. "I'll need to hunt in the Tynaan. I didn't have time to stock this place."

Tynaan? The foreign word invoked a full-body shiver as Kian ran a soothing hand down her shoulder.

"He means the forest."

She inhaled and sat, rolling her tired shoulders. The pain in her muscles eased, as if Kian had done a bit more than just heal her shoulder.

"Be careful," she said to Elias. "Please."

His head tilted. "Me?"

"Hex and Ace might still be in there. If they bite you—"

His expression softened as he wandered back to the bed, tucking a rogue curl behind her ear. "Shifter venom is lethal, but not to the royal bloodlines."

She relaxed a fraction, placing her palm over his hand still near her cheek.

"So Ace was telling the truth then. You're a prince too."

Elias glowered. "That was about the only thing he got right." He turned his hand to capture hers and brought her fingers to his lips, kissing the knuckles. "I'll be fine. If anything, I hope I see them; then I can put the animals down."

She shook her head, hating the way her hair bounced around her face. "Don't. If anyone is gonna kill them, it'll be me."

A dark look simmered in his stare as he smirked and pulled away, leaving her with Kian.

After a few moments, a distant door slammed, and Kian sighed. "We should get you cleaned up."

Taking his hands, Sylvie followed him from the sparse room into a giant en suite bathroom, the tiled space filled with luxury and pristine accessories.

A spa-sized tub stole her attention, resting against the back wall with a waterfall showerhead fitting above it. Flashes of Ace's torture filled her head, and she turned away. *Don't let him ruin this.* The vanity lit up as Kian flipped a switch by the door, and the tiles beneath her feet warmed.

In the mirror, she hardly recognised herself. Blood doused her washed-out skin and the purple-toned hollows under her eyes highlighted her hazel irises. She touched the red flecks on her lips and her scar. *Hex is all over me.* She shuddered, looking at Ace's abuse next. Her hair wasn't nearly as ugly as she feared. The waves she once had instead curled around her head with a gentle halo. The uneven layers around her nape would need a trim, but she could style it. She sighed and looked away. She really needed to get her priorities in order.

Opposite the vanity was an open shower space, which she slowly neared, pulling the lever to the hot water with shaking hands.

Kian drew a bath as she undressed and hovered before the scalding spray. Icy dread leeched the confidence from her movements until Kian brushed a thumb down her spine, soothing some of the fear. With a swallow, she climbed in, letting the water wash away her sins. She kept her face out of the mist, still unable to stop the barrage of violent memories when it touched her mouth and nose. Could Kian feel them? She really hoped he couldn't, and when she glanced towards him, her heart stuttered. Leaning against the vanity, arms crossed in front of his chest, Kian followed her every movement. Married or not, a blush crept across her cheeks.

The playful yet reserved quirk on his lips revealed some of his thoughts, too.

She inclined her head in question. *Coming in?* But he shook his head and turned to the bath.

She turned too, to the shelving hanging from the wall that offered shampoo and body wash, which she used ample pumps of until the water ran clear. Her hands trembled as she tilted her hair under the showerhead, using Kian's movements as a distraction.

The half-filled bath frothed with iridescent pink bubbles.

She turned off the shower and wrung her hair. "What's that for?" she asked as Kian approached, fully dressed.

"I thought you'd like a full spa treatment." A soft, knowing smile settled on his lips.

She regarded the body of water with shallow breaths. "Only if you come in with me."

He stilled for a moment before pulling his dark shirt overhead, then loosening his belt and letting the trousers drop to the floor. He took her pruning fingers and climbed in, guiding her against his chest. She lay on her side, her head tucked beneath his chin, tracing a finger over a scar that crossed the boundary of his trap muscle. He held her, the reciprocal tracing of his fingers along her body enough to quell the intrusive memories.

"You don't have to hide," she said, snuggling deeper into his chest.

"I know."

He reached his hand past her to a small panel with five silver buttons. The two closest turned on jets that bubbled around her feet. The pressure relaxed her soles.

"You don't have to either, Princess."

Kian gently turned her until her back pressed against his front and he massaged bubbles across her decolletage, breasts, and belly. Then trailed his fingers beneath the waters.

She clutched his free hand and guided it over her cleavage, the security in his grip letting her head fall back against his shoulder.

"I need to tell you what happened."

He stiffened, but his fingers continued their light tracing. "I felt it," he said.

She shuddered. Feeling every slice as Lazuli carved Kian's flesh would have killed her, and yet Kian held her, without pity or judgement, only peace.

"Maybe later then," she breathed, letting Kian's controlled touch meld her deeper into him. "When Elias gets back."

Yes. It wasn't a story she wished to repeat.

"If you're sure." Kian's voice dropped deeper as he kissed her head. "I can take more if you need." She sensed him probing her wavering emotions, the grief, the anger, but she shook her head. He'd taken more than enough. She would have to handle this one on her own.

"Just be with me. Like this." His finger brushed her clit, and he held it there, adding pressure until she nodded and lifted her hips. "Please."

And Kian did.

* * *

A light mist covered Sylvie's body as she jolted awake next to Kian, the waxing moonlight illuminating the hardwood floor at the foot of their bed. Sitting up, she skimmed a hand along her body, checking for aches or fever, but the wetness to her skin was foreign, like the nightmares of drowning that plagued her had crossed into the real world.

As the afterimages receded, she traced a finger across her lips and down the scar of her face, letting its tail guide her finger between her breasts, recounting all the ways Kian had filled her in the hours before. Those were the dreams to remember. Not Ace's violence.

Healing, Kian had called the moments between them. "Sex, intimacy, and blood sharing all act as a binding."

She palmed the mark over her heart, following the raised whorls. She needed a lot of healing. It was probably why Kian had drawn climax after climax from her.

"A mark is not something you receive and no longer have to earn. Like any relationship, bonds need regular upkeep," he'd said as he curled his expert fingers inside her—a reclamation. "If you don't maintain it," he'd said, nipping her earlobe, "it will fade."

She had melted then, against him, into him, her fears abating. It wasn't a hopeless fight against Hex. With enough loathing and distance, their "mate bond" would never amount to anything.

She shifted across the duvet and rubbed a thumb over her neck where Kian had grazed his teeth, the soft reprimand washing down her skin.

Stay with me. Don't disappear inside your mind.

"You okay?"

She jolted as Kian spoke from her side, his warm touch on her shoulder eliciting a faint electric shock.

"Yeah," she breathed, tucking her hair behind her ears. Damp.

"Did you go outside?"

She shook her head as she stood from the bed and padded to the sliding door, pulling the thick curtains aside. A light drizzle misted across the lawn, the moonlight hazy as the rain clouds bunched and darkened.

Kian's warmth kissed her back before his arms looped around her belly. Her gut twisted as she squinted into the darkness.

"Do you sleepwalk?"

"I don't know."

She pivoted in his arms. "Where's Elias?"

He hummed thoughtfully, kissing the furrow of her brow before guiding her from the bedroom. "He called earlier while you were resting. There weren't enough options in the forest, so he headed to Sterling to retrieve some of his stores."

She glanced around. The kitchen and lounge appeared relatively sparse, the stone bench tops and centre island shining under a trio of pendant lights, the glass shades giving off warmth. "We didn't have much time to move in," Kian said, guiding her to a tall stool by the island.

"It's okay."

She glanced at the dining area tucked behind a wall separating the spaces. In it sat a long table dressed with basic cloth and candles and a bushy plant in the middle. A smile tugged on her lips. *No time to move in, but enough to get a plant.* Beyond that room was a closed door, and she drew her gaze away. She'd go exploring later.

"How far away are we from Sterling?" From the shithole she'd called home since birth.

Kian filled an electric jug with water and set it on the stand to boil as he said, "About two hours. It's fairly secluded out here. Sagehill is the nearest town, but it's still half an hour away."

Sylvie blinked. *Sagehill?* She wasn't an expert on geography by a long shot, but she recognised the name.

"Isn't that a cult town?" There were a few on Erus, but they had little reach or influence. The western continent had far more, with most of the populace living the ways of the old gods. Or so Gold Broadcasting said. Thirteen primeval ancestors with supposed influence over worldly domains, meant to be honoured in every human interaction. Fire, oceans, war, and even sex. All male, unsurprisingly. It seemed like a lot of admin for Sylvie; when growing up was solely survival, there was no time to thank something invisible for her misery. It wasn't that people had to worship them, but non-belief was shunned in those "cult" communities. She'd always been an atheist. It was better that than believing a myriad of entities sworn to protect her had forsaken her. Plus the clergy of all thirteen gods vehemently opposed any literature about mythical creatures, which meant all of the spicy books that got her through many lonely years were banned in those towns. What would they do if they found out those "mythical creatures" were all real? Most of Sterling was the same as her anyway—godless.

Kian's chuckle breached her musing. "No, Princess. That's just good marketing. The locals know about our kind, but keep our secrets."

"Why would they do that?"

He drummed his fingers on his chin, elbow propped on the bench in front of her. "We keep the pests away."

She steepled her fingers and leaned towards him. "Are you intentionally being cryptic?"

His smirk was enough to give her butterflies as he straightened and moved through the kitchen, pulling mugs, sugar, and instant coffee from different cupboards.

"Shifters. I ward the towns against shifters, demons, anything with ill-intent. Half of the locals have some very diluted fae heritage from before the Division of the realms, and they want quiet lives. Shifters bring about chaos and violence, and Sagehill wants no part of it. They're good people."

Sylvie stayed silent as he made her coffee and slid it across the counter. She let the mug warm her clammy palms and tried not to implode from his statements.

"Do shifters attack people?"

Kian half shrugged. "About forty years ago, there was an influx of killings, mostly livestock and men. The town claimed a pack of extra large wolves were responsible, despite wolves being native only to northern Erus and the Iron Peaks. Once I warded the town, the sightings stopped. 'Animal' attacks are still reported along the roads here more than anywhere else in Erus."

He exhaled a faint laugh as she sipped her coffee.

"You inadvertently had us buy property near the largest and probably only surviving shifter populace on the continent."

Her stomach sank. It wasn't a fluke at all, if Elias's claims about sensing the bond were true. Something drew her to this place, to the ancient Tynaan forest and the beasts that lingered within.

Rowan-godsdamn-Hex.

Kian offered a knowing look before fixing her breakfast, a selection of cooked vegetables and mushrooms on rye toast and a bowl of carved fruit beside it.

"Are we gonna move again?" she asked.

"Do you want to move?"

No. Yes.

"I—I don't want them to take this from me."

Kian nodded, plucking one of her cut strawberries and eating it. "Then they won't." He took another. "I wish this could have been different for you. You deserve the world, Princess. I don't know why the Fates are determined to ensure you draw short straws."

Sylvie nibbled at the crust. "Maybe it's what I deserve." Kian's narrowing gaze had her straightening. That was an inside thought. "Sorry I—"

"Is that what you really feel?"

She pushed down the self-loathing. "No …" She paused, answer stilted. "I think I want to feel sorry for myself for a while." Rain picked up outside, the pattering on the roof rising to a steady thrum. Hopefully Elias wasn't driving the winding roads right then.

"Well, I'll be here when you're ready," he said. "The Fates wouldn't give you more than you can handle. There must be a reason you're the first fated in centuries. And the first I've heard with two."

Or three.

"And what's your hypothesis, Husband?"

Kian rounded the counter and lifted the toast for her to take a bite. She did, savouring the taste of mushrooms and garlic.

"I don't know, but the Fates don't make mistakes."

She rolled her eyes. Maybe her husband was a religious zealot, too. "What exactly is a Fate? Is it a type of god?"

Kian rubbed his face with a sigh. "Sometimes I forget how sheltered you were from our realms."

The frown she offered back had his hands lifting—placating. "The fae texts in my mother's library suggest they're sentient ancient beings from the conception of the three wider realms. Ilfaem, where all fae are born, as you know. Argyncia, more commonly called the Glass City by the vampires, and Beihllua—the shifter realm. Back then, the veil between realms was open for everyone. All you had to do was step through the fae rings they made across Erus."

"What about the western continent, or the rest of the world?"

He shook his head. "For whatever reason, the outer realms only border Erus."

"And what about humans? Could they travel through the fae rings too?"

"Yes. No adverse effects for travel, either. Portal sickness was a curse from the Division when the Fates segregated us, destroyed the fae rings, and stopped all interspecies mateships as punishment. Then same-species bonds faded. Some elders suggested it was from our twisted morals, others blamed the shifter rebellion." The toast grew cold in Sylvie's hand. *But they're allowing it now. What changed?*

"Why did they rebel?"

Kian shook his head. "I don't know. My mother said it wasn't a history worth knowing."

Sylvie brushed the crumbs from her fingers and slid the plate away, her appetite waning.

"The Fates are the closest thing to gods we have in Ilfaem. All of our texts have a level of influence from them. From visions or voices, or dreams. Prophecies. The last recorded fae to dream walk died a hundred years before I was born."

The air between them grew heavy. Oppressive. Sylvie straightened in her seat, downing the last tepid dregs of her coffee, and picked a flake of sleep from her eye. "Okay, well, whether I'm special can remain up for debate. For now, I want to move on."

Kian pressed his forehead to hers. "There's no rush."

She kissed him, the softness of his lips drawing her in. He always knew what she needed to hear. Even the warmth of his skin, his mouth moving with hers, melted away the darkness inside her. She ignored the way her hidden creature stirred and sucked his lower lip into her mouth, nipping the flesh between her teeth.

Before the moment could go further, the light chirps of waking birds surrounded them, and the front door slammed open.

EIGHT

"What do you mean, you need to leave?" Sylvie sat on Elias's lap as Kian packed a small duffel on their bed.

"Only for half the day. There are some things I need to complete the property's warding." He gave Elias a look that Sylvie didn't have enough time to decipher. She tracked that gaze and nudged her vampire. "You think it's a good idea for him to go out there alone? What if the shifters come back?" When Elias returned that morning, drenched and glowering, she had expected they would all spend the day together, making up for lost time.

Kian clicked his tongue. "I might not look it, but I can hold my own in a fight, Princess."

He did "look it." The symmetry of his muscles could only be from years of hard work.

She humphed and pressed her spine into Elias's broad chest. He'd hardly spoken a word to her all morning, mostly one word commands and a lot of gentle manhandling.

"Is it selfish of me to want us all together for one fucking day?"

She hadn't told them about anything yet, and by Kian's sad look, she wondered if him leaving now was intentional.

"I'll be back as soon as I can; then we can talk. I promise I wouldn't leave you if it wasn't important." He glanced at Elias again, as if communicating through telepathy. She frowned but relaxed into her cold vampire's touch, her ass brushing one too many times across his lap. The subtle stiffening and adjustment of her on his cock sent an obvious message. *Stop squirming.*

At his tightening grip, she craved to wiggle more. Instead, she settled for tucking her hips, hoping he would do something about her attitude as Kian zipped his bag.

Her husband kissed her temple and left the room, playing with the keys to the motorcycle she'd only just learned about.

As the engine's roar and pop of the exhaust filled the house, her pulse sped up. She'd never been on one, but that was going to change. The speed and open air. Exhilarating. The sound faded as Kian rode away and Sylvie zoned back into the slow exhales of the male at her back.

Her breathing quickened the longer they stayed in that frozen embrace until she couldn't bear the anticipation any longer.

"Elias."

"No."

She leaned forward to stand, but he held her steady a few moments longer.

"Elias—"

He finally let her go, and she turned to him as he buried his hands in the long, dark curls covering his forehead and held her stare. The silence grew unbearable, and she swallowed. "Talk to me."

He looked at her then, really looked, soaking in the hair, the dark circles, the sway of her still-sore body.

"Every time I look at you, I see my failure to protect you."

Her nose crinkled, the confession lingering between them as he stood, his height towering above her as his finger brushed a curl around her ear and traced a line along her jaw.

"I should never have left you alone." His jaw clenched. "I won't make that mistake again."

She shuddered, pleasure winding through her at the darkness of his tone, the hatred in his crimson eyes.

"They—"

"Not yet," he said, dragging his thumb over her lower lip and pulling it down as she inhaled sharply. "If I hear it, I won't stop until anyone who ever touched you is choking on their own blood."

Her inner flames seared away a fraction of the pain, his rage bolstering her own. "Good," she said. His anger flared, the grip on her face shifting around her chin, her jaw, her throat.

She sighed as he tipped her head to the side, his nose dragging along her scar, the sight of him over her consuming the memories of Ace doing the same. The shifter would not break her. She would not let him ruin her life.

"I want you to train me. To make me better. Stronger. I never want to feel that weak again."

Elias's fangs descended, the veins in his eyes spreading, his rage taking over. He stilled, letting his teeth return painfully slowly to their flat shape as he slid his hand into her hair. He had years to harness such mastery. She didn't have the same time.

"Show me how to use it. That rage," she said.

"Vīs," he rasped. "It's called vīs. If you don't have control, it will consume you."

Vīs. The affinity slotted into her awareness in the same way her fae sight had. She had felt it when she attacked Lazuli: the loss of self, the compassion—mercy. It was powerful. In her control, it would be deadly.

"Maybe that's what I want."

His grip tightened on the back of her neck, and she relished it. The touch of a male who would burn the world for her.

"I want you to mark me, Elias. I want to be yours."

His and Kian's alone.

Elias's grip tightened, the flare of his nostrils signalling the lapse of control as he flipped her onto the bed. His thigh nestled between hers, a hard weight settling on her pelvis. She ground her hips against it as his hands clawed at the duvet on either side of her head. His tongue dragged across his fangs.

"You aren't ready—"

But she shut him up by twisting her head and biting his wrist, hard enough to break the skin. He didn't pull away as she licked along the wound until it closed again.

"I'm fucking ready." She traced his spilt blood across her lower lip with her finger, puncturing it with a fang so their blood mingled. "Make me feel something." *Make me forget.*

He took one second to survey her—to drink her in before he tore her clothes off as easily as shredding paper. Her breasts prickled with gooseflesh at the sudden shift in temperature while his mouth sought to possess her, owning her lips, then her nipples, then lower. She hadn't had him that way yet, his dominating grip kneading her ass as he grazed his fangs along her inner thigh.

"Yes," she sighed, yearning to bury her fingers in his curls, but he gripped her wrists, pinning them overhead as he rose, drinking her in with irises the colour of carmine and rust.

"This is why Kian left, isn't it?" Even as she spoke the words, her mark hummed.

With a smirk, Elias drew back, crossing the room to a closed door next to the bathroom. A linen cupboard. "He knows as well as I do your needs, Kitten. Varied as they may be."

He has that right.

She propped herself on her elbows, observing his graceful movements as he pulled something from the narrow shelves.

"What's in there?"

Without answering, he turned and lifted the object between his hands—braided rope the thickness of her pinkie. Lengths of it.

Her brows rose along with her pulse. "What's that for?"

Again, he moved without speaking, his gaze flashing to a stout orewood beam above the bed and the silver snap ring attached to a thick screw secured there.

A raging flush pinked her cheeks as she sat up more, dragging the comforter across her bare lap. This was new. *New could be good.*

"Has anyone ever tied you up before, Kitten?" he asked, like her answer would determine many things. She settled on the truth.

"Handcuffs, once." *Half-truth.*

His expression flickered. "But not ropes."

"No." *True.*

He hummed, nodding to himself as he unravelled one end, letting the other fall to the floor. Then, grasping her ankles, he dragged her down the bed as she jerked the blankets tighter. She wasn't a prude, but this was another level of sex. One that would display her every imperfection, like the white hairline stretch marks along her hips, or the dimpling along the back of her thighs.

It was daylight, for fuck's sake. Humans designed that type of fetishism for the dark.

Elias shook his head at her white-knuckled grip on the comforter. "Off, now."

After two beats of resistance, she threw off her protection, tilting her head back at the vampire before her. *Her vampire.*

"Safe word?" he asked.

The lashing of the rope's tail atop her thigh stopped her mid-eye-roll.

"Ouch! Strawberries."

"Good."

She crossed her arms over her pebbled nipples until she noted his stare and the hand he held upturned between them. This time, she didn't pause. She placed her two wrists atop his palm, face up.

His eyes sparkled. "Good girl. Since you listened so well, you get a choice. Behind your back or in front of your chest."

"What does that mean—"

"Choose. Or I will."

She inhaled, clearing her throat on the exhale. "Chest."

He nodded. Pulling the end of the plaited rope through his fingers, he started an intricate binding around her wrists. Round and round, he wrapped, drawing her arms together until they melded as one. Three identical knots at inch intervals dotted her forearms, her mind jumping to a male she *really* didn't want to be thinking about. Three knots.

Three bonded males.

She shook the thoughts like clearing cobwebs, and Elias hummed. "Bring your arms in front of your chest."

"Yes, sir."

His motions stilted, but recovered quickly, and she bit her lip to stop the grin. Anything that ruffled him was a win.

The rough jute ropes followed the caress of his icy fingertips, then his lips after every knot.

"Stand."

She obliged, spying herself in the bedroom vanity, thoroughly flushed as he bound her tighter, a corset around her torso, accentuating the curves of her breasts and the new musculature of her arms until they were so snug against her body she couldn't manage a single movement. It should have scared her, being so restrained after the kidnapping, but something moved in her. Her back arched, her lids fluttering at the sight of her so beautifully bound by someone she trusted. Loved. *Worshipped.*

He pulled a small knife out from their bedside table, cutting the last section after knotting one last tie at her navel. The bindings warmed her skin from the friction, along with Elias's approving stare.

"You are the most beautiful being I have ever seen."

She flushed deeper, her head tilting as she let the sunlight filtering through the sheer curtains highlight the scar down her face. Her hair framed her eyes, bringing out the deepest golds.

"You're perfect." He dragged his fangs over her shoulder, standing to her side, the length of him pressing against her hip.

The silence between them gradually filled with heavy breathing and borderline whines as Elias curled his hand around her thigh to brush her clit.

"Yes, please." She leaned against him, holding his gaze through the mirror.

"Not yet, pet," he murmured into her hair, nipping the top of her ear and kneeling before her. She soaked up the image as he bound her left foot, his deft fingers creating a masterpiece up her leg, binding ankle to ass, her knee bent sharply. Her other leg wavered as nerves spun a web in her belly and her balance struggled to keep her upright.

"Just one leg for today. Perhaps we can try a more exposed position once you lose your shame."

She was incapacitated and naked, her body on complete display. *How much more exposed could I possibly get?*

He smirked at the defiance she plastered to her face even as she burned hotter. "Stop thinking. Lie back."

The last knot snuggled into her skin, and with her free leg she pushed herself onto the bed as Elias left the room completely. Without his watchful gaze she wriggled higher, testing the strength of his knots as she lay back, bound knee pointed to the ceiling. The likelihood he expected her to let it fall and bare herself completely was high, but she had appearances to maintain. She was his brat and he wouldn't forget it.

When he returned though, shirtless, a denser rope in one hand and a glass of thick red liquid in the other, she almost forgot. She lost her breath. "Fuck." Lifting her head up gave her a better view, but he moved far too quickly, his rippling abdomen catching the light. She itched to touch it. To run her tongue down until it reached the dark, coiled hair above his belt. To bite the tapered muscle.

Her hands curled in to fists as Elias grinned, taking a sip of blood and raising it to her, brows raised.

She dropped her head back with a wince. "No, thanks."

The only blood she would be drinking was his. And only once. After that, there was no need to consume that gelatinous, syrupy gore ever again. Even if Kian tasted like springtime and elation. If there were any perks to being a half breed, actual food was one of them.

Dropping the rope on the duvet with a thud, Elias slinked across the bed towards her, his shoulders shifting like a prowling beast.

Oh gods.

The moment he reached her knee, he threw it to the side and dipped his mouth to her soaked cunt.

"You're mine," he growled against her clit, sucking and flicking his tongue in languid circles. He pulled back just long enough to spank the exposed flesh of her ass cheek. "And I plan on showing you until you can't take another second."

* * *

Bound and suspended from the snap ring of the bedroom's centre beam, Sylvie balanced precariously on her toes as Elias curled his fingers inside her, drawing out the latest surge of bliss. Sweat dotted across her skin, her hair plastering to her cheeks as she whined.

"Please." Her teeth chattered as adrenaline coursed through her. "Mark me." The pains had already begun, a light roiling in her belly from the blood she had stolen. Maybe he would punish her, let her suffer for her thievery. But he backed away, lifting his fingers to his mouth and tasting her orgasm as she gasped and bucked. "Elias!"

"Are you ready to get down, Kitten?" He padded around her, trailing his forefinger across her belly to her breasts, pinching each nipple.

"Yes, please." She lowered her lashes. "Sir."

The smile that spread along her kindred's mouth could only be described as devilish as he undid the largest rope and lay her atop the bed. He worked in silence, untying each knot with a dexterity she could only dream of, until she lay free, her limbs sprawled limply. It's like he didn't want to mark her. At this rate, she'd be unconscious before she got the chance.

He undressed the rest of the way and climbed over her, letting his cock tease her entrance.

"Safe word?"

"Not yet," she groaned, lifting her hands to his hips and guiding them down to her.

With a sound that reverberated in his chest, firing a million sparks from her brain to her core, he gripped her wrists and threaded them behind his neck, nodding once when her fingers twined in the hair at his nape.

"I'll be gentle. Just this once."

But that wasn't what she wanted. She already had a gentle partner. One that considered her needs and took care of her soul. She wanted violence. Pain.

His gaze darkened as if her thoughts spelled themselves across her face, and his fangs slid free.

Without warning, his mouth dipped to her neck, the opposite side Kian had claimed, and his sharp needle teeth pierced her flesh. Her head reared back as a gasp tore from her mouth, tears prickling along her waterline.

She would get her pain.

But it shifted so abruptly as his cock plunged to the hilt inside her, his earlier foreplay giving her clarity. She needed to be drenched to handle his size. The stretch was considerable but bearable as she moaned and bucked to meet his second thrust. Third. Fourth. At some point, his mouth detached from her neck and claimed her lips, biting and sucking until she saw stars.

They moved in an erotic rhythm, the rocking of hips meeting in a mind-shattering collision as Elias pushed her closer to euphoria. Stroke after stroke, her body started failing her. Her teeth chattered, toes curling as bolts of pleasure pistoned through her, and her breath became laboured.

Blood roared in her ears until even his rasping, "Finish it, Kitten," barely broke through the haze. She let him cradle her nape, lifting her mouth to his bared throat as her lids fluttered to half-mast. Her gums ached in anticipation of the mark, and with a tentative prod of her teeth, she shivered at the sharpness of them, her second run through leaving her with a slice across her tongue.

Her lips parted against his throat as she floated atop a cliff above a churning sea. She leapt, arms wide, as she bit down, her mouth flooding with copper and ice. The flavour lashed her senses, throwing her into climax faster than she thought possible.

A dual orgasm shredded through both of them, and they groaned in tandem as their pleasure peaked. She swallowed a mouthful before pulling away and flattening her tongue against the wounds. The world grew sharp, her vision, smell, and taste firing heat into her brain, with the hottest brand scorching her chest.

She pressed Elias back, glancing at the new, deep crimson mark. Its patterns resembled Kian's, with one other addition—the single twining tail that united them. She hated the way there was a gap, that Elias's and Kian's marks each had a tendril that reached for something that wasn't there— that would never be there—but before she could let the thought settle, Elias pulled away from her. She immediately rued their distance, the emptiness chilling her, but the promise of aftercare staved off the cold.

She reached for him, for her scarlet-emerald mark carved across his heart, but he only smirked before flipping her onto her belly and plunging into her again. At first, she rose to meet him, the swelling beast prowling around her mind craving release, but after a dozen back-arching thrusts, she started unwinding.

"Elias! I can't ..."

"You know what to say."

"No!" Safe words weren't an option. She couldn't be weak. Not anymore. Not as Elias's mark throbbed on her chest. The tether between them was taut with rage and lust. She saw herself through his eyes for a moment—a phoenix alight after rebirth. The old Sylvie died when his mark seared into her flesh. She was made anew, and she would never bend again. Ice and fire fought within her as he fucked her into the mattress, her nails clawing the duvet until they pierced the fabric, tearing jagged lines. She screamed as his palm cracked against her bare ass, the sudden slap jolting up her spine. Again. Her back arched, her throat baring as she offered herself. He refused, slapping the opposite cheek, and she buried her face in the bedding. It was too much. She was imploding.

Wriggling only seemed to further capture his ire, his throaty tone cascading down her back. "No escaping, Kitten. You know what you need to do."

She lifted her head to breathe, but he forced her down, his finger hooking inside her mouth.

"No—"

She couldn't say it. It was weak. But her body wouldn't listen to her will, the tears coming before she could choke out in gasping sobs, "Strawberries."

He cradled her in an instant, his huge hands brushing the hair from her face before covering her with the untattered corner of their duvet.

"You did so well, love." The kiss he placed on her lips was nothing like the ones in the throes of passion. This one only succeeded in drawing more muffled cries.

"I failed."

His forefinger curled under her chin, his thumb brushing her lower lip as it trembled. "You did perfectly."

She sniffled, pulling her head away. "You did that on purpose, didn't you?"

His brows knitted together, but she sensed the deception down their bond. "It's normal to feel this way after an intense session."

"I don't want to feel! Not like this." More tears lanced through the sweat on her face. She swatted them away.

Swirling emotions electrified her nerve endings, her body trembling as he carried her to the bathroom and climbed into the shower with her in his arms. The scalding heat down her back did nothing to stop the spiral of her thoughts.

Elias held her against his chest, washing her as she tried to bury her emotions—tried not to picture herself drowning every time a drop of water flicked across her face.

"If you were mine," he said lowly, "only mine. I would teach you everything you needed to know about your vīs. I would stand at your side as you set the world on fire and hand you the kindling."

She hiccupped, her breaths uneven.

"But you aren't only mine. You are Kian's half too, and that means the parts of you that are pure and kind should be protected. I won't let you lose the elements of your soul that call to his."

Guilt swarmed all other thoughts as he washed her hair, his stare lingering on the choppy ends. She pulled back, jerking her head and whimpering as the shower spray misted over her mouth, the words she had been stowing away bursting out like they needed to be spoken.

"He cut my hair." Her eyes filled until she couldn't see past the unshed tears, her lower lip wobbling. Even without sight, she withered under Elias's shaking grip, feeling his sanity slipping away by the second.

"H-he held me under the water, over and over until I drowned. He tortured me for days."

"Weeks," Elias said, the sharp word forcing a chill through her despite the heat of the water. "He had you for two and a half weeks."

She crumpled into him then, barely feeling the lightness of his touch or the fury between their bond as he tucked her against him and didn't let her go.

NINE

"Find him."

She ran. The inky darkness full of biting branches and echoing howls closed in, but she ran. Soaked soil, foliage, and waterlogged sticks crackled underfoot as her steps thundered in time with her racing heart.

She had to find him. The Fates demanded it. "A triad!" they screamed as she pressed her bleeding palms to her ears.

One.

Two.

Three.

Heal the broken, so mote it be.

She ran. The swollen waxing gibbous shone, its last sliver hidden in shadow, yet its light barely reflected in her eyes. Throwing her arms out, she brushed the trees she passed, willing them to show her the way, their energy trails only visible if they so chose.

Darkness rewarded her touch this time, and she screamed in protest. "How can I find him if you won't show me the way?"

The shrieking winds whipped at her hair. "Call to him!" the voices of the Fates keened. "His blood already lives in you."

"Sylvie."

Her step faltered, her body jerking, hitting a wall, but her hands found nothing in her way. "What?"

"Sylvie!"

The voice grew insistent, but it wasn't who she was looking for—who she needed to see.

"Sylvie!"

"No!" she shouted back, trying to run again, only to be shaken violently.

Her jerky movements rattled memories in her brain. What the hell was happening?

"Wake up!"

* * *

With languid movements, Sylvie blinked against the afternoon sun as two faces stared at her sprawled on their bed, the top sheet barely draping over her naked body.

She sniffed a long, rib-expanding inhale and stretched her limbs in opposite directions until her joints finished their popping.

"What a weird dream." She stifled a yawn with the back of her hand.

"A dream?" Kian said. "Your eyes were open."

She blinked and peered at him then, tracing a nail over the marks on her chest. "No. I was napping."

Elias followed the trailing of her fingers as he said, "You had been. But when we came in here, you were talking to someone."

The leisurely thud of her heart faded, and a swirling unease gripped her increasing pulse.

"What was I saying?"

Kian's head tilted. "You really believe you were asleep?"

"Yes!" She sat up, wrapping the sheets around her chest, and was about to flip her hair over her shoulder before she remembered it was gone. Everything else that had temporarily fled her mind returned then too. Her throat constricted.

"You were looking for someone," Elias said.

Down the bond, a flood of emotions writhed. She couldn't distinguish any, or who they originated from, so she shut herself off from them before her turbulent thoughts strayed too far into her torture. They didn't need to know everything she was feeling yet.

"I was running through the woods."

Neither male spoke; they just held onto the silence, willing it to make her talk.

"It was just gibberish. Counting and voices and something about a moat—"

Kian gasped. "So mote it be?" His sudden outburst had her shuffling to the edge of the bed and searching for clothes to hide the thundering of her heart and the rising nerves along with it.

"Maybe. I don't know." She slugged a hoodie over her head and pulled on some sweatpants before padding towards the bedroom door. Elias blocked her path though, his hand cupping her jaw.

"I think it's time we talk."

She hardened her gaze, pulling her chin free, and slipped past him to the kitchen, snatching a speckled mug from the nearest cupboard and flicking on the electric kettle.

"I already told you. Ace tortured me." When she lifted her gaze from scooping the herbal tea into the metal infuser, she noted her males. Elias stood stiffly between the kitchen and the lounge while Kian sat at the breakfast bar, palming his hands across the counter like the world was tilting.

She dropped her focus down to the teaspoon in her hand. How insensitive could she be? Her torture had lasted two weeks maximum, when Lazuli had mutilated and abused Kian for years. As far as she could remember, Ace hadn't violated her in *that* way. She couldn't stand it if he had.

Still, there would be no mercy.

She fetched the kettle and filled her cup to the brim, letting the steam mist over her face. "How long was I gone?"

"Seventeen days," Kian answered, his bond tugging at her, as if to pull more of her pain. She shut him off. Shouldering this pain was the least she could do.

Elias, though—his tether to her sung with a vengeance so sharp she tasted metal.

"I'll skin that fucking bear."

She stirred and stirred. She would let him, as long as she could remove his head from his shoulders.

"And Hex?" Kian posed the question, but she noted how both marks twinged at the mention of the shifter. "Did he …"

He left the rest of the question unsaid, but she knew.

It was too hard to answer. Hex wasn't innocent. His touch just didn't illicit the same fear as Ace's. The hate, though, was fairly equal.

In silence, she lifted the scalding mug to her lips and blew, fighting the urge to down the boiling water in one gulp. Maybe that could cleanse her palate of the monsters. Perhaps recognising her thoughts, Elias appeared at her side, guiding the mug back to the sink, where he tipped a third of the contents and topped it up with tap water to cool it off.

"Answer him," Elias said, returning the warm mug between her hands. She regarded him as he hovered over her shoulder before sipping and shrugging.

Something tightened on her bond, making the tea slosh in her hands, and she jerked backwards, meeting Elias's glare with a scowl of her own.

"Say the words," he said.

"Stop it." She pushed past him and stormed to the front door, ripping it open and letting the crisp evening air cool her frustration. Moving past the porch swing, down the stairs, and onto the dewy lawn, Sylvie lifted her face to the slowly falling mist from the sky. Its soft touch quelled some of her turmoil as she breathed. Centred. Calmed.

The males' presence at her back grounded her until the words she had been holding back escaped with a sigh.

"He's my mate."

She blinked back a burning sensation as her marks flared. Rage. Disappointment.

Confirmation. They already knew.

"I will never accept him." She faced them. "Not after what he's done. What he let Ace do to me."

Kian had paled, even in the glow of the dying sun kissing his dark brown skin. "We wouldn't hold it against you if you did," he said.

"Speak for yourself," Elias growled. "He doesn't deserve to breathe, let alone be with her."

She fought the tightening in her throat with another swig of her tea.

"You saw what I did with him attacking his beta. Hex couldn't have known," Kian replied.

"Bullshit," she hissed. But it wasn't. At least not entirely. She had seen the same and loathed the desire it had spurred—the primal part of her that wanted to be loved enough to kill for.

She chugged the last of her tea to explain her blush and faced the forest once more, focus snagging on a pair of yellow lights beyond the rows of shrubbery and saplings. "Fuck you." She mouthed the words and stared until the lights winked out. *A trick of the fading sunlight. Nothing more.*

"He said the artefact could break the bond."

"There is nothing that can destroy a mated bond. And no one would ever try. It's sacrilege. It's *fate* we're talking about, Elias. Don't give me that look. Princess, it is your choice, but if you were to pursue the bond, blood share, or mark him, we would accept it." Kian's energy soothed her even as his words threatened to break the mask of composure she had been weaving since she returned home.

Elias curled his hands into fists. "I will not. Just because you feel comfortable trusting the species that slaughtered every born vampire trapped here after the Division doesn't mean I will."

"He isn't his ancestors. Just like you aren't your brother."

"Just stop." Her face twisted in their direction, disgust filling her even as Kian's words twinged something within her. "It's not happening. Ever. I'd rather die."

Kian's expression softened, and he closed the gap between them. "Forgive me. I won't push it anymore, Princess."

She leaned her forehead into his shoulder, breathing deep, but before she could say another word, a sharp sensation zapped through her scalp.

She jerked away, palming the offending spot. "What the fuck, Kian?"

Kian's eyes widened, then narrowed. "What is it?"

Elias brushed Kian aside then, much to her annoyance, and took her hand, pulling her in to place a hard kiss on her lips. The same thing happened, though this time, the electric pain made her teeth ache. "Ow!"

A noise akin to an enraged animal gripped his throat as he pulled back and searched her face.

"Did you blood share?" His irises flashed red in the dim light. "Did you?"

"No," she ground out between her clenched teeth. *But what if…? No. I would know.* She thrust her empty mug into his hand

and cracked her knuckles. This was getting out of hand. She didn't fight with Elias or Kian like this. The rage wasn't meant for them, so she drew calming breaths, letting a fraction of Kian's peace wash over her, but even that didn't have the same effect. She shut him off again.

"Let's go out," she said. "Take me to Sagehill. They have bars, right? Places we can dance or shop or something." *Anything.*

Elias shook his head, about to object, when that unfamiliar ire returned, and she was shouting. "Take me out, or I'll go by myself! I need out of this fucking house right now!" She shook the tangible energy from her hands, the fizzle at her fingertips filling her with fear.

"Too much gods damned testosterone in this fucking place," she finished as she stomped back into the house, burying her hands in her sweatshirt pocket.

She salvaged a decent outfit from the items stocked in their wardrobe and tucked her frizzy curls behind her ears. Jeans, a sexy, low-cut tank, and a cinched bomber. With one last dusting of blush across her cheekbones, she sauntered out of the bedroom and slipped on a pair of shiny, black platform boots by the front door.

"Let's go."

Elias's look was criminal, and she avoided his glare as she darted down the front steps and along the sweeping path that led to the three-door garage.

It didn't take long for them to hit the road. Elias's luxury car purred, hugging the corners so tightly Sylvie barely shifted from her perch in the back seat.

"You should rest," Kian chided her from shotgun.

"I'm fine." Sleep was not a respite anymore. It was a horror show.

Elias clenched the steering wheel, a muscle flickering along his clean-shaven jaw. "She's being a brat. Ignore her."

"Am not," she muttered, turning her attention out the window. Shadows danced with the trees, her vision catching flickers of light and insects under the fading dusk. In and out, darkness weaved between the trees, and she traced its path with her fingernail pressed against the glass.

The occasional conversation between Elias and Kian barely breached her thoughts as she puppeteered the shadows. They spun and jumped and flew alongside the car as if alive—corporeal. *Real.*

A wraith in animal form.

A dilapidated sign broke the monotony of the woods with a sudden whoosh. Sagehill. Cult town with a fae population. She could be herself there, whoever that was. Raised human, but not an ounce of human blood in her system.

Her gaze softened, the blur of trees in the creeping darkness merging into something else. Something beastly, its raven fur rippling with agile movement.

She leaned in, her lashes drooping when her forehead bumped the glass.

TEN

Find him.

The voices, breathy and inhuman, were familiar. At first, at least as a child, Sylvie assumed they were her own thoughts. The loathing, the needling ire, the demands. In Evergreen, they were different. The tone was deeper, rich and otherworldly. They'd pressed her. Incited violence. And now they were pleading for something else entirely, driving her to a different type of torture—a relationship sprung from darkness.

If they were Fates, like Kian claimed, she didn't want to meet them. She wished they didn't know of her at all.

Find him!

With a gasp so sharp she inhaled spit, Sylvie coughed and gripped her throat as she jerked her head off the warm glass window. Sweat beaded along her top lip and she continued coughing as Elias pulled into a well-lit parking lot and killed the engine.

When he rounded to open her door and cupped her cheek, she withdrew from the cold sting of his touch, shaking her head. "I'm fine!"

She climbed from the car onto shaking legs and dragged her fingers through the snarls framing her face. The hard concrete steadied her, as did every step away from Elias and Kian.

Flickering streetlamps cast misshapen shadows across the cracked pavement while a steady hum of traffic and occasional voices filled the air.

The town layout was quaint, featuring a central road ahead of the parking lot linked with a web of side streets looping around a mixture of old buildings. Not quite run-down, but on the way to it.

A tentative smile pulled on her lips. It wasn't Sterling, and she couldn't have been more grateful. Her favourite novels often were set in small towns, and Sagehill was as small as it could get in central Erus.

The nearest shop on the street corner, a gaudy diner, bustled with people all chatting jovially, the workers flitting around lightly on their feet. Too light for a human. Their perfectly symmetrical smiles lit up the space more than the sconces lining the walls as they took orders and whisked the empty dishes away. Sylvie finally turned to Kian with a raised brow.

He nodded back. "Fae."

She inhaled and dared a look at Elias. The gears turned behind his eyes as their gazes locked. He'd punish her later.

"Dinner?"

He slipped his hand into his back pocket and pulled out his wallet, then the iridium-banded debit card. She swallowed. Fuck. She'd never seen one in the flesh, but of course Elias-fucking-Ambrose had an Iridium. The rarest form of currency across the wider continents, a material mined from the depths of the Southern Ocean.

"On me." He held the shimmering rectangle between his middle and forefinger, the curl at the corner of his mouth a warning.

She bit her lower lip and closed the gap between them, reaching slowly for the fucking Iridium.

He let her have it and dropped his hand back to his side. "Lead the way."

She lowered her gaze in silent apology and crossed the road, peering farther down the street at the collection of shops: a boutique, a hardware store, and a small mall complex within a two-story building situated beside an eclectic church. Runes of the old gods lined the mantel above the bloodstained wood doors, candles flickering from behind the darkened windows. To its side sat a cemetery. She didn't let her gaze linger too long there. For a town so small, there were many dead.

The diner bell chimed as she pushed the door open, the sweet aroma of caramelised onions and the heat of the grills hitting her in the face as she searched for a seat. Kian stood at her side, not touching, but a soothing presence, as Elias stalked to a free booth, lifting a hand for her to follow. She did. Elias and Kian sat on the opposite side. Kian understood, even without the bond she could tell that, but Elias … Elias was pissed. They had just marked one another, and now his touch turned her feral. And not in a good way, either. But why?

Despite vehemently opposing the idea, accidental blood sharing was a better alternative to the other painful hypothesis flitting around in her twisted mind. Like, what if Hex's mate bond wasn't compatible with Elias's? They were supposedly enemies, after all. During the "heat" she got from Elias in Evergreen, Kian had been able to ease her pain with his touch. She'd never felt pain like this before. Her males didn't offer any clues either.

Once a server flitted to their table, Sylvie smiled tightly and ordered a burger, fries, and coffee before spiralling back into her head.

"Sylvie."

Her attention snapped to Elias and Kian, finally noting the steaming plate and mug sitting between them.

"Uh, yeah?"

"Do you want to talk?" Kian asked, stealing a fry.

She deconstructed her burger, letting the actions stall her response. Did she want to talk? She ate a pickle.

"Um. Warding." she finally said.

When Kian's brow rose, she elaborated, "What's the deal? I get you were helping the fae here, but surely there's other places that could use the help too, right?" He hadn't explicitly explained what warding was, but she could guess. A magical barrier of some kind, probably.

A passing server staggered, almost dropping a stacked platter of dirty dishes, and scanned their booth, bowing her head a fraction before darting to the kitchen.

"So much for anonymity tonight," Kian said with a wry grin.

"Sorry."

His brows drew down in a weak reprimand for the apology, but he dropped it almost as quickly. Elias did the opposite, his scowl deepening. He probably thought she was doing it on purpose. She wasn't, though. Kian just drew it out of her—the empathy.

"The veil between the realms is thin here," he said, lifting an onion ring to her lips. She bit it and sat back, not letting his fingertips brush her skin despite how much she wanted them to, especially after noticing the increase in alluring stares watching them throughout the diner—from the booths and the kitchens.

"Sagehill sits at an intersection of the continent's several meridian lines. Think of them like magic veins. There are other places, but this is closest to Sterling. It just made sense."

She accepted another morsel from his hand, ignoring the electric pain when his nail accidentally touched her. "But why?" she said through her chewing. "You can portal anywhere, right?"

He nodded. "But here, crossing is like slipping through a sheer curtain of mist. Everywhere else is breaking a door down with a sledgehammer. The bigger the hole I leave behind, the more unwanted followers."

She sculled the black coffee, hating the bitterness but needing the caffeine. "Makes sense."

A gorgeous server with raven locks and a dimpled smile appeared at the table, barely sparing her a glance as she bowed at Kian and said in a soft drawl to Elias, "You sure you don't want anything, sugar? We're used to varied requirements here."

Mine.

Sylvie hadn't realised how hard she was gripping the mug in her hands until the handle snapped off. The server noticed her then, and eyed her with a disdainful twist to her lips.

Kian recovered the broken porcelain, checking her over for cuts as he smiled close-mouthed at the woman. "I'll pay for the damage."

She bowed again. "No need."

A sound akin to a growl reverberated in the back of Sylvie's throat. The server inhaled sharply before flitting back behind the counter. Both marks hummed. One with concern, the other with desire. She avoided both gazes as she stood abruptly.

"I'm gonna go pay."

She twisted on her heel and paid quickly, smirking at the wide eyes of the cashier at Elias's Iridium. If it weren't for her males, she would never dream of flaunting it so openly. People killed for gold marks. Wars were started over iridium.

"Let's go." She breezed from the diner into the street, following the flow of locals and trying not to flinch at every chiming bell of customers weaving in and out of the stores.

So much noise. So much normality and joyful conversations. She beelined for the nearest shop, a second-hand store, and pulled the scent of old linen and dust into her lungs. It was an odd comfort. The door chimed behind her as Elias and Kian filed in and she walked around, fingering fabrics and dainty wooden figurines.

"See anything you like, dear?"

She lifted her head to the elderly storekeeper and smiled. "Just browsing for now."

The woman nodded, her glasses sliding a fraction down her nose before she pressed them back with a gnarled but beautifully manicured middle finger in a well-practised motion.

Sylvie pulled a handful of sundresses off a standing rack and held them to her chest. "Cute?"

Kian smirked while Elias's brow lifted.

"I don't need anything too fancy," she said. She gnawed on her lip, pulling a few knitted jumpers into her pile. "I might need to buy some workout clothes, though." Something to practise sparring in. The collection Elias had bought her and a few dainty dresses wouldn't do. One glance out the store window though, at all the people, had her stomach knotting. Another time.

She paid and headed for the door, inhaling the old scent again to prepare for the crowds when a cork board covered in odd papers caught her eye.

Community notices, lost pets, and job requests. Scanning the jobs, she homed in on a family needing a nanny ten minutes from the town centre. With a shrug, she ripped off the number and tucked it in her bag. It wasn't her first choice, but it was better than assistant work. As she darted back to the car and tossed the bags in the back seat, Kian appeared at her side, inspecting the torn paper she'd rolled in her fingers. "What do you know about nannying?"

She restrained a scowl. She'd looked after children plenty in the foster homes. Most families took on too many for greater income assistance, so once she turned thirteen, she became a live-in babysitter for the younger ones.

"More than being an assistant."

He chuckled softly and inclined his head back down the street. "Still want to go dancing?"

The streets quieted as the night settled over Sagehill, and the stars above shone far brighter than she was used to. Even the moon, swollen and distinctly golden, was high above them. Though tiredness curled around her bones, desperate for her to sink into the depths of sleep. She wouldn't. Not with the threat of dreams. *Prophecies.*

She swallowed. "Yeah. I do."

* * *

Thick darkness curled around her senses, body heat and cigarette smoke clinging to her skin as she climbed the stairs into the writhing club. It wasn't much, just another dilapidated building with crumbling wood floors, but the music was loud and with Elias's Iridium card, the drinks would be flowing.

The second she spied the dance floor, though, she balked. Bodies gyrated and pulsed to the lyricless sounds, lips and teeth meeting necks and chests as people had clothed sex on the stage. Though, calling it a stage was generous. Eight slabs of sheet wood on cinder blocks was more accurate. If she squinted, she could almost pretend it was another fae party in Evergreen, one nearing its climax. Literally.

She spun to Kian on her right and shouted, "Can I use one of your laptops when we get home?" Her mind kept returning to the nanny position. It felt right. Unlike replying to emails, caring for children would give her a purpose. She could make sure what happened to her never happened to them.

Elias answered her, "Your office is next to the laundry. I linked the computer to your work email."

She cringed and squeezed through a pair of sweaty bodies to the bar, their shots splashing her as they drank. The drop that hit her nose had her hissing, fighting a barrage of images until the bartender appeared, an amber bottle in hand.

"What'll it be, darlin'?"

She blinked the tortured memories away. "Three shots of whatever that is."

He looked at the bottle in his hands and nodded approvingly before lining up the shot glasses and sloshing the golden liquid inside them.

"Thanks."

"You're very welcome, darlin'." The bartender's smile died on his lips and he scurried away, scooping a stack of silver marks from where Elias had slammed them.

"You shouldn't be rude." She sculled the first shot, exhaling through the fire that licked the length of her throat.

"You wish to lecture me on manners to servers after growling in the diner?"

She flushed at that, not meeting Elias's gaze, and took the next shot. Elias didn't drink, anyway. It burned more than the first.

"I'm not working for you anymore," she said, picking up the last shot. It was for Kian. She was turning to look for him when her attention snagged on her vampire male.

Elias watched her, not touching, but coiled as if about to throw her over his shoulder and take her away. "No, you don't. You work with me. Half the company is under your name."

She almost dropped the shot.

"What?"

A cold sweat beaded down her spine, and she shrugged off her bomber. Kian was there in an instant, taking it from her shaking hands, and shot Elias a warning look. Elias ignored it.

"You are bonded to three leaders of their respective species." He left the rest unsaid.

This should be what you want. You were made for this.

But she wasn't "made for it," and it sure as shit wasn't what she had signed up for.

"You should have asked me first."

She eyed the last shot. Besides the burn, the other two had done nothing to ease her rising stress. Fucking useless. She downed it anyway, pulling her wallet out and shoving it towards Elias. "Your card is in there."

He took it as she lurched into the throng of dancing bodies. Heat, sweat, blood, and too-sweet perfume cloyed in her nostrils as she tried to find some variation of rhythm in the techno beats. Squeezed between so many bodies she could hardly move, she closed her eyes, letting the familiar, comforting tightness wash over her. But it wasn't comforting. A stray elbow nudged her ribs, a rogue boot squashed her toes, and the *sweat*. The sweat had her vision narrowing to pinpricks as every assault triggered visions of Ace's torture. Every time someone flicked their hair back, droplets would spatter across her face. Each lashing projected her back to the cells, to the showers, to her being held under and under and under.

And now Elias. The pressure. *The company? Is he fucking insane!*

She gasped for air that would not come, the tightness of the bodies around her, compressing her, stalling her lungs. She was suffocating. Her vision sharpened, then hazed over. Where was Kian? Elias?

She tried to push back the way she came, but the surrounding pressure swelled and her feet lifted off the ground. The swirling beast inside her screeched, its body twining around the fire that steadily dimmed, claws slashing outward.

She pushed and elbowed and shoved her legs out, but even with the scowls she received, they wouldn't let her go.

Please.

The roaring of blood in her ears and the slam of her heart against her ribs stole the last of her breath until she was choking. Choking.

Then she was yanked free, only standing with the help of Elias's grip around her elbow. A seizing, bone-aching pain radiated from his touch, but she ignored it as her breath shallowed.

"You need to breathe, Princess," Kian said, appearing at her side.

"Don't call me that!"

She wasn't a fucking princess; she was nothing, a half breed. Weaker than both, slower, dumber. She was no leader.

She was nothing.

Nothing.

Noone.

The ride home was long. Nothing breached her hearing but the sound of dripping water.

It plinked on her flames until they hissed. *Drip.*

The beast hissed too.

Drip.

Her hand curled around the car's door handle. Anything to stop the sound.

Drip.

Unlocked. She shoved the door open despite the dizzying speed of the forest whipping past. She needed air. Fresh air. *Drip.*

She should jump.

Find him.

"Stop her!"

A scalding grip latched on to her arm and dragged her back, the door slamming and clicking. She wrenched her arm free and fought the messy, angry thoughts as she faced the window, nails digging into the door.

"I hate this. I hate—" She swallowed, pressing her forehead to the window, unsure if she was directing the words at her bonded males or her reflection. "I hate *you*."

ELEVEN

"Take her to the unit."

Despite plunging in and out of alertness, Elias's words rang out in Sylvie's consciousness, loud and clear.

"What are you talking about?"

Images of the holding cells battered her mind as Kian pulled her from the car and up the path. He held the fabric of the bomber she had slipped on, but still she felt a twinge of discomfort at his proximity. If this was what her future held, being unable to stomach the touch of them, she didn't want it.

The Fates could get fucked.

Sylvie resisted as Kian led her past the house, but he held firm, walking down a slope towards a much smaller rectangular building nestled in the thickest area of the forest. Highlighted by the moon and a single warm-toned sensor light swarming with bugs, the "unit" looked abandoned, the curtained windows revealing nothing of its contents.

"Why are you taking me there? I don't want to go!" Her panic rose even as Kian's attempts at soothing washed over her.

"Trust me. You'll feel better when you see her."

"Who?"

Her words died in her throat, as did her struggling as a scowling Kerensa, princess of Ilfaem, stormed from the tiny front door and slammed it behind her. "What kind of hovel is this?" Her braids whipped around her head as she stepped off the small porch and narrowed her indigo eyes.

Kian let Sylvie go then, and she closed the distance, squeezing Kerensa in a one-sided embrace. Kerensa may have patted her once, but that was it.

"Fates, Hart. You look like shit."

Sylvie scoffed and zipped up her bomber against the frigid chill. "Gee, thanks."

Kerensa sniffed, adjusting the satchel she always wore on her hip, the tinkling glass bottles a reminder of what they had done not so long ago. "Trouble on the marriage front already?" She directed the question at Kian, but Sylvie couldn't help herself.

"You could say that again."

"No," Kian said with a sigh. "It's not that simple. I'm sure Elias debriefed you?"

Elias called Kerensa? Oh fuck, I really am a giant bitch.

"That he did. Pretty fucking foolish letting her get kidnapped, eh, brother?"

Sylvie snorted as Kian walked away, shaking his head and murmuring something about finding food.

When she glanced back at Kerensa, a ribbon of discomfort tied itself around her guts. "So. How long has it been for you?"

Kerensa's cheek twitched as she turned and headed inside the unit, with Sylvie trailing behind. "Not long."

Well, that didn't add up.

"I portalled here a few fae weeks after you did."

Sylvie's skin prickled at her tone. The slowness of it. The calculated words.

"Why?"

She took in the cramped space before Kerensa answered. The small table and chairs squished in a corner next to a bare kitchenette was their destination. Sylvie sat, dragging her nail across the layer of dust that had settled on the wooden tabletop. No wonder she had called it a hovel.

"Lazuli disappeared from the Stone Court."

Her finger stilled its tracing of a flower and tensed. If she could grow claws, they would be an inch deep in the tabletop. "What do you mean, disappeared? She isn't a realm crosser."

Kerensa worked her jaw. "No. She isn't. But I imagine she has connections to alternative methods of travel."

The orb Rheikar had used to summon the hybrids returned to her memory. She should've killed Lazuli while she had the chance. *Choices have consequences.* Her teeth ground together. She shut her mind off to the intrusive voices and added Lazuli to her growing list of problems.

"Have you spoken to them about what happened in the Stone Court?"

Sylvie blinked. Many things had happened in the Stone Court. Her attack on Lazuli. Rheikar's evening "visit." Neither were things she wished to rehash. "No. And I'm not going to. It's over. Let's move on."

Kerensa brushed her palm across the table and sneered at her hand as she rubbed the dust between her fingers, apparently unbothered by Sylvie's response. "You don't think it would be helpful for them to know what happened to you?"

"They know enough." Elias knew about her childhood, but that was inconsequential. Kian didn't need more baggage from her. She pinched the bridge of her nose at the growing ache in her head.

Kerensa leaned back in her seat, the shiny leather of her pants creaking in harmony with the wooden chair legs. "I suppose. Though any secrets you harbour will interfere with the bond."

Oh shit.

"How bad?"

Kerensa shrugged. "Enough to cause damage when it counts. You'll all be weaker. In power and healing. More susceptible to illness even. There are old stories in our holy texts about the closest pairs taking each other's abilities and growing stronger. Living longer. Healing each other by simply being close."

"So I won't be as strong as Elias or Kian. Fine." The beast inside her hissed again. She shooed it away.

With a gaze far too shrewd, Kerensa leaned in, hooking her fingers beneath Sylvie's chin. "So you blood shared with it, huh?"

Sylvie swallowed and pulled back. "I don't know." It was the first time she openly admitted it being a possibility, and the thought filled her with roiling distress. Anger. Fear. "Not on purpose."

"What are you feeling?"

She shook her head. "The kidnapping … it really fucked with me. I'm trying to hide it for Kian's sake, but a few days after I got back, something felt off. Their touch feels like I'm being electrocuted, and I have this rage inside me." She looked at her hands as they curled into fists. "I want to destroy everything." She wanted to take every word back, but it was too late, and she knew Kerensa heard what she didn't say. *I want to destroy myself.*

But instead of speaking, Kerensa just nodded and stood, offering her a hand. Sylvie took it. "Well then. Would you like to show me around?"

Sylvie's brows furrowed, but a lightness settled within her for a moment. One glorious moment. "Yeah. Yeah, I would."

* * *

"This is the kitchen, living, and dining. Our room." Sylvie choked, hiding it with a cough, when she spotted her sexy ropes peeking out from beneath the bed, then closed the door when a shirtless Elias strolled from the en suite. Her cheeks flamed red, but Kerensa only rolled her eyes.

"Anyway," Sylvie continued, "come." She padded down a short hall towards the laundry and her office.

"How many rooms are in this place?"

"I don't know."

Kerensa humphed. "Spoken like a true princess."

She couldn't stand the implications of the title when Kian said it, but Kerensa drew a laugh from her. It was more startling than anything, the sudden expression making her heart ache, along with the marks that branded her skin. Maybe the shots' effects were delayed.

"What's so funny?" Kian questioned, giving her a wide berth as he entered the room ahead of them with a small potted cactus.

"Nothing," she answered, shame replacing every other emotion. Kian deserved better. So did Elias. She wasn't the partner they'd signed up for.

"Just looking around," she added, voice wavering.

"Well, this is your office," Kian said. "I was just adding the finishing touches."

"Oh." She neared the doorway with apprehension, and his mark twinged. The sight almost undid her. Of all the rooms in the house, this one was the most decorated, with vast bay windows, a cushioned window perch, and a beautiful orewood desk with detailed panelling. Art adorned each free wall, the two large pieces displaying Tynaan from above. One was of trees, the expanse breathtaking, while the other had a lake in its centre, the crystalline waters painted so delicately she could've sworn the image moved with the ruffling breeze.

She stood at the desk, touching the slip of paper with the nannying contact information sitting in front of the keyboard, and closed her eyes. "Thank you."

"It was the least we could do," Kian said, not even chastising her on the improper thanking before drifting from the room in silence.

She had so much grovelling to do. Starting with scrunching up the paper and throwing it in the small woven waste bin. She wasn't on board with running Ambrose Enterprises by a long shot, but she would try. They deserved that much.

A long hoot sounded from outside and she shuddered, sleep still trying to lull her into bed. She clicked her tongue and faced Kerensa. "Do you want to do something?"

A tingling through her legs had her leaning from foot to foot.

"Like what? Knives, swords, hand-to-hand?"

Yes, yes, and yes. But— "I was thinking of a run?"

"It's midnight."

"Well, not too far."

Kerensa looked her up and down, a thoughtful expression settling on her face. "How about a walk? Then you won't need to change."

She glanced down at herself and the platform boots on her feet. She didn't even own any running shoes yet.

"Okay, deal."

They walked in silence to the porch, and Sylvie took two steps down the paved path when Elias's low voice had her heart leaping in her throat. "Where are you going?"

"Don't scare me like that!" She palmed her chest and rounded on him, his figure imposing from the bottom step of the porch.

"Don't disappear without telling anyone."

Her nostrils flared, the beast within her scuffing up dirt with an annoyed strike of its talons. "You aren't my keeper, Elias Ambrose. I'm going for a walk with Kerensa."

His gaze sharpened, the carmine hue of his irises cutting through the darkness as he palmed the back of her head, pulling her to his chest, the touch instantly transporting her to those cells—to those violent hands fisting her hair until her scalp bled and scabbed. She sucked in a shaking breath and ducked out of his touch, her breaths coming out in rapid succession.

"Sylvie, I—"

"I'm fine." She shook her head at him, willing the heat along her waterline to fade, willing her lip to stop trembling. Her hands. Everything.

"I'm sorry," she breathed, turning and walking away, gluing her gaze to the ground as a solitary tear cut down her cheek.

"We'll stay inside the wards," Kerensa murmured, even as the fae jogged to catch up.

She didn't speak again, and Sylvie was grateful. The metronome of her footfalls from paver to asphalt to gravel slowed her pulse and the thoughts until nothing mattered but her steps.

"Are you staying?" Sylvie finally said, crossing her arms around herself. With nothing but the moon to illuminate the path, her pace slowed to a virtual standstill.

"Until I find your runaway aunt."

Sylvie nodded.

"Do you—" Her voice snagged in her throat and she cleared it, peering once over her shoulder at the house, now just a speckling of light in the distance. "Do you know what's happening to me?"

When Kerensa said nothing, Sylvie glanced her way, stilling from her expression. The contemplation. *The pity.*

She masked it quickly, shrugging with a single shoulder. "I don't try to understand the whims of the Fates, and perhaps you'd have fewer troubles if you did the same."

A sinking feeling settled in Sylvie's abdomen as they stood betwixt the Tynaan, trees framing either side of the gravel road. "What are you saying? I should just accept it? Accept him?" The male that left her with a monster.

Ace is my beta. He does as he's told.

"In all the texts I've read and according to the oracles I contacted in the Sun Court, there are no accounts of multiple fated bonds, and now, when the realms are suffering and the species are dying out, you appear? Does that seem coincidental?"

"Don't put that on me, Kerensa."

"I have done nothing, Hart. I am stating an objective truth and asking you the question. Why would the Fates partner one female with three princes? Three leaders of species that have a violent, hateful history. Why would they do it?"

Sylvie's mouth dried. It was too much.

Heal the broken, so mote it be.

"I will not choose him." Even as she voiced the thoughts, a sharp jolt of pain ran from her head to her chest. She ignored it. "Not after what he's done."

Kerensa sighed. "Many terrible things have been done in the name of love, Hart. Kian and Elias are not innocent. Or you."

It was as if Kerensa had clutched her around the throat and pressed her face into coals of truth. They fucking burned.

Sylvie snapped her mouth shut and began the long walk back.

"I did not intend to upset you."

"And I didn't realise what religious zealots I was marrying into." She hated the bite to her words and the way Kerensa sucked air between her teeth. Kerensa didn't speak again, and Sylvie didn't apologise. She dragged herself to the porch swing, crawled onto the damp cushions, and curled up under the warmth of her shame, not once acknowledging the two golden lights that followed her the last hundred steps home, or why they didn't wink out as she let her eyelids fall shut.

TWELVE

Bound, gagged, and bleary, Sylvie writhed against a solid structure as the hazy light of the full moon barely pierced the trees above. Her wrists ached from the restraints, the pain radiating up her arms to her chest.

"He's coming," a disjointed voice hissed in her ear. Three voices.

As her vision adjusted to the dimness, haphazardly strewn logs at her feet stretching for rows and rows appeared. The scent of smoke and gunpowder filled her nostrils as her tongue worked at the cloth jammed between her teeth.

"Let him in."

She bucked and sobbed as the voices merged with the whistling winds, only stilling when a rhythmic one-two-thud echoed from the darkened path in front of her. In the distance, a blinking light appeared. Melting orange and yellow illuminated hazel-green eyes and raven hair. Fur.

A beast.

The light grew, and the popping crackle of the living flames danced behind her lids as she squeezed them shut.

Wake up.

Wake up.

"Open."

Twigs snapped and screamed as the beast prowled closer. Sylvie opened her eyes, crying into the cloth as the familiar gaze stared her down from a foot away, the flaming branch in its mouth close enough to scorch her arm hairs.

"Accept him."

The gag dropped from her face, and she spat at the beast. "No! Get away from me! I don't accept you!"

Hazel-green eyes turned molten gold. The beast opened his mouth wide.

Sylvie gasped as the torch slipped from his teeth and dropped onto the logs below, flames leaping from one to the next.

The flames licked her bare feet, and white agony drilled up her legs as the fire spread.

Her throat ached as the smoke tendrils from her melting skin invaded her mouth. Soon, nothing but screams filled her ears.

"Wake up!"

"Sylvie!"

* * *

"—Sylvie!"

"Don't touch me!" Sylvie screamed, striking the unknown assailant, every inch of her skin burning and doused with sweat.

The darkened room—her bedroom—glowed under the light of a rotund moon, the fullness of it flooding her senses with shock. It wasn't full when she fell asleep. Where was she?

"Breathe, Princess. It was a dream."

A dream?

"I'm burning! Put it out!" She screwed her eyes shut against the pain.

"I promise you, you aren't on fire, Princess. Open your eyes."

But she couldn't. The smoke seared and stung. "I can't. I can't!" She bucked and kicked against the blanket draped over her legs, pawing at herself with fingers curled into claws. They snagged on thick, pillowy fabric, not the jeans she had fallen asleep in. The fluffy lining clung to her skin and itched. It was melting into her flesh.

"Fates be fucking damned."

"That will not help her, Elias." Kian's anger spilt onto her and she twisted, writhing until she felt the edge of the bed and threw herself off it. She needed to put it out. The fall blew the air from her lungs and her eyes flew open as she gasped. Screamed. Kian crouched at her side, lips parted while Elias prowled at the foot of the bed, his fangs descended and ready to rip into something. *Me. Rip into me. Kill me.*

He stared down at her with open hostility, his head shaking like he'd heard the words. Felt them.

"This didn't happen when I blood shared with her," he growled, running a hand through his dark curls. She jumped when a freezing cloth touched her brow, a current travelling through it from Kian amplified by the water. The water. The cloth. Ace.

"Different species. She never fought this hard against your claim on her, and it's a full fucking moon!"

"You two couldn't have kept her unconscious for another fucking day?" Kerensa's voice pierced the fog.

"She broke through the sleep ward." Kian's lips moved, but the words were delayed. Delayed. *Delayed.*

"She what?"

Sylvie blinked back tears as the cloth dripped water down her cheeks into her ears, her nose, her mouth. She retched. "Please, help me!"

The blankets finally came loose, and she crawled across the floor to the nearest corner. *Stop.* It had to stop.

An agonised howl outside sounded, the noise piercing the closed windows and rattling the glass as her muscles seized and clenched.

"Kerensa, you need to leave."

"I'll get him." She turned and fled the room as Sylvie stared after her, blinking sweat from her eyes. Why was she sweating so much?

"Who?" she croaked, but neither male in her present company answered her. Elias just turned and slammed his fist into the doorjamb, the force vibrating the floor under her.

Kian rounded on him. "Stop! If you can't handle this, then leave. She doesn't need that right now."

Elias bared his fangs. "I'm not leaving her."

"He's coming."

"I fucking know that, Kian."

Sylvie shut them out. She couldn't do anything else as her head squeezed so tight she swore it would explode. Thoughts emptied until there was one voice—no, three.

Heal the broken, so mote it be.

She screamed, clawing at her ears. *Shut up.* "Shut up!"

"You cannot mark her."

Sound and pain compressed into a vacuum until Sylvie couldn't move. Breathe.

"Does it look like I want to hear what you have to say right now, Blood Prince?" The guttural response had pleasurable tingles shooting down her spine, but she curled tighter, her forehead against her knees.

"She's a vampire. It could kill her," Elias growled right back.

"Half," Kian snapped. "If they don't mark one another, this won't end. What do you think will happen if she can't stand our touch any longer?"

"Better that than dead, Kian."

She fell forward, her face pressing against the floor, fists clenched. She was already dead.

"Let me see her," the stranger said, voice nearing. With every approaching step, some of the pain eased. She could breathe again, and her skin cooled. She blinked, lifting her head until trouser-clad legs filled her vision. Then higher.

Taut abdomen, bare torso, fully tattooed besides a space over the left pectoral. Golden skin shone there, waiting for something. A mark. A mark he would never receive. The rage, the fury she had for her males streamlined into a single action, bubbling to the surface, her body responding before her mind could.

His primal gaze raked down her body as she stood, and with vampiric speed, swung her clenched fist right at his godlike face.

"Hello again." Hex caught her wrist without blinking, his tight grip cooling the burn of her skin and drawing a relieved breath from her lungs.

"I don't want you here." She tugged her arm away weakly, searching for Elias and Kian over his shoulder. His huge, tattooed shoulder. They would hate her for this. She hated herself. She hated how much she didn't fucking hate it.

"And I don't want you." His free hand brushed her hair from her face. She smacked him away. "But here we are," he said.

"You hurt me." She backed up a step, but there was nowhere to go. The wall pressed into her spine as Rowan Hex pressed into her front. She almost whined from the touch, the way it soothed her. "You burned me."

The green of his eyes melted to gold. "If you hadn't interfered with Ace, this would never have happened. We could have lived like we never met."

Wrong.

She winced at the voices and the name. Unless she was tearing out his throat, she never wanted to hear the name of Hex's beta again.

She slid along the wall, collapsing onto the bed, her breathing quickening as his legs slipped between hers, brushing the sensitive skin of her inner thighs.

What do I do?

More voices answered. *Accept him.*

Shut up!

The urge to hurt him filled her, and she scooted back across the bed until whatever easing their proximity had on her pain snapped. "Fuck!" She folded and groaned.

"Stop moving." He dragged her by the ankle, and she kicked his stomach with her free leg. Elias's chuckle warmed her.

"Don't test me, woman," Hex snapped, lowering his torso over hers, the touch easing her heat until she almost felt herself again. Almost. "You and your wretched kind hurt my people, and instead of grieving with them and protecting those left, I'm stuck here with you."

"Then leave," she bit out. "Never come back."

You must accept the bond.

She snarled at the voices. "I don't want another mate."

His body tensed as if she had struck him, and her mark ached. Kian's mark. She turned his way, but Hex's touch reclaimed her. His hands slid along either side of her face, cupping her head with light pressure, two outer fingers on either hand in her hair, his middle and forefinger stroking her cheek, and his thumbs near the corners of her mouth. With one movement, he could brush his thumb across her lips, and she didn't know if she had the resolve to keep them closed.

"Then you won't get one. We get through tonight and tomorrow we find a way to break the bond."

Her stomach lurched, as did the indigo whorls on her chest. She could almost hear Kian's distress. *Sacrilege.*

"Fine."

The beast inside her hissed, venom pouring from its lips.

Hex strained, apparently fighting the same inner demon.

"Fine."

She nodded, but wriggled under his weight, her clothes generating heat. "Off. Get this shit off me." Hex's jaw ticked as he raised one of his hands between their faces, the tip of his nail shifting into a long, black claw. She narrowed her gaze but nodded as he ripped through the layers covering her upper body, balancing on his forearm as he threw the tattered items to the floor. Her nipples pebbled under the fanning of his breath, and unlike Kian or Elias, who had kept their gazes off her curves before she accepted them, Hex did the opposite, drinking her in, then lowered his chest onto hers. The thumping of his heart tickled. She swallowed.

"What do you want?" he asked then, capturing her face again. "Tell me what you want."

"I want to go back in time to before I met you."

His hand traced along her ribs, squeezing her hip and shifting the waistband of her sweats aside. "And then what?"

She bit down a moan as his palm slid across the top of her thigh and nestled between them.

"Then I would make Elias and Kian stay with me that morning, and when you show up, I would tell them to kill you."

She tuned into the reactions of her males, the low chuckle and the soft intake of breath.

"You want me dead?" Hex's words drew her in, his nose only millimetres from hers.

She paused, her breath hitching as his cock pressed against her inner thigh through his pants. "I want you—" Before she could finish, he dipped to the erratic pulse fluttering at the base of her throat and licked a trail to her earlobe.

"You want me, what?" He nipped her soft skin, eliciting a warning grunt from one of her males. Elias.

"If you mark her, you could kill her."

Hex growled but didn't look his way. "Why would the Fates mate us if she couldn't wear my mark? Look at her fucking chest. There's a perfect space for my crest."

He was right.

"Bite her and I'll tear your head from your shoulders."

A surprising growl came from Sylvie's lips in the same instant her hands curled protectively around Hex's neck. She blinked, immediately releasing him, but his hand shot up to cup one of hers, his entire weight on his elbows.

He swallowed, his throat straining under the motion. She could just—

Hex broke eye contact. "Are you two going to leave, or would you prefer to watch me fuck your mate?"

It sounded as if he didn't have a preference and Sylvie clenched her jaw, fighting the lust wending through her.

"We aren't leaving her," Elias said.

Hex hummed. "I suppose I'll show you two how it's done, then."

"Shut the fuck up," Sylvie said, reaching for his trousers and pushing them down a fraction with her fingertips. After this, she would feel better. It was just sex. She'd had plenty of casual encounters before meeting Elias and Kian. It meant nothing.

But his weight on her and the possessiveness of his touch stopped her movements. It was just sex, but she would be in control. Not him.

"Wait."

He stared without speaking, nostrils flaring as she pressed against his chest.

"Get up."

"What?"

She clicked her tongue, pressing harder, her nails digging into the tattooed skin. "I said, get up."

He narrowed his eyes as Kian's words cascaded over them both. "The heat will return."

It already was. The more time they wasted, the more she sensed the impending agony. But this would only take a minute if he would just *listen*.

"I didn't say get off me, I said, get up."

When he still failed to move, she growled, curling her fingers around his throat, the other hand snaking down. "Up now, or the next thing I strangle will be your balls."

He stood slowly, her grip still firm around his neck as a smirk stretched over his lips. "Is that supposed to be a threat?"

Prick. With a smirk of her own, she crouched and snatched a bundle of rope from beneath the bed. She'd show him. On her way to stand, she dragged a hand up the inner seam of his trousers, flicking his crotch a little too hard with the back of her hand. She hummed, satisfied when he exhaled a grunt and curled her fingers in his belt loops, tugging him from the room. Sweat beaded down her spine as she pulled. "Hurry. It's too hot in here and I'm not fucking you on the bed I share with my *mates*."

She grinned, her back to Hex as he grumbled low. As they neared her intended destination, Hex's pace slowed until she was almost dragging him.

"You don't have the nerve," he said.

"Wanna bet?"

She ripped the front door open, letting the gust of night air slam it against the doorstop, and shoved him out onto the porch.

"Sit."

She made quick work of his wrists, tying three much messier knots than she had hoped, and wrapped the excess around the closest pillar holding up the pergola, pulling it taut until his hands were tethered above his head.

"These won't hold me."

"But they will," she replied coolly, slipping off her sweatpants and underwear. "As I recall, you were happy to leave me bound in your beta's truck so he could do what he wanted with me. It's only fair."

"I didn't—"

She cut him off, stuffing his mouth with her underwear. "I don't care what you have to say, Rowan Hex. This is just a means to an end."

Then she unzipped his trousers, pulled his cock free, and sheathed herself to the hilt.

THIRTEEN

It was too fucking big. Sylvie couldn't stifle the cry or push past the pain from her sudden joining with the shifter alpha. In an instant, Hex's hands held her hips aloft, the ropes she had bound him with hanging limply around his wrists.

"Don't touch me."

He spat the fabric gagging his mouth, and rasped, "Woman."

"Shut up."

The air between them shuddered. "Don't make me hurt you."

She sneered, holding her trembling arms against her chest. The less they connected, the better. Her marks vibrated, and she rubbed her palm across them. She didn't have to look to know Elias and Kian were close, likely reclined against the front doorframe, or perched on the porch swing.

"You already have," she said, almost regretting it when her bonds twinged with shame and rage. In that moment, between breaths, the beast inside her stepped into the light, its dripping fangs glinting. Its lips moved, and the word whispered against the shell of her ear filled her with resignation.

Mates.

She reluctantly placed her hands atop his shoulders, clawing her fingers into his traps as he rolled his hips.

"Fine," she said on a sudden exhale.

"Fine," he agreed.

It wasn't the same as her encounters with Elias or Kian. They put her pleasure first again and again before entering her, waiting until she was more than ready. But she never took her own pleasure into account when she led, and now she ached, the sharp stretching around the monstrous size turning the rest of her limbs to ice.

It—*he* started slow. Lowering her down. Lifting her back up. Almost too slow, until the pain melted and her muscles relaxed, her head lolling into the crook of his neck involuntarily, drawing a low rumble from his chest.

The depths he reached had her eyes rolling, and she pulled back to look at the face of her enemy. The one who kidnapped her and put her through hell in the hands of his beta. *Fuck you.*

You are, his eyes seemed to say. She struggled to keep hers open at his constant, undulating movements.

Blinding moonlight lit them up, highlighting every feature of their bodies, from the soft curve of her breasts to the roundness of her ass. With the shadows, Hex's tattoos faded into the darkness, and the full scope of his physique hit her. The depth of his core muscles had her itching to trace them, to drag her nails through every trough his abdomen offered.

His beard was scruffier, the lines of his eyes had deepened, and his hair hung around his face, tickling the tips of her fingers.

He was stunning. A wild, monstrous man. One far more animal than she was used to, and she should hate him. She did. But *gods,* she felt the pull. *Fucking Fates be damned, alright.*

"Faster," she said, hissing as her canines sharpened into needle points. *No.*

But as he bucked, his cock bottoming out inside her, over and over, she couldn't stop herself from running a tongue over them and savouring the sharp sting.

His pace never wavered, never lost control, but he tilted his head to the side, just a fraction, and the muscles under her right hand strained with tension.

As his eyes fell closed, long lashes grazing his golden cheekbones, the mask broke. His thrusts grew sloppy as her climax built with a suddenness she hadn't expected. It normally took more. But she—but she—

"Fuck!"

Before she could think or fight fate's pull with her rational mind, she bit him. She bit him really fucking hard.

Burying her teeth deep into the trap, she moaned as his fiery blood swirled on her tongue and down her throat. His strangled growl only turned her on more, forcing her body to take control.

All sound ceased as she trembled, her climax peaking. Unclasping her teeth, the blood dripping down her chin, her head flung back as she clenched over and over into oblivion.

Hex shifted beneath her, grabbing the back of her neck, his mouth latching on her shoulder when a loud shout and grip on her other shoulder shook her from her lust-filled haze.

"Stop!"

"What have you done?"

* * *

"What?"

Elias's glower and Kian's furrowed brow filled Sylvie's field of vision as she sat on the porch swing, a blanket hastily wrapped around her shivering body. *Where did that come from?*

Hex stood hunched on the front path where Elias had thrown him and dug his lengthening nails into the pillar they had just fucked against. "The bond is incomplete," Hex said.

"We know."

She glanced down at her marks and fingered the faint whorls between Kian's and Elias's. The lightest shade of gold dusted across her skin there, barely visible on her tanned chest. It would fade. Kian said without upkeep, they all would. And she wouldn't be performing any more fucking "upkeep" with that beast. *No matter how good it felt.*

She stood slowly on shaky legs and padded straight to Kian, palming his cheek even as his muscle feathered under her hand. It didn't hurt. *It doesn't hurt.* She hid the burn along her waterline by drawing him in for a slow, soft kiss. Relief surged between them, and he wrapped his arms around her as she pulled her lips from his.

"Let's go to bed." And finish this. She found unhealthy satisfaction in the gaze boring a hole into the side of her face.

Hex would never have her like that. Sex was one thing, but intimacy? Never. Her lips were only for Elias and Kian.

"You marked him, Princess. What were you thinking?" Kian's voice was low. Breathless. But they all heard. She could sense Hex leaning towards her, even as Elias hovered over Kian's shoulder.

"I wasn't."

Despite the incomplete bond, she could've sworn a tapering pain wove through Hex's mark. She scratched it.

Kian exhaled and loosened his grip, gingerly releasing her as she swayed on her feet. "I'll be back," he said.

Elias closed the distance between them, leaving the last inch of space for her to cross. To crawl and beg for forgiveness.

She teetered on her toes, twirling the blanket fibres between her fingers, not able to meet his penetrating stare. "I'm sorry for how I was acting."

Hex growled, but Elias's sharp glance quietened it as he brushed the hair from her face. "We'll speak of it later."

"And my people?" Hex cut in. "Will you speak of that later, too? Or do you leave that to your brother, Blood Prince?"

Kian appeared before anyone could reply, throwing a shirt and pants at Hex.

"Now is not the time for that conversation."

No, it wasn't. Sylvie's ire flared at the accusation in his tone. He was so quick to assume guilt and hate based on Elias's species when the only villain amongst them was the male Hex had put the most trust in. He was a hypocritical, stupid *dipshit*.

"Fuck you," she said.

Kian raised a brow at her but she just shook her head, a laugh laced with disbelief and disgust passing through her lips as she turned, her back pressing into Elias to face the shifter on her lawn. Where he belonged. *Dog.*

"Careful, Princess. The marking will have amplified your emotions."

"That has nothing to do with it." She scanned Hex with a loathing gaze. "Just go. I don't want to look at your fucking face anymore."

A muscle along Hex's jaw ticked as Kian walked towards him. "Let's talk."

Sylvie went to protest when Elias lifted her and headed inside, slamming the door shut with his foot.

"It's time for you to rest. We'll all discuss this in the morning."

He threw her atop the bed, ducking to retrieve the fallen duvet.

Cross-legged, she sat, scowling, with the creamy throw wrapped over her waist. "I don't want to discuss anything in the morning. I want him gone."

She needed to wash him off her first. Scooting off the bed, she slunk into the bathroom without saying anything to Elias, using the scalding burn of a wet washcloth to smear away the remnants of her night. She couldn't bear another shower. Ace needed no more real estate in her head.

Once she nestled back into her bed, Elias threw the blankets over her scantily clad body and leaned against the wall.

Her annoyance gradually ebbed until the space between them left her cold.

"Will you come in?" She lifted the blankets and after a drawn-out pause, he pushed off the wall and slid under the covers, though he still kept a distance between them. She hated it.

"I'm sorry," she whispered, nestling closer. He didn't pull away, instead with a flourish flipped her to face away from him and curled himself around her. Spooning. *Soon to be forking.*

"Why did you mark him?"

No forking then. She shuffled uncomfortably. "I don't know. I just had to—I wasn't thinking. Are you mad?"

He exhaled into her hair and toyed with the strip of skin along her belly between her singlet and underwear. "I'm mad at the situation. But with you? No. You have nothing to apologise for either, so don't even think about it."

The apology lingered on her tongue regardless as she curled deeper into his cool frame. Gods, she had missed his touch. It stirred the flames within her, and she was certain he warmed from it, too.

"What do we do now?" she asked quietly, shutting her eyes as the steady rise and fall of their chests in tandem lulled her.

"You sleep."

"Elias," she groaned his name, but he didn't bend. He held her still, his chin resting on her head, legs tangled with hers until all she could do was drift away into a dreamless sleep.

Morning came too soon. The mumble of male voices a distance away had her groaning, flinging her hand out to shush them when it struck a hard chest.

"Ouch."

Her lips peeled into a smile and she cracked open an eye at her vampire.

"I thought you'd gone," she croaked.

Sunlight streamed through the curtains, highlighting his form as he lay on his side nearest the window. His brows twitched beneath a rogue curl. "No, love."

Her stomach flipped at the admission, and she buried her grin in the pillow. Everything was back to normal. She could touch him. They could kiss. *Have sex.*

His next words were like an ice bath.

"Not yet, anyway."

The air between them fizzled as she pressed off the bed and sat on her heels. Rogue snarls grazed her cheeks, and she tucked them behind her ears. "What do you mean?"

He sat too, running a hand through his hair. "My home realm. Argyncia."

Even the name invoked shivers. Elias had once called it the Glass City. Perhaps that was why he chose Sterling as his first residence on Erus. Everything was glass there. And steel and rust and death.

"Take me with you."

He swallowed, the expression crossing his face one she hadn't seen before.

"I can't. Not until I know the travel won't kill you." He padded to the closet and pulled out a hoodie, tossing it her way as goosebumps prickled along her skin.

"And you'll discover that, how?"

His grim smirk had her answering for him, her voice laced with rage. "By not dying yourself? Elias, you can't be serious!"

"Hush. You'll wake all of Sagehill." He passed her a pair of jeans and she pulled them on, jumping a little to fit her thighs and ass inside. "I'll be fine," he said as she did up the fastenings.

"Do you have to?" She was selfish. So be it.

Elias arched a single brow, and she ached to kiss it.

"Are you not curious about the accusations the shifter placed on us?" he said.

She sighed, contemplating the closed bedroom door, then lifted her chin. "Not enough for you to risk dying."

He cupped her jaw, nipping her lower lip before stealing a kiss. "I said I'll be fine. Don't you trust me?"

"Of course I trust you. I don't trust him." Her arm flung towards the door Kian and Hex stood beyond. Chatting. About what was anyone's guess. He should've been back with his wild animals by now, not mingling with her fucking husband.

"I don't either, but be clever. Fate has a frustrating way of forcing things if it thinks its threads are being rewoven."

"Yeah, yeah." She rolled her eyes until Elias's grip tightened deliciously around her throat. His half-smile had her core turning molten.

"Watch yourself, Kitten. You might explore domination with Hex, but don't test me."

Her lips mirrored his, the gleam in Elias's eyes at the sight dazzling her. She bowed her head as far as his grip would allow. "Yes, sir."

Before he could say anything else, she pulled from him and headed for the door, ripping it open with enough force to startle the conversation beyond it. She sauntered into the kitchen, snatching a piece of fruit from the bowl Kian nursed between his forearms at the counter. Hex sat beside him.

"Did you sleep well?" Kian asked, lifting another morsel to her lips. She accepted it with a smile.

"Mhmm. Would've been better with you there, husband."

A playful grin danced on his face as he lifted a square of foil from a platter in the middle of the bench. Beneath it sat half a dozen grilled sandwiches stuffed with a decadent assortment of vegetables and herbs. "For you."

"You're too kind." She kissed him, slow and soft, swiping her tongue across his lower lip before pulling away. He sighed, clearing his throat as he positioned her on the stool he had been sitting on and dragged the platter closer.

"Eat up. Rowan has been informing me about his pack's predicament. I think you might like to hear it."

Rowan? She scowled and plucked a fried tomato from the top sandwich, shoving it between her teeth.

Elias graced the room with his presence, a tall glass of blood in hand as he leaned against the opposite counter. He too didn't seem impressed with Kian's casual reference to the shifter, and they shared a nod. She appreciated that one of her partners wasn't a traitor. Kian's mark twinged.

Too bad, Kian. Not cool.

Hex either didn't notice the tension or ignored it. "The kidnappings started when my father was alpha. Four decades ago or so. They were rare, but happened often enough to hurt us. They took our elders first, then my father's men, and recently our females. They're increasing in frequency now. This year they've attacked every month during the waxing moon."

The food in Sylvie's hand turned cold as she stared at the shifter, his story stirring unwanted sadness in her. *No.* Irritation. He was still blaming Elias for it, after all.

"We've killed a few of theirs. Tried to capture some, but they die even if we haven't touched them. They turn rabid and die."

"What?" Sylvie pulled the collar from her throat. Suddenly it was too hot inside.

"Desiccation," Elias said. "We can go without blood for a week until our vīs consumes us. It's not just for satiation. Blood sustains our strength, healing and glamours. Even a few days abstaining has consequences that I'm sure you witnessed. Madness and violence. Eventually we wither into husks."

"Ew." She was yet again grateful she was only a half vampire.

Elias chuckled into his glass as he took another swig.

Hex nodded slowly, probably storing the information away to use against them later. If Elias noticed Hex's demeanour, he didn't comment, and Sylvie trusted his judgement.

"Once they take them." Hex paused, swallowing as if tasting something bitter. "Once they're gone, we never see or hear from them again."

"And the mind-link?" Kian asked.

What the fuck is that? "Not even that," Hex answered. "It's dormant. Like they're cut off from us. We would feel it if they died, and none of them have."

"Not one?" Sylvie said abruptly. Her own voice shocked her, and she disguised her surprise by taking a bite of her breakfast.

Hex didn't answer immediately, his fingers digging into the thigh of his borrowed pants. "No. Not one."

Some of his people had been gone for forty years. She swallowed a dry piece of toast and coughed. Elias slid a glass of water across the counter to her and she accepted it gratefully, smiling at him even as her chest constricted.

If she had met Hex first—

She couldn't even let herself finish the thought. She didn't meet Hex first.

"Yet Argyncia has been closed off completely since the Division," Elias said. Hex tensed, his shoulders rolling like his hackles rose while in animal form.

"Well, you found a way, didn't you?"

Sylvie stood, her ass catching on the stool and making it screech, the beast inside her emulating the feral shriek. Rage blossomed through her like a budding weed, its roots so deep she wasn't sure where it ended and she began.

At Elias's warning glance, though, she bit her tongue. Hard. It bled.

Hex exhaled, but she couldn't look at him. If she did, she might do something that Kian wouldn't like. Like stab him.

"If Hayes found a way through, we could have a war on our hands, Elias," Kian said from Sylvie's side. His soothing energy probed at her walls, but she had grown attached to the rage. She could handle it.

He stopped trying.

"I remember we agreed not to speak that name again." Elias ran his tongue over his sharp canines, palming the counter. She rounded the bench to stand beside him.

"Your brother?" she muttered.

"My mother's other son. The king."

She clicked her tongue and leaned against him at the subtle attempt at a joke.

"I'll look into it," Elias said then, regarding all of them with a scrutinising gaze. "Anything else?"

She finally glanced Hex's way, startled to find he was already staring at her. She didn't look away, no matter how badly she wished to.

"Nothing," Hex replied.

FOURTEEN

Sylvie refused to cry, even as Elias took Kerensa's forearm on the front lawn and the fae and the vampire nodded at one another.

"If this fails, the pushback will hurt like a bitch. And if we somehow get in, you're still gonna be fucked for weeks," Kerensa said, ignoring her brother and the shifter to his side. "There's a reason I've only been there once."

Sylvie fought the apology slithering up every time Kerensa peered her way, but the fae didn't seem to notice. Or hold a grudge. That made one of them at least.

"I know," Elias answered.

Sylvie darted across the grass, threading her hand through the crook of his elbow, and pressed her forehead to his arm.

"I don't want you to go."

Kerensa released him for a moment, giving Elias enough time to kiss the top of Sylvie's head and wipe the ghost of a tear from the apple of her cheek.

"I know," he repeated, softer.

Kerensa interrupted any more shared words or lingering looks with a grunt. "We need to go while the moon is full or this will kill me."

With a nod, Sylvie backed away, returning to Kian's side and accepting the arm that wrapped around her.

Elias glanced at her one last time, even as Kerensa started invoking Ancient High Fae.

"I love you," he said.

The moment the words left his lips, he blinked out of existence along with Kerensa. A ring of mushrooms sprouted in their wake in the patch of grass where their feet once stood.

It took everything in her not to fall on the ground and sob, begging him to return. There was never enough time together. Never.

"This fucking sucks."

Kian's warm arms wrapped around her torso, his chin nuzzling into her shoulder as he sighed softly, his breath ruffling the soft brown curls beside her face. The morning sun kissed their skin, and the forest at their side hummed with wildlife like her world hadn't just been torn in two. With Elias gone, the tether between them dulled. She tapped it a few times absently before Hex cleared his throat.

Sylvie peered over her shoulder at him, not even bothering to turn. Kian forced her to, though, manoeuvring them as one unit. She dug her heels into the grass, but he was too strong. Clumps of mud stuck to her shoes.

"What are you still doing here?" Sylvie bit out. Kian squeezed her, almost tickling. *Prick!* She fought a giggle and stomped on his toe. To her chagrin, she missed.

"I will return in a month, then," Hex said, glancing away from their antics. Sylvie stilled.

"What for?"

"When your heat returns." He said it so casually, so flippantly, that she didn't process it until his body was cracking and morphing into a beast.

"What do you mean?" But he was already gone. He tore through the tree line and into the darkness beyond, the clothes from Kian left in tatters by their feet.

* * *

Four days passed in gentle monotony, but despite the quiet, Sylvie never found herself without things to do. With Kian's help, she moved the rest of their belongings into the house, turned down the garden for the nearing winter, and came. A lot. She lay in his arms, drawing patterns across his chest with a lazy finger. He never flinched from her touch anymore, even when she gently scratched her nails along his skin. He trusted her that much. She kissed him, pushing every morsel of gratitude and love into the motion, only noticing him stiffen after her caress moved to his face. She pulled back. "Are you okay?"

He swallowed. "That feeling, down the bond. What was that?"

"I—"

It would be so easy to say it, to tell him the three words he deserved, but the timing wasn't right. "I don't know." She kissed his nose, then each cheek, then his neck. "I'm just so glad we get this time together. It's been nice."

"Sylvie."

She paused her kisses. "Kian."

He gently lifted her onto his lap and sat, tracing the lines of her face with his fingers. "You won't like it."

Her heart dropped. "What is it?"

"I want to help the shifters."

He was right. She didn't like it. In fact, it made her sick. She slid off him, dragging the sheets up around her shoulders.

"After what they did to me?" She hated the weakness in her voice.

He cupped her cheek and searched her face. "No—no. It's not like that. Believe me."

"What's it like then?"

He worked his jaw, pinching the bridge of his nose. The action was so like Elias it made a pang in her chest.

"The beta is gone."

"What?"

"Rowan's beta. He's not there anymore. None of the shifters in his pack know about you or what happened. It was an isolated event."

Her throat dried up. The days—weeks—in that fucking hell returned like Kian had pressed play on the memories. How much had Kian and Hex talked about while she slept?

"I would never suggest this if I thought he would be there, Princess. I care little for killing, but if I ever saw him, he would understand the meaning of suffering intimately before you killed him." He gripped her shaking shoulders as her breath shuddered. "Let me help you," he whispered.

And this time, she did. She opened the fortress doors she'd been moulding around the deepest darkest chambers in her soul, around her flames and the beast that lurked in shadows. She let him in. He didn't touch anything but the panic. The fear. He coaxed it from the fortress and took it within himself, the hollows under his eyes darkening.

"Stop." When he kept drawing the fear out, she shoved him and slammed the fortress doors shut again. "Kian, don't."

"I want to."

"You've been through enough."

He tilted his head. "Is that what you're afraid of? Hurting me?"

She let his words hang in the air. Was that it? Somewhat. But also …

"I don't want to be fixed. How am I supposed to work through my shit if you keep saving me?"

The space between them grew cold, even as his warm touch trailed down her face. Her scar. For years, she'd suppressed who she was. The rage. The violence. Kian's siphoning of it was just another form of suppression. A permanent one that held consequences for him she didn't fully understand. Anger could burn through some of it, but where did the rest go?

"I understand," he said then. "But you don't have to suffer alone."

She exhaled. "Neither do you."

They wouldn't agree, but at least with the fear mostly gone, she could be objective. More curious.

"Why do you want to help them? How, I mean."

"I can ward against the vampires. From what Rowan said, they are unprovoked attacks, and violent. Undeserved."

She gnawed on the inside of her cheek. Maybe she was being too harsh. She only had experience with three shifters, all sitting at various positions on the scale from psychotic to bearable. Ace and Rose were at either end, while Hex had slid marginally up the scale since they first met.

"My mother always said the shifter history wasn't worth knowing, that they were no better than the lesser demons that slipped between realms. Monsters and animals. She was wrong."

"How do you know that? What about Sagehill and the attacks? What about Ace? They probably share his attitude."

Kian took her hands into his, threading their fingers together. He clinked their wedding bands.

"I believe him. Rowan. He shields his emotions well, but the ones I can sense are earnest." At her tilted head, he added, "Yes, his accusations are misplaced, but they come from fear. Not hatred."

She looked away. It was easier to hate him. If he hid his emotions, Kian probably missed something. Still, Hex's people were innocent. She couldn't allow further kidnappings when her husband could stop them. It would make her a hypocrite.

She shuddered. "Fine then, go ward the forest."

"I can't go without you."

Oh.

"I—"

"He left me the coordinates."

Sylvie untangled herself from Kian and stood from the bed, redressing and pulling her hair into a messy updo, thinking. Most of the short curls escaped, but it would have to do. *Actually* … "Does Sagehill have a hairdresser?"

Kian blinked, then stood and dressed too. "Yes."

"Take me there first, and then we'll go."

He blinked again, as if not believing what he was hearing. *It isn't that farfetched.* She wasn't an unreasonable cow. Was she?

"Shall we take the bike?" he asked.

She stifled a grin. "Fuck yes."

* * *

"And how much length do you want off?"

Sylvie smiled at the hairdresser, Tara, through the mirror. The pink-haired half fae floated around her, an assortment of items in her matching blush apron from scissors to combs to foil. From the moment they entered the dainty studio, Tara had made her feel right at home, drawing a laugh from her about the butchered "home job" she had done to herself. If only she knew the truth.

"As little as possible." Sylvie answered. "Just even it out, I guess. Maybe some, uh, some layers?" Truthfully, she'd never been to a hairdresser. Not as an adult. Most of the foster families she stayed with did it themselves, trimming off dead ends or shaving her bald—once, when she was nine. The lice infestation was too bad, they'd said. *Start fresh.*

"Perfect," Tara chirped. She started trimming the longest strands and Sylvie cast her attention to her husband reclined on the waiting couch near the window. His arms stretched over the back of the couch, one ankle over the opposite knee. *Divine.* He either didn't notice or ignored the eyes of every woman in the studio, his gaze settling on her flushed cheeks, her pressed lips.

"You okay?" he mouthed, leaning toward her with a furrowed brow. She nodded.

She wasn't a fan of being touched by strangers, or having a sharp instrument in such close quarters to her neck— especially after being carved from ear to ear in Evergreen— but Kian's calm lapped across her senses.

When the trim was over, Tara styled her waves and fingered some product through the ends before unbuttoning the nylon cape and brushing off any missed strands.

"Much better."

Sylvie couldn't help but agree. She glanced Kian's way and his smile proved he felt the same.

He paid, and they headed back to the bike.

"How long do you think the warding will take?"

"A week. Maybe longer."

She threw her head back and groaned to the sky. "Fuck, Kian. I thought this would be quick. What am I supposed to do for a week in the woods?" *Besides avoiding Rowan Hex like the pox.* Besides, she'd only packed enough clothes for three days—all the athleisure items she'd recently bought online. Moisture-wicking tights, snug long-sleeved tops, and a cute pair of black runners.

"You can stay with me."

She threw him a wry glance. "No offence, but I don't think plodding along behind you while you perform some magic vampire-stopping woo woo is going to satisfy me."

"Woo woo? How dare you." He placed the helmet in her hands, and she chuckled at his disapproving headshake. His lips quirked as she straddled the bike and pulled the helmet on, ruing the inevitable helmet hair.

"I'm sure we'll find you something," he said, climbing on in front of her and pulling her arms around his waist. She squeezed, nestling her cheek into the muscles of his back as he brought the engine to life and roared out of Sagehill faster than she could regret her choice.

FIFTEEN

Trees whipped past in a violent blur, only the brief shadows crawling within the twisted forest offering depth to the monotonous grey and sage.

Kian's motorcycle vibrated between Sylvie's thighs, the roar as he carved around the road bends sending tingles through her core. She gripped his abdomen, fingering the taut muscles through his jacket and the corded taper leading beyond his trouser fastenings. His belt.

He tensed, and she buried her smile in her helmet. Her mind wandered to the shifter residence as she toyed with Kian's top button. *What would they look like?* If the holding cells were anything to go off, they had electricity. But running water? Plumbing?

Flushable fucking toilets? She'd gone in a bucket in the holding cells.

She tilted her head to the side, blinking as the shadows merged and danced alongside them, a sleek raven shape winding through the trees parallel to the bike. Was that …

Kian decelerated. The darkness slowed, too.

With a narrowed gaze, she slid her fingers from Kian's waist to his thighs, scratching lightly towards his groin.

Her marks throbbed, and satisfaction rose through her as a bass growl sounded a fraction lower in pitch than Kian's bike.

Now, now. She smirked, muttering low and scathing, "Jealousy is unbecoming. *Mate.*"

The growl darkened, as did her expression. Just how good was shifter hearing?

She considered slipping her hand right into Kian's trousers to make a point, but they rounded a familiar bend, gravel scattering as Kian stopped.

No, no, no. Why would he send us here?

She shuffled off the back of the bike, standing on faltering legs as Kian flicked the stand and handed her the backpack from the seat compartment. She threaded it over her shoulders even as her arms shook, his posture tensing as he faced her.

"This is the place, isn't it?" Kian asked.

The holding cells weren't in sight, but she swore she could smell the building. Clinical, hospital-grade cleaner and the trace of deadwood. Rust and stagnant water.

Drip.

Kian took her helmet off just before she threw up her breakfast. She spat and sucked in a breath against the acrid tang of vomit, images assaulting what few reinforcements she had managed to carve into her mental fortress.

Ace's spirit hovered over her as she retched, scalding water pouring from her lungs, the breaths from her mouth rasping from internal burns. His hand curled into her hair, pushing her face back under again, then pinning her and covering her face with a soaked flannel before turning on the showers. Again. Again. *Again.*

"Come on, Princess."

A solid presence had her hand. It pulled her into the woodland, away from the crunching underfoot. Every step of crushed concrete flooded her system with dread. He was coming.

Her mouth dried out, breaths uneven.

"Rowan will be here soon," Kian said.

A furious growl, pitching into a whine, echoed through the orewoods as a wolf—his wolf—careened before them, his nostrils flaring as he took her in, then the place she had run from.

With four strides, he would be upon them. Sylvie's racing heart and churning gut twisted as the creature stalked forward, hackles raised. Saliva dripped from its maw and for a moment she didn't know who she gazed upon. Her mate or a wild animal.

Both.

He was bigger than she remembered, the gold of his eyes far darker, almost the entirety of his pupil blown out. Maybe it wasn't him …

"Shift back, Rowan," Kian barked, his voice hoarse. Her pulse spiked as she shuffled backwards, her sweating hand slipping from Kian's. The images of her abuse faded, only to be replaced by the feral glint in another beast's eyes.

She swallowed, shifting her gaze to Kian, noting the sudden change in his expression. Parted lips and raised brows to a thin grimace and narrowed eyes.

"What is it?" she asked.

Kian didn't reach for her again, but lifted his palm in a stop motion. She did. Hex didn't move, his predatory gaze locked on them, his body held so still she couldn't tell if he was even breathing anymore.

"He's lost control."

"What?"

Kian swallowed. "I don't think he can shift back."

Finally, some of Sylvie's faculties returned, and her breathing shifted from terror to frustration. "He looks like he's gonna fucking kill us, Kian."

"Not you," he whispered back. "Me."

Hex lunged, his lips curling as he moved like a bullet, spittle flying.

"No!"

Sylvie's scream staggered him briefly, but not enough. Kian shoved Sylvie back and as Hex descended, a red-furred missile barrelled into the wolf's side, knocking him into a nearby tree.

He whined once, shaking his head in a daze, giving their rescuer time to shift into her naked glory.

"Go west; I'll catch up with you once I deal with my cousin." Rose's body morphed before Sylvie could respond, and Kian bowed his head once before pulling Sylvie deeper into the Tynaan.

When it was clear they weren't being followed or hunted by a psycho shifter, Sylvie slowed their pace.

"What was that? Why did he try to attack you?"

Kian shook his head. "I don't know, Princess. I can't read his emotions in shifter form."

Sylvie raised a brow. Interesting. She had a lot to learn about the creatures.

Chirrups and a steady low hum filled the air as they plodded along an unbeaten path and she swirled a finger across her marks.

"Do you think Elias is okay?" she asked.

Kian interlaced his fingers with hers as he answered, "I think you may be more qualified to answer that, Princess." When she looked his way, he gestured to her marks.

"It's numb."

"Then he's fine. You'd know if he wasn't."

She nodded, continuing her caress. "Have you been there before? Argyncia?"

"No. Kerensa and I were born after the Division, and my mother made it unbearably clear that under no circumstances should Kerensa or I portal there. Erus is one thing, but Argyncia … it's like travelling through the eye of a needle at light speed. I can't believe Kerensa was even game enough to try. Though solar and lunar events offer more power. They'll have to wait there for the next one."

Maybe that's how the vampires did it. Travelled to Erus on the new moon, recovered until the waxing stage like Hex said and attacked, then portalled home with the full moon. But how did they get through in the first place? She voiced as much to Kian, and he offered an approving smile.

"Is that why Elias doesn't believe Hex?" she finished. Because what or who would have enough power to get them through other than Kerensa and Kian? The orb Rheikar used seemed too volatile to be a regular travel method.

"Exactly. The amount of portalling he's accusing is unbelievable even to me."

But he still wanted to help. They climbed over a felled log, careful not to disturb a small clutch of eggs curled into the corner of the wiry limbs.

"You know, I always wondered how you two met. Elias and you, I mean."

The question seemed to surprise him, a flurry of expressions crossing his face before settling on a half-smile. He lifted her over another felled log and reclaimed her hand as they found a dirt path through the foliage. "I was young, maybe fourteen. I hadn't got a complete handle on my affinity for portalling, yet, and ended up following a magic beacon to Erus while training with Kerensa. Every creature and place has its own energy signature, and I somehow found Elias's even through the Division barrier."

He laughed. "I landed in a pile of dead leaves and wood chips behind his cabin. It was more of a shoebox at the time. He said he took you there?"

Sylvie nodded, matching his smile. It was much bigger than a shoebox when she visited. It was gorgeous. Second only to their new home.

"At first, I didn't notice him," Kian continued. "He was covered in thick fur skins with only the red of his eyes exposed, then he tried to strangle me."

A noise crossed between a laugh and a gasp escaped her lips.

"Luckily, I was better with my empath affinities. I eased his fears." He traced his fingers absently across his throat, a faraway look in his eyes. "His expression still haunts me … the terror. He thought his brother sent me, somehow, to take him back. Once he realised I wasn't a danger to him, he let me go. We talked. Made wild plans to get rich in the growing city in southern Erus and I left."

And now Elias was back in the place that haunted him. Terrified him. A flutter of anxiety seized her.

"It wasn't until after … after Lazuli that we made those plans into reality."

Sylvie chewed her lip, swallowing the rising nerves, and leaned into Kian, brushing a kiss across his shoulder. "How old was he?"

Kian shrugged. "Born vampires age the slowest of all species. I don't even know his exact age. He looked sixteen, perhaps seventeen, but the years he had lived by then would probably triple that."

"Weird."

"I suppose by human standards. But there aren't any humans around, are there?"

"Shut up," she said, but she smiled. No. She wasn't a human, and despite it scaring the hell out of her, admitting that felt right. She'd never belonged in Sterling. Never fit in anywhere.

A scuffle sounded nearby, and she squinted, stretching her neck in that direction. The forest quieted until there were no signs of life, not even the warbling of birds.

She fiddled with the freshly cut ends of her hair and gnawed on her inner cheek. "Well, this sucks—"

"Sylvie!" Rose's voice carried from behind them, but her body was invisible until she was almost on top of them. Luckily that time, she sported a thin singlet and shorts, showing off her spattering of freckles and smooth, sun-kissed skin.

Rose nodded once to them both. "Follow me."

Kian followed without question even as Rose turned forty-five degrees off from where they had been trailing and started walking into the brush.

"I thought you said west," Sylvie muttered.

"I did." The flash of a smile over Rose's shoulder almost disarmed Sylvie. Almost. "I didn't want you stumbling on shifters without an escort. Rowan told me you were … guests, but no one else knows. Don't want you getting eaten now, do we?"

A silent question flickered in the shifter's eyes, but Sylvie ignored it.

"We're here to look into your vampire problem."

Rose bowed her head, though the unsaid words lingered between them. *How will I be of any help?* A fair question. Could she even "do" magic like Kian? She'd have to ask once they were alone. Didn't need her enemies knowing her weaknesses.

Ten minutes passed in easy silence before Rose said, "Almost there."

Then, a mix of raucous laughter and low, mumbling voices breached the woods.

"—don't play with it; just throw it in the tub."

"I am!"

"You're bruising them!"

"You told me to throw 'em, Maddissen."

"Fucking hells, we're already low on stores with this crop. Put it in gently."

Sylvie stifled a smile and a flaring of nerves as they cleared the tree line and two shifters, one tall, athletic, dark-haired female and a short but crudely muscular male, stared at them with narrowed eyes.

"Uh, Rose?" the male asked, his blue eyes phasing to dark amber.

"Alpha's guests. Kian, Sylvie, this is Alastair and Maddissen."

"Right," Maddissen crooned. "Well, tell Al to be gentle, or there won't be any unbruised spuds for dinner."

Al nudged her, but his eyes didn't leave Sylvie. "That ain't fair."

"I'm not getting involved," Rose said, ushering them past with a huff. "You two wanted me to do your dish duties after the banquet. Now you do my chores. Fair is fair."

Sylvie snuggled closer to Kian, vaguely amused and wary as Rose nudged them through the rows of raised beds full of fragrant herbs and dozens of staked plants and onto a narrow dirt path. Trees spattered all around with a cluster of modest wood cabins woven between them. Most of the front doors were open, and she struggled to drag her eyes away as they passed. It was all so nice. Muddy shoes beside the doorsteps, coats and umbrellas hung by the entryways. Small, bare lightbulbs glowed from quaint hallways that led to cosy living spaces.

Each cabin varied slightly from the same design until they reached a crossroads in the path. The left walkway disappeared into the brush beyond a forested bend. The right, though, featured a two story structure, more rudimentary than Elias's cabin, but equal to it in charm. Hanging baskets swung in a breeze along the stoop, and the tall orewood door was held ajar by a sawn log. Inside, a staircase obscured the rest of the space until Rose led them over the threshold. Then the roaring fireplace and pleasant living area came to life. An assorted mix of couches, rugs, and lamps warmed the space until Sylvie could think of nothing better than snuggling up in there and reading a good book.

"The rest of us are training or at work, so please settle in here while Rowan sorts himself out. Once he lets the pack know, you'll be free to roam."

All thoughts of relaxing washed away with a flare of annoyance. Right. This was the home of her rival. "What's wrong with him, anyway?"

Rose shrugged, gesturing for them to ascend the stairs. "Just a full moon thing. He'll be here soon-ish. The second floor has two guest bedrooms and a bathroom. Take your pick and holler if you need me."

Kian bowed his head. "We are grateful for your hospitality. If you would let your alpha know I am eager to speak with him, I would appreciate it."

Rose's cheek quirked and her eyes twinkled, but this time Sylvie didn't despise it. It wasn't attraction in the other female's gaze; it was amusement. Rose tipped her head and let her smile beam. "Alright, Charming. Seems I have a lot to learn about the fae. I'll link him."

Kian tugged Sylvie up the stairs after another bow and into the first free room.

Besides a bed and a couple of tallboys, it was sparse. She placed her backpack on top of the drawers and faced Kian. He traced his fingers over the walls and muttered something low.

"What is it?"

He shook his head, saying one more gibberish word, and faced her.

"Just ensuring we have privacy, and nothing malevolent can get in."

She blinked, settling onto the bed and massaging her scalp. The hairdresser barely touched her, but her scalp still ached. "Will I ever be able to do that? Warding?"

Kian's mouth compressed into a line, and he lifted a shoulder. "I've only known full-blooded fae achieve it. Plus, you'd have to pronounce Ancient High Fae."

She exhaled through her nose and faced the window. The answer was no, then. She had a hard enough time speaking Erucian, the language spoken throughout Erus, without stuttering over phrases or getting grammar wrong in her emails. The High Fae language would stay a mystery.

"Do you want to come with me?" Kian asked when the stomps of a new arrival sounded from the floor beneath them.

"No."

"Princess—"

"I'm good, Kian. You talk to him, I'll be here."

He padded over and kissed her head before returning to the bedroom door. "Be careful."

She was too drained to laugh, but the essence of a smile tinged her voice. "Always am."

SIXTEEN

"She's okay?" Hex's low tone wended into the spare room the minute after Kian left.

Kian left the door open on purpose. He must have. Without thinking, Sylvie stood at the crack, eyes staring at a scuffed spot on the opposite wall as her husband's response travelled up the stairs.

"That's rather relative," Kian replied. "And not why I'm here."

Sylvie bit back a snicker as he continued.

"I'd like to offer my assistance in warding your pack boundary against the vampires."

"It's a large boundary."

"I'm a strong warder."

Hex hummed. "It would take at least three days to walk the perimeter."

"I've got time."

Sylvie turned, leaning her back against the wall and crossing her arms. She had to admit their back and forth was a little entertaining.

The pair were silent for a few beats, and she craned her neck towards the opening. Had they gone outside? Had Kian warded the area, so she'd have to show her face? If he did, she would be so pissed, but their voices started up again.

"I would appreciate it. We're expecting them in a few weeks, but no matter how prepared we are, they always get at least one of us."

She hated how he stirred her pity. It wasn't fair. She was supposed to hate him.

He's my beta, he does as he's told.

She nodded, letting the disgust return and settle in as Kian said, "I'd like to start now, if possible." His voice dropped until it cut in and out. She caught "I go," and, "stay here."

He was probably talking about her. Oh well, the sooner he warded the area, the quicker they could return home.

"I'll have Elder Lonnie escort you. I have to prepare for tonight's meal," Hex said, his bass tone making her skin tingle.

A pause from Kian, then, "Alright."

"You will join us."

Sylvie could almost feel Hex's gaze drilling a hole through the floorboards.

"Both of you," Hex finished.

Like hell I will.

"We'd appreciate that."

She almost groaned aloud. Damn noble fae male.

Footsteps receded from wood floors to hard soil, and Sylvie slid down the wall, her head falling against her knees. Maybe she should have gone with him. Now she was trapped.

Her eyes closed, and she didn't realise she'd fallen asleep until the crash of metal, hissing oil in a pan, and footsteps on hardwood had her head jolting. The afternoon light outside cast the room in caramel, and she squinted before rubbing her neck. She stood, flexing her tired muscles and inhaled, her mouth watering at the scents curling through the space. *Right.* Dinner.

She rocked from foot to foot, ignoring the rumble of her stomach. It was rude, staying in the room while people worked tirelessly in the kitchen. She had to decide if she could live with it. She couldn't. With a sigh, she clutched the door handle and pulled, letting the rich garlic and spiced aroma cascade over her as the door swung wide.

With light footsteps, she padded down the stairs, expecting to see Rose, or a gaggle of middle-aged shifters, but stalled in the living area in front of the kitchen. It was Hex, and only Hex. When he said he needed to stay behind to prepare for dinner, she didn't realise he meant alone. Her teeth clenched, and she contemplated dashing back to the room, but he saw her, his hands pausing, one white-knuckling a sharp knife and the other poised around a thick carrot.

When he didn't speak, she gathered her courage and indifference and teetered forward on her toes.

"Need help?" she rasped.

His brow lifted, but he didn't speak. Instead, he pulled out a second cutting board on the opposite end of the bench and lay his knife on it, grabbing another one for himself from the second drawer.

The breath she drew was loud and more than a little shaky as she walked past him to the board. She wrapped her hand around the bone handle of the knife, noting the cold weight of it in her palm. She'd done it before. Stabbed someone. Her grandfather, Rheikar. Carving through his flesh was thick and gritty and disgusting, but doable. But then the shifters would go hungry, and it wasn't their fault their alpha was her mate, or that their beta had mutilated her thanks to his orders.

She bit down a sigh and picked up a large potato, cutting it in even chunks before dropping it in an enormous pot sitting in the sink. They cut vegetables in silence until the first pot was almost three-quarters full and he took it, washing them and filling it with clear water before lifting it onto the stovetop like it weighed nothing. She averted her eyes from his vascular forearms and kept cutting as he seasoned the broth and placed another pot in the sink.

The quiet was … nice. The monotonous work soothed the parts of her still thrumming with pain and anger. She'd almost lost herself in it when she reached for the last spud and her fingers brushed Hex's. She jerked back immediately, hand empty, and glanced his way, trying and failing to maintain a scowl. He said nothing. Didn't even look at her. Once he cut the last potato, he put the second pot on the stove and washed his hands, drying them on a folded apron he had tied around his waist. She swallowed and fought the butterflies fighting within her, the beast that prowled there pouncing on them and clawing the fluttering wings between its toes.

"Is there anything else I can do?" she asked.

He looked at her then, his amber-green eyes locking with hers. In the dappled lighting, they were beautiful—so different from the gold they phased to in shifter form. So … human.

"You could stir the stew until I get back. I need to start the fire."

She nodded and accepted a wooden spoon from him, hiding her expression as he walked away. Only once did they catch gazes again as he hovered at the front stoop, his iris flashing that animal gold. She turned away. He left.

A minute passed before she let out the breath she had been holding, the tension in her spine forcing her to hunch over. Minutes of stirring and seasoning passed, and she started snooping in cupboards. Flour, sugar, salt. She pulled them onto the counter and grabbed a glass mixing bowl. Maybe she could make the dough dumplings she ate as a child. It wasn't particularly nutrient dense, but it was filling and took on the flavour of the broth. Growing up in foster care, she couldn't afford to be picky. Regardless, they were delicious, and Hex's vegetables needed some extra oomph.

She eyeballed the measurements, mixing flour and water into a stiff, slightly sticky dough, then rolled out dozens of balls, lining them on the bench. Once the potatoes were almost fork tender, she dropped the dough in, poking them under the rich stock with her finger when a jarring thought filled her mind. What if the shifters hated them? What if she'd ruined everything? It was too late to pull them out. She'd already filled one pot to the brim. She put a lid on and turned down the heat, chewing on her thumbnail. *Please taste good.*

A scuff at the door jolted her as if she were guilty, and Rose's smile fell as she lingered in the entryway. "What happened?"

Not a "what did you do?"

"Uh, nothing. I just added some … some dough dumplings to the stew. Do you think they'll mind?" Rose crossed the living space and entered the kitchen, eyeing Sylvie with a look she couldn't place. She hadn't seen that look before on anyone. Rose lifted the lid and sniffed, picking up one of the floating balls of dough with her fingers before taking a steaming bite.

"Ooh, hot, hot." She blew air through her teeth a few times before chewing the dough and swallowing, her head nodding all the while. "These are great. Thank you."

"I—um. You're welcome." She palmed her cheeks and found them warm under Rose's smile. Her crinkled features held no falseness. Rose was genuine. It didn't bode well for Sylvie's decision to be anti anything shifter. She reluctantly smiled back.

"Now what?"

Rose turned off the stovetop, covered both pots with glass lids, and draped kitchen towels over the handles. "Now we take it all to the lake. Will you manage?" she asked, lifting one pot off the stove and holding it in front of her body, away from her skin. Despite her waifish appearance, Rose was freakishly strong. Sylvie carefully clasped the handles of the second pot over the cloth and lifted, glad she didn't buckle under the weight. It was heavy, but she could do it. At least for a couple of minutes.

"Lead the way."

Rose walked back to the crossroads and took the unexplored path, her steps slow and even on the silky dirt. More shifters followed behind on the trail, carrying pans and trays, pots and bowls of steaming items. Maddissen jogged over with a salad bowl, sniffing the coiling swirls of vapour pouring through the steam vent of Sylvie's pot.

"That doesn't smell like Alpha's recipe."

Fuck.

Rose rolled her eyes and peered over her shoulder at Maddissen. "No, it smells better," she said.

A blush burned across Sylvie's cheekbones, and she stayed silent. If Rose knew how Sylvie felt about her cousin, she wouldn't defend her so quickly. Maddissen just clicked her tongue against her teeth and strolled past, flicking her dark hair over her shoulder.

"Thanks," Sylvie murmured, her heart sinking before she remembered Rose wasn't fae. She could thank her and apologise with no repercussions.

Rose nudged her shoulder softly, perhaps noticing her flip-flopping emotions, and gestured in front of them with a jut of her chin. "Pop it on one of those tables and I'll get blankets."

"Okay."

She sucked in a cool breath as the path opened out into a cleared space, trees framing picnic tables and log seating before opening to a crystalline lake reminiscent of the painting in her office at home. In the middle of the space, surrounded by older shifters, was a bonfire, crackling and spitting embers as the flames ripped through the kindling.

Her steps lagged as she neared the table and Hex came into view from behind the flames, his shirtless form glistening with sweat as he swung an axe down on a thick log, splitting it in two. She froze, watching him. The flexion of his muscles and the contraction of his abs on the downswing … She nearly dropped the stew when his attention shifted to her, and the scalding metal burned her thighs.

"Woah there. Here, let me help." Rose swooped in, lifting the pot onto the table and giving her a once-over. "You okay?"

"Yeah." Sylvie swiped her sweating palms over the burning spot. "I'm good."

Where was Kian when she needed him? She sent a querying energy down the bond and sensed him a fair distance away. Still warding.

With a nod, Rose handed her a blanket and directed her around the area. She obliged, laying out blankets that shifters quickly occupied, all eyeing her with a wariness that bothered her more than she liked to admit. Like she was dangerous.

Something inside her wanted to prove them wrong. It wanted their trust. Her beast purred.

Once everyone settled in and flaming torches were lit as the sun set, Sylvie headed to the food tables, her stomach cramping. But bowls and cutlery were painfully absent. Resigned, she turned away, ready to give up on food, when

Rose stood in her path, a bowl and spoon in hand. She shoved them into Sylvie's palms with a grin.

"Here, take mine. It's bring your own plate, but I'm guessing no one told you."

"Oh." She half shrugged, holding the bowl back in Rose's direction. "I'm okay. It's your bowl—I don't want to be a nuisance."

Rose's brows shot up. "A nuisance? Don't be silly, you're our ... guest. Besides, I can just shoot home and grab another." With a quick wink, she turned and darted back towards the hidden path.

"Wait," Sylvie said, but she was already long gone. "Don't leave me here alone."

She gnawed on her lip and lined up at the picnic tables, taking a small helping from each platter. Salad, sandwiches, casserole and pasta. She bit back a satisfied smile at the two empty pots she and Hex had prepared. Not a single dough dumpling was left behind. The shifters bunched in groups, chatting, laughing, and eyeing her as she drifted towards the fire, trying not to shrink under their scrutinising gazes.

Swallowing a bite of bread, she perched herself on the edge of a log by the fire and leaned into the heat. This close, her eyebrows would likely be at risk of being singed, but it was worth it.

The warmth loosened the tension in her limbs and she stared at the amber heart of the flames as they danced. This place ... it was beautiful, and nothing like she could have imagined. The milling shifters edged inwards, and a handful of wrinkled faces appeared at her side, warming their bones too. An elder female smiled, her cheeks dimpling as she dropped a dough dumpling in Sylvie's bowl from the prongs of her fork.

Sylvie couldn't stop the smile as she tried the food she'd contributed and sighed at the taste. Perfectly seasoned and still warm.

She eyed the elder shifters and settled into the dirt, giving away her seat and scooting closer to the fire until her skin flushed. They inclined their heads at her, and she reciprocated before averting her gaze. Perhaps a few days here wouldn't be so bad after all.

SEVENTEEN

Sylvie was staring into the whorling fire, empty bowl forgotten on her lap, when a voice startled her.

"You alright, dear?"

She glanced sharply over her shoulder at the female who had offered her a dough dumpling and nodded quickly, drawing her knees closer to her chest.

"Fine. You?"

The elder smiled, sliding closer. A fuzzy shawl was curled around her shoulders. "I am well. Tell me, what is your story?"

Sylvie straightened. "Oh, um … well, my husband and I came to set up wards …" Her violet mark warmed. "To stop the vampires from coming here."

The female tilted her head. "That is certainly kind. I recall seeing your handsome male with Elder Lonnie a few hours ago. But what of you? What is your story?"

Sylvie sucked in a breath, her teeth gnawing the inside of her cheek as she cast her gaze around the space, from the fire to Rose pushing a bowl of food into Hex's hands by the tree line and a cluster of shifters darting into the dark waters of the lake. She winced at the splashes, her body stiffening as memories snuck through her defences. Turning back to the female, Sylvie shook her head, throat tight.

"It's a mess."

The smile the female offered held far too much knowledge. "Aye. But there is often joy in mess. Purpose." She sat still, waiting for something, and Sylvie shrugged, rummaging through years of mayhem.

"I was a foster kid and I—uh, started working for my husband. We didn't know each other at the time—" She ran through the most basic description she could of her time with Kian in Erus, leaving out Elias completely, despite the annoyance it stirred in her chest, and stopped before her kidnapping. The old shifter might've sympathised with Ace for all she knew.

The elder sat in silence for the duration, her expression never wavering from mild interest.

When Sylvie went silent, she spoke again. "And what is it *you* wish for? You share what has happened to you, but I seek to know who you are."

Sylvie swallowed, stroking the scar that marred her cheek. The action drew the elder's gaze, as did the motion of her hand falling into her lap. "I don't really know yet."

"I'd like to hear when you find out," the elder female said, her voice fading as a figure stole the breath from Sylvie's lungs. The reason for her suffering was sauntering around with her platinum hair and supermodel grin, chatting with a gaggle of shifters. Without thinking, Sylvie stood, Rose's bowl and spoon thudding to the dirt as she stormed towards her—towards Natalie.

Natalie was alive. And by the look of her unusually toned body peeking through a sheer cream shirt and the faint yellow glow to her iris, she wasn't human.

Sylvie closed the gap between them in ten seconds flat, the other woman turning too late as Sylvie let her fist fly, her first two knuckles connecting with a violent crack to Natalie's jaw.

A few shouts echoed as Natalie dropped, her body vibrating then shifting, tearing through her clothes as she transformed into a huge black cat. A panther. Her mouth curled into a snarl, but Sylvie held her ground. *I've lost my damn mind.*

"Woah!" Rose had appeared at her shoulder, then Hex, his aura imposing on everyone around them. He seemed bigger, his face morphing as a guttural voice poured from his lips.

"Shift back now, Natalie."

Rose hissed between her teeth, but the surrounding shifters didn't so much as lift their bowed heads as Natalie unfurled back into her human form. Someone draped a blanket around her and she slunk away, towards the lake. Tension dripped from Sylvie's pores. She itched to stalk after Natalie and tear the extensions from her hair.

"What was that?" Rose asked softly, holding her forearm with a steady grip. Sylvie sensed the steel in those fingers and wondered vaguely if she'd even be able to pull away.

"She sold me out." Bile rose in her throat and she spun, storming away. Rose let her go without a word. *Good.* She didn't want another enemy, but if she held on, there would've been violence. No one would control her anymore.

As she plonked down by the fire again, arms crossed and using the seating logs as a backrest, her fury simmered until a warm hand brushed down her spine. She sighed, leaning into Kian as he sat, his legs straddling her.

"Do you feel better?"

She exhaled through her nose, nestling into his thighs. "No."

His hands dropped to her shoulders, massaging lightly, and she sank lower into his embrace.

"Have you eaten?" she mumbled, the dwindling adrenaline and fire crackles lulling her into a state of deep exhaustion.

"Don't worry about me, Princess."

She let her gaze soften on the flames. "It's my job to worry."

He brushed his hand across her forehead, tucking her hair behind her ears in gentle strokes. "No, Princess. It is mine."

* * *

The bedroll Sylvie woke on was lumpy, the jersey tucked under her head giving her neck a crick as she sucked in a shocked breath through her nose and jolted to sitting. Awareness rushed back quickly, and she almost laughed at the fact that her sleep had been dreamless.

Shifters dozed around her, all in various stages of undress, and Kian was gone. The only other person awake sat opposite her, tending to the fire and stoking its embers with a long branch. Hex. He watched her through his lowered brow and she couldn't stop herself from preening a few stray curls and tucking them away from her face. His lip twitched before averting his gaze and she stood, stretching her arms overhead.

Rose wove through sleeping bodies and met her stare with a grin. "Morning, Sylvie. How are you feeling?"

Why do people keep asking me that?

"Um … fine."

"And your hand?"

She turned it over, revealing her healed knuckles, and Rose hummed. "While I don't condone violence, that was a solid punch."

Satisfaction swirled inside Sylvie as Rose said, "Would you want to join us for training after breakfast?"

From the side, Hex sighed, but said nothing, and Sylvie scoffed quietly. He was already learning his place. *Good dog.*

"I'd like that."

"Great. Meet back here at ten and I'll take you to the sparring squares."

She ambled back to Hex's house and salvaged some bread from the fridge, waiting for ten o'clock to roll around. To her relief, Hex didn't show up, and she changed into her activewear, tucking her clothes from the night before into her bags. It was just a few days. Then she and Kian could go home. Back to normalcy, and away from the crazy shifter forest commune. That was what she told herself as she jogged back to the clearing, anyway, meeting Rose with breathless excitement.

"You ready?" Rose asked, tying back her ginger hair in a simple braid. All the shifters were up by now. A few in the clearing were tidying scraps from the tables and Sylvie stalled, about to offer help, when Rose caught her gaze. "It's okay. They've got it."

"Okay then," she answered. "Hell yeah, I'm ready. What's first?"

Rose winked and linked their elbows together. "Hand-to-hand. Come with me."

They followed a small path Sylvie hadn't seen before through the forest opposite the cabins and popped out by rows of square patches carved into the dirt. The patches wove through the forest, careful to not disturb the root systems of the neighbouring trees, whose canopies brushed together, revealing tiny fragments of the sky. It was smart. Hidden in plain sight. Even if something flew overhead, they'd be invisible.

Sylvie lowered her gaze to the squares, each one containing a pair of shifters grappling, punching, and prowling in the soil. Their muscular bodies moved with animalistic grace as they collided in flurries of blows. It was like a dance, each shifter in complete control of their anatomy.

"Wow."

"It's something, isn't it?" Rose whispered. "We've always been interested in pushing ourselves to the limits, but after the first attack, it became a necessity. Strength and venom weren't enough to stop them from taking our people. So, we work, we train, we eat, and repeat."

"I'm sorry."

She meant it too.

"It's not your fault, Sylvie. Come."

Rose pulled her into a free square and hopped from foot to foot, sidestepping in a circular motion. "Copy me."

Sylvie did, and soon enough, she'd worked up a sweat, her heart thudding against her rib cage. It had been a while. But she had appearances to keep up, so she pushed through the fatigue. Rose raised her hands on either side of her face, and with a smirk Sylvie mirrored the pose, modifying the stance by widening her base.

"Good," Rose said. "You know any combos?"

"Some."

Rose's brows shot up like she hadn't expected that answer, and a smidgen of pride filtered through the usual snark. *Gods, I better live up to my own expectations right now, I swear.*

"Show me."

With one quick shake of her limbs, Sylvie approached, keeping her weight light on her toes and her core braced. "Full power?"

Rose grinned, a twinkle in her eyes. "Go on."

Without warning, Sylvie threw a hard jab to her head, forcing Rose's guard to rise and giving Sylvie the opening she'd hoped for. She rained hits on Rose's midsection, only getting in two blows before Rose leapt out of range and circled, offering a few jabs of her own. Unlike Sylvie, every one of her hits struck true, and pain leapt like fire from every point of contact.

"Fuck, you hit hard."

"You too," Rose said. "Not bad form either."

"Gee, thanks."

A few shifters watched from the sidelines and seemed to share the sentiment, except for one set of teal eyes, narrowed and brooding from afar. The beautiful strawberry blond attached to them stood with crossed arms and muttered quietly to another shifter beside her.

"Do you know any ground work? Grappling?" Rose asked, recapturing her attention.

"Uh, no."

She beamed. "Awesome, I'll teach you my favourites."

They moved through a variety of different holds, bars, and chokes, ensuring Sylvie repeated each position multiple times while listing them aloud.

By midday, they were both coated in dirt and sweat, and Sylvie's body was screaming for food and a wash. The crowd that had gathered was rather impressive too, the elder shifters nodding approvingly while Sylvie picked up on the grapples quickly and executed them smoothly. Just before Rose called for a break, Sylvie discovered multiple ways to manoeuvre through each hold with growing speed. The sweat helped her to slip free.

"Fast learner," Rose panted, wiping her brow with a forearm.

"Lunch is ready when you are, Rose," Al said as he passed the squares, his bulky torso glistening with perspiration.

"Thanks!"

Sylvie gulped air from her sitting position on the ground and used her nails to scrape dust from her tear ducts. "I'm gonna need a shower."

"Just jump in the lake. We've still got archery to go."

She sighed and let Rose pull her to her feet, suppressing the fear of the water as they trudged back to the clearing. One glance at the rippling lake, shifters splashing and diving within it, had her turning on her heel.

"I'll be quick," she said, dragging herself towards the house.

Rose called after her, but she kept walking, trying to suppress the dread, the shallowness of her breath. Why couldn't she get a full inhale? Every pant left her starving for air. It's okay. *I'm okay. I'm safe. Breathe. Breathe.*

This time Kian didn't come to save her, and she curled up on the bathroom floor until she could breathe again.

She missed lunch.

EIGHTEEN

"You're lucky vampires don't use guns. We finally found something you're bad at!"

"Shut up!"

Sylvie put down the pistol with a frown, shaking her hands to eliminate the recoil sensation. "I hate them." It was more than hate. She was no stranger to gun violence. By age seven, she had stared down the barrel of a gun twice in Sterling. Once in school and once inside a corner store with her foster father. All the guy wanted was some cigarettes. The shop owner killed him. She'd never forget the pop that made her ears ring or the thud of the body hitting the laminate floor. There was so much blood. She flexed her fingers.

"Can we go back to archery? I got pretty good at that after I figured out the distance."

"Maybe tomorrow. Come on, one more try."

She lifted the pistol once more, eyeing the notched wood targets wrapped in straw. The firing range was a few minutes beyond the sparring squares, and any missed shots would land in the lake. *Or not ...*

Natalie swaggered into the clearing, freezing between steps like a predator not wanting to be spotted by a prey animal. But she *was* spotted, and the roles reversed as Sylvie turned, angling the pistol at Natalie's lower half, fingers trembling.

"Sylvie," Rose said her name like a warning.

"Go, Rose."

Natalie pressed her lips and nodded, fighting tears. *Where were those tears when Hex dragged me from our office?*

Rose tried to speak again.

"I said go!"

She sighed and darted off past Natalie without looking back.

"You let him take me," Sylvie said. Backup would come, but she couldn't stop.

A fat tear rolled down Natalie's cheek. "But—but you're fine, you're here, so it turned out okay. I knew it would. He would never hurt you. He's—he's good."

Sylvie's head tilted, emotion flooding her senses until her sinuses stung. "Ace tortured me for weeks because of you."

"What? I—I don't know who that is …"

"Hex's beta. He beat me, and drowned me, pulled my fucking fingernails from my hands just to see how long it took me to heal."

"Oh, gods." More tears rolled down Natalie's cheeks as Sylvie fought to contain hers. She'd only told Elias and Kian about her time with Hex, and even then she didn't reveal everything he did. She didn't know why she was telling Natalie, either. Old habits …

"He cut all my fucking hair off, Nat. Look at it. And the thought of water touching my face makes me feel like I'm dying." The gun lowered to her side, but Natalie didn't move. She didn't run.

Her lower lip wobbled, the grown-out, chipped acrylics on her nails wiping away some tears. "I'm so sorry, Sylvie." Her head bowed like it was too heavy on her neck. "I got caught up in this future and I couldn't let you stand in the way of that. I didn't know his beta was a monster, I swear. He wasn't here when I arrived. I—I didn't know. And I know that isn't an excuse, but I'm really sorry."

Sylvie dropped the gun, her anger giving way to disgust in herself. She'd pointed a gun at this woman. This female who had been there while she acclimated to a hellish new career, who had made her laugh to the point of tears with her innuendos, who had made a mistake.

"I'm sorry for pointing a gun at you." She kept her gaze level even as stubborn tears spilt from her lashes.

"I don't blame you," Natalie replied, stepping closer. "Can we talk now without the threat of death?"

A small laugh escaped Sylvie's lips, and she wiped her cheeks. "For now. Though I think I'm more at risk than you." She closed the gap between them and stepped into an awkward embrace, waiting for the stab of a claw into her spine. When it didn't come, she relaxed, letting out a shuddering breath.

"Not a chance with Hex protecting you. I thought he was gonna rip my head off."

The beast inside Sylvie rumbled in satisfaction. She ignored it.

"Why did you want this? I thought you'd stick your nose up at anything outside of Sterling."

They pulled back and Natalie looked at her nails, a small smile playing on her lips as she sniffed and flicked off a chipped piece of acrylic.

"Are you kidding?" Natalie laughed then. The sound was sweeter than Sylvie remembered. Free. "I fucking hated corporate. The city. The people. As soon as I discovered the shifters existed, I knew it was what I wanted. To have no one judge how I look, how I talk, talk shit about my career choices, my partners, any of it. I just wanted the freedom to be me, and now I have it. It's only been a week and I feel more accepted here than I ever did in Sterling." Natalie's eyes misted, and she looked down, picking off another fake nail. Sylvie had misjudged her completely. She hadn't even cared to know.

I was too caught up in my own shit to connect with her.

Maybe if she had, Natalie wouldn't have been so quick to let Hex take her. Maybe none of this would have happened.

"I didn't know."

"You couldn't have. I couldn't remove the mask in that job—that life. I'm guessing you couldn't either."

She lifted a shoulder. "Not at the start. But things changed when—" Sylvie stopped. How much could she reveal here? The shifters knew of her relationship with Kian, but not that they were fated. The shifter Elias killed at the cabin had wanted them dead for withholding the artefact that would allow shifters mates. Unnatural or otherwise.

"When what?"

Sylvie shook her head, smiling faintly. "Nothing. Thank you for sharing that with me."

"Of course. Thank you for not murdering me, even if I deserved it."

A laugh resonated between them.

"You didn't," Sylvie replied, squeezing her hand. "Can we talk again?" She didn't know how to mend the connection, let alone build a friendship, so she held out the offer even if the threat of rejection stirred a fear so deep she thought she might vomit.

Natalie smiled though, wiping her cheeks of the last remnants of despair, and nodded. "Of course. Any time."

Sylvie's heart thundered, a wave of gratitude filling her as she stepped back, retrieving the gun and storing it in the black chest Rose had brought it in, snapping the lid shut and spinning the combination code.

"I guess I better go apologise to Rose," she said, glancing at Natalie. The other female offered a wry grin and waved her hand.

"Nah. I'll tell her you're finished with training if you want. It's almost dinner."

Sylvie's stomach took the opportune moment to growl, punctuating Natalie's sentence, and the shifter beckoned. "Come, I'll take you to the lake."

They wandered back, passing a few shifters who stared longer than usual, and Sylvie spoke from the side of her mouth. "What's it like here? Do you all eat together every night?"

Natalie chuckled, weaving through the trees with a graceful poise Sylvie envied. She belonged here.

"Not every night, but most. Every time they welcome a new shifter to the pack, they celebrate. Food connects us, and when we're all together, it's like the world is right. And training too, I guess. Hopefully, after the next attack, we'll all still be together."

With every word, Sylvie's steps slowed, her body filling with a foreign emotion. She couldn't fathom it. To be accepted by so many. To belong purely for existing, not because you're tied to another by fate. She'd never regret Kian and Elias. They had changed her path for the better, but they *had* to love her. The need for one another was scored into their souls.

"I will die before I let them take any more of you." Sylvie didn't realise she'd spoken aloud until Natalie touched her arm, a sad smile on her face.

"Me too," she said. "Me too."

* * *

Washing off the day with a scalding cloth in the upstairs bathroom of Hex's place, Sylvie's limbs hardly worked as the fatigue settled in with jarring clarity. The faded light outside signalled night was nearing, and a burnt sienna glow covered half of the room.

"Princess?"

"In here."

Kian appeared in the doorway with a tired smile. He paused, noting the dirt-caked towel and red raw skin where Sylvie had scrubbed.

"Are you alright?"

"Fine." She sighed, pulling on a pair of fresh underwear, pyjama shorts, and an old singlet she found in the drawers of their room. "I'm running out of clothes, though."

He closed the gap between them and kissed her head, probing at her mental fortress. "I said I'm fine, Kian."

"I know what you said, but I can feel your emotions even if you try to block them from me."

She sighed, lifting her face to stare him down. His eyes, although lined with bags, twinkled with mischief. He reached past her, tugging the shower nozzle to hot, and stripped off the last of his clothes. She worked her jaw and trailed a hand down his abdomen.

"My emotions are mine," she said, dragging her finger across his hip bones.

He smirked, kissing the tip of her nose, and backed into the shower, the water cascading through the divots of his well-defined muscles. She flushed, crossing her arms and staring at the perfection he was. He tipped his head back, massaging his scalp, the tight curls stretching under the spray. Old scars peeked around his shoulders and waist, but they didn't steal her attention—no, that was the hard appendage between his legs.

She bit her lip, dragging her gaze up to his chest, where her mark sat, right over his heart. She itched to lick it. To claim him again.

It took more than a few moments to realise he was staring at her, a curl to his mouth as he washed off the soapsuds that popped across his dark skin. She was jealous of the bubbles.

"What?" he said.

She tilted her head, humming. "Nothing. I was just admiring your beauty. Husband."

He pointed beside her and she followed his gaze, fetching the towel as he switched the shower off and took it, tying it around his waist. With every move, he stepped nearer to where she leaned against the wall.

"Is that so?"

"Mhmm."

With a soft grip, he took her chin between his forefinger and thumb, tipping her head to pepper kisses along her jaw to her lips. She draped her arms over his shoulders, twirling her fingers in the wet coils dripping along his nape, and melted into him.

"When can we go home?" she asked against his lips. Despite the question, she found herself less committed to it than before. Kian smiled against her mouth.

"I'll drop by home tomorrow morning to get you more clothes." A nonanswer, but one that gave plenty of information. They were nowhere near finished here.

She sighed and let him guide her to their bedroom. He dressed and crawled onto the bed beside her.

"What's the plan for tomorrow?" she asked him, sliding closer until they shared a pillow, his arm draped over her hip.

"More warding to the west. It's draining me more than it should, so I'm taking it slow." He kissed her, gently, before pulling back. "There's old magic here. Older than I've ever felt on Erus."

"Is it dangerous?" She pulled his hand from her side and kissed each knuckle.

His throat bobbed, his indigo-flecked gaze following her actions before he answered, "All magic has the potential to be dangerous, Princess. It's only ours to explore, shaping in ways we need, not own. True magic is volatile and cannot be controlled. It's in everything if you look close enough."

She believed it. When she used her fae sight, she could see the lines—the magic—running between everything. Nothing was more beautiful or free than the connections between the soil and its children. The trees, the plants, the grass, the air. Her.

She swallowed and tucked his hand beneath her cheek as she nuzzled into him.

"And what plans do you have tomorrow?" he asked hoarsely, adjusting his lower half.

"A run, I think." She toyed with the slight point of his ear, delighting in his shudder. "I wonder when they work."

Rose said they did, but so far all they'd done was train.

"Rowan's father made some good investments, buying property in the east. They don't have to, but many work over in the foothills of the Silverwood peninsula." *Silverwood.* That was where Elias's cabin was. That had to be miles away. She almost asked why they didn't just work in Sagehill and bit her tongue. Kian's wards. It had barely been a few days, and she was already forgetting the harm the shifters had caused. But that was years ago. Long before Hex and Rose, before Natalie.

She was slipping; she felt it. The Fates were winning, and she couldn't stop the overwhelming guilt as she lay awake in Kian's arms.

NINETEEN

Sylvie stretched with Rose and a couple dozen others by the charcoaled remnants of the fire, the morning sun warming her cheeks as she zipped up her jumper against the autumn chill.

She tied back all the hair she could manage, sighing at the tiny ponytail before hopping from foot to foot. "You won't ditch me, right?"

Rose peered at her, her wide eyes compressing under a smile. "Of course not. I always pace myself for the first hour, anyway."

"Hour? You're trying to kill me."

Rose just rolled her eyes. "You need to give yourself more credit. It's nothing."

Maddissen snorted from behind them and Sylvie shook her head. "Sure."

Hex arrived in running gear, the singlet showing off the swooping scrawls of ink covering his arms and hands and the grey sweats doing something disgusting to her body. She averted her gaze as he took the lead, jogging off towards the lake.

"That's our cue," Rose said, palming Sylvie's back and matching her jogging pace. They followed the lake's edge where silt met pebbles and she kept her gaze on the trees. She was safe. *No one will hurt me again.*

They turned a bend, and even with ten people between her and Hex, his enormous back still distracted her until she almost tripped headlong over an exposed tree root. She hissed, regaining her footing, and scowled at the tree. *Traitor.*

"Watch it." A sultry voice cut into her from the lakeside, the scathing quality not diminishing any of its beauty. The strawberry blond shifter with the teal eyes.

"Nice to meet you too," Sylvie said, increasing her pace until she was next to Rose. The female sneered and darted ahead, her long, tan limbs revealing swoon-worthy musculature with every strike of her foot on the ground.

She weaved between shifters, her ponytail swishing until she was shoulder-to-shoulder with Hex. He glanced at her, said something low, and she smiled, the light point of her canines flashing as she peered once over her shoulder. Right at Sylvie. Flashbacks of Lazuli flooded her senses until a potent jealousy turned her blood to ice. She had no right to be jealous. She didn't want Hex, but the words flew from her mouth regardless.

"What a fucking bitch."

Rose almost choked, and the shifters between them staggered, darting around the female as she froze on the path, her body twitching. It took a few seconds more for Sylvie to stop, almost skidding into her. Hex paused a few strides ahead as the female spun and stared Sylvie down with her two extra inches of height.

"What did you just call me?"

Sylvie held her ground. "From the look on your face, I'm guessing you heard me," she replied with equal venom.

"Say it again. I'm afraid my alpha was dividing my attention."

A humourless laugh passed through Sylvie's lips. "What's your problem? I don't fucking know you. You haven't got the decency to introduce yourself, so cut the bitchy attitude."

The female's voice sharpened, and the surrounding shifters lapped up every word. "And why don't you go find your pretty faerie boy, considering how obvious it is that you play favourites?"

Play favourites? What did she mean? Unless she knew Hex was her mate—

Her marks twinged as she processed the words, her fist balling and swinging, only missing by a hair when Hex dragged the female back and dropped her against a tree.

"Stop, Claudine," he growled.

"Yes, Alpha," she said, dropping her expression to perfect demure elegance even as she reined in her obvious fury, chest heaving. Sylvie had no such abilities. She lunged, prepared to move through Hex, but a grip held her back. Rose.

"Leave us," Hex bit out to the female, Claudine, and the shifters eavesdropping around them. "You too," he said to Rose when the others darted away. Sylvie didn't miss the scathing look as Claudine disappeared into the forest, or the reassuring glance Rose offered her after.

Then they were alone.

Hex said nothing, just stared like he was waiting for something, his shoulders rising and falling in shuddering waves.

"What?" she gritted between her teeth.

"What are you doing?"

She frowned. "What am I doing? What the fuck was that?" She pointed after Claudine. "You showed so much disgust over Elias and me when you had *that* waiting for you back home."

"She is not mine."

"Neither am I."

His golden irises flared. "Aren't you? Because that was a clear claiming. Unless something has changed, you don't get a say, and you don't hurt my pack. You are a guest."

She swallowed the hurt. "I thought I was your mate."

"To *them*, you are a guest." He swung his arms out in the direction the shifters went. "Guests don't go around and pick fights."

"She knows about me, though, doesn't she? You heard her as clear as I did."

"She only knows because she needed a reason I wouldn't accept her as my chosen mate."

Sylvie's throat seized. "What?"

He tilted his head back, exposing his throat, and rubbed his face before looking back at her. "The elders had picked the match. An alpha's duty is servitude, and without a partner, I can't give the pack what they need. No other leader has taken the title unmated, but when the vampires killed my parents, I had no choice. I had to serve them."

"That's why you wanted the artefact." She held his stare. "Do you want her?"

His expression twisted and he stormed forwards, pinning her between a tree and his chest. "Why do you care?"

"I don't care," she ground out. "This bond traps us together, no matter what I feel about it. If you want her, then—" She couldn't even finish the offer. It made her feel ill. He ignored it though, grasping at the other part of her statement.

"And what do you feel about the bond?"

What did he want her to say?

"I—I don't know. Just get away from me."

He backed up, eyes phasing from green and amber to gold. "You're driving me insane, woman."

"Ditto." She leaned heavily into the tree as Hex looked her up and down.

"Head back." He jutted his chin towards the clearing, speaking with such authority her hazed, hurt mind had no other option but to obey.

* * *

Sylvie stood over the bed, riffling through the clothes Kian had brought, and shook her head. Half were outfits for training and the rest were the dainty dresses she had bought at Sagehill. Rose had invited her to dinner for the autumnal equinox and told her to wear something nice. She wanted to decline, but Kian left her no choice. She couldn't wear tights again. The light outside faded as night fell, and the chatter of shifters carried on the wind. She'd managed a shallow bath earlier, so at least she was clean as she slipped on an emerald sundress. The sleeves billowed and cinched at the wrist, and the high neckline covered her marks. With a gentle spin, Sylvie savoured the brush of silken fabric on her thighs, the hem resting just above her knees. She slipped on a pair of strapped sandals and padded down the stairs, freezing when Hex met her gaze from the doorway beside Kian.

"Where's Rose?"

Hex straightened as Kian neared her, taking her hand as she finished her descent.

"Rowan has a few things to ask." He finished the sentence with a look that said, "be nice."

Sylvie rolled her eyes and crossed her arms. "Well?"

"Tonight you will be my guests for the equinox." There was that word again. *Guests.*

She fought a scowl.

"You will observe the first mating ceremony in over twenty years with the Animae artefact. It is sacred, and I expect you to behave with the utmost respect." He focused his gaze on her for the last part, and she felt hot.

How dare he?

"Together, we will bless the chosen unions, and you will stay at my side until the ceremony is complete. You both will," Hex added, turning to Kian, whose warm complexion seemed a fraction darker. Was he blushing?

Sylvie's brows rose, but she remained silent.

"With our combined blessing, I'm certain the Fates will allow the chosen unions to create offspring—"

"Wait." Sylvie raised a hand. "Why the Hel are you trying for children right now? Shouldn't you be focusing on stopping the vampires from taking the shifters you already have?"

Nothing triggered her more than children being brought into a world to face unnecessary violence and cruelty. She knew firsthand the effects that lingered from that kind of upbringing.

Hex exhaled through his nose, his frustration palpable. "We are, but we cannot put our lives on hold because of those beasts—"

"Beasts." He seemed to have forgotten that she was one of those beasts, and so was the male she loved. The same male risking his life for the ungrateful alpha. "So, let me get this straight. You hold ceremonies to make new shifter babies during what is essentially a war and turn humans, even though the survival rate is stupidly low. And you call us beasts."

"The humans always know the odds. They choose this life and gods dammit, they need hope!"

Sylvie snapped her mouth shut, the retort dying on her lips at his raised voice. She instead threaded her arm through Kian's and dragged him past Hex, not even deigning a response. If he was going to speak like that, then she had nothing to say. It didn't help that she understood his reasons. She hated that a part of her cared for the shifters, and she shoved it down before storming towards the clearing. They would observe the ceremony, bless the stupid cup, and then she would stay in her room until the warding was over.

"That could have gone better," Kian said.

Sylvie's reply was almost silent. "He shouldn't have yelled at me."

"I didn't say he should have."

She eyed him until Hex appeared at his side, head lifted proudly, and averted her gaze. The sight within the clearing wasn't much better. Males stood shirtless, their taut bodies rippling under the firelight with sweat dancing trails through their abs and into the loose grey shorts hugging their tapered waists.

The females' attire was worse. Their flowy shifts had enough opacity to maintain some modesty in the dark, but when the dying sunlight shone through it, she could make our every curve, dip, and spattering of hair on their bodies.

Each shifter was objectively beautiful, and she blushed as they caught her ogling. The shifters paired off, draping themselves over each other, enamoured. If love were a tangible entity, Sylvie would find it between those shifters. In the besotted glances. In the fraction of space between their heated bodies. She dropped her gaze, but a tattooed hand appeared beneath her chin, lifting it to meet his stare. Shock stopped her rebuke, as did the look on Hex's face. One that said, "Keep your head up."

He let her go, nodding at her straightening spine and raised chin, then turned, continuing his path to the bonfire, now roaring with new life.

The shifters drew nearer, as if Hex emanated his own gravitational field, and she found herself pulled into it too.

When he spoke, everyone fell silent. Even the wind paused its whispers. Sylvie swallowed. It was a lot. Where was Rose? Or even Nat? Kian remained a steady presence beside her, but he didn't feel the same way about Hex as she did. Kian liked him, she could feel it. And he trusted the Fates, which was more than she could claim.

"Welcome, everyone, to the autumnal equinox," Hex said, his voice projecting to every corner of the clearing. "To the mating ceremony, and the beginning of our turned shifters' new lives as mates." The shifters in the flowy clothing grinned and kissed, edging closer as Rose appeared beside Hex, a familiar metal chalice in hand. The Animae.

Rose handed the chalice to the closest shifter, who bowed his head in reverence, brushing his brow against the cup's rim before passing it along. Every shifter had their turn, even Natalie, who performed the action with a smoothness Sylvie envied. The cup came her way. *Shit.* Though the action seemed simple enough, she'd fuck it up somehow.

Kian took the chalice first as everyone stared, closing his eyes and whispering something in High Fae. Sylvie stared wide-eyed as he handed it to her. "It's all about intention," he murmured against her ear. Her fingers trembled, and she could only pray she didn't drop the thing as she raised its rim to her brow and closed her eyes. She scented blood and aged metal. *Um, please work and give the shifters mates.* Her body tingled, and a flash of foresight ripped through her.

A bed of leaves. Three males doting on her body, her mind, her soul. The magic in her veins calling to each, twisting and twining, merging with the trails of ultraviolet—the magic of the Tynaan. Of Erus.

She gasped, as did the crowd of shifters, then opened her eyes from where she'd landed on her knees. She hadn't even felt the fall. Fucking Fates. *You pick now to fuck with my head?*

As expected, they didn't answer as Kian tugged her to her feet and Hex appeared before her, cupping her elbow as she trembled. "I—I'm sorry."

Hex shook his head, taking the cup and watching her with just as much veneration as the first shifter who had touched the artefact. Then mistrust flared in his eyes. She flushed scarlet and leaned into Kian as Hex turned, calling for the first shifter pair. They spoke in hushed tones, repeating the same sentence as they cut their palms, filled the cup, and drank.

"By the Fates, I consecrate this totem. Whoever drinks from it will be blessed with a true mate bond."

At one point, Sylvie's gaze drifted into the wider crowd, catching the longing look that speared from Claudine and the nod Hex returned. There was understanding in that shared glance. And kindness. History.

Her heart raced as she dragged her gaze back to the shifters drinking from the chalice. Once the last one completed the ritual, they all ran, laughing and hooting, into the lake, losing their clothes in the process before shifting and disappearing sopping wet into the forest. Wolves, bears, a lion, and foxes. Most were the same species, but one couple was a lion-wolf pairing. *How does that even work?* Would it come out half-and-half? *Do they fuck in animal form?* Kian nudged her, and she realised the horror must've been written across her face. She smoothed her mask back into place until the loud moans and erotic screams started.

Oh. The responding flush that coated her from heat to toe had her staggering. She had to get out of there.

"I think we're sleeping out here again," Kian said against her hair, a smile in his tone. She'd be a liar if she said she wasn't *slightly* into it, too.

They settled by the fire, with Kian and the other shifters falling asleep early. She wasn't so lucky. After a heinously loud scream of pleasure, she stood, pacing away from the fire as the heat grew too much. The ceaseless moans hit their first crescendo, each shifter in similar stages of bliss.

She eyed the darkened forest. *I shouldn't. I don't need it.* But lust formed within her until she ached all over. More moans cascaded through the shuddering leaves like the soil felt the pleasure and revelled in it, too. Perhaps it knew release was imminent.

Fuck it.

She tiptoed into the tree line. It had been a while. With Kian exhausted after each warding, it was not like she could ask him. This was the selfless option. A solo tryst. Merging with the darkness, Sylvie fumbled with the hem of her dress before finding the part of her that sought release. Her fingers swirled in tight circles over her clit as the symphony of sex rose to its peak and she fell off with them, shuddering again and again against a tree. She panted, straightening her dress and pressed off the trunk, about to return, when a strange voice hissed in the dark.

"And what do we have here?"

TWENTY

Sylvie inhaled to scream, her fae sight flickering as a dark blond male prowled into the moonlight.

She barely got a sound out before Hex was at her side, shoving her behind him and lowering his stance. How long had he been standing there? *Gods.*

"Alpha," the male crooned. Dirt coated his face, highlighting every wrinkle and hard line of a person who had seen some terrible things. "I'm surprised you didn't invite us to your little get-together."

There was a harshness to his accusation.

"You chose this path, Matias."

Matias edged closer, the scent of death wafting from him. Sylvie peered around Hex to get another look. With her fae sight, the faint lines where human form combined with animal pulsed, the assuredness of his steps lining up with the forward prowling of an insanely big cat. Perhaps a tiger, though she'd only ever seen one on television. His gleaming blue eyes trailed up her body.

"What's this pretty thing you found, Alpha?" He spat after the last word, and Sylvie had to stop her flinch.

"Leave our borders, or you won't see the sunrise."

"You surely don't think you can take on all of us." Two, four, six, *twelve* pairs of eyes appeared in the near pitch-black and Sylvie squeezed Hex's shirt hem. They needed backup. "Your pack seems far too occupied to worry about little old me."

"What do you want?" Hex growled, edging closer to Sylvie as Matias took another step. Hex's muscles rippled as if on the verge of a shift, and Sylvie pulled on the surrounding energy to activate her fae sight. Her brain ached as she tugged Hex's top, the trees shifting the slightest bit inward at her nudge. Or maybe that was just the wind.

"Everything I deserve." Matias's grin widened and Sylvie's annoyance flared. She frowned. That wasn't her. With the slightest motion, she glanced over her shoulder and felt Kian's mark hum. He was close. Thank the gods. But why did he want her annoyed? Anger flared then until she tasted metal. *What?* Then it was like a wave of fury, one that forced her biting words out as Matias prowled closer. *Gods Kian, I hope you know what you're doing.*

She rounded Hex. "Who the hell do you think you are?" she snapped at Matias. "I've listened to you speak for less than a minute and can already tell you are a pathetic waste of air. Leave, or I'll make you." The threat was baseless, but Kian's gift of violent hate almost made her believe them. She had never felt so achingly irate—so murderous.

Hex took her hand, but she hardly noticed as she stomped forward, the trees bowing as she leashed them to her will. Blood spurted from her nose as she bared her lengthening fangs. She expected Hex to speak, to chastise, or pull her back, but he didn't. She reserved that surprise to unpack later.

Matias stilled but didn't retreat. "Well, the pretty lady has claws. Where did you find this one, Rowan? The gutter?"

She sneered. "Have you looked in a mirror, cunt?"

"Watch your mouth, whore." His body shook and Sylvie's ire rose.

"You watch it," she taunted him, pointing to her curved lips and spraying blood as she said, "Fuck. Off."

With that, Matias roared, shifting into a sickeningly huge white tiger with paws the size of dinner plates. She ripped one last time on her fae energy, the ground bucking, but her connection snapped, blood pouring down her face as Matias swiped. He landed the hit, but not on them. The force of his blow connected with an invisible foe that threw him to the ground, where he phased between forms and seized before flipping onto his belly and dragging himself away with a roar.

The eyes faded too, and Sylvie sagged into Hex.

"What was that?" he said, thumbing blood off her face. She didn't have the energy to pull away or snap at him. Her eyes rolled.

"Nothing. Need ... sleep."

"I'll take her," Kian said, appearing at their side. She closed her eyes as he lifted her, noting the reluctant release of pressure from Hex.

"What was that?" he asked again.

"I used her to distract them so I could activate a ward in this area."

"How? How did she know to do that?"

"I can take emotions away, and I can give them back. She burned through them, luckily, but she'll need rest."

That's good. I can lighten his burden, too. Good … good.

"No, not that. I would've expected that attitude from her," Hex said. Sylvie grumbled, eyes still closed, as her body started swaying with the motion of Kian's steps. "I meant the trees."

"I don't know," Kian answered, pausing a moment before walking closer to the crackle of flames. "Her affinities are still developing." He wiped something across her lips and chin, and she scrunched her face, burying it into his shoulder.

"Princess."

"Cold," she mumbled. "Fire."

"Yes, hold on, we're almost there." Heat licked at her chest and back as Kian lowered her to the ground, cuddling behind her. He kept his voice soft, but she still pricked her ears to hear him.

"Tell your people there were at least fourteen rogues. They're afraid enough to stay away for the night, but they're hungry and tired. I wouldn't put it past them to try again, and I'm still days from completing the wards. You're most exposed from the west and north, but with Granite Lake between you and the Iron Peaks, you're better off focusing your watch to the west."

"I appreciate the advice."

"Any time." Kian tucked her hair behind her ears as sleep doused her senses. She barely heard the murmurs between the males, but she held on. Just a little longer.

Kian spoke first. "You'll need to talk to her, eventually."

"I won't change her mind."

"You will. Show her who you are."

"It's too messy. She's too—"

Darkness stole the last words.

* * *

"Come on, Vee. It's been days. You should be better at shooting by now."

Sylvie scowled over her shoulder at a grinning Rose and a few other nosy shifters.

"I already told you I hate guns. Can't we just switch to grappling now? Or archery?"

Rose tutted and stepped towards her with a fresh clip. "If you hit the heart and head without running out of bullets, we can go."

Fine. Easy enough. Archery was like breathing. This should be no different.

Leaning forward and levelling the gun with the wood target about ten metres out, she took a smooth inhale, keeping her lips slightly parted, and narrowed her eyes. Her forefinger slid off the side of the barrel and curled around the trigger as she held her breath, lined up the shot, and squeezed.

As usual, she missed the point she was aiming at, instead skimming the edge of the target and sending straw and bark flying.

"Dammit!" She shot twice more, and somehow got worse, before a warm, tattooed hand cupped hers, lifting the gun up and to the left.

She hissed as Hex's breath tickled the hair around her ears. "Don't let your emotions control you. This is practise. These targets will not suddenly sprout legs and run. If you can't hit these, what hope do you have when we're attacked again?"

Not if. When.

She straightened her spine, not glancing his way, but noting the heat generated in the space between them. "I won't be using a gun."

His grip on her hands tightened. "If it's between nothing and a gun, you choose a gun. Do you understand me?"

She hated the way she shivered from his words. Hated how close he stood. How he breathed down her neck. How warm he felt.

"I'm no good at it," she said, edging away from him.

"Show me."

She looked at him then. He was closer than before. From this distance, she could smell the faint scent of smoke on his clothes.

"Fine." She repeated the motions, firing once, before he moved behind her, caging her arms between his. A flush erupted across her cheeks and she jolted forwards, away from the pressure of his chest on her back.

"Feel the wind on your face. The weight of the weapon. Relax your grip, woman, don't strangle the thing. Left hand under your right. Good. Now breathe. Slow."

Sylvie swallowed, trying not to shake as she followed his words, or lean into him as his lips moved near the shell of her ear. It was too warm.

Gods, move back.

"I'm not gonna have you there with me, so why can't I just focus on what I'm already decent at?"

"You will get better if you practise. Now shoot."

She scowled, but took the shot and blinked as the bullet struck true. The target's head wobbled under the force. Then, lowering her arms a few inches, she shot again, hitting its dead centre, this time without correction.

"Good."

She shuddered as he released her, a mixture of frustration and disappointment settling into her belly and lower. *Gods dammit.* She needed Kian. He could help her with her minor sexual frustration problem.

"Well, I'm going to do what I want now," she said, daring him to contest her. He didn't.

"And was is that?"

His expression remained open. Curious. Gentle. She worked her jaw, fighting every instinct in her to like this male. "Rose said I could join the sparring shifters."

His brow lifted, and he faced a sheepish Rose. "And who are you suggesting she spar with? It's the tournament."

"Why do you think I brought her to gun training first?"

Sylvie placed the weapon in its lock box and faced the cousins with folded arms. "What are you talking about? You never said anything about a tournament. I want to join."

The breath Hex expelled through his nostrils made Sylvie's mouth flicker as Rose filled her in. "Sometimes we arrange small competitions to see who the best fighter is. No big deal."

This time Sylvie did smile, turning to march straight towards the training squares, staggering when a grip circled her forearm. "What?" she snapped, jerking her arm back from Hex. "It sounds like fun."

"You can't fight against them—" He looked physically pained.

"Why not? It's just sparring."

"And gambling, and prestige." Rose raised her hands placatingly at her cousin's withering glare. "You know it's clean fighting. She can always leave the square."

"Yeah, I'll be fine."

Hex's eyes flashed. "It's not you I'm worried about."

Her lips curled despite herself, and she took off with Rose in tow towards laughter and cheering. She tried not to think about the parting look she caught before turning away. The half-grin or the resignation. *I don't like him. I don't like him. I don't like him.*

The fighting was already in full swing as they entered the area. A few shifters sat along felled logs with bloodied noses and ripped clothes, but the majority still surrounded the fighting pairs. Sylvie searched for an opening but came up empty. *Come on …*

"Hey! What are you doing here?" Natalie said, appearing through the crowd with a grin and a sheen of sweat across her upper lip.

"Sparring?" Sylvie said, raising her brow in silent question at the platinum blond. Natalie's mouth dropped open, and she rocked on her feet, about to bolt. "Come on, Nat. You've got shifter strength now. It'll be fun."

She laughed, but nerves made her cheek twitch. "But Alpha will kill me—"

"I'm nothing but your ex-coworker, and you're gonna fight me."

Natalie's gaze flickered over Sylvie's shoulder to where Hex and Rose stood.

"I never took you for a chickenshit."

"Fine! Fine. Get in the square."

Sylvie bit her lip to contain her excitement and shook her limbs as she jogged into the closest free square.

Rose followed beside her. "This is a clean fight. No shifting, no weapons. Tap outs must be honoured, and if anyone exits the fighting square, the round is over. Got it?"

"Yes." Sylvie faced her opponent. Natalie's posture alone proved this wouldn't be a challenge. But she wouldn't underestimate her. She'd never make that mistake again.

Raising her guard, they circled each other, watching the other's movements. Sylvie waited for Natalie to lunge, but she didn't. *Fine. Me first.* It might have worried the old Sylvie how easy it was for her to hurt people. To hit first and ask questions later. But the old Sylvie was dead, and if she ever saw Ace again, she'd be ready.

With a quick jab to test her distance from Natalie, she followed with a hard cross to the face and three more strikes to the abdomen, forcing Natalie to fold over her winded belly. Sylvie took the opening and moved in with unexpected speed, twisting her body around Natalie and hooking her elbow around her neck, executing the perfect sleeper hold.

Waiting for the tap, Sylvie spotted Hex's heated gaze from across the square and her cheeks warmed from the silent praise. Hopefully, the vigorous exercise excused her blush.

Natalie tapped out, and the round was over before it even began. Rose cheered, and Natalie rubbed her neck with a grimace.

"Guess I deserved that. And I should probably train more."

"Possibly." Sylvie laughed, still catching her breath as the adrenaline faded and an unfamiliar elder shifter waved from the sideline.

"Will you join us for the second round? We have someone without a partner." The elder and Sylvie glanced at Hex, hovering with folded arms, who nodded once, and Sylvie jumped up. She wasn't waiting for his approval.

"Of course. Lead the way."

TWENTY-ONE

Following the first round, Sylvie forced two more shifters to tap and knocked another unconscious.

Unlike Natalie, though, the recent fighters had got in some kicks, one even splitting Sylvie's brow. Everyone froze as she lifted her head, wiping the blood from her eye, but she forced her partner to continue despite Hex's low growl from the sidelines.

"Treat me like everyone else," she said. And they did. Her bruised ribs and tender jaw proved it.

"Alright, move in," Josiah, the elder in charge of the betting, said, calling the remaining fighters over. Two males and one female, who—of course—was Claudine, stood before him.

"Sylvie will fight Claudine, and Alastair will fight Denny. The winners from this round can choose whether to tie or take the chance. Rules are the same. Enter your squares when you're ready."

Kian appeared out of nowhere, pulling Sylvie to the side with a curious expression. "Look at you, my little warrior. What are you doing?"

"I dunno," she said with a wince, his hug too tight for her aching torso. "But I'm gonna finish it."

A surge of calm passed from his arms to her, and she smiled at him. "Thank you."

"Insufferable. Be careful, or Rowan is going to have an aneurysm."

Over Kian's shoulder, Sylvie spied the male in question, suppressing a scowl as Rose chatted beside him animatedly. She pulled her gaze away before his eyes found hers and spun to face a sneering Claudine.

"Let's finish this."

"Don't underestimate her," Kian breathed against her neck. Sylvie smiled and brushed his cheek with her fingers.

"Never."

The second her feet entered the square, Claudine was on her. Her fists flew for every bruised spot on Sylvie's body. Unable to return a hit, Sylvie shoved Claudine back and shook her head to clear it. A flood of adrenaline hit her, and she spat a glob of blood on the ground.

"What? Giving up already?" Claudine said, not a hair out of place.

"Not a chance." Sylvie sprang forward, feigning a jab before dodging right and gripping Claudine's wrist, twisting it around and forcing the other woman to the ground.

Before Sylvie could jump on her back, though, Claudine kicked outward, the blow clipping the inside of Sylvie's knee. She fell, twisting away from Claudine's rolling form, then stood, trying not to hobble from a sharp pain in her thigh.

Again, they circled.

Punching, evading, kicking and parrying, Sylvie heaved breaths into her lungs as the round stretched longer and longer. Claudine had barely broken into a sweat. This was child's play for the experienced shifter, which pissed Sylvie off more. With a well-placed kick, Sylvie tackled Claudine to the ground, where they grappled and swore through their teeth, each landing a few elbows and knees as they curled around each other. If Claudine could shift, it would be over, but Sylvie's swelling adrenaline kept her in the fight. She grew numb to the impacts, even as Claudine pummelled the same spots repeatedly. Flashes of Ace's violence flitted into her vision only to be swept away. Presumably by Kian.

"You won't win," Claudine growled, grabbing and twisting a chunk of Sylvie's hair in her fist, exposing her throat. The effect was immediate. Panic lanced through her until she couldn't breathe and she was back there, held aloft by Ace with a knife glinting seconds before it sawed through her hair. She blinked back tears as Claudine's other arm reached around to choke her. To end it. To kill her. *No. No. No.* With the last of her strength, Sylvie twisted her head away, throwing a punch straight at Claudine's nose. The shifter's face flew back, blood spurting forward and coating them both in slick, fiery crimson. It stunned her.

Holy fucking—

Sylvie shot forward on hands and knees, aiming for another blow, when a cloud of dirt flew into her eyes, blinding her, and an excruciating strike crunched into her throat.

The wind whooshed from her body as she flew onto her back, her mouth gaping as she desperately sucked in slivers of air still mingling with dust plumes. With each breath, she coughed. Choking. Shouts and animal roars filled her ears. Someone or something blocked the light behind her lids, and she struck out, hoping she'd somehow keep Claudine off her.

No way that bitch would win.

"It's me," a deep voice said, their minty breath hitting her face and clearing some of the dust. "Get her out of here now," it said then.

"No, wait …" Sylvie's voice came out strangled. Barely a wheeze. She wasn't done. She didn't want anyone to touch her or take her anywhere. It wasn't fair. The fight wasn't over.

"Move back," Kian's voice echoed from her side.

"Alpha is with her—"

"I don't fucking care. That is my wife!"

She coughed, reaching for Kian, and he clasped her hand in his. She fingered his signet wedding band and blinked against the scratchy dirt in her tear ducts.

"Didn't … tap … out."

"Princess."

She pried open her eyes in time to see Hex's pained glance at Kian. They shared something undecipherable through the look, and Kian's grip loosened.

"Rowan will take you to their healer, Amira, and check you over," he said.

"I'm fine." A coughing fit stopped any more words, though, and Hex scooped her aching body into his arms. Tears leaked from her eyes as she tried to swallow, the pain finally kicking in as Kian's gifted adrenaline dissipated.

"The fight is done." Hex's fast gait jostled Sylvie's injuries, stealing her focus as they moved away from the squawking masses.

She sucked in a shaky breath, wincing at the painful swallow. "I wasn't done."

"No," Hex conceded, wiping the tears from her cheeks. "I was done. If you had continued, I could not have stopped my wolf."

She shook her head, shuddering at the strain along her throat. *What does that even mean? Are the animal sides to shifters sentient?* She had believed they were a primal addition to the shifter experience, wild and pure animal. They didn't think like the human form, did they? Why else would Kian not be able to read their emotions, unless they didn't have any?

Whatever. It's not my problem.

She shut her eyes, trying not to snap at every jostle and jolt. The rest of her was aching now. Her ribs especially. That would teach her not to push the limits on her first try. Arrogance was a killer, too.

"Flower girl, what have you got yourself into?"

She blinked through grit at the elder female who had fed her on her first night. The one who asked for her story. Amira. Plants and dangling crystals wreathed the doorway she stood in, while vines decorated the thatched roof.

"Nothing—"

"Claudine," Hex said, cutting her off. Normally, she'd snap at the interruption, but every word she spoke crunched down her throat like glass.

"Ah." Amira nodded and waved them in.

On either side of the main room, solid workbenches stood covered in books, mortar and pestle, potted plants, and tubes filled with pastel liquids. The main room had one door, and Sylvie assumed it led to a bedroom, but it was closed tightly. Two long stretcher cots with papery sheets sat parallel to the back wall, and a full glass cabinet sat opposite. It was a mess. Hex laid her down on one of the tall stretchers, the sheets crinkling under her back as she stared at the ceiling. Dark burns scorched the wood panels, thin lines running between each one. A constellation, maybe.

"She's a quick healer, but she's in pain."

"Aye, I see that. Go wait outside, Rowan." His name sounded more like Rao-an from her lips and Sylvie exhaled a quick puff of air through her nostrils, the closest she could get to a laugh at his banishment.

He shot a look at the elder, but didn't argue as he left the room, closing the door with a soft snick.

Amira prodded her from head to toe, applying salves to the bruises and a warm poultice to the smaller abrasions. The creams tingled across her skin and she fingered the tacky substance, playing with it between her finger and thumb. "What is this?"

Amira flitted about the room, screwing lids on and storing things in their places, not even glancing to see what she was talking about.

"Harnweed, ternbarb, and a shaving of heartwood from a grevin tree."

All the names were unfamiliar, but she tucked them away for later as she sat up. "Thank you for helping me," she said, rubbing a thick spot of paste on her ribs.

"You're no fledgling to pain, Flower. This was for the pup hoverin' outside."

"I can hear you, Amira—"

"Don't I know it."

Sylvie pressed her lips to stop the grin as Amira winked, returning to her side and rubbing one last dab of yellow cream across her brow.

"There. All better."

She tapped the end of Sylvie's nose and padded away, leaving her to brush her fingers over the spot. Her cheeks warmed at the loving touch and she stood, tucking her shaking hands under the opposite arms.

As she wandered to the door, the softest voice curled around her ears—the whisper: alive.

"You need not fear the mark, Flower."

Sylvie turned to ask Amira what she meant, but the shifter was gone. With a shudder, she pressed the door open and staggered through, right into Hex's torso.

Instead of fighting or jerking away, she blinked tiredly at him. Maybe it was the fading of adrenaline or the salves working their way into her bloodstream, but she couldn't rile the hate for him she used to. She swallowed, lifting her hand to him, ignoring the way his eyes widened, his hand trembling slightly as it took hers.

"Will you take me back to the main house? I need to lie down."

After a few stumbles, his arm looped around her waist, not once jarring the bruises blooming there, and held her as they walked. Amira's cabin sat alone, a thin path leading from it to the side entrance of Hex's house, which he bypassed for the front door. *Because the front door has fewer stairs, not because he wants to hold me longer.* Her inner beast scoffed at the proposal.

"Hey, hot stuff!"

Sylvie glanced up as Natalie jogged over from the main path, ponytail swinging and a grin lighting her face. "That was so—" She cleared her throat and looked between Hex's face and the arm around Sylvie's body. "Can I have a minute with Sylvie, Alpha?"

She nodded even as Hex grunted out, "Make it quick," and lowered her to a sitting position on the front steps of the stoop. Everything groaned in protest, but at least the lingering sensation of being on death's door had faded. She could even manage a soft laugh without tasting blood.

Hex disappeared into the house as Natalie raised up and down on her toes, her teeth nibbling on her lips as if to keep the words in. "That was the most insanely epic thing I've ever seen in my fucking life. You put Claudine on her ass."

Sylvie scoffed. "Hardly." It was one good punch in a fight that was a scramble to stay two steps behind in.

"She cheated. You won me a lot of marks today, and I reckon I'll be off dishes for a month!"

Sylvie laughed, then groaned as her ribs screeched. "Where's my cut?" she said through a grimace. "And where did she end up, anyway? Everything got blurry after the dust cloud."

"Holding cells. Alpha's orders." Natalie spoke the words like they were a common occurrence, not seeming to notice the chill they caused to ripple through Sylvie. *Alpha's orders.*

And those cells. She lowered her face onto her knees and sighed.

The air between them went quiet, the sun beating down from overhead.

"You need to spill your secrets. Seriously. How did you get that good? Were you secretly an enforcer the whole time?"

Gods. *What a thought.* Erus's enforcers were brutal. Tactically trained law enforcement that the government controlled and harnessed to maintain order and beat the ever-living shit out of people. Usually the poor. She'd stayed under their radar for the greater stretch of her life, only having one close call when she'd shoplifted some risqué undergarments from a shopping complex. Fifteen-year-old Sylvie had gotten into a lot of shit, but she was fast. That had saved her ass from the enforcer that chased her. At the time, she thought he must've been having a bad day when he couldn't scale the fences through the downtowns slums of Erus, but it was probably her vampire blood that made her quicker. Slippery.

"No. Fuck no." Enforcers were bastards. Monsters of the human variety. She'd never claim to be one of them. "Vampire."

"Oh, shit!" Natalie didn't look disgusted, though. Only curious. That pressed Sylvie onward.

"And dryad."

"What the hell is that?"

Her throat dried, and she swallowed. "A type of fae. Think trees."

Natalie glanced over her shoulder at the woods beyond and whistled. "Can you like—" She chuckled softly, perhaps not quite believing what she was about to ask. "Can you control them? Like, use the vines to cut people's head off and shit? You know, hero stuff?"

Sylvie's brows knitted as she rested her chin on her fists, elbows atop her knees, a smile creeping across her face. "Sounds more like a villain."

"You know what I mean."

She let her gaze fall to the ground by Natalie's feet, snagging on a small weed stretching its wiry tendrils through pebbles and bark.

Something *had* happened on equinox night. And her fae sight had evolved. To what extent she didn't know, but the tension between nature and her body had tightened, like what happened after targeting an untrained muscle. Maybe she could control it. Maybe with a bit of focus …

"I think that's enough, Natalie."

Sylvie lifted her gaze to Hex at her side, accepting his calloused hand as he pulled her up. Natalie offered a quick farewell before skulking off, the sudden silence both a comfort and a source of dread. She didn't want to talk to Hex, especially after hearing where he sent Claudine. It reminded her of what he was capable of, and that she could never forget what Ace had done.

Alpha's orders, after all.

When they made it to her room, she levelled a stare his way and muttered a low "Thanks," before pushing the door shut. She didn't miss the bob of his throat or the subtle flex of the hand he'd held her with. But it didn't matter. It didn't matter at all.

TWENTY-TWO

It took two days, between training and sleeping, before Sylvie's focused staring finally made a single vegetable twitch. Her gasp had jolted Maddissen right out of her harvesting, only to look bored when the difference in the cucumber's length was less than an inch.

"You're bleeding again," Maddissen muttered as she returned to her task. Sylvie wiped her nose across her sleeve and sighed. Natalie had suggested weaponising nature, and while Sylvie was determined to explore that aspect eventually, the pack's food shortage had snared her attention instead. Her training was inherently selfish, driven by a crippling fear of weakness, and the shifters had already done so much for her. Housing her, feeding her, and mending her wounds. The least she could do was help provide for them.

So—growing vegetables.

It wasn't going well.

With a sigh of resignation, she stood, wiping her hands across a spare pair of Rose's overalls, and grabbed the wheelbarrow Maddissen had filled.

"Hold on a minute," Maddissen said, pulling two more beets. She dumped them atop the pile and wiped the back of a gloved hand across her brow. "Thanks. Just put them in the alpha's cellar."

Sylvie blinked. "Where's that?"

"Under the stairs, next to his room."

"Okay." She tried not to stall on the reason Maddissen knew where Hex's bedroom was and pushed the wheelbarrow along the garden path. But the male in question leaned against the wall of a small cabin, chatting with Alastair, his relaxed posture and wolfish grin doing something to her insides. How many women—females—had he seduced with that wild face? That body?

"Watch out," Rose said, wrenching the front of the wheelbarrow back onto the path and away from the wooden post Sylvie was heading towards.

"Fucking hell. Where did you come from?" Hopefully, the startle explained away her rapid breathing and light dusting of pink across her cheeks.

"Came to invite you to dinner. You hungry?"

"Yeah, sure. I'll uh, I'll meet you there."

Rose nodded, darting off as Sylvie pushed the wheelbarrow to the side entrance of Hex's place. She fetched a scratchy burlap sack from the kitchen cupboards and transferred the beetroot into it before dragging them into a cold room beneath the stairs. The cobwebs were large enough to have her scurrying straight out and slamming the door with a cough. She stood there, wiping dust from her palms, when her thoughts wandered. *Next to his room, right?* The door immediately behind the staircase had always been closed and was painted the same grey as the walls, but there was no mistaking it now. Hex's bedroom. She wouldn't peek. Yet. They'd been there for the better part of two weeks, and she wasn't sure he'd even stayed there once. The undisturbed dust settled on the floor proved it.

Sylvie stared at the unassuming door handle for a few seconds until her legs grew leaden. She shouldn't. She wouldn't. But …

"Princess."

She spun so quick her stomach lurched.

"Kian. Hi!" With a soft chuff, she threw her arms around him and kissed his lips. Perhaps a little too hard.

He stiffened, unpeeling her clammy hands from his shoulders and cradling them on his chest. "I wonder if you owed that kiss to someone else?"

Sylvie's mouth dropped open, guilt presumably written across her face. How long had he watched her staring at Hex's unopened door? She pulled her hands free. "I would never kiss you and think of anyone else."

His lip quirked as he shook his head. "I didn't mean it that way." A look flashed across his face, and she frowned. "You know that," he finished.

With a huff, she barged past him to the kitchen, swiping a dirty bowl off the counter and piling it into the sink. "You insufferable smug fae. If you don't want to kiss me, then fine!"

She turned the water on and squirted a line of dishwashing liquid into the stream. The turbulent waters frothed.

Playful energy surged against her back, and she gnawed on her cheek to stop the smile.

"And I think your brattiness is also meant for someone else, as my wife wouldn't dare call me names."

"It was hardly a name—" She jolted at the slap that bit into her ass cheek and spun, spine digging into the counter, finger aloft and pointing. "Watch it, pretty boy."

"Oh? You think I'm pretty, wife?" His mouth twitched, each corner threatening a grin as he stalked closer.

When hot water scalded her back, she turned quickly, turning the tap off before it flooded the kitchen, but that was all the time Kian needed.

By the time she faced him again, he was on her, ducking low and scooping her onto his shoulder as she yelped and gasped with laughter. "I need to do the dishes."

"The dishes can wait." A smooth stroking of his hand up the back of her thigh had her melting. The dishes could wait, indeed.

Their bedroom had gained more items during their stay: clothes from Rose, weapons, and a handful of potted plants along Sylvie's windowsill—gifted from Amira. Most were herbs and medicinal flowers, but they were also the perfect source of practise.

They remained bright and healthy, but hadn't grown any more than a regular plant might. Maybe the best she could hope for was being a decent gardener.

Kian threw her atop the bed and remained standing, his adoring look filling her with heat. "You're beautiful," he said.

"So are you."

He lowered himself above her, placing his palms flat on either side of her head as a cage.

"The full moon is nearing. Do you feel the effects yet?"

She pressed her lips to the inner crease of his wrist, right over the scar she had given him in Elias's office so many weeks ago. Nothing happened. No ache, or zap, or pain. "I don't think so."

"Good," Kian said, peppering kisses along her jaw, her neck, her chest. "I've been feeling your lust all week, and I'm about to explode."

She hissed, fighting the shame, the desire and hatred, but he covered her lips with his, diverting all thought.

Between breaths, their clothes fell away until there was only skin and warmth. When he entered her, it was peace she met, and lingering bliss. They moved in rhythm, his undulation in time with the steady rock of her hips, the grip of her thighs around his waist. Her feet interlocked behind him as she opened, welcoming him deeper. With synchronised breaths, Sylvie's desire mounted, a subtle quaver to Kian's inhale spurring her straight over the edge of oblivion. Visions of his proclamation during the tournament filled her mind and soul until warm tears cut down her cheeks. *That is my wife.*

She moaned, burying her face in the crook of his neck.

I am his wife.

He pulled back, just enough to thumb the tears from her cheeks. "Why are you crying?"

Their lips met once more in a conversation. One of love and longing. Need.

"I love you," she murmured against his lips, smiling when his pace staggered, his breathing ragged. "I've known it for a while now. I love you, Kian."

Her heady whispers turned to moans as he shuddered and groaned and released inside her, his body roiling with tension, then nothing. They stayed linked as he rolled to his side, palming the side of her face with a tenderness she'd never thought she deserved.

"I have always loved you," he said, twirling a strand of her hair between his fingertips. "Always."

She grinned as they kissed again, a tangle of limbs and bed sheets.

When she pulled back, Sylvie took in his face, his rich umber skin, and dark eyes with mulberry stripes. He looked better. No bags lined his eyes, no tired wrinkles were etched into his skin. Her mind shot to the night with the tiger shifter and the shared words between Hex and Kian while she had almost fallen comatose. *I can take emotions away, and I can give them back.*

"What are you thinking about, Princess?"

She lifted her head to glance at the windowsill again, at Amira's gifted plants shimmering from a draft.

"After dinner, I need your help with something, and you aren't allowed to say no."

"Well, that's ominous."

Hours later, after a generous helping of dinner, Sylvie and Kian found themselves in the shifter's garden beds under the light of the moon.

"What is it you'd have me do here, Princess?"

Sylvie knelt by a tired pumpkin patch and curled her fingers around the tendrils twining from the stem. A few flowers had formed tiny pumpkins, but they were a long way from harvesting.

"I need you to do to me what you did on that night with the intruders."

Kian rocked back on his heels, possibly preparing for a quick getaway.

"You promised you would help me," she said.

"You had an outlet then. You could burn it off."

"Yes." She cupped the baby pumpkins. "And I will have an outlet here too. Please, just try. If I can't do it, then you can just take it back." When he was silent, she added, "The rage, I mean."

"I know what you intend, Princess, but I don't want to hurt you. The darkness I take, it's a burden I never want you to shoulder."

But he could. How was that fair? She had shouldered many, many dark traumas. He had no right—

No, no. That is not you talking, that's the incomplete bond. Breathe.

She took a stabilising breath and nodded at him. "I hear you, but I want this. I want to do something good, something meaningful, and if it takes a little darkness, then so be it."

He sighed and looked off into the forest, but nodded as a wave of darkness and anger lapped at her feet. Hatred. With a sharp inhale, she tapped into her fae sight, taking a moment to bask in the glory that was her power. The energy between things—the magic—was bright and pulsing. From the soil to the stem to the flower to the tiny fruits, she let Kian's power surge, and she pulled and pulled and pulled. The blend of darkness and delight flooded her senses as it worked—*it worked!*

She barely registered Kian's gasp as the pumpkin before her grew too heavy to hold with one hand. His outpouring emotions pulled back as she lowered the monstrosity to the dirt and rubbed her shaking palms on her thighs.

"I did it."

Kian's focus wasn't on her. It was farther along the patch. She followed his gaze and gasped, her laughter bubbling until she couldn't contain it anymore.

"I think you'll need a bigger wheelbarrow," Kian commented.

It wasn't just one pumpkin. The entire plant and all its flowers had ballooned, the fruit bigger than Hex's head in wolf form. Her laughter filled her body until she felt lightheaded. Kian took her chin between his fingers.

"Are you alright?"

"Perfect." And she was. Kian's influence had pumped her magical muscle full of stimulants until using her affinity was as simple as breathing. No bloody nose, no headaches, and Kian's load was now lightened. Win-win. It made perfect sense that fate had bound them together. If she were to believe in that …

Days passed the same way. Kian warded, Sylvie trained, and by night they bolstered food production until the shifters started commenting on the size of the fruits she forgot to pick and store in Hex's cellar before sunrise. Even Maddissen offered her a smile. Golden lights followed them from the tree line, but never breached the gardens. She ignored them.

"Elias will be proud," Kian said, kissing the spot below her ear that made her breathless.

"I don't think so." She rolled onto her back, pulling him atop her in their dark room. "He'd probably rather I let them starve."

"Both things can be true."

She grinned.

Sleep dragged her down as thoughts of Elias wove into dreams.

Then screams. She jolted awake, bed empty, and searched blindly for her strewn clothes as the telltale raucous clashes and signs of fighting echoed through the moonlit room. The waxing moon.

Shit, shit, shit.

"Kian?"

But she was alone. Gods, he better be okay. Refusing to think on it any longer, Sylvie sprinted from the room, dual knives in hand, heading towards the furious shouts before barrelling straight into a solid mass of flesh.

TWENTY-THREE

"Get back in the house and hide," Hex shouted, grabbing Sylvie's shoulders to steady her on her feet.

The immediate desire to shout a resounding "no" bubbled in her throat, but an incoming mass froze the words on her tongue. Hex spun. His clawed fist captured the vampire's throat, squeezing until blood spurted from his eyes. The vampire swiped a sharp knife at him despite the pressure crushing his larynx, and Sylvie used the distraction to sprint towards the softer screams.

With her fae sight, the luminescent light trails brightened, weaving along the path towards the lake, and she ran, bolstered by Hex's guttural howls. A dying fire illuminated a heinous scene as the trail opened into the clearing. One shifter lay dead. Her blood blossomed around her as a vampire knelt at her side, lapping at the ground like a starving kitten on milk. Two other shifters writhed beneath giant glittering nets reminiscent of spider silk coated in morning dew. The remaining vampire flitted about the space, gathering the corners of the nets. Strange, brown, skin-like tactical clothing clung to the vampires' flesh, with scales over their chests and groins while their arms remained bare. The only telltale sign of their species was the bright ruby glow of their eyes.

"Move, Jeric. Come and get the Fates-damned panther."

The vampire, Jeric, lapping at the ground lifted his head and hissed. "If death is coming for me, I will die fed."

"You won't die."

Jeric lifted his arm just high enough for the light to catch the massive bite wound, black twining lines already running under the tactical vest he wore. Bitten. The first vampire hissed as Sylvie ducked behind the trees, edging closer to the trapped shifters. Natalie and a wolf she didn't recognise. Maybe she should've brought a gun, but Hex stored those away. A twig snapped underfoot and the vampires' heads snapped towards her as she stoked her rage—her vīs. *Shit.*

"I see you, little mouse."

Just slow enough for her fae sight to catch, Jeric darted towards her, clamping a hand on her biceps and ridding her hands of her knives long before she could stab him with them. *Double shit.*

"This one has pretty eyes. What kind of shifter might you be?"

She shrank back, pulling her eyebrows up and together and shaking her head as the blood-drenched vampire dragged her closer to the nets. *That's it.*

"Answer me, wench." He shook her roughly, and she whimpered, closing her eyes to search beneath her feet for something. Anything. She found it, the end of an orewood root twining a metre deep. She'd never tried, but it would work. *I will die before I let them take another shifter.* Even when she said the words to Natalie the first time, she meant it. She'd protect these people with everything she had. More than she had. Without Kian's additional power, it would fall on her. Her own rage would have to do, and one look at Natalie, wide-eyed and shaking in panther form, was more than enough. Her inner beast snarled in delight.

"Pathetic," Jeric sneered.

She pulled on the roots, holding on despite the throbbing behind her eyes, and shoved her foot into his chest. Jeric staggered backwards at the same time the root breached the dry soil behind him and impaled his heart through his back. The world stilled except for the fine line of blood dripping from her nose. Jeric's eyes bulged. Fluid gurgled from his mouth. Her fae sight snapped from her hold, and Jeric fell to his knees, then slumped to his side. Dead.

"What did you do?" The other vampire stared with an expression so filled with sorrow, Sylvie's fury withered to a husk.

She tapped into the fae sight once more, pulling the exposed root from Jeric's body and holding it aloft, pointing the sharp end towards the other vampire. Her brain screamed in protest.

"Don't try anything," she gritted out, her sight flickering between the energy lines and fire-tinted sepia. *Hold on.*

She kicked the metal nets beside her, nudging them over Natalie's paws and head, keeping the living stake ready to strike. A viper of wood in her control.

"You killed a born vampire, the last of his line."

She suppressed the guilt and threw the last of the chains off the wolf shifter.

"He had a wife."

"He was a dead male anyway," Sylvie hissed, fighting the sensation of thick grief in her stomach. A shifter bite would kill a vampire. She only sped up the inevitable.

It was a mercy. The trio of whispers did little to quash the rising weight on her heart, and with a smoothness she didn't feel, she rounded the slumped form at her feet, staring the vampire down.

"Where are you taking the shifters?" Her voice held steady, and she clung to that strength even as her throat constricted, salt running down the back of it as she sniffed.

The vampire's expression darkened as he withdrew towards the lake. Natalie and the wolf shifter flanked her with soft growls, their movements slow, clearly weakened from whatever laced the nets.

"I do not answer to you."

"Why then? Why do you need them, and how are you getting across realms?"

His throat bobbed as he took another step away. The distant screaming had quieted, and Sylvie could only hope that the other vampires had failed.

"The pack will get here soon, and if you tell me what I need to know, I could help you. I could ask them to be lenient."

The wolf at her side whined, and Sylvie could only guess they were questioning her sanity as she lowered the root and released her hold on her fae sight. She had to, or her head would explode.

"Just tell me something. Please."

The darting of the vampire's eyes and uneasy slinking of the creatures at Sylvie's side raised the hairs on her arms. The forest wasn't just quiet. It was silent.

Before he could utter another word, a shadow leapt from the tree line, engulfing him in its jaws and crunching down with a cut off shriek and squelch, then a thud. The animal turned, blood and viscera dripping from its jaws, a familiar gold hue homing on Sylvie, then dropped to the vampire at her feet.

The wolf's hackles rose and body shuddered like something was burrowing out from beneath its sleek coat. That was accurate, in a sense. Hex stretched to his full height, the transition jerky and flooded with primal intent. Nothing but blood and death adorned his body, smearing over tattoos and hair as he growled something at Natalie and the wolf, who whined and scampered away.

They stared each other down in the silence. Hex's approach was slow, the fire illuminating every twitch of his muscles, every clench of his jaw. She was in trouble. *So is he.* Why did he waste a perfect opportunity to question the fucking vampire?

His attention flickered over her shoulder, and a low rumbling reverberated from his chest—a warning. She didn't turn, but her indigo mark hummed, a soothing energy sliding down her back as she palmed it. How dare he shoo Kian away?

Her teeth chattered as the last of her adrenaline faded and biting night air nipped down her spine. "Why did you kill him? We could've got some answers."

"Why didn't you hide in the house like I told you?" He didn't yell, but she bristled at his intensity.

Maybe it was the cold, or the shock, but she latched on to the bobbing of his throat, the clenching of his fists.

"I helped," she said. "Isn't that something? I did what I thought was right."

But then a coppery scent dragged her burning vision to its source. A vampire. Dead. Eyes bulging, papery skin covered in black veins.

She'd killed a person. Again. Her own kind.

"What was right?" Hex echoed, incredulity in his tone. She hated it. "You could have been hurt, or taken. They could have killed you!"

Her head was shaking. Everything was shaking. Why was that all he saw?

"I did it for you—for the pack."

She buried her fingers into her hair and clenched her fists, homing in on the sharp sting, the pain, so she didn't just float away. It would be so easy to disappear. To let the guilt consume her. Jeric had a wife.

She'd taken him away from her.

If someone had killed Kian or Elias, she would destroy the world. She turned, searching for her fae mate, but a warm grip encircled her forearm. "Don't walk away from me," Hex snarled.

But she was drained. "Let go."

"No." He spun her, his blood-smeared hands clasping her face. The acrid scent turned her stomach.

"Let me go."

Cutting night air skittered over her bare arms until they flared with goosebumps, and her eyes stung. Hex pulled her close with a grunt just as a voice called from the path, "Alpha. There's another scent beyond the western borders, headed this way."

"A second wave?" Hex asked back, his whole body coiled as if preparing to shift at any moment.

The shifter shook their head. "I don't know."

"Find them," Hex said then, releasing her and tying his hair back. Her teeth clacked from the sudden coldness. Without permission from her mind, her arms lifted his way, searching for something. Warmth. Comfort.

His brows drew inward, his hands lifting before he flew backwards through the air and a cool embrace clutched her instead.

The splash of Hex in the lake's depths broke the silence of the clearing, the crackle of dying flames and the chirps of insects returning the same moment her eyes met red.

"Elias?"

"Love," he rasped, lifting her shivering form into his arms. "You're freezing."

"Elias."

Hex stormed from the water, cleansed of death and shouting unintelligible threats as he closed the gap between them in all his naked glory.

Elias bared his fangs his way. "What did you do to her?"

"She did this to herself," Hex snapped back, shaking even as his eyes lingered on her face. She didn't know where to look.

"Where's Kian?" Elias asked, glancing over his shoulder.

"On the way to my place."

Elias's head tilted, a predatory glint in his stare.

Sylvie blinked again. "Elias?"

"News?" Hex asked over Sylvie, his attention shifting between her and the vampire holding her.

"Perhaps."

The one-worded conversation muted every other noise from her brain until she numbed. Her shivering stopped. Breathing slowed.

"And?" Hex asked.

"I'm uncertain it's worth sharing."

Sylvie slipped her finger along Elias's chiselled jaw, a faint zap setting her mind alight with clarity. This was real. He was back.

"Elias," she breathed, leaning into his neck to inhale him. He smelled like home.

Hex stepped closer. "Tell me what you discovered."

"That I need to return."

Alarms tolled in Sylvie's head and she wrenched back, her hold tightening on him enough to divert his attention. Finally. "I'm going with you."

He looked poised to say no, but she scowled, pressing her finger into his chest.

"Yes."

His nostrils flared, the challenge rising between them, but Hex interrupted. "When do we leave?"

Elias turned, still carrying her, and walked away from the lake, Hex behind him. She never broke Hex's gaze, instead letting her chin rest on Elias's shoulder to prolong the staring contest. She would win against him. Hex's attention flickered, and she tuned into it, captivated by the lightened hue of his eyes. Beautiful wild male. She hated him.

Elias exhaled, something akin to a laugh jostling her body as he answered.

Whatever his answer was, she probably wouldn't like it.

She was right.

"The next full moon."

TWENTY-FOUR

"They didn't take anyone last night, thanks to you," Natalie said, slapping Sylvie on the shoulder beside the roaring campfire. The elders tending the flames had shifted the log seating back as the heat scorched her eyelashes, but the warmth wouldn't penetrate. "Like you promised."

Sylvie chewed a hangnail. Everyone was eating lunch, but she couldn't get herself to dig in. Eating repulsed her. After Elias had taken her back to the main house, he shared about his travels. He'd spent days recovering in a cave with Kerensa, then snuck into the main tower in Argyncia. They found nothing. No fresh sign of the shifters. Their scents were everywhere, scattered inside the city walls, in the cellars and the lower halls, but he couldn't pinpoint a single one. A solar flare got them home, and he recovered at the house for a few days. Days when she could've been back home, too. Not under Hex's gaze. She'd chewed him out on that fact, but he'd shut her down quickly. "I was in no position to protect you, Love. You were safer here."

"Why couldn't I feel you?"

She'd tugged her shirt away to check his mark. It was faint. "Upkeep," she whispered. They'd spent the rest of the early morning performing the upkeep until she was satisfied with the warm crimson hue of his mark on her chest.

Kian had watched, and gods did that fire her up. But now, staring at the patch of dried blood and the flaccid root drying out, she couldn't think of anything but the thud of Jeric's body hitting soil.

"The shifter that died?" she rasped. Jeric had lapped at the shifter's blood like a male starved.

"Rogue," Natalie said, smoothing white paste over her skin. For the nightbane, a plant sap the vampires smeared across their silver nets that weakened the shifters. "The vampires dragged her here after they caught us and she killed herself."

Sylvie inhaled sharply, swallowing as her mouth filled with saliva. *Don't puke.* She stood and started for the running path around the lake, but Natalie shuffled up behind her. "You okay?"

"Walk," she muttered back, splaying her hand across her chest as her heart squeezed like it was preparing to stop dead.

The walk turned into a run and then an amble before she stopped beside a juvenile orewood and stared at the claw marks down its trunk. Her mouth dried, throat clenching as she saw the flashes again and again. The vampire—staked, mouth gaping, eyes wide in disbelief, a red bloom widening through his vest, staining the scales that were supposed to protect him.

He had a wife.

She was a killer. And she didn't know if she was imploding because she'd done it or because she didn't feel as bad as she should. The tree swayed, and she stepped closer on shaking feet. Maybe she just needed a respite. Elias was still recovering from the travel, Kian had wards to complete, and Hex—it didn't matter. She could just merge for a while. It would be fine. With a trembling hand, she reached for the bark. It would welcome her. It wouldn't judge her blackening soul, the one that killed without a second thought and used her abilities for cruelty. The tip of her finger grazed the trunk when a grip hoisted her off her feet and dragged her back.

She screamed and kicked, leaning to throw an elbow at the attacker's head when they dropped her on the edge of the pebbled lake. She scrambled to her feet, about to run when she saw who it was. Who she should've known was there before his skin brushed with hers. But whose presence she ignored so strongly that the golden mark on her chest had faded until it was as light as dust.

"It was you or him," Hex said then.

She froze, body turning rigid.

"Just leave me." She reached again for the tree, but Hex stopped her, this time with his hands holding her face, his torso pressed against her.

"Listen to me."

She shoved the heels of her hands into his stomach, but he wouldn't budge.

"He would have died anyway."

Her face contorted as she pulled and twisted in his grip.

"You know that," he said, pulling her closer.

She didn't know anything anymore. She wanted to be trained, to be strong and violent, so males like Ace couldn't hurt her anymore, and it worked. Even her mind didn't assault her as strongly with the memories of his abuse. She'd filled her days so completely that by night she was too drained to even dream. But then she had killed someone—someone with a family and a life. A vampire like her.

"I betrayed my kind."

He shook his head, searching her face. "Blood means nothing. Your family are the ones that choose you, and who you choose, woman."

She blinked back the heat searing her waterline.

"Because you are their world." He gestured towards the clearing. "My pack is not my blood. They are not even all my clan, but I would die for them. And I would kill for them. For you," he finished.

She blinked, lashes fluttering, and let her forehead fall into his chest, the rapid beat of his heart tickling her brow. Her breathing deepened. Resignation. That's what it was. That's why she clasped a hand around his belt and tugged the buckle. It was the full moon soon, anyway.

"Wait." His hand cupped her elbow, but from the way he trembled at every point of contact between them, waiting was clearly the last thing he wanted. Her beast curled around her legs, purring.

The belt hung open, and she started on the button, then the zip, then—

"Wait, woman!"

He pulled her wrists to the side and she gasped, wrenching her hands to her chest as realisation set in. What was she doing? The heat behind her eyes surged until tears flooded them to cool the sting.

"It's the bond," he said.

"No. I shouldn't have touched you like that—I …"

"It's the moon. It's not your fault."

She shook her head. Tears flew. "It is my fault. I shouldn't have." Maybe she was no better than the monster who had touched her without consent. *Monsters.*

A sob cleaved her in two as she fought for ragged breaths, tears searing her cheeks.

Hex's expression softened, then, a mixture of pity and pain. "If I hadn't wanted your touch, you wouldn't have got close. But if you have me, it won't be out of spite or surrender. You will *choose* me, or you will not have me at all."

She couldn't help but glance at the swollen moon still hanging low over the lake.

"Full moon not inclusive," he added.

She flexed and interlaced her hands, twisting them until they cracked and popped. "What if I did? What if I wanted you?"

It's the moon. It's just the moon.

But Hex just shook his head. "You wouldn't have to question it. Come."

But she couldn't move. Her legs had taken root.

"Agh, fates."

Hex scooped her into his arms, his heated skin bringing a flush to hers. She stared listlessly ahead as he cut through the trees at a confident pace. Even without a path, his steps never wavered. He was in his element. And she was out of her depth.

She felt Kian and Elias before she saw them, the telltale questioning down the bond clear. Then a flare of irritation. It didn't take a mate bond to guess which emotions speared from who.

Hex placed her on the stairs of his front stoop, but didn't move away. He left that last separation to her. With Kian appearing at the threshold with open arms, she did quickly. Though not painlessly. Fates, moon, bond, or not, something flickered within her at the touch of the shifter. She just wasn't sure if it was worth the suffering it inevitably brought. Or the monster she was becoming.

Tears slid down her cheeks as Kian turned her chin left and right, checking her over. He sighed. "I wish I could have been there last night to stop you," he whispered, pressing his forehead to hers as another cry escaped. That one closer to a whimper. He spoke the words without judgement or disgust. Instead, understanding snaked down the bond. Even when it was necessary, killing was something Kian wished to spare her from, but she ran straight to it.

"Shall I take the guilt?"

She lifted her face to meet his stare and shook her head even as tears flowed. "No. I deserve it."

Hex growled low at her back. "Those vampires have taken hundreds of my people. Your justice was merciful."

"She was raised human; her morals are not like yours," Kian said as he wiped damp strands of hair off her cheeks.

She disappeared from the conversation, weaving under Kian's arm and into the living room, where Elias leaned against the kitchen bench. It wasn't like him not to come to her aid or offer sharp quips at Hex's expense, so she scanned him as she ambled onto the couch and curled her legs beneath her.

His pale skin shimmered, the darker veins more prominent along his bare arms and the exposed skin of his neck. He watched her with predatory intent, but his movements were slow. Tired. The travel was still affecting him then. The full moon was less than a week away. How was he going to survive another trip to Argyncia when he already looked half dead? He sat beside her and she shuffled closer, curling into his chest, hand splayed between the buttons of his dress shirt as she toyed with the soft, inky hair. A faint ache radiated up her fingers from the caress, but the full moon's effects could fucking wait a minute.

"Can we talk?" she whispered, leaning over to kiss the spot where her mark branded Elias's skin.

"Of course."

She waited, heart pounding, until Kian neared, perching on the edge of the sofa next to Elias. Hex had gone, his footsteps receding down the steps and path as she let the guilt wash over her like a spring tide.

"I need to talk to you both. Some things you might know, others I've kept to myself, but I love you both and I don't want anything blocking our bond." Kerensa had told her secrets could impair a bond, and if she wanted to be at peak form in Argyncia, she needed everything they offered. Perhaps it would help Elias's healing, too.

"The night Rheikar died, he came into my room and tried to assault me."

Elias stiffened, and Kian's skin paled.

"He thought I was his fated. My grandmother."

"No excuse," Elias gritted out between lengthening fangs.

"I know. I stabbed him. The—the Fates wanted me to kill him, but I couldn't."

Kian's brow rose.

"I've been hearing them long before the dreams started. I just—I didn't know what they were until you explained them."

Kian's throat bobbed, but he didn't interrupt. Elias didn't have the same consideration. He swore and dragged her onto his lap completely, like he could protect her from the faceless voices in her head.

She retold the history of her childhood, the abuse at the hands of a foster father and the way she ended his miserable life after he had a stroke above her. Kian's expression almost destroyed her then. The raw knowing. The shared trauma. He knew how it felt because he'd lived it for years. Elias just held her. He'd heard it already, and his comfort anchored her. She recalled her attack on Lazuli next, when her vīs took over long before she realised what it truly was.

"I wanted her dead. I probably should have done it." Now her aunt was missing from the Stone Court, presumably up to something. Neither male judged her for the violence. If anything, both shared pride. Ace's torture came next with almost every sordid detail, omitting the brief things she'd shared in their home. She relayed all the violent abuses even ones she'd forgotten about, like the skin he flayed from her thighs just to see how long it took to regrow. Or the molar he twisted and ripped out before shoving it back in with his half-shifted claws. A bottomless howl sounded from the woods. A prick of fear wove through her, but she stifled it.

Kian glanced at the window once, his mouth pressing into a line as she continued, "And that vampire … I had to kill him. I know I did, and the Fates didn't ask me to, but I—I could feel their—their satisfaction in what I did." She could've said pleasure, but the thought of higher beings taking that level of delight in her violent actions sent shivers through her.

It was a mercy. She cringed at the repeated whispers.

"They speak to you? Even now?" Kian asked, reading her face.

She nodded, unpeeling herself from Elias as the ache from her bond to Hex grew into a sharper sting.

"I'm sorry I didn't tell you all of this sooner. I think I'm just used to keeping it all inside and dealing with it by shutting it away, but I don't want secrets from you two. We might die travelling to your shitty ass vampire realm and I won't have regrets." And gods, it felt good to share the burden of her thoughts.

Elias smiled ruefully, tipping his head back to the ceiling. "It is shitty," he said. "Are you sure you won't stay behind?"

She poked his ribs, suppressing a smile at the sudden scowl aimed her way, and stood from the couch.

"You never have to apologise either, Princess. Ever. Not for things like that. You've been through enough."

He held out a hand, and she took it, flinching at the burn of his skin on hers. She pulled back, a wan smile crossing her features.

"Both of you have," Elias added, holding back from touching her with clenched fists.

Kian swallowed and looked down, his own secrets bubbling beneath the surface as she glanced between them, then to the open doorway.

"Maybe you have things to discuss, too."

She stepped away from her males, letting the placid wind toy with her loose waves as she edged towards the front door.

"Where are you going?" Elias hovered a hair's breadth away. He already looked a little stronger.

"I need to blow off some steam before the full moon comes."

"I'll come with you."

She shook her head. "No. You rest. Both of you. We need to be at full strength for portalling. Plus, I don't want to lose my shit at either of you. I'll stay with Rose."

Kian nodded even as she drifted away, the rising agitation pushing her out the door. *Damned Fates.* They felt more like a curse than beings deserving of devotion.

She dashed down the front stairs with a quick, "I love you both," before searching for something to fight, stab, or shoot.

TWENTY-FIVE

"Hey."

Drenched in sweat and rage, the glacial air of autumnal twilight settling into her skin, Sylvie spun about to swing on the intruder. Claudine. The other shifters had left the fighting squares for dinner, but Sylvie's energy was far from burned out, and the sight of her mate's "chosen female" did nothing but reignite her fury. She pulled the punch, then swiped her forearm across her face and squinted.

"What do you want?"

Claudine's lips curled, and she bowed her head a fraction. "I heard what you did for us during the attack."

That wasn't where she thought the conversation was heading, and the reminder of her crime flashed inside her head until her jaw ached from clenching it.

"I don't want to talk about it. If that's what you came here for, then—"

"I came to apologise."

With a scoff, Sylvie returned to training, lifting the long bow and drawing back the arrow, but when Claudine hovered at her side, she sighed and lowered the weapon.

"Why? It was training. Shit happens."

The shifter's teal gaze narrowed to slits while her mouth pinched into a reluctant smirk.

"Not for that." She turned, straightening the arrows in their quiver atop a makeshift log bench. "My time cleaning the holding cells gave me clarity. He isn't mine to claim, and I know if I found my mate, nothing would stand between us. I'd kill anyone that interfered with the bond."

Sylvie snorted, but the revelation settled in her gut like a weight. She had cleaned the cells … Could she smell Sylvie's fear in that place?

"So … I appreciate your mercy."

Sylvie's brow quirked. If the shifter wanted to, she could rip Sylvie apart. Perhaps following her thoughts, Claudine added, "Hex would've killed me if you asked."

"No, he wouldn't. I saw the looks between the two of you. He likes you."

Claudine's laugh scared a handful of birds from nearby branches. She followed their flight path with her eyes as she answered, "Yeah, as friends. We grew up together like siblings. It was the elders that suggested our match, and we tried, but … no. We aren't compatible." She glanced sidelong at Sylvie. "Obviously."

Despite herself, Sylvie managed a weak smile. "Fine. Apology accepted."

She went to return to training, but Claudine remained, and the heated emotions inside Sylvie's skin bubbled. She tilted her head back and closed her eyes.

What now? Couldn't everyone just leave her alone? Rose had noticed quickly how standoffish she was lately and gave her a wide berth after fretting over her lack of appetite. Sylvie had scarfed down a whole bowl of stew in less than a minute to get the fox shifter off her case.

When she opened her eyes again, Claudine stared at the targets where Sylvie's arrows had found their mark.

"You're getting good."

Sylvie followed her eye line. "I guess."

Claudine faced her once more, an openness to her expression despite the indifference she seemed eager to paint back on her face.

"Do you want to learn to use a staff? I could teach you." She ducked to a bag at her feet Sylvie only just noticed and pulled two exquisitely crafted and darkly stained wooden staffs, each as thick as a gold mark and just as beautiful. Was this her plan all along? She took the one Claudine offered and ran her hands along the smooth surface, thumbing a pattern of swirls and distinct lines at the thickest end. They reminded her of something.

"Show me," she said.

Claudine grinned. "My pleasure, Alpha."

* * *

The next few days passed similarly. Kian and Elias visited occasionally to remind Sylvie to eat and rest as the moon swelled, the faint yellow glow of the beauty's full face reaching her as she ran along the carved path beside the lake. Granite Lake, Rose had called it. Under the rising moonlight, it embodied its namesake, the waters still enough to reflect the stars. It was as mesmerising as a slab of flecked stone.

Footsteps followed her for some time, the occasional snap of a twig or crackle of crisp leaves reminding her to keep moving, to use her fae sight to see the curves in the path as clear as day. Any unruly tree roots encroaching on the path would get a quick nudge back into the underbrush, and so far, no nosebleeds. Her temples pulsed as she crammed a thick knot down, the corded surface roots fighting against her shove, but it relented and the pain eased once again. She couldn't deny her growing strength or the pain spiralling from her chest where the shifter's mark should be. It had completely faded, but a tether as fine as hair still linked them. It wouldn't snap, but the more she pulled away, the sharper the sting became, like the twining bond would slice through skin and bone to keep them together. Her beast toyed with it.

"Hex."

She folded as a wave of lancing heat ripped through her abdomen, the movement driving her to her knees.

"I know you're there," she panted through gritted teeth. Golden lights danced through the trees like fireflies as she clasped her arms around her stomach. Her fae sight shut off as stars burst behind her eyes, the agony so visceral she didn't know which way was up anymore.

A whimper reached her ears as she curled in dirt and leaves.

"I'm here."

And he was. Naked and coated in a fine sheen of sweat, his tattoos shifting and flexing as he scooped her off the ground. Her legs twined around his waist, hooking behind his back as he buried his face in her neck.

"Don't mark me."

"I won't." He pulled away with a hiss, his nose pressing against hers as their bodies vibrated with need. She slipped from her clothes until nothing separated them but barely maintained restraint.

"I should hate you," she whispered as he lowered her atop her discarded clothes, his face close enough she could see herself in his eyes. Flushed and needy.

"Why?"

"Because of what we are. We're enemies." They were supposed to be, and maybe once she had hated him, but the infernal scale she kept had him sliding closer to tolerable.

His growl rang through her at a frequency she could barely hear, but Fates could she feel it. "I am not your enemy."

She shivered as they locked eyes, their fogged breath fanning around their heads. The ruggedness of his features did nothing to diminish his perfection. There was a symmetry in the wildness. *Beautiful.*

He inhaled sharply, his hardness sliding against her. Every movement had her writhing, her fingers digging into his ass— his perfect fucking ass—to get him closer, to make him fill her.

"Woman," he breathed into her flesh, his teeth grazing her collarbone. She arched her spine, breasts pressing into his chest.

"I'm no woman."

"No, you're a goddess."

Fucking hells.

Her groan almost undid them both, Hex's responding growl shaking the ground.

"Fuck me. Now."

He didn't wait or tease. He hoisted her legs over his shoulders and slammed himself inside her to the hilt, releasing her pent-up frustration, need, and pain. Over and over, he buried his cock pelvis deep, until her moans turned to ecstasy-laden screams.

She bit her fist to dull the sounds, but Hex pulled it away, pinning her hand over her head. Heat rippled through her at the action. Everyone would hear her. And when she bit her lip hard enough to silence herself, Hex thumbed that free, too. He wanted them to hear.

"Look at me," Hex said, grabbing the soft skin of her hips and squeezing. She reciprocated with a firm grip around his throat and a bite of his nipple.

"Don't tell me what to do."

His rhythm faltered as a groan escaped. The fierceness in their joining, the bucking of hips and scratching of dulled claws across skin, had her cries echoing until she clamped around him in perfect rapture. This time, though, she needed more.

They pulled apart, and she dipped her fingers to her clit, circling quickly until the friction made her shake.

"Wait," Hex groaned, dragging her hands away. "Let me."

A full-body flush rippled through her as he shuffled down her body, his mouth lining up with her core. "No. You can't."

"Please," he begged, kissing along the soft skin of her inner thighs. It was the first time his lips had touched her skin in that way, the softness of his mouth contrasting with the rough hair of his beard.

He hovered before her as a chorus of moans, pleasured cries, and heavy breaths erupted around them.

"What is that?" she breathed, but she knew.

"The pack," Hex said against her, the warm air making her jolt. "The full moon amplifies sex for us all."

A scorching, wet pressure slid up her centre. "Fuck!"

"They must like what they hear," he said, repeating the action until the world fell away. She cried out.

"Good," he purred. "You should never be ashamed. You are divine."

With that, the subtle edging ended, and he descended upon her, tongue lapping where her fingers had been. Even as she writhed, he held fast, suctioning his lips to her and caging her thighs in his arms. His hands splayed across her belly as she traced the swooping patterns on his shoulders. Where had she seen them before? His next movements stole the thoughts. He hummed against her, the throaty vibrations driving her off the edge.

"Come for me," he said. But she was already there, already falling. Down. Down. Down.

"Don't tell me what to do," she panted, even as his soft chuckle eclipsed her, his wet kisses trailing from her navel to her neck.

"You think you're the alpha, don't you?"

She stiffened. Claudine had called her that, too. At the time, she thought she was just being snide, but the title pleased her beast. Ridiculous.

"With you, Rowan Hex, I am." She shoved him off her, nudging him onto his back as she lifted onto her forearms. He swallowed hard, turning his flashing gaze to the spattering of trees above them and the clear sky over the lake. She copied his movements, letting her rapid heart rate slow. The song of sex around them climaxed and ebbed, a hot flush keeping Sylvie warm as she stargazed. Too weary to speak, she focused on the rhythm of her breath and keeping her eyes off the male body at her side.

Maybe if she made a list of the shitty things he'd done, she could stop the feelings that were growing inside her, but what had he really done? Everything she had seen while living in his home negated her initial thoughts. He served his people; he was just, and kind, and loved.

The one answer she didn't have was about Ace and the motives behind his torture. She needed to know before even considering him being a possibility.

"I need to ask—oh my gods, did you see that?" she gasped as the remnants of a star streaked across the sky. Long after the tail faded into darkness, she pulled her eyes away, dropping them to the place her hand gripped Hex's. She let go.

"I've never seen a real shooting star before," she said.

His sculpted profile shimmered under the moon's glow, every feature holding a sharpness, from his straight nose to his angular eyes and square jaw. Even beneath the beard. He was beautiful in his hardness. Another hardness caught her eye as it rested against his thigh, still glistening from their shared climax.

"Make a wish," he said.

She sighed, letting her lids flutter shut as she fought the pull—the need—and made her wish.

With an inhale, she stood, pulling her crumpled sweats off the ground, about to dress, when a spear of pain drove through her chest.

"Gods!"

She folded in half, almost dropping to her knees as Hex appeared in front of her. "What is it?"

"Your mark," she panted. "Why is it still hurting?" Last time, one climax was all it took. She fucked him and went to bed with Elias like nothing happened. This hurt worse and didn't bode well for them portalling to Argyncia in the morning.

"Maybe the Fates aren't happy we didn't complete the marking."

She grunted, losing control of her legs as Hex lifted her against his chest. Even the nearness eased some spasms.

She scowled, screwing her eyes against the pain even as Hex's words settled in her gut. If the Fates were that involved in her choices, she had bigger things to worry about. She worked on fortifying her mental fortress against them as she swayed in Hex's arms. It wasn't until the gentle slosh of water reached her ears did she realise the sway wasn't him rocking her gently back and forth, but walking into the endless depths of the lake.

Her eyes sprang open the same instant the lukewarm waters submerged her toes, and she panicked. Her mind exploded in a vision of Ace, the concrete cell, the plink of water on cold floors. Heart skyrocketing, her pulse hammered in her throat, mouth drying, limbs shaking, lips parting. But nothing happened. She couldn't speak. She couldn't move.

"Hey. You're safe. It's warm. See?"

As the tepid waters consumed her, the visions flared and her sight faltered until nothing reached her but the distant sound of a male's voice.

"Down," she managed to whisper between chattering teeth. "Put me down."

Her toes brushed the pebbled ground, but a slick material stole her balance and she slipped, swallowing a mouthful of water. She didn't flail or cry as she plunged beneath the waters. It was like sinking into a dreamless sleep. Falling into an abyss. Into silence. She glanced towards death, hand outstretched, ready to be consumed when a grip dragged her into the harsh air, breath reluctantly refilling her lungs as she disappeared outside of herself. Above herself. Blue lips. Glassy eyes. Empty.

"You didn't tell me you can't swim."

Hex thumbed water droplets from her face, searching it like he could see that she was missing. But he wouldn't think to look up to where she drifted.

He wiped her face again. Tender. Afraid. "I've got you." He walked them both from the water, retrieving her clothes and carefully dressing her even as the fabric clung to her saturated skin. "Did Rose ever tell you the story of Granite Lake?"

She didn't respond. Couldn't. The pain of the bonds didn't touch her any longer.

He picked her up again. "The humans that lived here first welcomed my people after the Clan Wars. They helped us settle, shared their histories, and hid us from the rest of the human world. We offered them a shifter life in return. Some of the pack supposedly descend from them. They say back then, the Fates were still generous with mate bonds and childbearing."

She felt herself sinking as he walked, floating towards her limp form. "They told us stories of this lake and its creation. Millennia ago, volcanoes riddled the land, coating the soil in ash and death, cleansing the continent as the gods saw fit, but the people of the Tynaan were a spiritual people. Witches. They used their collective power to beg the goddess Ira to protect them. She took pity on them and breathed life into the Tynaan, into the land, and when the volcano erupted, the magic forced the mountain's fury down into the soil, protecting its people and those throughout the continent. The woods became known as the lungs of Ira and they have protected us ever since."

She'd never heard such a story, and neither had the rest of Erus, probably. Even the worshippers of the old gods never talked much of a goddess. Perhaps that was the old magic Kian spoke of. Goddess magic.

Slowly, slowly, her hovering form settled into her skin, her head dropping back with the weight of the return. She blinked, vision spotty. Hex was there, in her face, relief clear in the softening of his brow.

"Thank the goddess," he breathed. He swallowed as his home came into view and the waves of fury down her other bonds jumped out with stark clarity.

"What the fuck did you do?" Elias stormed over, shoving Hex after he handed Sylvie to Kian.

Stop it.

Kian gave her a painless once-over as she blinked at him tiredly, sensing the gentle siphoning of her lingering fear. She shook her head at him, wriggling to stand on her own, and he lowered her, a mixture of shock and pride slithering down the bond. She could handle this. Hex had helped her back, even if he'd put her in the situation in the first place.

"What did you do?" Elias demanded again, shoving Hex. He didn't even fight back.

"We washed off in the lake and she slipped under. I didn't know she couldn't swim."

Realisation flashed in Elias's eyes, then rage.

"She wasn't catatonic because she can't swim, you worthless mutt—"

"Elias, stop it," Sylvie rasped, her anger flaring.

"You're fucking beta drowned her, again and again, when he tortured her. He held her under until she couldn't hold on any longer—"

Sylvie shoved her hands against her ears and mumbled unintelligible sounds to block the words. To stop the descriptions from taking root inside her again. She knew what happened; she lived it, and she didn't need to hear it retold ever again. Hex needed to hear it, though. It was the one thing that had held her back, and she needed answers, confirmation he wasn't the shifter she had believed he was, but the male she now knew from her time with the pack. But as Elias spoke the words, tension and disbelief muddled in Hex's expression, and he visibly recoiled.

His lips moved, head shaking, eyes darting to her, then away. Shame. *Disgust.* Sylvie blinked. Swallowed. Heart breaking, her beast slunk into the shadows, whining. Her hands dropped from her ears as Hex backed away, saying, "I can't."

I can't.

Then, with a gut-wrenching groan, he turned from male to animal and darted away into the dark, not looking back once.

She stared after him, then at Elias as he returned to her, touching the hair plastered to her face. "I should've come sooner."

She shook her head, facing Kian as he frowned down at her, lips pressed. "Come in and rest. We leave tomorrow at noon," he said.

She dropped her head and trailed behind him to their room, Hex's last words echoing in her mind. *I can't.*

The rejection stung more than the lingering ache of their unconsummated bond. He'd left her when she most needed comfort. When he finally heard the truth about Ace's abuse, he ran.

He didn't cause the harm, but he couldn't face it either. He couldn't face her.

I can't.

TWENTY-SIX

"Let's go already," Kerensa grumbled from Hex's spare bedroom doorway. "It was bad enough, just Ambrose and I. Now I need to take you, Hart, and the wolf?"

"I'll be helping, Kerensa. Stop grumbling." Kian closed the door in her face as Sylvie pulled on her clothes—toughened activewear from Rose, with tactical scaled armour over her chest.

A tad overkill, but Elias insisted. After she slipped her feet into her boots, Kian gestured for her to sit and began tying her laces.

"You okay?"

She sighed, wishing at that moment he couldn't feel her emotions. "Yeah."

After a long sleep snuggled between Elias and Kian, the heartbreak of Hex leaving her after hearing one of her greatest pains had dulled to a steady ache. Soon it would fade to her regular distaste of the shifter male, but for now, it hurt.

The door opened, and Elias peered in, his attention shifting between the pair. "Are you ready?" Sylvie nodded as Kian tied the last bow and stood, walking to take the vampire's outstretched hand.

As they crossed the front door's threshold, a gaggle of shifters blocked their movements. Hex chatted amongst them, his back towards her. Amira, along with the other elders, shared furrowed glances and pinched expressions as Hex spoke. They weren't happy with him leaving the pack, it seemed. A month was a long time. Without him, the next attack could leave them with more shifters taken. Sylvie gritted her teeth. That wouldn't happen, regardless of whether he wanted her. The shifters didn't deserve it. They would get the stolen members back and finish the wards when they returned, and if any more were taken while they were gone, she'd find them too. She could do it.

Kian laced his fingers with her free hand and she squeezed, only realising how odd it likely looked to the crowd of shifters after they peered sidelong at her and the hands both males gripped. They weren't stupid. Or blind. Only Claudine knew she was Hex's mate, but the others would have heard them having sex. What would they think of her?

Amira nodded with a soft smile, a look of knowing on her face. Sylvie reciprocated the gesture, finishing her descent to where Kerensa stood, arms crossed and frowning. Hex dismissed most of the other shifters and faced them, a pack slung over his shoulder. Dark circles lined his eyes like he hadn't slept a wink. *Serves him right.* Kerensa and Kian had backpacks too. Provisions to last them a week while they recovered from the travel. After that, they would have to scrounge to survive.

"Hey, Vee." Rose darted over, a bright smile lighting her face. "Show 'em who's boss, okay?" She gripped Sylvie's shoulder and squeezed.

"Yeah, stay alive," Natalie added, keeping her gaze downcast and body just out of reach of Elias.

Sylvie nodded to them both. "I will. Be careful while we're gone." She gnawed on her lower lip before saying, "If anything happens and you need a place to hide, head to my home. It's warded and there's a spare key in the hanging flowerpot closest to the door."

Kian's grip on her hand squeezed with a rush of love, and she squeezed back. With his pack wards only half completed, their home was the only place fully protected from the vampires.

Elias's hand cinched around hers for an entirely different reason, his attention fixed on Natalie.

Rose took Nat by the wrist and followed the disappearing crowd of shifters, offering one last wave as they faded through the trees.

"Relax," Kian said to her vampire mate, who was emanating a wall of hatred.

"She betrayed her."

Sylvie shook her head, the weight of the gun she had pointed at Natalie a phantom in her palm. She untangled herself from Kian and clenched the offending hand. "She apologised. We're good now."

Elias grunted and pulled her closer to his side, but didn't press the issue as Hex glanced between them.

"Finally." Kerensa guided Hex to Kian's side and closed the circle with a tight grip on his forearm. "Hold his arm, for fate's sake."

Hex did, although reluctantly, and Sylvie nestled them all closer, careful not to brush against the male on Kian's other side.

"Don't lose your grip on each other or you'll get lost in the liminal realm, and I'm in no mood for an impromptu trip to Hel."

Sylvie's grip on Kian and Elias tightened until her fingers ached. She didn't want to travel to Hel either. She'd seen glimpses through Rheikar's portal in the Stone Court, and that was more than enough.

"Kian, channel all your portalling affinity between them to me."

"Now?"

"No, yesterday."

Kian clicked his tongue and shuddered, a pulse of energy shooting through Sylvie, forcing her back to arch at the sharp jolt. Elias gripped her wrist tight, his forearms tensing as the power travelled through him too. Kerensa absorbed the surge, her eyes rolling back until they turned white, and she gritted her sharp teeth. "Don't let go."

In a single breath, the world tilted on its axis and Sylvie floated in an abyss of darkness. Her only tethers to reality were the bodies pressing against either side of her.

A faded groan drew her attention somewhere to her left, but it withered away in a maelstrom of wind and growing light, the outline of a structure twinkling in a violet glow.

"Hold on," a voice wheezed, and then they landed in a pile of sprawled limbs and cerulean foliage. Sylvie coughed as her males rolled off her and blinked up at the canopy of unnatural trees. They certainly weren't on Erus anymore.

She patted herself down and sat waiting for the pain that travel to Argyncia promised, but nothing happened. Beyond a slight ache forming over her brow, she felt normal. Her fingers slipped to her marks. Maybe her plan worked after all. Even her full moon escapade with Hex would have strengthened her half-done mark. Or maybe the portal effects were accumulative and she'd feel worse on the way home.

Whatever. They made it.

"We're along the western borders," Elias muttered, dragging himself to sitting as if the action was the most laborious task. "The cave is close."

She touched his cheek, worrying her lower lip. "Okay, let's get to the cave. Can you walk?"

He nodded, but the movements stalled and jerked. Kian and Kerensa were only a little better, their skin lacking the usual umber glow. The only other person seemingly unaffected was Hex.

Sylvie tucked herself under Elias's arm and helped as Kerensa led them to a crack in the land, muttering High Fae phrases the whole way. The staged foliage made the cave entrance disappear in the pastel landscape. The bark of the trees they passed varied in texture from velvet to spongy to spiked, and the colours were unlike anything she had seen, the blends mixing in mesmerising hues. They slipped between the cracks of ochre rock and slid down into a wider sanctum, the pocket of space just wide enough for them all to fit inside. More tunnels led away from the area, but the light from outside didn't reach them, and when Sylvie threw a pebble into the darkness, a splash echoed.

Just my luck. More water.

Elias leaned heavily against the cave wall with a bag of blood to his lips. "We'll need a new way in. I imagine the tunnels we used last time will be heavily guarded."

Hex slung off his pack, setting it at his feet. "And why is that?"

Kerensa snorted as Elias answered, "Because I killed half a dozen of them trying to find the shifters."

Sylvie shuffled back, copying Elias's posture. "And you found nothing?"

"Nothing of note. There were turned vampires roaming at night, so we searched during the day. But each morning, the shifter's scents were everywhere."

"Do you think the vampires are using them for something?" Sylvie asked.

Hex growled from her side, but she kept her gaze off him.

"If they're overrun by the turned vampires, it would make sense, but I couldn't deduce anything from the guards. They've been compelled so deeply I couldn't break them in the time I had."

"You broke them alright," Kerensa murmured.

Sylvie sighed, accepting a piece of fruit from Kian as they fell into silence, all eating a few morsels.

Kerensa broke the tension. "This feels different from last time. Easier."

Elias nodded, eyes closed. "She's unaffected."

Sylvie glanced his way, then Kerensa's as the fae female narrowed her gaze towards her.

"It's probably the bond," Sylvie said with a shrug. "Ilfaem was worse."

Kerensa nodded, though her expression remained guarded, if not a little disbelieving. "Stay in the cave. I've warded our scents, but my incantations are weaker than usual."

Hex was the only one irritated by the request, but Sylvie didn't care. In fact, it pleased her.

Elias caught her attention as he stowed away the empty blood pack, a faint flush to his cheekbones. She sniffed and glanced sidelong at Kerensa before humming.

"What?" Elias cracked open an eye.

"Last time you didn't take a bag. How did you get blood?"

Kerensa shuffled and straightened as Elias peeled open the other eye, a twitch spasming in his cheek. It didn't take emotional reading to tell he was laughing at her.

"Did you drink her blood?"

Kerensa made a disgusted sound. "It was barely anything, and I used magic to make it go farther. Don't make it into something it's not."

Sylvie smoothed her features into cool composure. "I wasn't." She tilted her head. "But I don't know how I feel about it either."

From the way Hex adjusted himself, she knew her clashing with another bonded was affecting him. It should've annoyed her, but it only made her stomach tighten.

"I drink other people's blood all the time," Elias said lowly, though humour laced his tone.

"From a bag."

She stared him down. If he wasn't so weakened from portalling, she wouldn't have pushed it, but he was, and her mood needed an outlet. He broke first, half-smiling as he tilted his head against the cave wall, eyes closed once more.

"Don't do it again," she added last, hoping he couldn't scent how turned on he was making her. The anticipation of future punishment was enough to fire her right up. Even her inner beast rolled onto her back, stomach exposed and needy.

Kerensa groaned before lying down and facing the wall. She couldn't scent it, but Sylvie's face was usually an open book, one that Hex seemed to be reading. She caught his stare and levelled a look of her own, one that revealed how much she didn't give a shit about him. He looked away.

Good.

* * *

Days passed quickly. They burned through their supplies in five, so Kian and Hex took to hunting in the deep woods. The hunting turned to scavenging when the animals were too cunning for the traps they laid, setting them off every time and leaving them empty, so they survived on fruits, wild vegetables, and a squishy substance Elias called fiorns. They tasted a bit like mushrooms. All of which were for the humans that once called Argyncia home. Being an eternal feedbag didn't sound appealing to her, but each to their own. On the ninth day, Kerensa and Kian returned to full strength, and they sat around a small fire, eating the fiorns with wild apple.

"In the morning, we'll head to the wall and find a way in. We can lie low in one of the abandoned homes in the outer city, but we'll need cloaks first," Elias said, drinking the last of his blood bags. Unlike the rest of them, he'd packed enough for the fortnight, which was good because she couldn't feed him without finishing the process with a hard screwing, and that wasn't happening in the cave in front of her sister-in-law. It was fine. After everything that happened with Hex, she hadn't felt the urge to be intimate anyway. They hadn't spoken once, which helped some of the hurt fade into distaste, but it wasn't quite enough. She'd soothed her bruised ego by snuggling between Elias and Kian every night.

Morning came quickly. They left the cave, leaving no trace of their visit as they headed for the city. Kerensa and Elias stayed ahead, while Hex and Kian walked behind Sylvie. She didn't question if the guarding formation was intentional.

A few hours passed before they came upon a twenty-foot wall of stone a hair's breadth from the woods that blocked every sight and sound of the city within.

"Why aren't there any guards?" Sylvie asked.

Kerensa groaned. "There will be if you don't keep your voice down."

Elias shot Kerensa a sharp glance and palmed the stone, his hands coming away with crumbling rock and dirt.

"No one goes beyond the walls of the city any longer." An unmistakable sadness filled his tone, and Sylvie stepped to his side, lacing her fingers with his. "It wasn't even here when I called this place home."

She squeezed his hand. He must have been gone for a long, long time.

"Back when I was a youngling there were thousands of us within the city. It was the only haven for born vampires, and while some explored the wider realm, none found a home like this. The farther from the city, the harsher the elements. My mother thought it was the 'gods" way of containing us. That we were borne of a dark god's whim and the realm was their masterpiece to toil over."

Sylvie hummed. It wasn't very different from what the humans believed in many parts of the world back home.

"We trained in these forests when they teemed with animals, explored the caves and cliffs to the north for minerals to carve into spending tokens. The wastes on the other side of the city were once a salt lake where humans swam and fished. Those same humans trapped here after the Division were turned or kept for food, and the lake ran dry. It wasn't a large realm, but it was mine."

The wall, corroded and withered by the elements, looked almost as old as the woods at her back.

"It certainly isn't anymore," he finished.

Sylvie leaned against him as Kerensa waved them over to where she stood investigating the wall. "We could try the cellar entrance," she suggested, walking along the border but not touching the stones. Sylvie followed with the males at her back, their footfalls virtually silent on the ground. She dropped her gaze to the plant matter underfoot and her brows lifted. Instead of grass, dirt, or stone, small floral vines made up the foliage, with milky flowers creeping across the ground and snuggling tightly against the tree roots of the forest at their side. Some tendrils snaked along the wall, but none climbed it, as if the stone repelled the beauty.

"The cellars would take us past the old turned quarters," Elias answered.

Kerensa shrugged. "Then there won't be any guards."

"They won't need guards if the turned wake and kill us all."

Sylvie adjusted her collar and tried not to think too deeply about Elias's ominous words as they made it to a pair of double doors flung open with enough force to rip one of them off their hinges. The thick metal lay strewn on the vines, and Kian made a low noise in his throat. "They're sleeping for now," he said. "But this isn't your best idea, E."

Hex growled. "What's down there?"

"Yeah," Sylvie agreed, "I'm not descending into a dark hole with things that will kill me until I know what your plan is and what the hell they are."

Elias stared hard down into the darkness as he answered, "Turned vampires were once human, so they have similar needs. Eat and sleep. We used to house them in the dungeons to keep the born vampires safe, but the tunnels surrounding the cells are riddled with them now."

"How can you tell?"

"The heartbeats," Hex answered for them, and Sylvie shuddered.

"They're usually docile during the day if they've fed recently, and they can't stand sunlight, but I won't risk you anymore than we have to. While we're in there, no talking, and watch your step." Elias's attention focused on Sylvie, but he glanced at Hex, too.

"And once we're inside the walls, you will all need to walk ahead of me with your heads down."

Sylvie's brows rose. What good would that do?

"I'll monitor their sleeping patterns, but if they wake, I'll portal us out, then you run." Kian cupped Sylvie's chin, and she nodded, even as Kerensa rolled her eyes and strutted past to the darkened stairwell.

It would be fine. If Kerensa could walk in fearlessly, then so could she.

With one last steeling breath, she descended into the thick, inky gloom.

TWENTY-SEVEN

Sylvie padded down the concrete stairs with soft repetitive scuffing, her vision adjusting to the dimming light as she caught up with Kerensa. Her males followed, their presence a balm in the eerie quiet. The stairwell led into a narrow tunnel, and all traces of light faded with every subdued step until only mildew and the faint echo of trickling water assaulted her remaining senses. Sylvie's heart thudded in her chest. A wintry chill charged the air, and she leaned into the warm presence at her back. Kian. He clasped her hand as she reached for him. Two stars of indigo glowed where his eyes would be, and she exhaled shakily. He could see. That was something, at least. Elias's blood-toned irises shone in the darkness too as he slipped beside her, threading a warm, but clammy, hand with hers—Hex's.

She tensed, wanting nothing more than to jerk away, when Elias's cool grip clasped her shoulders, stilling her movements. Hex was a shifter, an animal—without light, his wolf eyes wouldn't be of any use either. She nodded. Fine. The two liabilities would stick together. With exaggerated steps, Sylvie followed the gentle pressure of Elias's hands, holding fast to Hex even when his fingers squeezed hers so hard her knuckles ached.

The warmth of her males enclosed her as if they'd stepped into a smaller passage, and she drew on the closeness to keep her calm, especially when the sudden whooshing of multiple creatures' breathing sounded. Their collective exhales blew stale air from all angles and Sylvie tried not to gag from the foul scent of fetid blood. She closed her eyes and reached for her fae sight. Anything to light up the undying dark, but Kian's sudden squeeze of her shoulder stopped her dead. *Don't.*

In the pause, a sharp sniff to their side filled her gut with dread. Before she could move, Hex's body rounded hers, his arms cradling her, his chin on her head as Elias curled protectively around her back. Kian's embrace came from behind Hex, and even in the dark, she could picture them—a bundle of muscle and power shielding her from the bleary red stare of the turned. Kerensa and Kian whispered a ward around them as the creature lurched nearer, the light of its eyes flickering. Blinking.

Please go. Don't hurt them.

Like it collided with a wall, the turned bounced off an unseen shield and continued its lumbering gait away from them, muttering foreign whispers under its breath.

Once the steady breathing steadied from the slumbering turned and Sylvie's heart dislodged itself from her throat, Elias and Kian pulled back, their hands returning to her shoulders. Hex held on a beat longer and she swallowed, hating how good it felt. She pulled away first, reclaiming his hand loosely, and resumed her slow, trembling pace.

After an eternity, a faint glow filtered from a staircase before them and she released a restrained breath.

Elias's hand slid down to her lower back in silent praise. They did it.

Ascending the stairwell, Sylvie led them to a carved door, palming the frigid metal with both hands. It gave her a reason to detach from Hex and cooled the lingering burn his touch left behind. "What now?" she whispered.

Kerensa stepped beside her, offering a reproachful look, and tapped Sylvie's chin before pushing it towards her sternum. *Keep your head down.* That's what Elias had said. She did, clasping the handle and wincing at the hideous shriek its hinges offered, swallowing a scream at the collective moans of waking turned.

"Move," Elias hissed, cramming them through the door and slamming it behind them. Purple orbs lit the space, and silver cages lay empty, bracketing a thin passage. Elias shoved his back against the door as it bulged.

"We're in the dungeons. Run straight to the end of the path and turn left. The door up the stairs leads to the main halls. The instant you're clear, I'll meet you," he finished, clearly noting the storm clouds brewing on Sylvie's face.

"You better." She turned and ran, her bonded males and Kerensa surrounding her as she met the wall, spun on her heel and darted to the stairs Elias had directed them to. The walls were tight, brushing her on either side as she scrambled to the top. Kerensa stretched a hand over Sylvie's shoulder and muttered a phrase in High Fae in front of the locking mechanism above the handle until a heavy thunk sounded. Sylvie peered back over her shoulder. "We're clear," she hissed, hovering her hand over the handle.

The wind gust of Elias's presence filled her with relief, and she swung the dungeon door wide open and clambered through, landing in a hall with polished floors and a crowd of shocked vampires. *Shit.*

Elias slammed the doors behind them all, and the vampires scattered. She barely stopped her mouth from dropping open. What the hell? She waited, expecting guards or an attack, but nothing happened. All was still.

Once the halls cleared, she turned to face him. "What was that?"

"Nothing," he said. "Remember what I told you to do?"

She rolled her eyes but nodded, dropping her gaze to the floor and shuffling forward.

"Left," Elias said. Lower he asked Hex, "Can you mind-link here?"

"No."

Sylvie glanced back as Elias sighed. "I don't understand it," he said, then paused, running a hand across his chest, right where her mark branded him. She frowned. There was something off about her marks, too. They were quiet. Asleep.

"What has he done?" Elias whispered.

She thought to question him when voices carried down the hall, and Elias growled, "Move," he said, his voice taking on a tone she hadn't heard before. Dangerous, and not the fun kind. She followed his orders despite the unease spiralling through her, the floor becoming the object of her scrutiny once more. The polished stone slabs sat inside frames of silver, the corners twisting in delicate arches and climbing up the floor to ceiling windows. It was so much like Sterling.

Even with the glass walls, the realm beyond remained obscured, distorted and hazy, like a fog swirled within the panes. Within the building, legs pattered past them, sharp in their movements aside from the half-second pause each one made when seeing Elias before darting away down the sun lit corridors. Everything was so odd. No one said anything. *This doesn't make sense, unless …*

"I should have guessed." The voice was painfully similar to Elias's, but resonated in front of her. "My guards turn up dead and no one raises the alarm. In fact, they suggest I appointed the punishment myself. And now you've woken the younglings."

The younglings? Those monsters were their children?

Sylvie tentatively lifted her eyes, daring to disprove her theory because it couldn't be true. They couldn't be. But the male took her breath away. *Twins.*

"Nothing to say, brother? It has been an awfully long time." The male who looked scarily similar to her kindred angled his head, the slightly shorter hair hanging limp against his face. His effortless charisma lured her in while the seething arrogance had her leaning back into a rigid wall of ice. Elias. He pushed her to Kian's side, who tucked her against him, a subtle rage humming between them. She let a sliver of fear seep through her as their movements captured the feline gaze of Elias's brother.

"Aren't you a treat?"

She held his gaze for a beat, not shrinking when his lips pulled into a surprised smile. Hex growled and Elias manoeuvred him to Sylvie's side so roughly he stumbled.

"Enough, Hayes," Elias snapped. "Let us take our leave."

"Your leave? And I thought my brother had turned mute. Instead, you make a mess of the royal guard, distress the slumbering turned, and dangle these little beasties right under my nose without so much as an offering." While his voice never changed volume, steel laced every syllable. Sylvie lowered her stance, preparing for violence, but instead of lashing out, he smiled. His eyes crinkled and his posture relaxed enough to disarm a fraction of Sylvie's warning bells. *Nuts. He's got to be.* Hayes glanced over at them all and inclined his head.

"I apologise for my outburst. We are scarce on fresh blood these days."

That was the cost of not feeding. Madness. Elias had spoken briefly of it once. Without blood, the vampires would wither away to nothing. Desiccate.

In the dragging silence, Hayes's demeanour shifted again to one of impatience, his hands clenching into fists at his side.

"Well? Care to explain why you did not wish to enter through the front door?"

Elias held the silence for a beat too long, and even Sylvie had started sweating when he finally said, "With the state of the realm, I wasn't certain what I would find behind the twenty-foot monstrosity encasing the city. The turned were a familiar comfort."

Comfort was laughable. She could only hope Hayes didn't see through it, but by his stare at Hex, perhaps he already had.

Hayes nodded. "Very well. Take leave to your quarters. At least that remains unchanged." A vague sense of sadness lingered in the air as Elias nudged the group around Hayes, offering the slightest of bows.

"Oh, and brother?" Hayes's trailing voice sent icy tendrils crawling up her back. "Don't let your pets out of your sight. We wouldn't want a frenzy on our hands."

Elias nodded and continued shoving them along like they were no more than a nuisance. His pets. They followed a wide hall to a double set of stairs, one going down—to freedom, the other upwards.

To her frustration, and Hex's based on his throaty grumble, Kian tugged them up the shimmering silver stairs after Elias as Kerensa lagged. At the top of the flight of stairs, another hall led to multiple sets of elaborately decorated metal doors. A familiar pattern framed each one, and Elias headed to the one farthest from the stairs, pushing the door open with a creak and holding it as they all filed in. Sylvie glanced his way as she passed, a question on her brow, but the space beyond stole every thought, every question, along with her breath.

Tapestry-lined walls danced in the softest breeze from a barred window, jagged glass pointing up from the base of the frame, while ornate rugs drew the eye to the canopy bed in the room's centre. Rich maroon fabric draped around the pristinely made bed, big enough to fit a dozen people. It didn't take a genius to surmise its uses. Sylvie flushed. She needed a bed like that back on Erus. Kian untangled from her as she craned her neck to admire the high cathedral ceilings and the three crystal chandeliers with giant purple bulbs suspended at the apex.

"A mimic of the sun," Elias said from her side. She leaned into him and continued her ogling. "Hayes must have added them after I left."

"Lets see what else he left," Kerensa grunted, running her hands along the walls directly opposite from Kian as he muttered warding in High Fae.

Sylvie inhaled and glanced up at Elias, who held a finger to his lips. *I know that.* She rolled her eyes and scowled, and he checked her with a rough ass grab. *Bastard.* As if hearing her thoughts, he picked her up, his forearm under her ass like a seat and the other hand gripping her jaw.

"This is my wing, but you will stay here. The bathroom is there." He pointed to a door next to a wardrobe. "I suggest you get comfortable, as these will be your permanent lodgings until we return home."

"Um—" Sylvie started to reply, but her words cut off as he threw her onto his bed, the mattress sinking beneath her while she choked on breathless laughter. She stared up at the velvety canopy and shook her head. While getting comfortable sounded perfect, they had a mission.

"We can speak freely now," Kerensa said, slumping on a velvety upholstered armchair. It was so large that the fae appeared childlike, curled in its cushioned luxury.

"We are not staying in here," Hex said immediately. His anger flared through the room. "We need to find the shifters and I can't do that stuck in this tomb."

"I will find them," Elias said, pulling off his outer layers and storing them on hangers in his wardrobe.

"Do you honestly think I'll sit by while you look for *my* people? Your brother is the reason we're in this mess."

Sylvie didn't miss the shift in blame, but ignored it. It was too little, too late. She agreed, though. They would not stay in the room while Elias risked his skin.

"Just say we need walks or something," she said. "The shifter scent is outside and in the lower halls, right? So we need to get down there."

But Elias and Hex argued over her until her suggestions were little more than wasted vibrations on the wind.

Hex attempted to sidestep Elias. "Get out of the way."

Elias spun him with a sharp grip on his elbow. "Even if I were to take you, it wouldn't be now. You smell like death."

"Good. Then I won't need to worry about your kin draining me dry."

"I wouldn't touch you with a ten-foot lance, but frenzied vampires have no such reservations."

Their voices rose until Sylvie's eardrums throbbed.

"Just get me down there and I'll find them," Hex grated, his fingers shifting into black claws.

"Sit down."

Sylvie groaned, throwing her head backwards into the mattress again until her sounds shifted into an exasperated scream. "Stop yelling!"

To her relief, the arguments ceased, yet Kian's chuckle drew her gaze.

"What?" she demanded.

"You're the one yelling, Princess."

Elias raised a brow at her, lips curling while Hex looked away, hiding his flushed cheekbones and a deep scowl. Each reaction had her insides churning. Warming. Wanting. She clenched her teeth as Kerensa stood abruptly, the chair beneath her scraping the floors in a hideous screech. "I'm going to make this abundantly clear. I do not wish to see, hear or smell any of you breeding, and if I even sense you lot giving each other the eyes, I'm portalling back to Erus without you."

Sylvie stretched her arms overhead before sitting up and giving Kerensa her best indignant look. "For one, shut up, and two, when can we portal next?"

"Next full moon. Two and a half weeks, give or take," she said.

"Alright," Sylvie replied. "So we explore the city, find the shifters and get them out the day of the full moon. Easy." The sarcasm bounced right off Elias's stern expression.

"It's not safe for you to go outside. I will find them. We'll head to the wastes and then we'll portal home." Elias crossed his arms, and she crossed hers, holding his glare until her brow hurt from the furrow.

"I'm going to the restroom," she finally growled, storming to the bathroom and slamming the door behind her. If he wanted to treat her like a child, then she would act like one. And damn, it felt good to be a brat.

TWENTY-EIGHT

Much like the bedroom, Elias's bathroom transported Sylvie straight into a fantasy novel. The toilet, basins, and clawfoot tub were a blend of silver metal and heavy, carved wood with swirls identical to the marks on her chest. There was no mistaking whose room she was in. With a bit of fiddling, she managed the taps and stripped, her anxiety rising as the water did. *I can do this. I'm safe.* With clenched teeth, she climbed into the half-filled tub and waited for flashbacks as the rushing liquid played around her ankles. They never came. With a steadying breath, she sank to her knees, her fingers digging into the lip of the tub as the water rose past her belly button before then caressing her lower ribs. *Drip.*

That was enough.

She swallowed, carefully releasing the tub's edge and reclined, letting the water lap up her body to her neck. *No. No. Too much.*

She sat with rapid breaths, already shivering from the loss of heat across her torso, and settled on scooping small handfuls over her shoulders to trickle down her back.

Once her heart evened to its normal rhythm and her muscles started relaxing, Elias let himself into the room. The pile of clothes atop his hand could have been mistaken as a peace offering, but the closing of the door behind him and heated stare stole any assumptions of truce.

"Did you think you would get away with that?" He stalked closer, dropping the clothes on the floating bench next to the basin, and pulled a dark wooden stool from underneath it. Sylvie eyed him warily as he sat.

"Did you think your challenge in the caves would go unpunished also?"

No. She quashed the desire with a frown. "I'm not a child, Elias. Don't treat me like one."

His eyes flashed at her casual drop of his name, and she averted her gaze.

"I am treating you like a person who knows nothing of this realm, which is the case, and you slammed my door."

She sighed, splashing the water over her shoulders once more when goosebumps pricked her skin. "Fine. I'm sorry for slamming your door, but I'm not apologising for anything else. We're a team, right? That means we do this together. I didn't come with you to sit on my hands while you risk your life here. I saw how sick portalling made you. You aren't bulletproof."

"I think you'll find I am."

"You know what I mean."

His lips curled, and she ducked her chin to hide her smile, hissing when water cascaded down her back from a foreign source.

"It's just me," Elias said, and she relaxed her cheek onto her knees as he cupped and poured water down her spine. Her gaze softened on her kindred, and his expression pinched as he meticulously kept her hair dry.

"What happened with your brother?" she whispered. "Why is he like that?"

Elias's gaze slid to hers, a discontented line creasing his brow. "There is no simple answer, love."

She thought that was the end of the conversation, but Elias continued.

"Perhaps if my mother favoured him instead of me he would be different, or if my father had named him heir. Maybe he was born selfish. Rash."

"Why would she favour you?" She could already see why, but maybe Hayes wasn't always a monster; maybe he was made.

Elias slowed the soothing rinsing of her back, lathering her in soap before washing suds away as he spoke. "I learned quickly how useful self-control could be. I mastered compulsion very young and blood never frenzied me the same way it did him. My father named me heir when we were boys, but I saw the pain it brought my parents, the grief when the Fates decided to forsake us and the kindred bonds. When every pregnancy ended in death …"

Sylvie hung on every word, though the revelation of him being the rightful king wasn't surprising at all.

"I let Hayes step in for me during our tutor's lessons occasionally, so he knew enough of what it took to lead the realm, and when our parents died from a revenant attack, I abdicated. Although Hayes was erratic and sometimes cruel, he had the innate desire to lead. I didn't. And when the realm heard of my decision, whisperings of rebellion filled the city. So I left, and then the Division happened, and I wasn't able to return. It gave them no choice but to accept Hayes, luckily before they gave him cause to destroy me."

"I'm sorry about your parents."

"I am too. It was the first time we had seen that kind of creature in the flesh—a second-generation turned vampire. They're monstrous. A sin of nature and magic. With the degeneration from the turning, their bones fused and hardened until they were almost impossible to kill, and their flesh and eyes melted away."

"So, how do they hunt without sight?"

"I'd guess scent and sound. Body heat. They consumed everything: blood, bones, marrow, and soft tissue. We never found out who let it in that night."

Sylvie shuddered, rubbing her fingers over the bumps that pricked her skin. They made turned vampires sound like a dream. Thank the gods they hadn't stumbled upon them in the cave, as she had no desire to be torn apart and eaten by vampire zombies.

They lapsed into silence, the bath cooling, and Elias stood, fetching her towel.

She dragged herself from the milky water, lightly clasping herself about the waist, and traced circles on her body with her fingernails. "You would've been a good king."

Elias's eyes snapped to hers, and his mouth twitched into a reluctant smile, followed by a smirk. *Uh oh.*

"Then I wouldn't have met you."

A flush coated her cheeks as he draped the towel over her shoulders and tugged her into his chest, their lips lining up as her breath fanned the rogue curls framing his eyes. In a motion too swift for her to counter, he lifted her from the tub and flopped her across his thighs as he dropped onto the wooden stool. The cool kiss of air blew against her ass before his rough squeeze did, and she buried her curses in her cupped palm.

"Everyone will hear," she gritted out, peering over her shoulder at him. Smug. He was way too smug.

"Only if you can't keep quiet," he said.

A loud knock startled them both, and Kian spoke through the closed door. "We have a problem."

Sylvie unpeeled herself from Elias's lap, cheeks burning, and secured her towel around her breasts while Elias stowed the stool back under the sink and hovered at her side. "What?"

When Kian cracked the door and peeked in, he homed in on Sylvie's flush first, then the heated glare Elias was sending her direction. His throat bobbed. "We've been invited to dinner."

* * *

Elias held Hayes's clothing offerings in clenched fists, his scowl scaring away the servants as soon as they dragged in the chest of luxury goods. Kian and Hex had found suitable attire after a wash, the pair adorning matching brown vests made with the same material the vampires that had attacked the pack wore, and tight—*strangling*—pants that showed off every bulge and divot. Sylvie glued her eyes to the varying shades of green spilling from the chest to stop her mouth from watering.

Kerensa changed into a modest sage gown, the only slit carved between her cleavage, while her legs remained hidden beneath half a dozen layers of silken skirts. Just thick enough to hide her weapons.

Sylvie had no such luck. The last option in her size was a two-piece set. The top barely hid her breasts behind two strips of cloth, revealed her midsection, and the lower piece looked more like a loincloth than a skirt. Well, it did, before Elias tore it to scraps. He dropped it in the chest and handed her a male's shirt to put on from his wardrobe. She smirked, taking the rich cream dress shirt, and slid her arms through the crisp fabric. Not quite long enough to call it a dress. A decent one at least.

"She can't wear that," Kerensa said, knocking Elias to the side and riffling through the chest. "It will draw more attention to her than the dress."

"Too late now," Hex muttered, tugging the laces of his boots tighter.

"I don't care about what clothes I wear." Sylvie moved to Kerensa's side as she dug through the piles of mismatched clothes. Maybe they missed something.

"We need to keep your marks hidden," Kian offered when Elias started grumbling. "If Hayes sees them, it would be a direct threat to his rule and a danger to you."

Sylvie sat back on the bed, accepting a billowy moss gown with thick straps and threaded her legs through it, pulling it over the dress shirt and turning so Kerensa could secure a thin belt to cinch her waist. "Why can't you just glamour it like you did when I was kidnapped?"

When no one spoke, she glanced up at Kian, blinking at his tilted head. "What?" he said.

"When Ace took me to the cells, you glamoured my mark."

Kian's brows pinched. "Why do you think that?"

"Because when he made me undress, he didn't see it." A rippling anger flooded the room from everyone in it. Even Kerensa scowled, a muscle in her jaw feathering.

Once Kian found his sense of calm again, he asked, "Are you sure he wasn't looking at something else?"

"He looked straight at me, Kian. My mark felt weird, and when he looked across my chest, his face went all slack and his eyes glazed. He couldn't see it."

"I didn't—" Kian swallowed, an apparent sense of awe stealing his voice, and Kerensa took over.

"A bonded's mark cannot be glamoured or warded. They are immune to the magic of every species."

What about the magic of the Fates themselves?

Sylvie left the thought unsaid, but it seemed to ripple through the group, anyway. Elias finished adjusting his cuffs angrily while Hex rocked idly from foot to foot, impatient. She fluffed her hair and shrugged, making sure the dress shirt hid the marks still dormant on her chest.

"Let's not keep the king waiting," she said.

As they trailed single file down unfamiliar halls, the sun shot distorted beams through the hazy glass. Servants with dark red attire hanging off their bony frames scurried past, bowing and squeaking their greetings once they spotted Elias at the head of the group. In his regal maroon suit, he looked every bit the king he was meant to be.

"In here," he said, strolling through a door held by a dark-haired servant. The servant kept his gaze down, but inhaled audibly as Sylvie passed. Kian nudged her through the door, his body shielding hers from the vampire, and she tried to fight the way the servant made her skin crawl. Surely the vampires wouldn't try anything, not with the giant males around her exuding their best killing auras. She wasn't to be trifled with either, but the flouncy dress and shirt combo wasn't doing her any favours.

The room opened into a regal dining area, the table a cold silver tone with thick vases of syrupy blood and an assortment of dishware in its centre, with patterned draperies lining every wall. Hayes stood at the head of the fifteen-foot dining table, straightening one of his five knives and forks. Why a vampire needed cutlery was anyone's guess. Probably to throw at guests that overstayed their welcome. She lowered her gaze and followed Kerensa to a seat. Servants pulled the chairs back and Sylvie sat herself between her sister-in-law and Kian, while Hex took the chair opposite her and Elias took the head.

Kerensa sniffed from beside her and Sylvie glanced sidelong as the fae folded a napkin in her lap and interlaced her fingers atop it. Then Kerensa bowed her head. Sylvie followed in slower, precise movements while keeping her attention pricked towards the monster at their side, trying not to startle when he finally spoke.

"Thank you for joining me this evening." A twinkle of humour filled his voice. "Though you could have spread yourselves around. I understand you are my brother's pets, but I don't bite."

Like Hel you don't. But she pressed her lips together in an apologetic smile regardless.

"Oh well," he said, pouring and sipping the viscous liquid from a silver chalice. The servants brought in more glasses with pink bubbly liquid, placing them in front of everyone as Hayes raised his chalice. No one in her group touched theirs.

"Animal blood," Hayes said through a lazy smile, taking another long swig. Sylvie's stomach turned. *Animal blood.* Did he mean shifter blood? Hayes's attention slid to her as she fought with her rage, replacing it with a level of demureness she didn't feel. She dared a glance at the shifter across the table. Head down, hands hidden in his lap; Hex hadn't reacted, so maybe the king was being forthright this time.

"Were my seamstress's clothing choices not to your liking, brother?"

She sensed more than saw his leering stare move off her.

Elias sighed. "What do you want, Hayes?"

"What do I want?" He laughed, but it was void of humour this time. "You steal into here, kill the royal guard, and refuse to speak cordially. You tell me, brother."

When Elias didn't offer a response, the servants moved in synchronicity, steaming dishes in each hand, which they loaded onto the table in front of the food-eating guests. Despite herself, Sylvie's mouth watered. Delicate caramelised fruits, steaming roasts, and fresh loaves filled the air with a heady aroma—enough to make her stomach growl. She glanced towards Elias, catching Kerensa's rolling eyes as she, too, looked Elias's way.

"Eat," he said, and Kerensa heaped food onto her plate until it overflowed.

"Yes, take as much as you'd like." Hayes nodded her way, tipping the chalice to point at the buffet. Sylvie waited until everyone else had taken their share and Elias had drank a portion of the "animal blood" before tentatively serving herself.

"So well trained. How precious." She hated the condescension in Hayes's tone. Hated his swallowing sounds too as he downed the last of his goblet. From the corner of her eye, she watched his every move, from the refilling of his cups—which he always did himself—to the sluggish way he leaned in his high-backed chair. If she didn't know any better, she'd assume he was drunk. He had gorged himself.

"You're a mutt, aren't you, little one?"

Sylvie swallowed a chunk of fiorn, fighting the cough that spasmed her chest as she again looked to Elias for confirmation.

He nodded, and she turned back to Hayes. "Yes."

"Yes, what?"

Shit. "Yes, Your Majesty."

He hummed, the dark line of red smearing across his lips as they pressed slightly. *Did I pass?*

"Do you have a name, little one?"

Eugh.

Elias spoke before she could. "Sylvie. She is accustomed to fae lore and will not reveal her identity because of it. She did not mean to offend."

Was he offended? Had she not masked her expression well enough?

Hayes seemed satisfied with Elias's answer, regardless. "Ah, yes. The way of the fae. I was musing about why you had two in your cadre. Well, two and a half, I'm guessing. Quite the collection indeed."

Sylvie's skin crawled as he sniffed, then sighed. "You always were rather eclectic in your tastes."

She fought every urge to roll her eyes. *Says the vampire who kidnapped dozens, if not hundreds, of shifters for half a century.*

Switching off from the conversation, she instead focused on the foreign flavours her tastebuds explored. The fruits blasted her with a rich sweetness bordering on tart while the vegetables had a kick. Some purple garnish gave off enough heat to make her skin redden.

She reached out to take a palate cleansing slice of what appeared to be flatbread when Hex's hand brushed hers and she jerked back, fingers coiling into a fist while he shakily picked up the slice and placed it on her plate. Did he expect her to scold him for doing so? Instead, she watched him as she plucked the bread off her plate and pulled it apart to eat it in dainty sections. He dropped his gaze first. For once, she rued the submission. Without meaning to, she tuned back into Hayes and Elias's tense conversation.

"Perhaps you would like to see the state of our home. As you well know, much has changed. We've resorted to melting most of the city's silver to fortify against the revenants. It's a marvel the glass city still stands."

Goosebumps danced across her skin.

"You can bring the faeries too. Perhaps they will prove useful."

"Not today," Elias replied gruffly, standing abruptly and gesturing for the rest of them to do the same. The servants swooped in to help with their chairs.

Hayes stood too, a thin smile on his lips.

"Fine. Another time."

Sylvie turned to follow Elias when chilling words cascaded down her back.

"A word of caution. Don't go outside after sunset."

TWENTY-NINE

An eerie quiet filled the night, and Sylvie hardly slept, wedged between Kian and Elias. Hex slept on the floor in wolf form while Kerensa took the seat by the window. "Close your eyes," Elias murmured against her hair and she did, though sleep never came.

By morning, the slow hum of bustling servants at the door woke her companions, and she exhaled the tension that had coiled every muscle in her body. Every time she tried to drift off, her mind conjured different apparitions of revenants tearing through flesh and bone—her mate's flesh and bones.

Some had black eyes and needle teeth with claws, others had detachable jaws, and the last monster her mind created moved so quickly it had ripped Elias's guts out before he could even react. She curled into her kindred, dragging his arm around her waist.

"Did you sleep well?" Kian asked sleepily from her other side.

She hummed in his direction, tilting her head and letting her bloodshot eyes do the talking.

"It's strange," he said. "Not being able to read you easily here. Whatever magic Hayes is using, it's potent."

"Yeah," she murmured, burying her face in the pillows. At least now the sun was up. It would be safe enough to rest. The door to their chambers swung open and servants flitted around, serving food and supplying clothing for the day on a huge rack they carried in on their shoulders before standing between the bed and the door. Wishful thinking.

"Your Highness, the king has requested an audience in the royal aviary, present company included."

Sylvie muffled a groan and sat, picking the sleep from her eyes, grateful the sleep shirt Elias had given her covered her mate marks as a gaggle of gaunt, red-eyed vampires gave her a once-over.

Everyone else accepted the help to change, but when they neared Sylvie, Elias hauled her back, much to the servant's surprise.

"My fae pet will dress her," he said, taking the waiting gown from a fair-haired servant and handing it to Kerensa, who managed a smile. If Sylvie didn't know her, she would've believed it. But the tightness of her muscles as she guided Sylvie behind the changing screen was unmistakable.

Despite her manner, Kerensa dressed Sylvie with ease, her fingers deft with the laces of her undergarments and corset. When Sylvie's brows rose at Kerensa's soft adjustments of the bodice and shawl, she offered a genuine half-smile. "I am still a royal after all," she muttered, low enough Sylvie had to strain to hear it. "My mother taught me." The curl to her lips fell, and she stepped back, nodding once. "You're ready."

"Follow us, Your Highness," the first servant said and led them from the room. The walk was quiet. Sylvie let her gaze roam, trying to memorise each room they passed and every stairwell they scurried down, but after the seventh passage, she gave up. Elias knew this place. It would have to do.

The last hall led to a silver arch with a grated door. The servant pulled it open, and Elias nodded. "I can make it from here, Willa."

"Yes, Your Highness." She bowed before scuttling past, her steps faltering at Sylvie's side as if captured by an invisible tether. Sylvie turned her head to follow the vampire's movements, but she was already gone.

"Stay together," Elias addressed them all. "You are free to explore the aviary while I speak with my brother, but don't leave the area. Understood?"

Sylvie nodded along with the others and gasped aloud as she crossed the arched threshold. The aviary roof domed overhead and a collection of plants, trees, and crawling vines blocked any view of the outer confines. Purple orbs hovered in three-foot intervals around the ceiling perimeter and silver chains stretched from wall to wall. Creatures with membranous wings and oily bodies flitted above, using the chains as a perch, only moving when disturbed by a much larger animal, its wingspan wide and see-through, with colouring reminiscent of an oil slick lining the wing's darker sections. The larger creatures' bodies fluffed as they keened, the sound closer to a whine than a bird call. Sylvie closed her gaping mouth and clung to Kerensa as they took a dissecting path from Elias. Kian and Hex followed closely behind.

They didn't speak, but with one glance in Hex's direction, she knew what to do. Her sense of smell wasn't as good as his, but with all the surrounding nature, her fae sight could show her something. The soil held memory, and if she could find tracks, she could lead them to the shifters.

With rising excitement, she tuned into her fae sight, inhaling sharply when it barely stretched beyond where her soles touched the dirt. "Shit."

"What?" Hex whispered, coming to her side in an instant.

She shook her head. "It's not about them. My fae sight is so weak here."

"It's some kind of warding," Kerensa murmured. "Keep trying."

"I will."

They spent what felt like hours discreetly searching the space for any sign of the shifters, sitting and milling in between pacing to avoid suspicion. Elias returned to them after the first hour, watching as they explored the area. Servants brought them lunch, which they ate on a blanket under a flowering tree. Sylvie pushed on her fae sight until her head ached.

By the time they returned to Elias's rooms, it was late afternoon, and Hayes soon summoned them for dinner. It started and ended the same way, with Hayes's welcome and request for Elias to visit the wider city, which he refused, and they all returned to the room for a fitful sleep.

Days turned to a week of the same ritual before Sylvie snapped, her brain throbbing from lack of sleep and overuse of her pathetic fae sight.

"I think we need to admit they aren't here," she said.

"They have to be," Hex snarled. "Their scent is everywhere."

The closest hint they had gotten was from a vent near the back corner of the aviary, but it led outside and the royal guards, dressed in the familiar brown scaled armour, had already made it clear they weren't permitted to wander.

"Have you seen a single one?" Kerensa said, stowing her sharpened dagger beneath her skirts.

Hex growled, storming to the bathroom, and slammed the door behind him.

"Testy, testy."

"Don't annoy him, Kerensa. We need to find them," Sylvie said, smoothing her skirts. "Take up Hayes's offer."

"No," Elias said instantly.

"Yes. Get him to take us all out of the tower and into the wider city, so we have a better chance." She crossed in front of Elias, placing her hand on his folded arm. "Please. We're running out of time."

After a long pause and a disdainful sigh, Elias hissed through his teeth. "Fine. Let's go."

* * *

"Have you reconsidered my proposal, brother?" Hayes asked, sucking a glob of blood from his teeth at his usual chair in the dining room.

"Yes. But we go together. All of us."

Sylvie's heart increased its pace, the anticipation of a real chance at finding her people—Hex's people … *Where did that thought come from?*

"Nonsense." Hayes's tone broke her free of her thoughts. "The mutt is far too delicate. Even the shifter wouldn't stand a chance."

Hex growled until Elias slammed his hand on the table and all movement ceased except for the flapping of Hayes's mouth. "Just look at them, brother. Surely you would not suggest exposing them to the townsfolk at this hour. Their blood—"

"Alright, enough." Elias stood, throwing his napkin on the table with a grunt.

Say yes. Go with him. Please. She sent every ounce of begging down the dormant bond she could when she noted his straightening spine. "Make this quick. I trust Willa will escort my remaining pets to my rooms."

"Certainly," Hayes replied, holding a hand out towards a darkened corner of the room. A dark-haired vampire scuttled forward, the same one who held the door for them each night, holding a pillow with a chestnut, oval-shaped stone atop it. Kian and Kerensa stood, following Elias to Hayes's side as he plucked the stone and cradled it in his palm. Sylvie didn't miss Kian's swallow or Kerensa's clenched jaw. Whatever it was, they'd seen it before. Sylvie slid her chair back to stand, but a firm grip circled her forearm. In the time she looked away,

Hex had moved to her side, his gaze holding a warning almost as firm as the grip on her arm.

"What?" she hissed, but the flash at her side was the answer. When she spun back to where Elias, Kian, and Kerensa had stood, they were gone, along with Hayes, leaving behind the grinning servant.

"What was that?" Sylvie demanded as she stood, pulling Hex along with her. They had portalled, but how? And why was the servant so smug?

"Don't worry," the servant crooned, his red eyes flashing. "The portal key only works within the realm. They'll be back shortly." He smiled, his canines lengthening as more glowing stares emerged from the corners of the candlelit space. Even Willa, the fair-haired vampire that dressed her companions each morning, was there, a lethal gleam in her stare.

"Back off," Hex snarled, pulling Sylvie back and pinning her between him and the table. *Bad idea.* She squirmed out of his grip and faced the table instead, kicking at the flash of red peeking from beneath the embroidered tablecloth and the taloned grip reaching for her ankle.

"This is a trap. We need to find them," she said.

"We need to get out of here," Hex countered, gripping her arm again and tugging her towards the door. Towards the hungry vampires.

"Let go of my arm!"

They closed in. The scent of copper and noxious air coiled in the space between them and the vampires. Flakes of blackened skin peeling around their collars and cuffs fluttered to the ground, rotting. Her heart dropped. These vampires weren't just hungry. They were starving. And every night they had watched their king gorge himself on blood while they served drink after drink. Platter after platter.

"Fine," Hex yelled as he released her arm but dropped his shoulder into her stomach, wrapped a vice grip around her thighs, and threw her over his shoulder.

"Bastard!" She could handle herself.

"I don't mind if you hate me," he grunted, holding her still as he slashed his free arm at a nearing vampire. "As long as you're safe." With that, he barged through the thinnest group of vampires, giving Sylvie enough time to punch one in the face when it bared its fangs towards her, and darted from the room. Once they were clear, he broke out in a run, jostling her so much her food threatened to come back up. She lifted herself, using his belt to stabilise, and yelped at the wall of feral vampires stalking after them.

"They're gaining!"

"Stop squirming then!"

She stilled, but shouted, "We would be faster if you put me down!"

Another glance revealed the desperation on the vampires' faces. Their bodies strained against one another and the glass walls as more joined the fray, the volume of creatures slowing them a fraction. When one vampire fell, the rest broke through the line and trampled their body as they wheezed and screamed. Sylvie squeezed her eyes shut. "Hurry."

Without their king around to control them, the vampires had dissolved into madness. Hopefully, Elias, Kian, and Kerensa were faring better with the bastard than without him.

"Hold on." Hex grunted, twisting down one last corner and through Elias's doors, dropping Sylvie on her feet and slamming the door behind him. He locked it and pressed his palms flat against it. "Grab something to block the door with."

She glanced at the chair Kerensa had slept on and was heading that way when the silence pricked her ears.

"They're gone."

"Just grab something—"

Sylvie rolled her eyes, dragging the chair across the floor, and stood back as Hex wedged it under the handle.

"I'm telling you, that's pointless."

He snapped at her, "They might be gone now, but there's no guarantee they won't be back. Maybe they're finding another way in as we speak."

She shrugged. "Then we take them."

"Take them?" he asked as she padded past him to the door, pressing her ear against the surface.

"You know ... fight."

Hex's furrowed brow turned to a scowl, his hazel-green eyes flashing gold as he grabbed her arm and pressed her back against the wall. "That is exactly why I didn't put you down."

"Back off."

But he only caged her in more, his heaving chest pressing into hers with every furious breath. "A part of being an alpha is knowing when to fight and when to save yourself for another day."

"Sounds like cowardice to me."

Hex snarled. "You have a desire to run towards danger, but I won't let you get yourself killed. I—I can't." His words choked off slightly at the end, but it only spurred Sylvie's rage.

"You can't? Like you couldn't stand to hear what Ace did to me? Like you couldn't look at me, so you ran? Running seems like all you're good for, *Alpha*." She sneered at the title.

His sharp inhale pressed them so close she could feel his racing heart thudding against her chest. "*That* is not why I said that."

She rolled her eyes, shoving him. "Now is not the time for this. We need to find the others."

Hex tilted his head back and groaned as if she'd eaten away the last of his patience. "Haven't you been listening at the dinners? The king wants fae wards. He needs help. Why would he hurt them?"

She hadn't been listening much, and he was probably right, but she wouldn't let him know that.

"Let go of me."

"I can't."

I can't. There were those words again. She hated them. But then Hex slid his hands down her shoulders, lacing his fingers with hers in a gentle motion, the suddenness completely disarming. Despite every fibre of her being that held onto rage at the shifter, she didn't move, or speak, or fight. The beast inside her, which had been rather quiet, stirred under Hex's touch.

"There's a part of me that says we shouldn't be mates."

Sylvie's beast whined as her heart fumbled over itself and squeezed. He really knew how to crush her.

"My pack needs me, and I've been neglecting my duty because of the bond."

Because of me.

His grip on her fingers tightened, and through the touch, she felt his slight tremor.

"I didn't leave you that night because I couldn't look at you. I left because I couldn't control my shift."

She swallowed.

"If I didn't go, my wolf would see Kian and Ambrose as a threat to you. I couldn't hurt you by hurting them." He hung his head. "The day we got the artefact and I realised what Ace did to you, I wanted to kill him. More than kill him. I would have destroyed him for you. Mutilated him. I should have known what was happening—should've listened to my gut when I heard the fear in your voice—"

His voice hitched before he continued, "Trusting him will haunt me forever. I—I hunted him for days until the heat came and drew me back to you." That night returned to her with aching clarity. The way the pain fled from his touch. Or how he let her take command. How the alpha had submitted to his mate.

His brow leaned into hers. "I wanted to lay his head at your feet, but I was too late. He just vanished. The blood trail ended, and I assumed he was taken here."

Gods. *Gods. Ace is here?* A flurry of emotions engulfed her until her heart beat so hard she could hear the blood rushing in her ears. And Hex's words. The devotion. The rage. It was everything she wanted to hear, but … but …

She closed her eyes and inhaled. "I—"

"I've made so many mistakes with you, and I can only blame my nature for some of it." His forehead lifted from hers as she opened her eyes and studied his face. The rawness to it. The pleading.

"And I don't deserve it, but I would beg for your forgiveness for the rest of my life if it meant you would stop looking at me like you hate me."

Time ceased. Nothing existed but Sylvie and the shifter baring his soul. Heart to heart, they stood, and even with the broken bond, she felt him. He was a part of her just as much as Kian and Elias. Fates or not, he was hers. The air fled from the room in a vacuum and Sylvie's lips parted in a soft inhale. "Rowan."

His own sharp inhale flooded his chest, the pressure of his body on hers filling her with longing.

"I don't—"

His gaze dropped like he was preparing for rejection. "Sylvie," he whispered, ragged, desperate. "Can't you feel how much I need you?"

Even though his hands shook where they were clasped in hers, he let her go, backing up two steps. She grew cold in an instant, her breath struggling to fill her lungs in his absence. How dare he say something so—so …

Beautiful.

"Rowan."

He looked up, their gazes locking at the command in her voice. She had never used his name, but it felt right on her lips. She didn't want to stop saying it.

Without breaking eye contact, she tucked her hair behind her ear, exposing her neck with the rapid flutter of her pulse on display.

There was no fear in the motion.

"Show me," she said.

THIRTY

Sylvie and her alpha mate stared each other down in Elias's bedchambers, the air sizzling in the two feet between them. His gaze dropped to her neck, and he swallowed as if waiting for her to take back the invitation to complete what she had started all those weeks ago. She wasn't going to.

"Don't tease me," he rasped.

Instead of answering, a smile curled her lips, and she pressed off the door, striding towards him and gripping his nape to draw him in.

"I thought you liked teasing," she whispered into his sternum, kissing the base of his throat where a spiral tattoo flared into broken lines, dipping beneath his scaled vest and up into his beard. Up close, the detailing stole her breath, the meaning behind them unknown but heart-stopping, regardless.

"What do these represent?" Every hushed word summoned waves of goosebumps across his skin, his head falling back as her touch undid him. His hands stayed at his sides, fingers shifting between human and animal, flexing and coiling.

His throat bobbed. "It's my history. My people. My pack. Ancestors—"

With every word, she kissed another spot on his neck, letting her fingers twirl in his hair as his words grew shakier, his thoughts clearly muddling.

"They're beautiful," she said.

He shivered, and she bit her lip to stop the smile. She shouldn't let the power go to her head, but gods, she loved the way she affected him.

"But I think they're missing something." That time, she grinned, dragging her fingers down the ties that secured his vest and unbinding each one, letting the fabric hit the floor with a heavy thud. His chest tattoos rippled with tension as she eyed the one patch of virgin skin left just for her. For them. There was a risk in her decision to do this. Elias had drilled that into her, but something Rowan's healer said returned to her with sudden clarity. *You need not fear the mark.* She hated siding with fate, but there had to be a reason for their connection. They wouldn't pair her with a male whose mark would kill her.

"Mark me, Rowan."

His groan forced her skin to flush and tingle, his hands finally moving to her hips, gripping tight enough to ache. "Say it again."

"Rowan." She popped the button of his pants next, never breaking eye contact, even as his irises flickered between the mesmerising hazel-green to gold. "Mark me."

A second-long pause had them nose to nose, breath filling each other's lungs until she didn't know where she began and he ended, their souls connecting with desperate longing, then their lips collided. And everything else. His hands gripped her ass, lifting her around his waist as she savoured him, finally giving in to the urges she had repressed.

He tasted divine. His rich, heady scent of clove and embers mingled on her tongue as she opened herself to him. Palming his cheek, she used her thumb to tug on his chin, forcing his mouth to open and let her tongue dance with his more deeply. His growl answered her dominance as she lost herself in his kiss—his touch. The other males in her life swarmed to the front of her consciousness and she sighed against Rowan's lips. They would be fine, pissed when they returned probably, but Kian had said from the beginning they would accept whatever choice she made. They would accept him, just like she had.

"Rowan," she rasped against his lips, "put me down."

He pulled back, chest heaving, and lowered her to the ground at her insistence, although painfully slow, like losing her touch hurt him.

She sighed at his falling expression, pinching his chin between her fingers. "Undress me."

His focus homed in on her again before he curled his fingers around her nape and tugged the laces, letting the fabric fall off her shoulders and pool at her feet. Nothing but a thin slip separated her bare flesh from his hungry stare, and she flicked each spaghetti strap until that too adorned the floor.

"Goddess," he breathed.

"Take off your pants."

He reached for the zipper.

"Slowly," she amended, loving his thick swallow and the slowing of his deft fingers. One inch at a time, he slid the pants off his hips, the deep V diving into a thicket of dark hair, then farther until the fabric hit the floor. There they stood before one another, bare, and she couldn't take her eyes off him.

When he broke her stare, she chided him with a tut. "Look at me."

With a swallow, he closed the space between them, guiding her to Elias's bed and laying her atop it, his gaze raking down her nakedness like she would slip through his fingers and disappear if he didn't drink his fill.

She did the same, a memory flashing of a time when their roles were reversed. When he asked her a question she'd hated the answer to. His weight had crushed her bruised ribs as she'd tried to escape him outside the cells. Back then the insinuation of his question infuriated her, but now it flamed another heat, right between her thighs.

"Rowan?"

"Mhmm?"

"I want you to beg."

His expression flickered as the memory returned to him too, and a slow smile settled on his lips.

"I want you to beg me to let you inside me," she said, shifting her hips until his cock brushed the wet flesh of her pussy. "Beg to mark my flesh. To make me yours."

His breathing grew shaky, the twitching of his bobbing length revealing how quickly his control was slipping.

"Please," he started, rolling his hips once. "Please let me fuck you, Sylvie. You are a goddess." Her stomach fluttered at his tone, and she ran her fingers over his tattoos, grounding herself to him. To the stories in his skin that had brought him to her. "Let me be yours forever and I will never stop worshipping you. Let me show you I belong to you. I am yours."

Heat lanced through her body, forcing her back to arch, breasts pressing into his chest. "You're mine," she echoed. "And I am yours, Rowan." She dug her fingers into his ass and pulled him inside her as they both groaned. He rocked his hips, filling her, and she met him thrust for thrust with movement of her own, crying out at the delicious pressure of him within her walls. Mouth dipping to her neck, Rowan kissed the spot where his teeth would claim her, warning nips driving her closer and closer to bliss.

"Yes. Do it." She sensed a faint hesitation from him and twined her fingers in his hair. "It's okay. I trust you."

His curse filled her with desire until nothing else remained but a shared climax so potent her eyes watered. She clenched again and again as he finished what she'd started. Finally. *Finally.* The sharpness of his canines splicing into her neck barely registered as she squeezed him in a vice grip, fiery heat blossoming across her torso to her heart. They pulled apart, both staring at the mark on her chest, a brilliant gold with a tiny vining coils connecting him to Elias and Kian. They were one. Gasping, she found her mark on his skin, filling the space his tattoos had left. Crimson and emerald. Identical to her other bonded, and just as deserved. He slid out of her and searched her face, eyes widening as she broke out in a sheen of sweat. The burn on her torso spread until she warmed inside and out.

"What's happening?" she said.

Rowan fetched her a pitcher and glass from the bedside table, filling it with water as she used her discarded clothes to dab the sweat.

"What does it feel like?" he asked.

She offered a weak smile, trying to diffuse some of his nerves she could feel through the bond, but he only grew paler.

"Warm," she replied, fanning her face. But it was far more than that. Power swirled in her veins and every sense amplified in the space, the beast within her skulking closer to the front of her consciousness. Or grew more corporeal somehow. Death became a distant memory as she smelled the faint sweetness of detergent still on the glass she sipped from, and the loamy minerals in the water itself. "I'm not gonna turn into a shifter now, am I?"

He blinked, disturbing a piece of dust the size of a pinprick on one of his lashes. It settled on his cheek as he took her empty glass and put it down on the side table.

"I—I don't think so. Turning requires a lot more blood loss and magic. Even I don't understand it completely." Stroking the sweat from her brow with his thumb, Rowan swallowed.

"But, as far as I know, there hasn't been a mateship like this before. The magic that binds you to me, to the others …" He traced each mark and sighed. "Well, I know little about that, too."

She brushed the dust from his cheek and wrinkled her brow. "And what do you know then?"

The green—moss and olive—of his irises sparkled in the starbursts within the hazel tones. "Well," he said, "I cannot claim you are mine if you don't wish it to be, but I know I love you. I think I loved you the moment you threw your heel at my face."

Laughter burst from her chest as she covered her face with her hands. When the fit finally passed, she took his hands and kissed each palm. Then his shoulder, to his jaw, before stopping in front of his nose and giving it a light peck.

To her shock, the feeling was mutual. It elated her and scared her all at once. A male she should've hated—her natural enemy—that she loved.

He must've read her expression, as a smile lit his face, followed by kissing in a clash of teeth and giggles until voices echoed from the hall and her previously dormant bonds hummed.

"Oh shit. Clothes!" she hissed, shoving Rowan off and scampering from the bed, exhaling hushed laughter as she hurriedly pulled her dress on. Rowan had only secured his pants when the door flew open, throwing the chair they had propped against it straight into him.

"Fuck!" he groaned.

Sylvie pressed her lips to stop the chuckle as Kian, Elias, and Kerensa entered, glancing around the room accusingly.

Kian smiled instantly, hiding it with a hand as Elias's gaze narrowed on her and the alpha dragging the chair back into its usual place.

"Vampires chased us," Sylvie bit out, clasping her hands behind her back and swaying from foot to foot. They all stood in silence, poised to speak, but no one did. Her marks itched.

Kerensa was the first to break, her eyes rolling. "Animals." She stormed straight to the bathroom and slammed the door, muttering low under her breath. Something about being gone for less than thirty minutes. A fraction of humour laced her tone, and Sylvie's eyes watered from restraining herself.

"You risked her life?" Elias said coldly, closing the bedroom door slowly, as if his grip on the handle was the only thing stopping him from launching himself at Rowan.

"I'm fine." She dashed between them. The warm pressure of Rowan's fingers on her hips brought a flush to her cheeks. She felt like a teenager again, caught by the head librarian for making out with a boy in the last row of the library stacks. "Look at me, Elias. I'm fine."

Kian tutted and brushed past Elias, giving him a look. "May I see?" he asked, pointing to her chest and offering a knowing grin. She obliged, dropping the unlaced dress off her shoulders and catching it just above her breasts. Kian traced his fingers over the interlinking marks, with Elias scowling over his shoulder and Rowan over hers.

"They're connected now," Elias muttered.

"Yeah."

Kian smoothed his expression, thumbing her neck where Rowan had bitten. "Any pain or lightheadedness?"

She shrugged. "I feel warm and—I don't know—heightened somehow."

Kian hummed, dipping his head to kiss her, and glanced over his shoulder at Elias. "She's fine. If she were to have any adverse effects, it would've happened by now. Her neck is healed and there are no signs of infection. No venom trails. So relax."

Elias's scowl lingered as Kian nodded towards Rowan. "Welcome to the family."

Sylvie snorted, catching Kian's wink, and shuffled before her vampire mate. "Are you mad?"

She kept her gaze down to hide the smile, and he sighed, lifting her chin with his forefinger. The furrow of his brow softened, and he worked his jaw. "I'm not mad."

"Good."

"I'm disappointed."

She scoffed, slapping her palm into his chest. "Oh, come on!"

But his lips curled as he sauntered towards the wardrobe, pulling a night gown free and placing it in her arms. "Get cleaned up."

She did, switching with Kerensa in the bathroom as the fae female groaned about the state of her sleeping arrangements. The chair was scuffed and one arm cracked from the force of the door throwing it into her mate.

Rowan's voice carried through both rooms, his question forcing hairs to rise on Sylvie's arms. "What did you find out?"

Kerensa laughed once, her tone turning dark. Sylvie had suspected it, but the answer filled her with unease all the same. "That they're fucked."

Sylvie padded from the room, drying her hair with a towel as Elias elaborated.

"Revenants. They're organising, orchestrating attacks on the city in waves. The born vampires have resorted to day walking and hiding in the night."

A chilling shriek filled the night air, piercing the room through the barred window opening, like his words had summoned them from the darkness.

They stood in uneasy silence as the creatures screamed and hissed, their movements far too close. Inside the city walls.

"Elias?" she whispered, but he was already there, pulling her towards his bed.

"Get in," he murmured, gesturing to the group. Sylvie climbed in first, followed by Kian, then Rowan on her opposite side. Between them, she started sweating from their body heat and kicked off the blankets.

"You too, Ren," Elias said, jutting his head towards the mattress. Sylvie smiled at the casual nickname as Kerensa shook her head vehemently.

"I'll take my chances."

The screeches outside garbled, then merged into a single low keen. Shivers spread across Sylvie's skin even as she melted between her hot-blooded males.

"They will scent you," Elias said then, a seriousness in his tone she hadn't heard before. Fear.

The heat quickly grew too much, and she scrambled over Kian on shaking limbs, nudging him to Rowan's side and snatching a few pillows, creating a wall beside her. "Here, get in. I promise no touching."

Kerensa stared at the bed, scowled, then stormed over, climbing in and building the pillow wall higher.

"Good," Elias said then, plucking one of the purple light orbs off the bedpost and climbing in between Kian and Sylvie. He handed it to Sylvie before pressing a button behind the headboard. Silver panels slid down from a hidden compartment above the canopy, slamming into the floor with a solid thunk on all sides. The sudden ceiling-to-floor containment startled each of them. As did the darkness. While the orb gave off a cool lilac glow, the metal walls sucked out the light and dampened the sound.

"I thought vampires sleeping in coffins was a human-made construct," Rowan said, nestling down at Kian's side.

Elias gave him a withering look before lying beside Sylvie and pulling her into his cool frame. "Hayes added these in every room after our parents were killed." He took the orb and hung it over the headboard as she curled into him with a sigh.

"Get some rest," he said. "By morning, we can come up with a better plan to find the shifters."

Rowan hummed his agreement. Besides the muted cacophony of monsters outside, she could almost pretend everything was normal—if having three males you were irrevocably in love with and your sister-in-law all together in a giant bed was normal.

"Night, everybody," Sylvie whispered, her marks humming with love at their responses. Even Kerensa managed a grunt. It would be fine. The revenants wouldn't get in, and tomorrow they would make a plan and find the shifters in no time.

THIRTY-ONE

Bear shifters pawed through the creeping plants, tearing deformed heads from bodies, the barbed collars on their necks laced with nightbane their only concern. One spun as a monster latched on to its spine, biting its rump with needled teeth.

A tiger leapt next, catching a creature seven feet in the air before crushing its windpipe with blood-drenched canines. How many more could there be? They seemed to be growing smarter, hiding.

Fourteen lions hunted in the wastelands, chasing the scent of a wounded monster. Yes, the bite would eventually take it down, but any failures, any more leech deaths, could mean another one of them becoming food.

Rogue wolves stalked a creature outside the city walls. This one had been elusive for weeks, killing a half dozen leeches, the tattered navy dress still hanging off its deformed frame. They were organising themselves. Packs of them. They were hunting—

* * *

Sylvie woke, eyes bulging and stomach churning at the remnants of the dream still darting through her brain. Her males shot upright beside her with sleepy stares of alarm, while Elias immediately searched for breaches in the silver tomb.

"What?" Kerensa groaned, her leg strewn over the pillow wall slowly retreating into her self-imposed boundary line.

Sylvie shook her head, closing her eyes and breathing until the waves of nausea subsided. If it wasn't dawn yet, vomit encased in silver walls would not be fun.

"Princess?" Intuition stifled Kian's tone, and she squashed it with a firm headshake.

"Just a dream."

When she opened her eyes, everyone was sitting and Kian had folded his arms, his dubious look catching Rowan's attention.

The shifter peered between them both. "What? What's wrong?"

She dived back into the pillows, not glancing at anyone. "Can't we just talk about it in the morning?" she mumbled into the mattress.

"Sylvie has prophetic dreams and I won't let her dismiss them. What did you see?"

With a groan, she rolled onto her back, staring at the canopy ceiling. "I was looking through their eyes." As she let her head fall to the side, Rowan caught her gaze. He edged nearer, sitting by her legs, enthralled.

"They were hunting the revenants for the vampires. I knew if I failed—if they failed, I'd become food," she said.

"Now we know why the vampires are taking them," Kian said, pulling the duvet up as Sylvie's skin broke out in gooseflesh.

"They wore silver collars with poison in them. Some kind of mechanism as a failsafe, I imagine," she said, adding, "but it was just a dream, remember?"

"It's more than we had before," Rowan said, running a palm atop her shin.

"We need to explore the city," she said, and to her relief, Elias nodded.

"Is that what your *dreams* are telling you, Hart?" Kerensa said, sarcasm pouring over the pillow wall between them. The gentle teasing eased a fraction of Sylvie's nerves and she hummed back, knocking the pillows down with a lazy fist.

"Shut up before I tell my protective males you like to cuddle in your sleep."

* * *

"You'll need to keep up the act of obedient pet," Elias said quietly after catching her giving Rowan a morning kiss. She sighed, smoothing her dress and bumping into him lightly.

"I know that, grumpy."

"Grumpy?"

"That's what I said—" Before she could add another new pet name for her vampire, he hoisted her into his arms until they were eye to eye.

"I'm keeping you safe, my little brat. I barely succeeded in convincing Hayes you all should visit the morning markets. Don't test me."

A blush erupted across her cheeks when Rowan's chuckle reached her from the bathroom.

"And if I do?" she demanded.

Kerensa's words were like a bucket of ice over them both. "What did I tell you when we got here? Keep it away from me."

Elias's cheek muscle jumped as if restraining a smile, and he returned Sylvie to the floor as they embarked on the long walk to the aviary.

Hayes greeted them at the aviary door, his sweeping gesture falling short as he took in Elias's appearance.

"Welcome, brother—my, you look ghastly. When did you last feed?" With that proclamation, Sylvie's act of demure pet fled, and she stared up at Elias's face. He had seemed fine that morning, perhaps a fraction paler and colder, but not "ghastly."

"I'm fine," Elias grumbled while Kian tried to tug Sylvie back into line with a strangling grip on her dress. She dropped her gaze when Hayes's attention burned into her, but stayed at Elias's side. He needed to be at full strength to get through the next week and the return portal home. He needed to feed.

"Forgive me, Master, for not noticing sooner," she rasped, tilting her head to expose the unscarred side of her face. "Please."

Hayes hummed as Elias curled his icy hand around her nape, holding her still while her mate bonds thrummed with fear.

"Intriguing. You let them offer themselves? I always thought of you as a taker, brother. Maybe I should teach you how to handle your pets properly."

Elias lifted her in his arms like he had in his room, a growl roiling from his lips. "She's mine."

Instead of tearing into her neck like she assumed, he captured her wrist, lifting it to his mouth and pressing his lips there in a silent kiss before sinking his teeth into her skin. She hissed at the initial sting, though it dulled as he pulled blood from her in even swallows. How much was too much? Already a lightness swarmed her body, and her vision warped. Would he know when to stop? Could he stop? The look of reckless abandon on his face seemed to state otherwise. She sighed, leaning into him as the scent of copper laced with something nauseatingly sweet overcame her. Was that what they were always going on about? Her blood smelled like Evergreen's flower gardens, intoxicating and wild.

A distant clattering of metal shocked her to alertness, and Elias pulled back, detaching his fangs from her as clarity returned to his expression.

She applied pressure to the two small pricks and slumped into him, noting the subtle thumb stroking across her back as Hayes spoke.

"Really, brother, it isn't like you not to share. She's frenzied the servants."

Elias held her tighter. "I never shared. You just took."

Sylvie glanced up as Hayes blew air from his lips and two royal guards dragged an unfamiliar servant from the aviary, head sagging on her shoulders. "Semantics."

Hayes didn't look towards the servant getting dragged away or the four royal guards marching towards them as he brought his hands together. "Well, follow me."

The winding path through the aviary led to a door of frosted glass four inches thick with a silver frame.

"Our people will be wary of all your strange guests, brother. And hungry. Let's save feeding off that little mutt until we return, shall we?"

Elias scowled his direction but said nothing as he nudged Sylvie between Kian and Rowan. Kerensa muttered a warding in High Fae and followed close behind as the royal guards strained to push open the doors. It wasn't until she spotted the pockmarked, crispy vampire wedged against the partially opened doors that she understood why. Its eyes had popped inside the sockets, and black liquid had bubbled from the orifices and stained the hands that curled under its chin. The arms and fingers were far too long, reminding her of the hybrids in Ilfaem, not the humanoid creatures they'd woken in the turned quarters. And the smell. Without the seal of the glass, wafts of garbage and baked shit assaulted them long after they scurried past into the city streets beyond.

Hayes's steps crunched along a shimmering path that looked suspiciously close to diamonds. "The less time we linger in the stench of that turned, the better. Dispose of it, Horuk."

"Yes, My King."

Sylvie refrained from glancing back. There was no way in Hel that thing was *just* a turned vampire.

"Stay close," Hayes said. Three royal guards accompanied them. The fourth, Horuk, stayed behind to clean up the dead as the rest flanked Hayes, keeping their gazes fixed ahead. Only once did Sylvie catch one of them glancing at Elias with a look in his eyes she couldn't quite place.

The path led through a stone arch and over a footbridge that hovered twelve feet above a rushing stream, the water a ruddy brown with streaks of black and red. Sylvie tried not to think of what might contribute to the colour when the high rises of the city stole her breath. Apartments upon apartments, towers and buildings that blotted out the lilac sun. It was so similar to Sterling. She shuddered. Through the shrouded windows, shadows watched, glows of red flashing, then blinking out of sight again.

A bell tolled ahead where the apartments opened into a flat expanse of paved ground, and the city came alive with chatter, hammering, clanging pots, and squeaking wheels. Before their eyes, life breathed into the realm.

The paved area bustled with people—vampires—with stalls, carts, and tables covered in poultices, trinkets, bloodred vials, parasols, and patchwork linens.

"Oh, blessed Fates—"

"It's the king!"

"Hush!"

Hayes raised his hands, nodding as he guided the group through the layers of vampires. Up close, the frailness of their bodies was clear, their veins dark and skin paper thin. They were in a worse state than Hayes's servants.

"We are simply here as customers," he said. "You may treat us as such."

Their skittish glances, sliding from the king to his brother, drew a low grunt from Hayes. "I assume most of you remember my brother?" Accusation dominated the sentence.

A few brave vampires nodded, but the rest dropped to their knees, heads bowed. "Continue on your way, then." Hayes waved them on and rounded to the group. "Explore if you wish. I will be back to collect you to the north of the square in an hour." With that, he disappeared into the crowd like a wraith, guards close behind, and Sylvie swallowed the lump in her throat.

"Easy," Elias muttered, positioning himself at the front of everyone and digging a hand in his jacket pockets. The thimble-sized tokens he withdrew caught the eye of every nearby seller, and Sylvie accepted a handful, as did Kian, Rowan, and Kerensa.

Kian jostled Sylvie slightly before veering to a stall filled with fabrics and dyes. "How much?"

The shopkeeper's eyes bugged from his head. "Fae? Oh, uh … blood. A vial would do—"

Elias hissed, moving in a blink to drag Kian back to the safety of the group, his imposing form casting the entire stall in shadow.

"My—my liege! F-f-f-forgive me … I meant no offence."

"Do. Not. Touch. What. Is. Mine." Elias scanned the market, his wicked glare forcing everyone to bow their heads in submission. Even Sylvie suppressed the urge to avert her gaze. Instead, she moved to his side, subtly brushing her fingers against his and burying her smile when his pinkie hooked her index finger.

"Let's keep looking," she said.

He held the shopkeeper's gaze for a fraction longer before pulling Sylvie away, interlacing her fingers with Kian's.

"Once you've used up your tokens, return to me. I'm one call away."

Sylvie offered a faint smile and nodded, leaning into Rowan when Elias faded into the throng of market goers. She glanced Kerensa's way and scoffed at the look of utter disdain on her face.

"You coming?"

Kerensa scowled. "Yes. Hurry up and pick something. The sooner we spend these, the sooner we can leave."

Sylvie detached from Kian and Rowan. "I'm going with Kerensa. You two go see what you can find." They nodded and spread into the western stalls, scanning for the shifters while Sylvie and Kerensa took the eastern side.

Kerensa beelined through the maelstrom of frail bodies towards a carriage stocked with vials of iridescent liquids.

"Anti-desiccation, jikir root, hunger suppression. Any potion you can dream of, I have," a vampire purred from the open wing of her metal carriage. Her honeyed voice dripped over them, and Kerensa's scowl softened. She perused the elixirs as the vampire spun to face her, black hair cascading over her back. She revealed her fangs in a smile. Kerensa returned the sharp grin.

"Hello, pretties. You are the king's pets?"

Kerensa didn't answer, and the vampire's gaze shifted to Sylvie.

"Oh." Sylvie shook her head. "No. Elias's."

The female blinked slowly, her lips pressing into a downturned smile. "As I said."

Sylvie's newly enhanced hearing barely picked up the fleeting whisper, but when it did, she homed her attention in on the vampire. A treasonous sentiment. Even after all this time, Elias still had supporters in the Glass City. The vampire's eyes flashed a warning as she said, "What would you like to buy today?"

Kerensa leaned farther over the vials, brow lifting. "Do you have any flora occisor?"

"Ah. The deadly sort. Hmm. I recall a vial in the back inside my inhibitor solution." She reached over, her breasts almost brushing Kerensa's wandering fingers. "Why might you need it?"

Kerensa scoffed, throwing a sideways glance at Sylvie. "My stocks have been depleted."

The vampire nodded, pulling a tube filled with clear liquid and, within that, a smaller vial of pure white. The flora killer. She accepted all of Kerensa's token without question and slipped the potion into a small brown bag before handing it off, her focus shifting to Sylvie again.

"And you, child? Pick your poison."

Sylvie straightened, flicking her gaze over the vials. She gnawed on her lip before asking, "Do you have anything to help with sleeping?"

The vampire's attention pinned her to the spot, her head tilting and eyes sparkling. "In what manner? Are you looking for a deep rest, an instant one, or something more permanent?"

Sylvie's lips parted, her silence giving her brain time to conjure distinct possibilities that could be more useful than the selfish desire to not have prophetic dreams anymore. "Instant."

The vampire grinned, again flashing her bone-white fangs, and plucked two purple vials from a tiny hidden drawer compartment in the carriage. "This one," she said, rolling the duller-coloured vial in her fingers, "must be inhaled. Smoked or snorted will do. More so for recreational delights. While this one only needs a single drop on the tongue to do its job."

The shimmer in the second vial danced in the morning light as Sylvie peered between the options.

"How much for that one?" She pointed at the sparkling purple vial.

"Depends."

Kerensa clicked her tongue, but Sylvie spoke over her. "What do you want?"

"One drop."

Sylvie glanced over her shoulder the way Elias disappeared and sighed, shushing Kerensa's growing unease with a wave of her hand.

"Hurry," she said, shoving her arm towards the vampire. In less time than it took to blink, the end of a needle pricked her fingertip, the silver edge gleaming for a moment before returning to the females pocket. She swiped her finger across the bead of blood and ran it along her teeth and gums.

"I know that bloodline," she muttered, her eyes growing wide. "You should go, but if you are successful in your plans, come and find me. I have a message for you."

"You can't just tell me here?"

She bowed her head and began closing her carriage up. "Too many listening ears."

Kerensa grabbed the vial Sylvie paid for in blood, stowing it with the occisor in her dress pocket. "Let's go," Kerensa grunted, pulling her. But the vampire's last words breached the distance between them as they turned to leave, dousing her in ice.

"It's about your father," the female said. And then she was gone.

THIRTY-TWO

Sylvie settled on spending her tokens on a thick emerald cloak and gave the rest to a beggar, her mind still reeling about the mysterious vampire's knowledge of her birth father.

Kerensa had promptly told her to forget about it. That the likelihood she knew Sylvie's bloodline was next to impossible without magical affinity, and vampires didn't have that kind of power.

"What if she's like me?" she asked.

"I don't think anyone can claim that honour," Kerensa replied with a subdued smirk.

They found Elias brooding along an empty wall, and Sylvie walked straight into him. She smiled against his side, savouring the coolness through his shirt as he tucked her inside his cloak and held her.

"Where's Kian and Rowan?" she mumbled into his ribs, laughing softly at the twinge of movement he made away from her. Grumpy vampire prince was ticklish. Before she could trail her fingers down his sides and explore the newfound knowledge, Kian's voice drew her from her hiding spot. "Here, Princess. Let's go."

She uncurled from Elias's body and followed behind as they wove through the markets to the north edge. The stones gave way every dozen steps to solid silver grates in the ground, embellished with engravings similar to the tower floors. Each time they passed one, Sylvie's gaze lingered on the space. The beast that slumbered at the front of her mind awakened, its ears flickering as if picking up sound. Whatever it was, it was too low for Sylvie to hear, but the strange niggle grew.

They passed another and her beast cooed, rubbing its long back along the mental fortress she had created with a longing she never thought possible from the creature. Her steps slowed, but by the next grate, they reached Hayes. He tracked her movements for an unusually long time as she scuffed her feet over the grate and stone alike. She needed to get closer. Whatever was down there was calling her, but she had to be smart. If Hayes realised what she was doing too soon …

"Follow me," Hayes said, finally tearing his eyes away from her and turning on his heel.

She immediately searched ahead for the next grate, and then something to use as a distraction.

Her cloak was new. And long. The hem dragging along the floor could be the perfect source of trouble. She lagged behind Kian and caught Rowan's eye, giving the briefest headshake before flicking the cloak around her ankles and stumbling headlong with a yelp. To her relief, Rowan didn't save her, and Kian was just far enough away that his outstretched hand missed. She landed hard atop the grate, palms scraping along the rough slabs on either side until they stung. Then burned. She stared between her hands at the small holes hidden in the design, inhaling decay and animal scent. It was a tunnel. Maybe sewers or storm water, but the pull in her heart and mind grew. They were down there. They had to be.

"Ow." She whimpered for good measure as she stood and held her shaking hands aloft, pearls of blood beading in the cracks of her palms.

The dawning understanding on the staring faces of her bonded only held her attention for a moment before the silence of the markets behind her forced the hairs on her nape to rise. That and the rage growing on Hayes's face. Then dread on his guards'.

A collective inhale, then pained screams surrounded them before someone shoved her and they were running. She hoisted the cloak into her arms to stop it from truly tripping her and followed Elias as the guards ran behind them, screaming commands.

"Halt!"

"Stop, now!"

The sounds of cut-off words and squelching followed. Then slurping.

"Gods!"

"Just keep moving!" Kerensa shoved her again, muttering a ward as her feet slapped the crisp stones.

"Here!" Hayes waved them over to an open hatch nestled in the side of a building, his teeth bared and face a mask of fury aimed straight at Sylvie. He shoved Rowan and Kian down first, their bodies hurtling into darkness after two steep steps. Kerensa jumped down next while Elias scooped Sylvie into his arms, sensing her hesitation, and darted after the rest of the group. Hayes slammed the hatch shut behind them, plunging the freezing hole into darkness and locking them in with a sickening screech. The faint drips of water echoed around them as the desperate cries of the vampires became nothing but a distant nightmare.

The fizz of a flint strike catching a torch alight drew Sylvie's gaze towards Hayes once more, and she blinked against the fire's brightness.

"I should have let them drink her dry. Wretched bitch."

Elias lowered her to the ground and dragged a growling Rowan towards them before he could shift and rip the king's head off.

"Shut your fucking mouth, Hayes," Elias replied, giving Rowan's hand to Sylvie.

"Why? She's just a pet, isn't she? Your favourite clearly, but I could buy you a dozen more far prettier and less moronic."

She gnawed on the inside of her cheek to stop the words that flooded her mind as her blood boiled. *Fuck you.*

She bit hard enough to make her eyes water and hoped her sniffling and red eyes hid the way she wanted to kill him. His guards were all dead. Four to one was good odds. But Kian dropped a hand on her arm and shook his head. It wasn't the time. They needed to get back and then find the shifters before anything happened to the realm's king. Even if he deserved it. She looked around at the chamber, squinting at a darker arch dead ahead. Tunnels.

"They've tasted blood. They'll be insatiable now and the desiccation will only hasten, thanks to that clumsy little bloodwhore."

Elias's jaw clenched so hard she was certain he'd chip a tooth before he chewed out, "If only you hadn't turned every human left in this realm in your selfish desire for younglings, you would've had a source of nourishment beyond the dregs you scrounge from animals."

Sylvie swallowed a hiss. Animals. They were dancing a very fine line, and she was certain Hayes already knew exactly what they were doing. But why he hadn't done anything to stop them was anyone's guess.

"Shut your mouth. You don't know what we suffered when you fled." The torch in Hayes's hand sputtered and flared as he swung it towards the opening behind him and started walking.

He left space for Elias to answer, but neither male spoke again, and the echoing patter of their footsteps drowned out their breaths. As Sylvie's anger dulled to a low simmer, another sensation slid over her in soft waves. Rot and stagnant water overpowered the faint animal odour, but the beast within her started pacing. She fixed her gaze on the ground and listened. Listened. Listened. The beast rumbled low in its chest, the feline steps turning frantic.

Nothing. Besides the water droplets assaulting her mind like a knife piercing into the memories she had carefully stowed away, there was nothing. No talking, no screaming, not even the scurrying of rodents, or whatever creatures this realm had. But the lingering sensation remained. Then grew. On her mind's fringes, right out of the beast's reach, thoughts entered and swirled around the blankness. Thoughts that were not her own.

Help us.

She gasped, drawing everyone's gaze, but she waved them off.

"A bug," she breathed.

Once Hayes turned away, she caught her mates' glances, touching her ear with one brow raised. Elias shook his head once, understanding her question easily, while Rowan mimicked her movement, touching his own ear with a frown.

Kian hid a smile and shook his head too. They hadn't heard what she had.

Maybe it was all in her head.

Help us. We're here …

She straightened as a set of stairs materialised from the darkness and a gust of wind blew the torch in Hayes's hand to embers. The whispers returned, riding on the breeze as Hayes opened the door atop the stairs and gestured for them to enter. She lagged to the back of the line and gazed towards the gusting air. It had to lead outside. It must be how the shifters got out at night. But how could she get to them?

Hayes drank her in as she passed, his leering attention dampening the voices even as they cried one last time.

Don't leave us!

Then the door slammed shut and the connection died. They were in a kitchen space. Dusty and dark, with rotten cupboards and a centre island with chunks carved out of it. Hayes's hungry glare followed as she let herself scheme. She'd found her access to the tunnels. Now all she needed was to convince everyone about the means.

* * *

"No fucking way."

"I wasn't asking permission, Rowan."

Elias's clenched fists looked prepared to punch through solid silver as Sylvie relayed her idea in his room, rolling the tiny purple sleep-aid vial between her fingers.

"It's a good plan, with one amendment," Kerensa said, reclining in the corner seat. "I go with you."

"Fine."

Kian shook his head. "He won't fall for the seduction."

"No," Elias said, slamming his palm against the bed's canopy post. "He likes to break things, that's what he does. What he's always done."

"Then we let him get close enough to think he can break me, and we knock him out. The tunnels are right beside that fancy alcove with the view above the aviary. I just need to get him there and Kerensa and I could handle him."

Rowan looked at her hard, then away. It wasn't the safest plan, but it was all they had. With the next lunar event looming, they were running out of time.

"Unless you offer an alternative that gets all of us out alive, I'm doing this. Only I heard them, so it's safe to say only I can find them."

"You mind-linked?" Rowan said from the bed, leaning against the bedpost Elias had abused.

"I—I don't know," she replied. "What exactly is it?"

"Threads that link us—like a web. If I want to communicate, I focus on a single thread and send a thought down it, but it's blocked here."

Sylvie pressed her lips and shook her head slowly. "It didn't feel like that. Their voices just sort of appeared in my mind."

"Like with the Fates?" Kian asked, a mask of concern settling on his brow.

Shit. *Shit.*

"It was, wasn't it?"

She frowned. "I guess. Either way, I have to hope it leads me to the shifters. The Fates pushed Rowan and I together. There has to be a reason."

Elias ran a hand through his hair, disturbing the curls that brushed across his scowl. "I should tie you to this bed and find them myself."

"Eugh." Kerensa stormed past Kian and slumped into the broken armchair.

Elias's gaze flickered at the movement, jaw clenching. "The thought of his hands on you ..." He trailed off as his knuckles whitened. "You need to stop the pet act."

"Oh?"

"Nothing riles him up more than stubbornness."

She smirked. If it was a brat he wanted, she would provide.

Elias sighed at her look, but it was Rowan's curling lips that drew the full smile out of her. Kian crossed the space and cupped her chin. "Tell me more about your plan. You and Kerensa go first. Then what?"

She beamed up at him, clasping her hands together.

"Okay. Here's my idea."

* * *

"Open it, now!" Elias's violent fist thump shook the bedroom door on its hinges.

Sylvie steeled her breath, smiled wryly at Kian and Rowan poised on the bed, and ripped the door open before storming past Elias at breakneck speed. Hopefully, the servant was spying again. Willa—master of whispers. Sylvie's bare feet slapped across the floors, but before she could plummet off the top of the stairs, Elias's rough grip hoisted her up and over his built shoulder. The air whooshed from her lungs at the force, dampening the squeal when his slap across her ass cheek was far harder than expected.

"Ow!"

He spanked her again as he stormed back through the bedroom door and slammed it shut. Only then did he rub a soothing circle on the tortured spot.

"Did you have to spank me so hard?" Sylvie huffed.

He hummed as he lowered her onto his bed between her two bonded. "You shouldn't have slapped me at dinner."

She chuckled lightly, scurrying back behind Kian to avoid another smack, then rising to her knees and using her fated as a fae shield. "Hey. You told me I needed to act like a brat."

Kerensa clicked her tongue from the window seat but buried her nose in the book Elias had supplied about ancient vampire lore as he replied, "Even I have my limits." He snatched her wrist and plucked her from behind Kian like she was a ripened fruit, nipping at her neck as she wrapped her legs around him.

"Don't forget whose brat you are," he murmured lowly. Sylvie shuddered. It was not the time to be getting frisky. Soon, she'd be staring into the dead eyes of the vampire king, attempting to incapacitate him without alerting any guards. She detached herself from Elias and straightened.

"Are we ready for tomorrow?"

Days of feisty dinners, putting on shows in front of the servants, and irritable glances across the table were leading to that moment.

Kerensa hummed, closing her book with one hand, twirling a dagger with the other. "Ready when you are, Hart. You know what route to take?"

"Yeah. I got it."

Rowan came to Sylvie's side, palming her cheek. "Are you sure about this?"

"I'm gonna find them."

A muscle in his temple jumped as he nodded and placed a feathery light kiss on her cheek.

"Don't take any risks," he murmured into her hair as Kerensa cleared her throat.

"You need rest. All of you. After Hart and I get into the tunnels, you'll need to haul ass to catch up before someone alerts the guard. We won't wait." For Sylvie's plan to work, Hayes couldn't sense the males nearby. He'd never let his guard down if he thought she wasn't alone.

"We know," Kian replied, interlinking his fingers with Sylvie's. "And if anything delays us, we'll catch up."

He lay both their hands atop his chest where her mark thrummed, and her lips quirked. In completing the trio of marks on her chest, their link vibrated with a new awakening. Still duller than in Erus, but enough to track, like a hair-thin string of twine.

"We won't get delayed," Elias grumbled, unbuttoning his shirt and stalking to the bathroom. Delayed or not, the plan was in motion. With a grim smile, she climbed into Elias's bed for the last time to stare at the canopy for eight hours as marrow-eating monsters prowled outside.

THIRTY-THREE

Daybreak gifted silence to the realm, and Sylvie slunk towards the alcove by the kitchen with Kerensa ghosting behind her. The farewell with her bonded had brought lingering sensations of grief, but the goodbye kisses steadied her resolve. Nothing but trust poured from them. Fear, yes, but pride too.

The rosy gown she wore pooled around her slippers as she padded down the winding stairs. Servants sporadically darted past, some glancing her way but not registering her presence as Kerensa's weakened glamour settled around them. When Willa flitted down the hall, though, Kerensa dropped it, and the vampire glanced sharply at Sylvie as she rounded the last corner, sniffling and concealing the lower part of her face with a trembling hand. The act seemed to work, and Willa picked up her pace, disappearing quickly behind a slamming door.

Sylvie settled on the balcony overseeing the aviary while Kerensa nestled in a small, cushioned, hollow space nearby, invisible. Sylvie searched the empty alcove for a few moments. If she didn't know better, she could swear she was alone. She turned back to the aviary view. From above, the flying creatures didn't notice her as they dived around the space, perching on branches or screeching at intruders. Even the servants with bundles of food for them weren't safe from their snapping maws. Little monsters.

A whisper of wind caressed the curls brushing Sylvie's shoulders, and she softened her expression. It was time. The scent of him engulfed her before he spoke a word.

"Elias," she said, breaking the silence as she clasped the vial of sleep potion in her pocket. She sighed, giving him the opening.

"You speak my brother's name so freely. Do you have no respect for your master?"

She repressed the shudder that travelled up her limbs as she turned, keeping her face blank at the three guards flanking the vampire king. Four to two.

Not good odds.

"No, I—" She dropped her gaze to her feet. "I should go back to his rooms." If she could get closer, maybe she could use the knife Kerensa had strapped to her thigh. The dark, predatory eyes of Hayes's guards locked on her throat as she swallowed. They were starved. Hopefully, that meant it wouldn't take much to kill them. She winced. Incapacitate, not kill.

"Should you?"

She met his stare then, squinting at the lightness in his tone. The playfulness attempting to mask the cruelty. He shared Elias's face, but that was where the similarities ended.

"You are certainly brazen, pet," he spat the title. "Meeting my eyes like that. Who are you?" His hand launched at her throat, stopping the retort dead. "You certainly had Yasmina under your thrall at the markets. Unfortunate I had to kill her—treason and such."

Sylvie's eyes bugged as he lifted her off the ground, her empty hand clawing at her throat, the other desperately holding onto the vial. The knives attached to her hip would have to stay hidden if she wanted to continue playing the part.

"I must give her props for keeping the information about your father in her death." He lifted her until they were eye to eye, her lungs burning with the lack of air. Her strangled cries fell on deaf ears. Even Kerensa did nothing to help. Good. If she came out too soon, their plan would fail before it even began. And besides, Sylvie was no stranger to violence.

"So," Hayes continued, "now I must rely on your input. Who are you?"

He released her, the sound of her feet slapping the ground enough to force his lip to twitch. She staggered back for added effect and clutched her sternum. Couldn't show he hadn't ruffled her.

"I'll tell you," she answered low, sucking in a breath as she glanced over his shoulder. "But only you."

He huffed. "The guards stay."

"Please. It's important no one else knows. If they did—" She let the insinuation hang between them, not enough to give any answers, but enough to pique his interest. Hopefully.

"I trust them." Maybe not.

"Well, I don't. Why do you think Elias keeps me hidden?"

He leaned against the wall of the corridor, crossing his arms, the motion so human she could almost forget he wasn't a man.

"And if I just kill you?"

She exhaled a quick puff of air through her nose. "Then the secret dies with me."

Shallow breaths from the guards at Hayes's back sounded, then a rustle of fabric as he lifted his hand and gestured for them to leave. She tried so hard not to smile, to show the hand too soon, but the second the guards were out of sight, she bowed her head, nodding, a smirk tugging her lips upward.

As she looked up, Kerensa appeared over Hayes's shoulder, her forearm wrapping steadfastly around the vampire's throat. In the split second before his realisation kicked in, Sylvie punched his nose hard enough her knuckles sang and shoved the vial in his open mouth. He pursed to spit, and she drove her fist into his jaw in a violent uppercut, the act smashing glass and purple matter inside Hayes's mouth. Blood dribbled down his chin as she plucked a smooth round stone from his pocket—the portal key—and shouts exploded from the end of the corridor.

"Better luck next time," she crooned. Kerensa released the king as he dropped to his knees, hatred pouring from him, and then he fell to the side, unconscious, head cracking on the polished ground.

"Quickly." Sylvie kicked him one last time in the balls for luck and shoved Kerensa to the dilapidated kitchen door as the guards returned in droves. Not as covert as she had hoped, but fairly satisfying.

Kerensa warded the door behind them and threw a bag at Sylvie. "Change quick. It won't hold long."

Sylvie stripped the prim dress and pulled on pants and a flowy shirt, finishing it with the same scaled tactical wear the vampires wore. The shoes Elias had found were one size too big, but the thick socks he gave her along with them made them comfortable enough.

"Treason!"

"The king needs aid."

"Find blood. Hurry."

"Lock down the tower!"

Sylvie strapped two more knives to her thighs and nodded to Kerensa. "Ready."

"Good. Move it."

Together, they darted for the tunnel door, shoving it open and snatching the extinguished torch Hayes had placed against the steps. Sylvie held it still as Kerensa lit it with a strike of a match, its spitting hiss singeing a few eyelashes.

"Do you think the others will be okay?"

Kerensa nodded, descending farther into the darkness. "They'll need another way out, but they'll be fine. We'll meet up in the wastes."

The tunnel was as damp and gusty as Sylvie remembered, the occasional scuttling and chirrups of tiny creatures the only evidence of life. Minutes passed in drafty quiet as her nerves rose. The beast within her prickled with awareness, its yawning maw tilting to the right.

Show me the way, please. Where are the shifters?

Voices carried from behind them, and they increased their pace to a run down the endless tunnel.

Turn.

She dug her feet into the ground, almost sliding on slick goo, and pointed the torch to her left and right. Sure enough, the glistening walls gave way to a wide archway.

"This way."

"You sure about that, Hart?"

Hurry!

"Yes, I'm sure."

With a grunt, Kerensa followed behind her as they picked up the pace.

Here.

Sylvie tried not to think about the inflection of the voices in her mind and how she couldn't tell who or what they belonged to as she made another turn. Four more insistent demands later, and she found herself before an antechamber with a gloomy light filtering from a small doorway.

She signalled for Kerensa to put out the torch as a pair of red eyes scowled in the dark. Kerensa didn't wait. She pulled her dagger from its sheath and threw it at the vampire's head, where it sank deep into the glowing eye socket.

Alarmed whispers filled the much larger space, and behind thick silver bars that split the room in three sections stood dozens, if not hundreds, of shifters with wide eyes and ghostly pale skin. Their faces were indistinguishable behind layers of grime, and their bodies appeared to be in varying states of malnutrition underneath relatively tidy clothes. Sylvie swallowed her shock and darted to the fallen vampire, looking for keys, trying not to check for the one shifter that deserved this fate. She found them clipped onto the vampire's belt, tearing her arm back when he groaned and pawed at her. Kerensa finished the job as Sylvie fumbled through the key ring, ignoring the squelch of blood and snapping tendons.

"It's that one," a soft voice spoke, pointing a mud-encrusted nail at a simple gold key. Sylvie glanced up at its owner and smiled until she noticed the blood-smeared collar flashing silver around her neck. Just like in her dream.

"Thank you." Sylvie slid the key home and with one twist, the lock disengaged. The door swung open. "Let's get you out of here."

"Who are you?" another shifter asked. His wary, dark eyes flitted across her face.

She glanced over her shoulder at Kerensa and gestured to their necks. "Once we get those off you and escape, I'll tell you everything. For now, all that matters is Alpha Rowan sent me and we're gonna take you home."

Kerensa raised her hand towards the collars and spoke in High Fae, giving Sylvie time to scan the crowd again as they fell to the ground in muted clinks.

"Are you looking for someone?" the first shifter asked, her smile revealing a wisdom that reminded her of the elders.

Sylvie swallowed, glanced once more behind her, and dropped her voice to a whisper. "Ace."

The shifter hummed thoughtfully and shook her head. "Gone. A woman came to speak with him and a few other rogues and they never returned."

"A woman?" If Hayes had a partner, he certainly omitted the fact at the dinners.

The shifter shrugged. "The richer leeches have unusual tastes and the funds to acquire them."

Sylvie nodded once as Kerensa returned, swiping her hands on her thighs. "It's done. Let's get out of here."

The idle shifters stood and stretched, a few much older pack members needing more help than others as Sylvie led them from the cells.

"You take the front. I'll be at the back," she said quietly to Kerensa, waiting for the weaker shifters hobbling from the cell. Not one ounce of fat coated their wiry bodies. Many had visible bones through their loose clothing.

She ducked under the arm of an elder, and her new acquaintance did the same.

"I'm Grace," she said, kissing the older shifters' temple. "And this is Kui."

"Sylvie."

They jogged as one unit, their motions almost silent, the action clearly familiar to the shifters. Even Kui kept up with a bit of stability from Sylvie and Grace.

Light swarmed the tunnel, and in an instant, the entire pack was outside the city walls. Cracking salt flats and dust stretched between them and the horizon, and Grace blinked again and again, her irises almost milky. The shifters squinted, hands over their eyes at the brightness of Argyncia's sun.

"I haven't seen daylight in years," Grace said, a mix of awe and fear in her voice. "Where are all the guards?"

Sylvie squinted against the light too, the memory of Hayes at her feet replaying in her mind. She sneered. "With their king, probably. Hold on to each other, okay? We need to run."

They moved as one, breathing in sync and stepping with assured footfalls even as many shifters moved with half-closed or covered eyes.

"Where are we headed?" Grace asked.

"As far away from the city as we can get before the moon rises, then we'll portal out of here."

"We can't be out here at nightfall. We're completely exposed."

"The falls," Kui rasped.

Grace sighed but bowed her head, then addressed Sylvie again, "We'll show you the way."

"Thank you."

They jogged on, and Sylvie glanced back to the city, its ancient walls staring with judgement. Stony silence emanated from the streets and the market square as her thoughts lingered on the vampire that had a message about her birth father.

Yasmina. Dead. Another crime the vampire king would atone for. But she had already resigned herself to never knowing her parents. Nothing had changed. And then there was her bonded, nowhere to be seen. The single tether that stretched between each of them thinned unbearably, but she let the worry fade. They had promised they would find her. She turned back to the flittering mirage on the horizon and steeled her resolve. Time to go home.

THIRTY-FOUR

Scorching sunbeams burned the shifters' backs as they jogged across the endless wastelands, not a single vampire in sight. Sylvie's anxiety brewed in her gut as the tether between her and her males strained, as if one more step would snap them. She rubbed the marks in slow circles before having to lift the elder Kui's arm higher over her shoulders as she stumbled yet again on the cracked ground.

"I've got you," Sylvie wheezed. The older shifter bore most of her own weight, but her balance teetered more the farther they ran from the city walls.

"Only a few more hours, I think," Grace said with a grunt, her posture stooping. "Then we can rest."

Sylvie's stomach cramped, but she nodded. The shifters continued with a stoic grace that she envied, despite looking like they hadn't enjoyed a filling meal in a decade. Perhaps some hadn't. She silently cursed her growling belly.

"Thank you for trusting me," she said, adjusting her grip again. "I know I probably wasn't who you were expecting."

"After this long, you learn not to expect anything, yet be prepared for everything," Grace replied. "Where is Alpha Rowan, anyway? They took me when he was still a boy."

Sylvie smiled faintly. "He's here. Well—he got held up, but he'll be here." She rubbed her chest again when her marks heated.

"Mates," Kui breathed, her milky gaze following the path of Sylvie's hand.

Grace stalled, as did the shifters ahead of them, their heads swivelling like they operated with a hive mind.

"Impossible. You're not a shifter."

"There haven't been mates in so long."

"Who are you?"

The voices blurred into a hum of sound, the dirty faces of a hundred shifters staring down at her as the beast within shifted uncertainly.

"He's my mate," she replied softly, straightening under the narrowing stares, the gasps and gaping mouths. "But so is the fae prince."

Grace frowned. "What?"

"And the true king of the vampires." Sylvie's lips thinned into a grimace. It sounded kind of stupid when she said it out loud.

Kui hummed as the other shifters descended into chaos. Liar, polygamist, and cheat got passed around a fair bit before Kerensa appeared between the crowd, her brow set in a hard scowl.

"What is the holdup? We don't have time to stand around, Hart."

"I told them about my bonded."

"Impeccable timing." The sarcasm was palpable. "We're still out in the open. Do you want the guard to catch us like rats out here?"

"They will not come," Kui's voice held a strength as she addressed them. "Living like humans has aged and weakened them. They would not risk travelling this far, not with dusk approaching."

Sylvie focused her attention on the elder, despite the continual murmurings.

"She is his mate. I can sense the alpha within her. We will not waste precious daylight squabbling over the possibility of her existence. If fate has intervened on our behalf this once, then so be it." The voices quieted, and the shifters milled as Kui smiled at her through crinkling eyes. "Take us home, dear one."

Reluctantly, the shifters turned away, resuming their trek towards the horizon.

"Thank you," Sylvie whispered, the weight of Kui's arm across her shoulder now far easier to bear.

The hours dragged. Sylvie's legs shook with exhaustion, her muscles flickering, preparing to seize. Rock mounds covered in spindly gorse gradually rose around them on either side as the sky turned a murky grey.

"It's just around that rock," Grace said, wiping sweat from her upper lip. Sylvie followed her gaze, looking ahead of the dozens of bodies to the monolith splitting the path, rivulets of water arcing around it and rejoining into one stream that careened past on their right side. The shifters took turns taking sips of the crystal waters and she followed soon after, gently leaning Kui against the imposing rock. High above them on either side, giant ochre walls filled with cracks and small caves wrapped around the space, reminiscent of the canyons in the Iron Peaks of Erus. A bowl. *Or a barrel.*

Once the bone-cold waters trickled down her throat, she followed the leading shifters deeper into the canyon, the sight of the roaring falls knocking her back, awestruck. It was an oasis in a barren desert, the waterfall blanketing the overhanging basalt cliff face.

"How did you know this was out here?" she asked, returning to Kui.

"Before the collars, this was where we escaped to."

"Until we ran out of food," Grace said, taking Kui's hand. "They fed us well enough, healed our sick, and clothed us. It wasn't luxurious, but it could have been worse." Grace's words, followed by a wry smile, took Sylvie aback. How she could rationalise being taken and finding positives within such a terrible transgression shook her. It was so far from what she was used to. So pure it tightened her throat. These were the creatures every other species turned their noses up at. Kian's mother certainly thought their stories weren't worth knowing, but she was wrong. How many other things were the fae wrong about when it came to the shifters? And Sagehill? What if everything about them was a lie?

In contemplative silence, Sylvie and Grace walked Kui to a formation of flat rocks and helped her sit as the rest of the shifters filled the area, some forced to wade through the bulging waters of the falls to find a place to recline.

The hairs on Sylvie's neck stood, the beast within bristling, but her scans of danger provided nothing. Now all they could do was wait for her bonded and hope they made it before the moon was in position.

Kerensa stepped over and met her expression with a nod. "I'll start a perimeter ward."

"No." Sylvie scanned the cliffs around her once more. "Save your strength for getting all of us out of here."

"And if something finds us before that?"

They shared a long look. It was a possibility, but one they couldn't linger on. Her bonded would find them first, and every shifter in the canyon would be free. She couldn't stand any other option—wouldn't.

"Hey," a croaking voice called from a patch of thistly plants by the water. "Josiyan berries."

"Those are tiny, Setka."

"I can see that," Setka, a curly haired, dark-eyed shifter growled back. Beneath the muck, his bronze skin peeked out and radiated warmth. "But there used to be food here. Maybe there's more."

Grace smiled and shook her head. "Always dreaming of food." She spoke just low enough for Sylvie to catch. But Sylvie didn't scoff at Setka's sentiment. She eyed the bush with tiny, ruby-coloured berries and wove through the sitting shifters.

Once she reached the male, she paused at his side, tapping into her fae sight gently. Unlike within the city, the power swarmed into focus, saturating her vision with glorious hues of bioluminescent light. The beams almost blinded her as the power settled in her veins, stronger than ever before. Her body relaxed, a joy heating her skin. She didn't know what changed, but she'd never look a gift horse in the mouth.

"So these are edible, huh?"

"They are, but only at five times the size," Setka said, glancing at her from the corner of his eyes. The shifters were wary, and it was fine. If she had to prove her worth, then so be it.

"What about ten times?" she asked with a wink as she lowered onto her knees and palmed the soil around the plant's base.

She vaguely heard Setka's confused reply, "Never seen 'em that big," as she tuned out of the world and into nature. This time she prepared for the beams of light and softened her gaze, using her newly trained internal strength to surge power into the plant. It shimmied, and the berries swelled before her eyes. Air and blood whooshed through her ears and the faint, metallic scent of blood stained her tongue, but her nose didn't bleed, nor did her head ache. As she pulled back with melon-sized berries rolling before her, satisfaction almost made her feel drunk.

She plucked one and held it to Setka. "For you. "

He took it with trembling hands, but his expression wasn't fearful. Tears rolled down his cheeks as he bit into the supple flesh and handed it off to the nearest shifter to share.

When he turned back to her, he kept his gaze lowered. "Blessings of Ira to you, Alpha."

She swallowed, a wave of unfamiliar emotion filling her chest. Her beast seemed to swell with pride, strutting back and forth with the title.

"It's my pleasure." She slowly dipped her fingers beneath this face, and when he didn't shrink away, she lifted his chin until he met her eyes again. "Please, call me Sylvie."

The inner beast's neck arched, head tilting and lips curling back as if saying, *"What, bitch?"*

She exhaled a faint laugh between her teeth and glanced beyond Setka, where Kerensa stood watching. They locked gazes, and Kerensa lifted both hands to her scalp like she was handling an invisible crown, offering it to her with a subtle forward tip of her hands.

Sylvie bit the inside of her cheek and gave a gesture of her own, involving her longest finger. Kerensa's head tilted back as she laughed, the sharp points of her teeth catching the last of the sunlight as she walked away. Sylvie smiled and settled by the water's edge, her head facing the entrance, waiting for her bonded. That was all she could do.

* * *

Sylvie faded between alertness and daydreaming, her gaze never leaving the path into the canyon. Shifters huddled around her, staving off the chill since Kui had vehemently forbade fire. A silvery light haloed the clifftops of the basin as the moon rose and cast them all in an eerie grey hue.

"Come on," she mouthed silently. Her marks warmed, but nothing suggested her bonded were any closer. They were running out of time. A few hours they could manage, but another month here with little food and in revenant territory would likely lead to needless death. They needed Kian to help open the portal. She needed her males with her and safe.

"Hurry."

A shuffle from beyond the basin had her ears pricking, heart swelling with hope. The shifters' heads swivelled towards the sound as it grew clearer. Over the echo of rushing waters, the dragging of feet through cracking earth was distinct. It wasn't her bonded. She stood as Kui's whisper spread like wildfire.

"They're here."

"Where?" Not what. Sylvie knew exactly what was coming. She followed Kui's opaque gaze to the top of the cliffs, where the rocks and shrubbery trembled, undulating under an absent wind. Time suspended as memories of hybrids scaling the hedgerows in the Stone Court flared in her mind. Lesser demon and fae halfling creatures. They'd coveted her dryad blood, hunting her by sight and scent. Skeletal deformities that clawed themselves from Hel's depths through the gaps Kian's portalling had left behind. But there were no demons here, and the top of the cliff had no shrubs. It was—

Sylvie's lungs squeezed in her chest. *No.* It was worse than she ever imagined.

Revenants. Hundreds of them.

Sylvie shook, her vision stalling on the leathery bodies dragging their way down the cliff, in and out of the caves and squeezing through the cracks.

"Get in the water," she breathed. No one moved. Despite the revenants' blindness, they navigated easily towards the basin, which reeked of flesh, pumping shifter blood, and burning body heat.

"In the water, now," she hissed, pushing the nearest shifters towards the edge. "Behind the falls."

Slowly, they moved, their motions jerky and breathing laboured at the sight of so many creatures clawing themselves closer to a feast. She caught Kerensa's attention, who nodded at Sylvie's command, guiding the shifters into the deeper waters and under the curtain of the falls.

Unlike in the city, these revenants moved in total silence. Beyond the rustle of their bodies shuffling across sand and rock, their skin stretched so tightly over bone, there was a void of sound. Sylvie dragged her eyes from them and guided the rest of the shifters into the water, threading Kui's arm over Grace once more before they waded in too. The waterfall consumed everyone, and even with the revenants almost breathing down her neck, awe filled her at the scope of its size. Then panic. *I'm okay. He can't hurt me here. He's gone.*

"It's shallow, Hart. Walk to me." Kerensa appeared from the falls, body drenched and hand reaching. Sylvie glanced around. She was the last one. She could do this. Twenty steps and she'd be safe. She started with ten. Ten steps and she was waist-deep before the terror flooded every sense, flashbacks pushing themselves through the gaps in her defences. Her beast fought bravely against them, but she stalled, heart beating so fast she could feel its vibrations in the water.

"He's not here," Kerensa said. "Move!"

The irritation mingling with concern was enough to draw her back into herself, just enough. "I'm coming."

"A little faster would be good."

She waded, keeping her hands above the rising froth, and barely kept a grasp on her breathing as they neared the falls together.

"I've got you," Kerensa said, taking her wrist. Sylvie slid her hand into the other female's and squeezed.

"I'm okay." The rushing waters deafened her, but before it could beat down on her head, half a dozen arms shot out, creating a doorway to duck through. The mist still slicked her skin, but her mental fortress kept the memories of Ace at bay as she slipped inside.

"Thank you," she panted, gulping down lungfuls of air as they let their arms drop, the waterfall blanketing them again. The water reached her sternum, and she searched in the near pitch dark for Kui. The elder was so much shorter than her, and if Grace grew too tired …

"Kui?"

"She's here," Grace said a few feet away, and Sylvie came to her side, leaning her back against the rough basalt rock. A shrill keening cry pierced the falls, and the shifters collectively held their breath. A responding call followed, then a cacophony of shrieks so similar to the nights in Elias's chambers that her skin chilled. They were going to find them.

"I'm sorry," she whispered. Her fists clenched as she searched with her fae sight for anything to protect them with. The hazy glow of lilac light illuminated the cavernous space, accompanied by growing hisses and screams.

"What is—"

"Kui!" Grace's cry from her side had her gaze snapping to the elder shifter slowly slipping beneath the churning water.

"No!" Sylvie grabbed Kui's torso, hoisting her up. "Hold on."

"I've got her," Setka said, looping his arms under her armpits, letting Sylvie turn back to the lights. They bobbed and significantly brightened, lighting up the features of every hiding shifter. With shaking breaths, Sylvie opened her arms to shield as many of the shifters from what was to come and screwed her eyes shut as the screams outside curdled her blood.

The purple light seared an image behind her eyelids of her bonded. God, how she wished she could see them one last time. And as a giant pair of hands gripped her sides and dragged her through the falls, she finally screamed.

THIRTY-FIVE

"Open your eyes."

Sylvie bucked and fought as the rushing waters beat down on her and the creature that gripped her. She kicked, gasping for air as flashes of torture stole every other thought but fight. No one would hurt her again.

"I'll kill you!" she snarled, swinging blindly.

"Sylvie!"

"Princess, open your eyes."

That shocked her to stillness, her heart still thudding wildly as she blinked the water from her eyes.

"Rowan?"

Tears filled them.

"Kian?"

"I'm sorry we're late," Rowan said, kissing her brow and squeezing her so tightly she thought she would burst. A small noise escaped her, something between a laugh and a whimper, as she pressed her forehead to his.

"Everyone is behind the falls," she breathed.

He pulled her away from him, swiping her hair off her face with a look of pure adoration. "You did it," he said.

She bit back a sob, spraying water droplets from her hair as she shook her head. "They did it. Now let's get them home." She peeked over his shoulder, face crumpling when Elias came into view. The purple orbs of sunlight surrounding the water haloed his dark curls as they held back a much smaller number of revenants.

"They're headed for the city," he said.

The unprotected city, thanks to her freeing their only means of killing revenants. And feeding. She could sense the Fates' pleasure with her, but guilt still lingered. She shook the thoughts away as Rowan placed her back down right in Kian's path. The icy waters rippled around them as she accepted a soft kiss from him. Through it, his pride pulsed, then restlessness.

"Is Kerensa behind there too?" Kian asked, glancing sidelong at the falls, now glowing a bright lilac.

Sylvie nodded. "Near the middle."

"I'll be right back."

Sylvie wrung her fingers as Kian pulled away from her, disappearing behind the rushing wall of water. She hovered a moment, letting her body grow numb to the cold before facing her vampire.

"I thought you weren't going to get delayed." She kept her expression coy for a beat, but couldn't control the quiver of her lip as he cut through the water to get to her.

"My little brat, come here."

With a choked laugh, she threw herself into his arms. He lifted her, almost completely out of the water, and buried his face in her neck, breathing her in. "The guards were in quite a state after your performance. They locked down the tower within a minute of finding him." He kissed her throat. "Kian didn't want to waste any power escaping, so we clawed our way out the old-fashioned way."

"You didn't kill everyone, did you?"

She sensed more than saw his smile.

"No love. Not everyone."

She palmed his cheek and tilted her head back to the sky. The rotund moon was in full view, its blueish tone casting the world in an otherworldly hue.

"Let's get out of here."

The shifters emerged like wraiths through mist, each taking in their alpha, then Sylvie in the arms of another. One that looked identical to the male that had enslaved them for a generation.

Some shifters bared their teeth, fire flaming in their eyes, but Kui, now safe in Setka's grip, shushed them. "It's not him," her soft voice stated.

Rowan bowed deeply to her, his hand to his heart. "No. Ambrose is not his brother. We will discuss everything once you are safe within the pack lands. Please hold on to one another." Sylvie tensed in Elias's arms and wondered briefly if the proclamation meant as much to him as it did to her. He was *not* his brother.

Rowan didn't look their way, his posture faintly submissive as he turned to Kian, who nodded, hands joined with Kerensa. Sylvie didn't miss the straightening of Elias's body then. She palmed her warming cheeks and checked for revenants again. A handful hissed and scratched at the bow of light arcing near the rocks, but the clifftops were barren. Thanks the gods—and goddess. As Kian and Kerensa began chanting High Fae, a swirling light appeared on the surface of the water between their clasped hands. The moon reflected in the spiralling waters, and Sylvie craned her neck to see within it. The faintest scent of orewood spread over the water and she gasped, a wave of fear flooding her senses.

"Swim through it," Sylvie said. Quietly at first, but when Kian inclined his head her way, she spoke louder. "Swim into the light. It will take you home."

Unease rippled amongst the shifters, but Grace straightened and waded straight over, giving her a tight smile as she stood before the fae.

"I trust you," Grace said. Sylvie held her unyielding stare, suppressing the fear of what would come next. She would be okay. *And so will I.*

"Hold your breath," Kerensa bit out and Grace did, diving under and disappearing, a light winking behind her. Relief muddling with tension filled Sylvie's chest as she peeled away from Elias and shepherded the shifters closer.

"Keep going. You're almost home."

The other shifters followed suit, and it wasn't until they were sixty shifters down did Kian and Kerensa falter. Their skin turned wan, limbs shaking and eyelids fluttering as they dragged their tongues over High Fae like they were swimming through tar.

They weren't all going to make it. Sylvie ushered shifters faster when a warmth in her vest pocket had her pausing. She reached inside for the smooth stone she had almost forgotten about. Stolen from the king. With the portal key in hand, she waded closer to her husband and held it towards them. "Will this help?"

Kerensa nodded weakly. "Throw it in the water between us."

As she did, the portal strengthened, light arcing outwards and warming her face, but it wasn't enough. Not for every shifter and themselves.

"Take some of my power," she said, hand planting on Kian's shoulder.

"Princess, no."

Rowan appeared at her side in an instant, followed by Elias. "What are you doing?" the latter demanded.

"They need more power or we won't all make it."

"I won't use you," Kian bit out, even as his muscles seized.

Elias steadied him and glanced at the last thirty shifters still to cross. "Then use me."

"Us," Sylvie growled, gripping Kian's wrist firmly. "I can do this. Get us home, okay? All of us."

Kerensa nodded, overriding Kian's resistance. "This will hurt bad. Don't let go."

And it did. Her mind floated far above her body like a spectator, but the last of the shifters found their way to freedom as her skin felt like it was tearing itself apart stitch by stitch. Cell by cell. A circuit ran between them all. A live wire tearing through her flesh until her bones screeched. Teeth clenched and grated. Their channelling would tear her apart. She wouldn't survive it. "Hold on!"

She couldn't tell who was speaking. Yelling. Screaming.

"Go, now."

The pain ceased like it had never been there. Sylvie swayed on her feet, confused. "What?"

"Go through the portal! Hurry."

She didn't know who spoke, but she followed, moving in stilted steps, accepting Elias's and Rowan's hands. Standing before the swirling light and orewood-tainted air, she gulped a breath—perhaps her last—and plunged headfirst through the portal home.

* * *

Sylvie burst through the surface of Granite Lake, coughing and clawing at the hands that held her aloft. Not to hurt them, but to pull them closer. Her marks screamed with connection, the dampener from Argyncia completely gone. It was elating. Soul exploding. Every feeling surged between them like a tidal wave and the agony that had consumed her fled her consciousness completely. Rowan laughed, accepting her handling, while Elias staggered closer out of exhaustion. Portal sickness.

"I'm okay," he soothed when fear darted down the bond. "It was far worse last time."

But Kian … she eyed the waters like a hawk, waiting for the last travellers to make their way through. Seconds passed. Minutes. They weren't coming. Why weren't they coming? Did they get stuck? Did they run out of power? This couldn't be happening. How could she get back to save them?

"Where are they? Come on."

Rowan tried to walk to the bank with her, but Sylvie dug her feet into the loose pebbles below.

"Kian! Kerensa!"

Her breathing quickened as she faced her bonded, pulse skyrocketing. "Where are they? What's taking so long?"

"Fates, Hart, what are you crying about now?"

With a yelp, she spun back to a very dishevelled Kerensa and Kian, pulling them into the group hug and squeezing.

"We did it. We actually did it," Sylvie laughed through the tightness in her throat. She scanned each of their faces, and when she was certain they weren't in imminent danger of dying or passing out, she let her body relax. A moment passed where they simply breathed each other in before Sylvie nodded for shore and the mass of shifters milling around it.

"We should get out."

"Are you sure now? I do so love the feeling of lake algae in my underwear," Kerensa quipped.

Sylvie managed a smirk and hummed. "Now that you mention it, no, I definitely need one more minute of holding you all."

Kerensa moved to push her when Rowan's growl rippled through the waters.

The fae rolled her eyes and sauntered away, flapping her hand in the alpha's face. "Good doggy. Guard the pretty princess."

Rowan grumbled, but wiped some droplets from Sylvie's cheeks. "You okay?"

She knew what he meant. "Yeah, I think so." She took a full breath. Then another. "Maybe one day you could teach me." When his head tilted in an adorable wolfish way, she amended, "To swim."

That had his spine straightening, the trust from her flooding his every sense until gratitude shot right back.

"I would be honoured," he said, hand over his mark.

Kian searched her face, concern pulsing through his bond. "Are you feeling alright?"

"Fine. Groggy maybe, but fine."

"I took a lot from you—from all of you. Are you sure you're well?"

She tuned into her body, flexing her fingers and toes, and used her fae sight to strengthen the root system in a nearby bush. It came to her just as easily, if not more so, like whatever muscle it took to control her abilities had been supercharged. With a satisfied sigh, she palmed his cheek and nodded. "I feel great, Kian." When he still looked dubious, she clicked her tongue. "Maybe I'm just stronger than you thought, Husband."

He half-smiled then as Rowan said, "I always knew you were strong."

By the time they reached the bank, the pack was waiting in silence. The elders, including Kui, were nestled around the roaring fire, while the rest of the rescued shifters were eating an assortment of food off paper plates. Rose waved, tears in her eyes as she flitted around, handing out more food to the hungry. Natalie trailed after with blankets, and Claudine scanned the water as if expecting an attack.

"Kerensa and I will need to finish the wards and make sure nothing follows us through the portal tears," Kian said in her ear as her shaking feet crossed from pebble to compact soil. She nodded, offering a chaste kiss as he disappeared into the forest, but not before Rose shoved a platter of food in his hand.

The shifters stilled as Rowan mind-linked with them, their attention far away, unfocused. Once he was done, the conversations resumed, and he smiled down at her, noticing her stare.

"We'll have plenty of time to debrief with everyone later. For now, you need rest."

She tilted her head at him. "Rowan."

He shivered, like her saying his name invoked pleasure. Based on the tingling down the bond, it probably did.

"I don't want rest. I should be here."

"But—"

"This is what I wished for the night of the shooting star. The shifters' freedom. For them to be safe and home. For me to be home." She met his eyes and found they were glassy. "You are all my home."

He grabbed her shoulders and pulled her in, drawing the breath from her with a kiss. A kiss that had the shifters cheering. A kiss that solidified everything. They all knew who she was to him, Elias, and Kian, and they cheered regardless.

Rowan broke apart first, breathless. Tears carved a line down his cheeks and into his beard. "I will never deserve you, but by the goddess, you are everything this pack needs in an alpha."

She laughed against his lips and kissed him again, lingering in the slowness. The love. The power she held over the shifter alpha.

"You actually fucking did it!" Natalie's voice drew them apart and Rose threw herself between them in an iron-tight embrace.

"Don't you two ever scare us like that again. I thought the whole lake was about to explode, and then Maddissen's aunt appeared like—well, like magic." She took two blankets from Natalie and wrapped them around the pair of them while speaking. "And then everyone else ... goddess, some of these shifters have been gone from before I was born. Lucky I told everyone to make extra food just in case, but—"

"Rose, breathe," Rowan chided, patting her face like an older woman might with a child. Sylvie bit back a laugh and kissed the fox shifter's cheek.

"I hope we didn't worry you too much," she said.

Rose flushed pink. "No—no you didn't—I … I'm just so glad you're home."

"Me too." Sylvie pulled the soft fabric tighter around her shoulders.

"What about the vampires?" Claudine said suddenly, appearing at their side. "How do we know they won't return and take them again?"

Murmurs cascaded through the space.

"We should increase watch around the pack, order in more weapons," she continued.

"We could move some of the pack," Alastair suggested.

To Sylvie's surprise, Rowan didn't immediately shut them down. It wasn't until a rustle from the fires sounded did she understand why.

Amira stood, wrapping an elegant shawl about her shoulders. "Perhaps we should address why their realm is dying rather than the symptom of them taking our own."

Most of the returned shifters held a solemn energy while the others turned hostile, distaste written across their features.

"Why should we care? They drained our people."

"This is ridiculous."

"They deserve everything they get from here on out."

"Let them burn!"

Sylvie's face grew hot. "Stop it." She didn't yell. In fact, it came out closer to a whisper, but the shifters silenced like she had pushed a mute button.

She cleared her throat as it squeezed unbearably tight and focused her attention on the elders. "Let me be clear that I don't condone the actions of the king and I don't want to hurt you with what I say next." She looked at Grace and Kui. "Any of you."

"You won't," Grace said.

She stood taller. "I would never tell you how to think or feel about any of the things that happened. But the rest of you need to understand that if you condemn all vampires, then you condemn me, too."

Uncomfortable silence came from the others.

"The shifters being stolen from their homes and their families is wrong, and no matter how well the king and his guards treated everyone, you didn't deserve what happened to you. Even if I know why they did it, it doesn't make it okay."

"I'm sensing a but," Claudine interjected.

Sylvie barrelled on, voice strong. "*But* the vampires in the city were starving and weak, and I'm willing to bet they didn't know the shifters were even there."

She glanced at Kui again, fearful she'd offended her. When Kian first told her he wanted to help the shifters, despite what Ace had done, it hurt. But these shifters were not selfish like she had been. Kui bowed her head first, followed by Grace and Setka, then the rest of the returned. She couldn't help but find Amira in the crowd, her crinkled smile filling Sylvie with warmth. In that second she felt more seen that she had in a lifetime, their first conversation swarming to the front of her mind with sudden clarity.

I think I might know who I am now—or who I want to be.

Amira winked.

"They're living in fear because they turned all the humans though, right?" Claudine said, stealing her focus back to the pack. The shifter glanced sharply at the crowd, then at Sylvie.

Sylvie's beast narrowed its gaze and sat on its haunches. *She's testing me.*

"And why is that? Why would they do such a thing?" Sylvie said, testing her right back.

Setka raised his hand, and Grace swatted it. He spoke anyway. "They wanted children."

"Like us," one female who had been a part of the equinox mating ceremony said, palming her flat abdomen. Hanna.

Sylvie nodded. "Like us. Until we know the wards are complete and it's completely safe here, anyone who wants extra protection is welcome to stay at my place. It's not far."

Rowan brushed against her. "If anyone wishes to move, we go together in the morning. For now, there are plenty of free cabins, or you can sleep under the stars."

Most of the returned shifters nodded emphatically at the second option. After decades trapped in a dank cell until night where they were forced to guard the city and kill monsters, it made sense they'd seek the complete opposite.

"Now rest. We can talk more later," he said, pulling Sylvie away from the crowd.

"Is that alright?" he said then. "About coming to your house …"

Sylvie took in Rowan's face—the lower lip slightly drawn between his teeth, the faint tinge of pink splashed across the gold of his cheekbones, and the anxiety wending through the bond.

"Of course. That's your home too now, if you want." She quickly peered at Elias, who dipped his head in silent affirmation.

"Only if you're sure," Rowan said.

She answered him with a kiss, but pulled away when the scent of hot food filled her nostrils. Rose had returned with two large platters and now guided the pair to a blanket by the fire.

"You can come sit too," she said to Elias when he hadn't moved.

He hummed, inclining his head a fraction before saying, "I have something I need to attend to." With a chaste kiss across Sylvie's brow, he disappeared into the woods, heading towards Rowan's house. He didn't speak a word, but Sylvie sensed discomfort from him, and a sliver of annoyance. The portal sickness had to be taking a toll. She sent love after him and leaned into Rowan as they ate in silence.

As dawn broke over Granite Lake, the lack of sleep finally started dragging Sylvie under.

"Let's go," Rowan said into the shell of her ear.

"I'm fine." But even she could hear the way her words slurred.

"I'll take her." Elias's voice startled some of the nearby shifter conversations, and Sylvie barely had the energy to blink up at him. He scooped her into his arms and she nestled down, lids heavy.

"I should stay."

"I need to speak with you."

That woke her as if he'd doused her in ice water. The "we need to talk" line never went down well. At least not with human men. But Elias was no man. And Sylvie wasn't the same woman she used to be.

He carried her to the shifter gardens and sat her on a short log bench, crouching in front of her as she gnawed on the inside of her cheek.

"What's wrong?" she said.

His icy blues flashed red. "I do not want another moment where others question who or what you are to me, in any realm, city, or pack."

Her head tilted as he lowered onto one knee, taking her ringless hand. The other, adorned with Kian's wedding band, shook and clutched her blanket for dear life. Oh, goddess. Was he …

"Sylvie, love, be my wife." His firm hand remained steady as he reached into his pocket and pulled a black box into his palm, thumbing the top open. She bit her lip to restrain the sob as the vintage iridium band shone her way, featuring a glistening carmine-coloured stone in its centre. It was so *him*.

The bloodred sheen was the same hue as his eyes and her mark.

"Will you marry me?"

She laughed breathily and let him thread the ring over her finger before throwing her arms around his neck.

"About time."

He laughed then, too. "Brat."

"Your brat." She kissed him.

"Yes," he said against her lips. "Mine."

THIRTY-SIX

Two weeks later.

"Is it bad I want to rip that dress off you and ravish your body right now?"

"Yes, Rowan, it is bad, and Elias would kill you."

Rowan chuckled from his reclined position on the bed in Sylvie's home, picking at the polished buttons on his dress shirt. "I never liked these things. Too easy to shred."

"Well, that's too bad. It looks great on you." Sylvie padded over, lifting the tulle skirt so she could lean in and kiss him. "And don't you dare shred that shirt. It was expensive."

He grinned. "No promises."

She rolled her eyes and returned to the standing mirror in the room's corner. The A-line vintage style dress, the colour of the first frost, swished around her as she swayed and turned. Her full figure, bond marks, and new muscles peeked out through the slits along the thighs, low neckline, and short sleeves. "Are you sure it looks alright?"

She followed Rowan's wolfish gaze as he eyed her hungrily. "There are no words for how perfect you look right now."

With a flush, she faced him again, and carefully climbed onto his lap, straddling the hard bulge in his pants. "Be careful. You might make us late for the party."

"We wouldn't want that. Especially since your vampire is just starting to tolerate me."

"Rowan."

He shuddered, his cock twitching against her. "No fair," he whispered. "You know what that does to me."

She did, and that was exactly why she said it. After weeks of refusing to even think of him by his first name, she found using it to be addicting—intoxicating in its potency. Many nights since their return, she had used that new power to bed the shifter alpha. With a smirk, she slid off his lap and stood, arms crossed, her fingers drumming on her biceps. "It's just the engagement party. We can be fashionably late."

"After I'm done with you, there won't be any fashion left."

"Rowan Hex, that is filthy," she said, burning hot, loving the laughter that flowed from his mouth. Her beautiful, wild male.

"Alright, that's enough," Kian said, entering the room after a single knock. "This isn't a shifter ceremony until sundown, and unless you want to be taken in front of everyone right now, I suggest you tone down the erotic energy."

Well, not everyone …

"Princess."

"Sorry."

He clicked his tongue but didn't push the rule of no apologising to the fae. After she'd said goodbye to Kerensa a few days earlier, he was the only one who could use her words against her.

"Well, if you both aren't going to let me have my fun, then let's go eat," she said.

And they did. Elias took her hand from the threshold of their home and walked her towards the lawns where the shifters had set up tents and a fire pit, food tables, and picnic blankets. Rose hollered at the sight of her and many other shifters followed, applauding as Elias spun Sylvie in a circle. Her mate marks flared with desire, and many eyes glued to the spot on her chest.

"It's real," someone whispered.

"The Fates really blessed her."

"Thank you for coming, everyone," Sylvie said, ignoring the stares that made her feel like a human circus attraction. Rowan mind-linked the pack, and they promptly stopped their gawking before he turned on some music. The quick instrumental had many swaying while eating and as the night went on, the dancing started.

Hanna tapped Sylvie on the shoulder as she was downing her drink and leaned in close to speak over the music.

"I just wanted to let you know the mating ceremony worked."

Sylvie dropped her gaze to Hanna's abdomen, then back to her face. "You're pregnant?"

"We all are."

Every single shifter pair? What were the odds?

Sylvie's eyes burned as joy overwhelmed her senses. "Congratulations."

Hanna stroked her belly with affection. "It's all thanks to you. You're bringing new life to this pack."

Sylvie shook her head. "No—no, that's all you, Hanna. I can't claim that honour." She probably never would either. It wasn't in her to be a mother. But maybe there was something special about that night. Something magic in the blessings she bestowed with the pack.

Hanna smiled, a hand leaving her belly to palm Sylvie's cheek. "There are other ways to bring life than becoming a mother, Alpha."

Compassion rolled off Hanna in waves, and Sylvie bowed her head in respect. They had different desires for their lives, but neither judged the other for her choices. It differed from how people often were in Sterling. Different was good.

As the sky darkened, the elders said their goodbyes, heading down the newly warded path to the pack, followed by most of the returned. While many had eaten and trained enough to be almost at full strength, their aversion to the dark had become incapacitating for some. Amira taught her what herbs to blend to help with the nightmares. Most nights Sylvie would be with the returned, providing sleep tonics and ensuring the fires around their cabins never died.

Claudine wandered over, a drink in hand and a staff in the other. Her way of helping the shifters was to always be ready for an attack. "So, when's the wedding?"

Sylvie accepted a drink from Rowan, waving him off when he gave Claudine a warning look.

"When everyone is safe."

They hadn't planned anything yet, but she was leaning towards a tiny ceremony—maybe even elopement in some legal building in Sterling. She had a big wedding in Evergreen with Kian and it was beautiful, but it wasn't her style, or Elias's.

"So, never then," Claudine said, sipping her drink.

Sylvie snorted and shook her head. "You're funny."

The look Claudine gave her flickered between surprise and fascination before the shifter patted her back firmly and walked away, her last words lingering on the wind. "You'll make a good alpha."

"You look so beautiful!" Rose rushed over, grabbing her hand and squeezing while Natalie nodded from her side. The pair had grown inseparable.

"Yeah," Nat said. "About time for the shifter part of the night, right?"

Sylvie choked on her drink, catching Rowan watching her from the same pillar she first fucked him against. "What?"

A bright flush rose under Rose's freckles. "Natalie!"

"What?" Natalie raised her brows at her, then wiggled them for Sylvie. "It's a rite of passage, and no shifter party would be complete without it."

Sylvie's inner beast uncoiled and stretched before rolling on her back and purring. *Slut.* It growled right back.

Elias appeared at her shoulder and enfolded her against him as Natalie and Rose scattered like frightened rodents. "You can say no."

She peered up at him, breathing in his scent. Woody cologne and something deeply vampiric that had her mouth watering. "Do you want me to say no?"

"I didn't say that."

Holy—

"You want to fuck in front of people?"

"Not in front," Rowan corrected, sauntering to their side, followed by Kian. "Just around."

Her lips drew down in a contemplative line as she toyed with her bond marks, enjoying the responsive inhalations from her husband, fiancé, and mate. She was no stranger to the ways of the shifters. Sex wasn't nearly so taboo as it was in Sterling. Here it was a shared gift. Something beautiful, and not once did she feel dirty about it. Plus, they were all adults. Tension budded into arousal as she dragged her fingers across her marks and between her breasts.

"How about a game first?" she said.

Rowan's posture changed as if the animal within him was leaping at its confines.

Her anticipation heightened, suspense building with every second. "Hide and seek?"

Kian clicked his tongue at her, but from the heat in his stare and the waves of desire rolling off him, his approval was palpable. "My wards extend a mile in all directions, but the path to the pack lands is narrow and marked with ropes. Don't cross it."

"Obviously." She turned to Elias, body thrumming with scorching need. The beast paced and threw its lean body against every sharp edge of her mental fortress, looking for friction. She pressed her thighs together.

"So?"

Elias scrutinised her, a ghost of a smile creeping along his lips.

"Run, Kitten."

* * *

Orewood sentinels stood watch overhead as Sylvie tucked herself into the nook of an overgrown bush. She dragged in air through her nostrils to suppress the panting from the run and palmed her fluttering belly before dipping her fingers lower. Maybe she could get the party started sooner. But when shrill, delighted squeals reached her ears from surrounding shifters getting caught by their respective partners, she homed in on her power. No way were they going to catch her that easily.

She scanned the energy lines, and after confirming her bonded were nowhere near, she darted out of the bush and up a spindly orewood, jamming herself between a junction two stories up. The squeals slowly turned into pleasured moans and she pressed her forehead to the rough bark, strangling the thickest branch with one arm and touching herself with the other.

Up so high, most of the forest floor remained obscured as she panted against the trunk and luckily, none of the other shifters stumbled across her. She wouldn't like to see what her bonded would do if someone other than them tried something with her. Or maybe she would …

"I can hear you breathing, Kitten."

She stopped touching herself in a rush and pressed her lips together, holding back the laugh that bubbled.

"She's excited." Kian's mirth filled the darkness. She tuned into her fae sight and followed each of their prowling forms as they surrounded the orewood she nestled atop.

"She smells so sweet," Rowan crooned.

Reaching overhead, she grabbed a branch for support and peered at where they stood, directly beneath her.

Elias spied her first, then Kian. Rowan lingered longer with his eyes closed, breathing deeply. Her beast purred with delight.

"Come down, now," Elias said.

Kian winked. "We win."

Sylvie laughed and leaned out as much as her tight grip on the branches would allow. "I wonder if they can tell I'm not wearing any underwear." She murmured the words low enough that they'd need to strain to hear, but based on Rowan's sudden scrutiny up her tulle skirt, they did.

"If you don't get down here, I'm coming up," he growled.

She poked out her tongue. "You have to catch me first."

With that, she leapt to the nearest tree, scaling down with the sound of tearing fabric following behind her. She dived the last few metres onto the soil, grateful for her bare feet as she landed hard and rolled over her shoulder before standing again and racing through the darkness.

Her bonded's low chuckles forced her legs to pump harder even as her beast whined and urged her to return to them.

"Not so fast, Kitten." Elias appeared directly in front of her, and she dug her heels into the ground to stop from careening into his rigid form. Before he could scoop her up, though, she dropped to a slide, getting beyond his grip and back to her feet in the near pitch dark.

Her fae sight resumed with every foot strike, and she used it to dredge up roots from below. One by one, she drew the older roots from the ground, flattening the tips to steps and climbing them higher and higher until the nearest orewood was in reach, its long arching limbs spiralling around it. She let the roots drop, cutting her bonded off from following her, and caught her breath within another junction of orewood branches. The exertion had her swaying, mouth tasting faintly of blood, but she held on, testing the branch to the next tree with her foot.

Rowan prowled below as a breathy laughed passed her lips. Elias and Kian had disappeared, and with her focus on walking the bowing branch, her fae sight didn't help her see them either. Too late, Sylvie's error grew apparent, the branch splitting with a sharp crack. She had no time to turn around or catch herself, instead plummeting to the ground. Her scream died in her throat as she twisted to land on her feet, but instead slammed straight into Elias's waiting arms.

She sent a mental apology to the tree, its branch dangling limply as he tossed her over her shoulder and palmed her ass.

"That wasn't very safe, was it, Kitten?"

"Why would I need to be safe when I have you to catch me?"

She kicked her legs to keep up appearances, but the absent-minded stroking of his fingers along her inner thigh drew a traitorous moan from her lips.

Each pass grew dangerously close to her bare flesh, the tears in her dress doing very little to cover her.

"Not always," Elias said, dropping her onto a thick pile of crushed leaves under a blanket.

"Did you do this?" Tiny bobbing lights surrounded the blanket, illuminating the tucked-away nook created by a crescent of tightly woven orewoods. A basket of assorted items sat against a twisted root system, too. Linens, water, lube.

Rowan snorted. "We knew it wouldn't take long to find you."

Kian rubbed his chest in affirmation, the bonds stringing them together humming with a satisfied, harmonious note. Each male gave off their own tone, the blend radiating tingles through her body until she could almost see them in space through it, no matter the distance.

Elias took her forearms and tugged her to sitting, ripping the rest of her dress from her body and throwing the mucky, torn garment aside.

"Elias!"

"I would buy a thousand more dresses, each one more expensive than the last, just to tear them off you, Kitten. Don't question me."

Her head rocked back, a wave of desire flooding her senses until she spoke the words she knew he wanted to hear. "Yes, Master."

Through her half-masted lids she took in his clenching jaw, pussy throbbing at his satisfied grumble. With a fluid grace she always envied, he unbuttoned his dress shirt, folding it and depositing it in the basket. Kian and Rowan followed at the same time. Their matching expressions, fuelled by unbridled lust and adoration, quickened her breathing until the rapid rise and fall of her chest enthralled each pair of beautifully coloured eyes. Just then, a flash of her bonded pleasuring and possessing her came to mind. The same vision as the one she received the night of the mating ceremony. The one that brought her to her knees before the entire pack—a gift potentially from the Fates themselves. She shook the faceless witches from her head and took in her bonded again.

"Elias?"

"Yes?"

"Will you tell me what to do tonight?"

His irises flashed carmine, a flash of his lengthened canines catching the light from around the blanket as he answered low. So low. "My pleasure."

Rowan's groan broke the silence, his hand hidden beneath his waistband. She grinned, letting her knees fall apart slightly to bare herself to him. Kian, as expected, showed more restraint. His hands stayed at his sides, but his zipper strained under the force of his erection.

"Kian will have you first while you suck the shifter's cock."

Rowan met Elias's stare, holding it for a silent beat before rounding her side and dropping to his knees.

"Yes." She freed him, curling her fingers around his width. Velvety soft yet rigid with the need for release. She drew him closer, licking him from base to tip.

Kian undressed completely, settling between her legs and warming her goose-prickled body with his gliding touch. He spent a long time over each erogenous zone, stroking and circling, kissing and sucking until she ached for him.

She pulled away from Rowan's cock just long enough to plead, "Please, Kian. I'm ready."

He slid himself along her pussy and filled her as Rowan stuffed her mouth. For minutes, hours, aeons, they rocked inside each opening. She shuddered, curling her fingers around whatever part of her males she could find, holding them closer. Closer. Closer. They switched and she writhed at the different sensations Rowan offered. The taste of her own pleasure from Kian's cock. Rowan pulled himself free as Elias directed her once again. "Get on your hands and knees."

She obliged, even as her muscles trembled, her arms buckling under the weight of her body.

"Hold on to him," Elias said, angling his head at Rowan, and she did. With a moan, she curled her arms around his neck, her face pressing into his bare chest when Elias slammed inside her from behind. She cried out, the power in his thrust filling her with aching need.

"Elias!"

"Don't let go."

He grasped her hips as he fucked her into oblivion. Rowan held her firmly, his form never wavering even as his lips dipped to her neck to draw out more pleasure with his teeth and tongue. Kian observed from the sidelines, his perfectly sculpted abs catching the flickering lights as he leisurely stroked himself. A bead of cum glistened on his head as she writhed under Elias's nailing. Elias's hand slid from her hip to her clit, his fingertips circling perfectly over the spot with just the right pressure to have her eyes rolling back. Just when her orgasm neared and she was poised to leap into oblivion, the ministrations stopped and she screamed in protest, arching her back.

"Don't stop!"

He slapped her ass and bit her shoulder as she leaned backwards into him, the sharp slice spearing her closer to bliss.

He flipped her over, directing Kian and Rowan to either side to kiss her, suck her nipples, and stroke her as he plunged deeper. Sweat drenched her skin and the primal sounds of shifters finding their own climax flooded her with heat. With want. With overstimulation. She cried out, begging for release.

"You know what to say," Elias said with a growl.

"No." She wouldn't use the safe word. Not a chance. Instead, she splayed her arms wide, her nails raking the soil and calling deep into the land. The world lit up with millions of energy flows, many of which surged between person to person. Every shifter that basked in the soil, connecting within the forest, sent out tendrils of honeyed light, but nothing was more breathtaking than her bonded, their streams of desire—purple, red and gold—writhing around her in a vortex of devotion. She let some of her own energy flow into the soil, through the coloured streams of her bonded, to ease her overstimulation, and Elias's gaze fixated on her. "What are you doing?"

She grinned at her minor rebellion as Elias unravelled slightly and breathed, "Don't stop, Master."

His expression hardened, but he didn't waver as he snatched her hips, thrusting faster and deeper until her pleasure hit another glorious peak and climax neared. She inhaled until her lungs swelled, suspended in a moment of pure euphoria. Then, like a pebble dropping in the centre of a sleepy pond, ecstasy rippled out from her, through the soil, her bonded, and the shifters, the delicious moans echoing in a rising crescendo. Ropes of hot cum lanced her sides and stomach as her bonded came as one entity. She let her fae sight fade and sighed contentedly while Kian and Rowan watched her with wide eyes.

"What the Hels was that?" Rowan said.

She let her eyes flutter closed and her lips pull into a smile as she said, "I don't know. But let's do it again."

EPILOGUE

Two days after the full moon, the pack was still. Calm. The vampires didn't come.

Sylvie pulled her hair into a short pony, slid on some runners at the front door of her home, and accepted the apple from Kian's waiting hand as she stepped onto the stoop.

"I have a list of herbs Amira needs me to buy from Sagehill. Do you have any requests, Wife?"

She bit into the apple, chewing thoughtfully while thinking, then kissed his cheek. "Maybe you could take down the part of Sagehill's wards that are anti-shifter?"

Kian smiled, his hand brushing a stray curl off her forehead. "Of course."

With the added load of the returned shifters, keeping the pack close to home for work or errands seemed the most logical. Even if the vampires never returned, the fear would likely always linger.

Rowan agreed, though many shifters had already decided against leaving the pack wards at all. They had food, water, and power. They wouldn't risk going out in the open.

"Have you spoken to Elias this morning?"

Kian nodded, biting a chunk of her apple. "He's finalising some contracts with Goldtech's managing director, but promised he'd be home tonight." Kian thumbed her brow when she frowned.

He'd been away a lot. Busy with the businesses—their businesses. But he hadn't pressed her to return to Sterling or work. He had to though, if they wanted to keep the pack running smoothly and add more buildings for the growing populace.

The night after their engagement party, he had offered to fund the pack, which was more than she could've hoped for. Rowan tried to refuse, but Elias didn't bother listening. "It's for my kindred. Not you," he had said.

"Well, I'm gonna run to see Rowan. I'll see you later?"

"Stay inside the wards."

She rolled her eyes but smiled against his lips when he kissed her again.

Throwing the tiny apple core in the front garden's compost, she started a brisk jog down the grassy hill and into the Tynaan. Through her golden bond, she could picture Rowan fussing with the fire by the lake, his torso glistening with sweat as he sliced wood and stoked the dying flames. He'd started clearing areas closer to home for more cabins and buildings to bridge the gap between the pack and house, but today he was a world away. She picked up the pace along the roped path, birdsong and insects enlivening the space as she flew over sticks and debris. Her beast stuck its head out a castle window, the wind flowing through her fur. Sylvie grinned inwardly and palmed a few trees as she passed in a rough high-five.

At almost a third of the way, face flushed and hot under the glare of the sun blasting through the canopy, the noises of the Tynaan stopped.

The ropes that lines the warded path hung limply, their frayed edges littering the forest floor. She paused and reined in her breathing, scanning the path and the space ahead. It was dead silent. Down the bond, concern swirled, and she sent it back more potently to Rowan. Trouble. She felt more than envisioned him heading towards her, but even in wolf form, he'd still be over twenty minutes away.

She backed up, keeping her footing light, and was zoning into her fae sight when a crack sounded from outside the path.

Her head whipped that way, stance widening as her heart stalled in her chest.

"Just the bloodwhore I've been waiting for." The tattered face of her living nightmare twisted into a cruel smile. "The king isn't finished with you yet, but when he is, I'll be happy to resume where we left off."

Only a second of horror muted her before her faculties came back online.

She swallowed dread. Clenched her jaw. Breathed deep. "I'm not going anywhere with you, Ace. We're warded."

"Are you?"

A sinking sensation threatened to drag her away, but she bared her teeth, letting her vīs out from its cage. One of them would leave this forest on a pyre, and it wouldn't be her.

Fighting stance established and power surging through the root systems below her, she sharpened each spear of wood to a violent point.

Ace grinned, displaying his cracked front teeth. "Don't you want to hear what I have to say?"

"Fuck you."

"Not even about the traitor in your midst?"

She wouldn't fall for it. Not for one second. As the roots spliced through the soil, Ace raised a long spear-shaped weapon, levelling it at her head.

She sneered, drawing the roots up in a slithering spiral around his feet. Then higher, swarming his calves, then his waist. How much force would it take to squeeze the life out of him? Power coiled through her as she sent a jolt of warning through Rowan's bond. He had to be close. Kian had turned around too. Plants bowed inwards around them as Ace's expression flickered from malice to uncertainty. Then nothing, as if wiped clear of emotion. Devoid of feeling. Dead inside. Oh well, he was about to be dead on the outside, too. She raised the spears higher, each an extension of her fingers as she curled her hand into a fist.

"Come with me, bloodwhore. The king isn't finished with you yet. And when he is, I'll be happy—"

"You already said that, cunt."

"—to finish what I started."

She let her vīs swell, her beast growling so loudly her own chest felt like it vibrated, desperate to break free of the mould that was her skin. The roots shivered from her rage, trees arching back, away from the fury in her veins. She lifted a finger and curled it in a mocking come-hither gesture. "Try me," she said.

ACKNOWLEDGMENTS

Here we go again. This was my favourite book to write in the series, both in drafting and editing, and I'm so excited to share it with you all.

Thank you to my editor, Courtney. I couldn't have done it without you. Your meticulous eye for detail and ability to honour my author's voice is astounding.

To my family—I love you always and you're not allowed to read this, so put the book on your shelf and walk away.

Dad—you need to stop telling everyone my pen name. It's supposed to be a secret!

Uncle Matt, here's your shout out. You're famous now.

Uncle James, you don't know this, and I also hope you don't see this, but I fell in love with fantasy because of you. I'm both so embarrassed and happy that you know I write and are proud of me for it.

Aunty Amanda, thank you for all your support and guidance in the parts of publishing that had me fleeing in terror.

To the gals at work who I talk to this about, thank you for listening and gassing me up at every milestone.

To my freaky friends at circus, here's to you. Sorry about the cliffhanger … again.

Juls—you know how I feel.